Something told me I would regret my next words.

But I didn't want his death on my conscience.

"You can't stay out there all night like that. My tent isn't big, but I can make room for you. If you want."

"God, yes. Thank you." He flung off the rainfly and trotted over. Rainwater splashed under his running shoe-clad feet and clung to his bare shins.

Face obscured by a ratty beard and his hood pulled low over his nose, rando dude dove for the entrance to my tent.

"Hey. Hey. Slow down." I held up a palm. "Take off that jacket and your muddy-ass shoes and leave 'em in the vestibule. Otherwise it's going to be as wet and nasty in here as it is out there."

"Okay. Okay." He stomped and shivered, slipped off his rain shell, and sat in the entrance unlacing his shoes with shaking, wrinkled fingers. Water pooled on the tent floor around his ass.

"Shit. You're soaked. Take off everything before you get all the way in here."

He glanced over a shoulder and a pair of deep blue eyes gazed into mine. "You're not trying to take advantage of me, are you?"

A zing of electricity shot through my chest and settled at the apex of my thighs. For no good God damn reason.

"I'm trying to keep you from dying out there. So, hurry up." I snagged my pack towel, wiping up the puddle inching toward the foot of my sleeping bag.

He hesitated, teeth chattering. The musty smell of damp wool filled the tiny space.

"I promise I won't make fun of your tiny peen. If that's what you're worried about, we can chalk it up to shrinkage."

WILD at HEART

Stacy Gold

Onyva Press

Cover, print layout and ebook design: Brian Kannard

Icons provided by: Vector Vectors by Vecteezy
https://www.vecteezy.com/free-vector/vectory

Print ISBN: 979-8-9856460-0-9
eBook ISBN: 979-8-9856460-1-6
iBooks ISBN: 979-8-9856460-2-3

Printed in the United States

Thanks to my amazing dev editor, Elizabeth Nover at Razor Sharp Editing, who helped me troubleshoot early drafts of this story. Without her guidance it wouldn't be even half as good as the book in your hands.

DEAR READER,

Thank you so much for taking a chance on my backpacking romance, Wild at Heart. This book means so much to me, because it's the type of story I wish I could've read when I was younger.

You see, I got my first backpack for my sixteenth birthday. While I'd been car camping with Girl Scouts and boyfriends, I'd never camped overnight on the trail. Definitely not alone. I also didn't know any other women who had, so I had no examples to follow. Still, it only took one trip for me to get hooked.

This led to a degree in Resource Management and Environmental Education, and a position as a U.S. Forest Service backcountry ranger. Being out in the wilderness with everything I need on my back makes me feel confident and secure and incredibly happy. I adore the solitude, the stunning scenery, and knowing I can take care of myself.

I've now spent my adult life skiing, whitewater raft guiding and kayaking, mountain biking, and hiking, mainly in the company of men. So, with my romances, I want to show women as smart, capable, and competent in the outdoors—not damsels in distress. And also as beautiful, desirable, sexual people totally deserving of love (even if we don't need rescuing).

I hope you enjoy reading it even half as much as I enjoyed writing it. Please do let me know what you think by connecting with me via email, my newsletter (sign up at stacygold.com), or leaving a review.

Happy reading!

Stacy

CHAPTER 1

JULES

"I'm so jealous, Jules." Bryn perched on the end of one of the beds in our hotel room at Cascade Locks, watching me pack gear. The thin, gray light of pre-dawn filtered through a crack in gold curtains that'd seen better days.

I tucked a bag of snacks and my rain jacket into the top of my backpack, cinched the drawcord, and buckled the lid with a solid click. "Of what, twelve guys dumping me for their exes in a row? I'm sure we could arrange that for you too. If you ever really start dating again."

"Ha. Funny." She toed my calf. "You're taking five weeks off to go backpacking solo. Who cares why?"

Tingles of excitement zoomed around in my chest and I flashed her a grin. "Yeah. Dealing with zero assholes and zero clients for more than a month does sound pretty heavenly, doesn't it?"

She grinned back. "Like I said, totally jealous. At least of your trip." Her expression went serious. "I still can't believe the next guy you date is gonna be unlucky number thirteen, though."

"Yeah. I've thought about that. Probably too much. Definitely enough to jinx the next one for sure. So, I'm swearing off men for at least a year to restart the count." I hesitated, the excitement buzz fading. "A year is enough time to consider it a clean dating slate, right?"

"Wait. You mean you're swearing off dating, or swearing off sex too?"

"Yes. Both. All of it." The last eight years had been nothing but suckage on the relationship front. It'd probably take more than a year to fix my shit. But nothing would change if I didn't change something.

Bryn eyes widened. "You're serious."

"Dead." Bending, I tugged the rough nylon laces of my left boot. The well-worn leather snugged around my foot. "I'm never gonna figure out anything buried in too much work plus too many bad dates."

"When did you decide this?"

"Last night." I shouldered my pack and adjusted the straps until the familiar weight settled on the tops of my hipbones. "What I've been doing isn't working. It's time to take a big step back and focus on myself for longer than just a few weeks."

"I guess that's one way to break the pattern." Bryn opened the door and we stepped outside into early morning stillness. "And yes, a year is definitely long enough to clean your dating slate."

Fog tendrils drifted from the Columbia River across the half-empty parking lot. The air hung thick with moisture and cedar and the sweet mustiness of damp soil. The best smell in the world after too many days breathing city fumes.

"I sure as hell hope so. If not, at least maybe I can figure out what to do about my business. I can't keep working this much."

We strolled across the lot side-by-side, the chill air nipping my skin through my nylon hiking pants and shirt, waking me up. The sky glowed marigold behind the inky silhouettes of the mountains.

"You'll come up with a plan. You always do."

"Thanks for the vote of confidence." We crossed the empty highway, walked a few hundred yards and turned off. Gravel crunched under our soles. "And thanks for driving me down here from Seattle. And picking me up at the other end."

"Of course. That's what best friends are for." She wrapped a hand around my arm and leaned in, hugging one of my few body parts not covered by my backpack. "Though I still wish I was going with you. I could use a break from assholes and clients, too."

The first golden rays of sunlight slanted through the tree branches, lighting the dirt road ahead. "We'll have to plan a girlfriends' trip once I get back."

"I'm holding you to that." Her warm hand tightened on my biceps. "Maybe we can convince Aly to come with us for once."

I snorted. "We'll get Aly on a backpacking trip when pigs fly. But I'm all for trying."

A handful of parked cars and a dark brown trailhead kiosk appeared, marking the southern end of the Pacific Crest Trail through Washington. And my starting point. And the start of five weeks of solitary bliss in one of my favorite places in the whole world.

Bryn pulled out her phone. "Hey. Let me grab a shot of you in front of the sign, to commemorate the moment."

"Okay." I took a few steps back.

"Say, single life."

I popped a hip and smiled for the camera. "Single life."

"Perfect." She slipped her phone into her pocket. "I love you, girlfriend. Stay safe out there and call me whenever you hit civilization."

"I will." My throat tightened. "I love you, too."

I was totally looking forward to hiking solo. To enjoying time alone and figuring out my craptacular situation with no distractions.

But, for a second, I couldn't help wondering if I should've taken Bryn up on her offer to hike this first section with me.

Deep down I knew it would be a distraction, though. I needed alone time, in the woods, to find my center and do a serious assessment of my life. Especially my love life. Because I kept picking the same kind of winner, over and over, and I was done losing.

"See you in a couple weeks." With a wave, I pivoted on my heel and stepped into the emerald glow of the Pacific Northwest rainforest. Happy with my choices. And looking forward to not having to do anything, at any set time, for anyone other than me.

EVAN

Sitting cross-legged on floor, the hardwoods cooling my thighs, I thrust another stuff sack into the flimsy neon green nylon bag that passed for a backpack. The idea that everything I needed to survive for a week in the woods would fit securely in this thing seemed optimistic, but the salesperson at the outdoor store swore it was the best for going fast and light.

Three loud thuds reverberated from my heavy, dark-stained oak front door through my uber-sleek loft apartment. I grabbed another piece of improbably small and light gear, ignoring the door. If anybody talked me out of this trip, I'd never get up the guts to do something like this again, and I needed to do something.

Even the thought of staying in Boston, marrying Lainey, and finding another Financial Analyst job made me nauseous. I had to get away and go somewhere totally different, if I was ever going to figure anything out. Because I didn't know who I was or what I wanted and staying here hadn't generated any epiphanies.

The booming faded. I exhaled into the silence.

"Come on, Evan."

I jumped. *Fucking John.*

"I know you're in there. I saw your car outside and the lights on." His knuckles tapped the door this time. "Talk to me, bro. You haven't been answering your phone. I'm worried about you."

The plaintive tone in his voice pressed on me. A few tiny chunks of my limited resolve crumbled. I wedged my water filter and cook stove into my pack.

"At least let me know you're all right."

Setting down my titanium pot with a clank, I crossed the living room and did the last thing I wanted to do. Or maybe the second to last thing since Lainey wasn't the one standing on the other side of the door. I turned the knob.

My brother loomed over me, lips pressed in a thin line, eyebrows pulled together, fist raised to knock again. *Stay strong, Evan. Stay strong. You can do this.*

I crossed my arms over my chest. "You don't need to break down my door. I'm fine, I promise."

One thick shoulder shoved against me and he barged into my apartment, waving at the pile of multicolored bags and bits piled on the floor. "What's all this?"

"A backpack. And gear."

"What's it for?"

"Backpacking."

"No shit, Sherlock." He spun to face me. "You haven't been camping since Cub Scouts. You're not planning to pull a Chris McCandless and die in the wilderness, are you?"

"Fuck you." *Stay strong. Stay strong.* "For your information, I have been backpacking since then."

"When?" He lifted his chin.

"Boy Scouts, when I was twelve. The year you went off to Stanford." I held my rain jacket and pants folder over the top of my pack and flipped the lid to lock everything in place. The buckle didn't reach. I pulled and shoved. "Those were some of the happiest days of my life, so please don't try to talk me out of this trip."

"Does Lainey know about it?"

"I wrote her a note." I pointed at the counter.

"Now I know you've cracked." John lifted the paper off the granite kitchen island and scanned it. His eyes widened. "You're going backpacking in Washington State? Couldn't you go somewhere closer to Boston? I mean, doesn't the Appalachian Trail go through part of New England?"

Annnnnnnd…This is why I haven't told anyone my plan. I gritted my teeth and laid my stomach across the top of the pack, striving for maximum compression. The tips of the buckles almost touched. *Damnit.*

I rocked back on my heels. "Anywhere in New England is not far enough away from here."

"What about the Rockies? Isn't Colorado far enough?"

"Colorado is too rugged and high elevation. Besides, I've always wanted to check out Portland and Seattle."

He shook his head. "Well, at least I know where to send the search and rescue team."

"Very funny."

"Are you sure this isn't just unemployment depression talking, bro?"

"Positive. Honestly, losing that job was a relief more than anything else." I tossed the rain pants aside, folded my jacket flat as possible, and laid it on top. Balancing the pack between my legs, I strained to clip it shut, praying it wouldn't burst at the seams—here, or on the trail.

"So, let me get this straight. You've got a hot fiancé from a wealthy family who's about to make partner at her law firm—"

"She's not my fiancé anymore." I growled. The buckle clicked. I rocked back on my heels and glanced at the ball of black nylon on the hardwood floor. *It's August. Even in the Pacific Northwest, I can survive a week without rain pants.*

His eyes went wide. "What? Seriously?"

"Seriously." John's stare pulled the words out of me. "I'm dying here. That job, my relationship, they've been sucking away my soul."

"Damn. I knew you weren't super happy, but I didn't realize it was that bad. I figured you were finally learning how to toe the family line without losing your mind."

"I'm not like you, John. I wasn't born to be the golden boy of the Davenport clan." I hoisted my pack onto my back, the weight digging into my shoulders, and tried to remember the right order for adjusting the straps. "I'm not sure what I want to do with my life, but I know this isn't it and I don't think I'm ever going to find it here."

"Mother and Father are going to freak the fuck out when they hear you left."

A bucket of ice-cold guilt poured over me, cooling some of my resolve. "They're going to be even more upset when they hear I left Lainey."

"Yeah, and they'll call me when they can't reach you. So will Lainey. What should I say?"

This time the guilt hit more like a thick, icy blanket of snow. The kind that traps you and suffocates you if you aren't careful. I ran my fingers over the bumps and ridges of the stones of my leather brace-let—the one Uncle Martin gave me the year he died—searching for confidence.

"Tell them you don't know any more than what is in my note. I'll be home in ten days, so it's not like it's the end of the world. And right now, I have a plane to catch."

"I'm guessing there's no cell service out there."

"You guessed right. Besides, I got rid of my phone."

"You wha—?"

"Don't." I held up my palm. "I'll explain it all later, but I really have to go."

John crossed his arms, eyes pinched at the corners, and blew out a breath. "Fine."

"I owe you one. Seriously, you get the award for world's best big brother for this one."

"Gee, thanks. Just don't blame me if you come home to a serious shitstorm or three."

I grabbed my duffel bag of extra clothes and opened the door. "I'm well aware the only person I have to blame for my shitstorms is me."

CHAPTER 2

JULES

Tiny raindrops pattered on my nylon roof. Tucking my dirty hiking boots into the corner of my vestibule, I butt-crawled inside, shimmying out of my damp rain pants along the way.

Belly still warm from a hot dinner of tuna mac, I pulled on long johns and fresh, dry socks. I slithered into the cozy cocoon of my sleeping bag with a deep, contented sigh. The rain picked up steam, hitting my tent like a line of drummers at a halftime show. Laying back, I stretched long, shifting around to work out the kinks in my back.

Four days in and my life had already settled into the familiar rhythms of the trail. Wake before the sun heats the green walls of my tent. Make a hot breakfast. Break camp. Hike through spectacular scenery. Eat snacks. Hike some more. Eat some more. Set up camp. Make a hot dinner. Sleep. Repeat.

Nobody to deal with. Nobody else's problems needing solving, or egos needing stroking. Not even any real decisions to be made beyond when to eat and when to make camp.

In other words, total fucking bliss.

Not that I'd gotten very far on solving my own problems. But I had miles and hours and days of thinking time ahead. I could afford to relax and just be for at least a week. Get back in touch with the me I was when I was alone, instead of always being somebody's graphic designer, consultant, coach, armchair psychotherapist, or goddamn ex-girlfriend.

Tension that wasn't from carrying an almost thirty-pound pack crept into my neck. I grabbed my book and set my headlamp on medium, reading until I couldn't hold my eyelids up. Which took about three minutes.

Lights out, surrounded by sighing forest and tapping rain drops, sleep sucked me in the way it had every night so far—hard and fast. No dreams, just thick, heavy, total relaxation.

My eyes snapped open for no apparent reason. I held my breath, listening through the rain drumming my tent.

A man's voice rang out from feet away, the tone somewhere between exasperated and hopeless. "Seriously?"

Nylon rustled and shifted outside my tent, loud even through the rain.

I exhaled. *What kind of dumbass tries to set up a tent in the dark, in this weather?*

A branch snapped. "Fucking goddammit!" This time his voice hit a note somewhere between pissed and despondent. Nylon crackled and shushed.

Snuggling in deeper, I covered my head with my bag to block out the noise of my new neighbor. The rain's tapping lulled me. My eyelids drooped like they had weights attached and—

"Sonofabitch."

I flipped over and stared up at the night-dark ceiling, listening to continued cursing, crinkling, and crumpling. The guy wasn't setting up his tent, he was in a full-fledged, mixed martial arts fight with it.

"Fuck. Me." Scrabbling for my headlamp, I unzipped my tent and aimed the beam across the small clearing. Raindrops formed silver lines, obscuring my view.

My light caught a bit of reflective material. And a bare leg. And what looked like a pile of fabric thrown over a boulder but had to be a rainfly tossed over the asshole who woke me up.

"Um, helloooo. What the fuck are you doing out there?" My breath hung like a ghost in the beam of light.

"Oh, nothing. Just trying to get some shut eye. Except my tent just broke, it's pouring rain, and I'm soaking wet."

"And why, exactly are you setting up in the middle of the night in a rainstorm?"

"Because I need somewhere dry to sleep."

Fuck. I knew I shouldn't have asked.

"Don't you have rain pants?"

"If I had rain pants, don't you think I'd be wearing them?" The pile of nylon shifted and settled, and the bare leg disappeared.

"You're going to go hypothermic dressed like that."

"Tell me something I don't know." The rain pounded down. "Are you going to turn off that light, or what? I am trying to get some sleep over here."

"Sure thing." I clicked off my headlamp and sat in the dry comfort of my tent, staring out into the dark, wet night.

The chances of my random neighbor getting any shuteye out there were pretty much nil. Ditto the chances of me sleeping through the night with his periodic shifting and cussing.

The chances of him getting hypothermia dressed like that in forty-five-degree rain, on the other hand, were pretty damn high.

I clicked on my headlamp. "Aren't you freezing?"

"Pretty much."

Something told me I would regret my next words. But I didn't want his death on my conscience. "You can't stay out there all night like that. My tent isn't big, but I can make room for you. If you want."

"God, yes. Thank you." He flung off the rainfly and trotted over. Rainwater splashed under his running shoe-clad feet and clung to his bare shins.

Face obscured by a ratty beard and his hood pulled low over his nose, rando dude dove for the entrance to my tent.

"Hey. Hey. Slow down." I held up a palm. "Take off that jacket and your muddy-ass shoes and leave 'em in the vestibule. Otherwise it's going to be as wet and nasty in here as it is out there."

"Okay. Okay." He stomped and shivered, slipped off his rain shell, and sat in the entrance unlacing his shoes with shaking, wrinkled fingers. Water pooled on the tent floor around his ass.

"Shit. You're soaked. Take off everything before you get all the way in here."

He glanced over a shoulder and a pair of deep blue eyes gazed into mine. "You're not trying to take advantage of me, are you?"

A zing of electricity shot through my chest and settled at the apex of my thighs. For no good God damn reason.

"I'm trying to keep you from dying out there. So, hurry up." I snagged my pack towel, wiping up the puddle inching toward the foot of my sleeping bag.

He hesitated, teeth chattering. The musty smell of damp wool filled the tiny space.

"I promise I won't make fun of your tiny peen. If that's what you're worried about, we can chalk it up to shrinkage."

"No. I'm wondering how we're both going to fit in here."

"You're not that big."

"You don't know that." The corner of his ashen lips quirked, but he peeled off his shirt and reached for his waistband. He lifted his hips off the floor, the muscles in his back rolling and flexing. And just like that, a naked, quaking stranger filled my tent.

If I didn't get this guy warm soon, I'd have a bigger problem on my hands. I scooched to the side and opened my bag. The damp nylon wall pressed against my back. I shivered. "Zip up the door and climb in."

EVAN

Trembling and chattering, and eternally grateful, I crawled into her sleeping bag, burrowed my head under the covers and curled into a shaking ball. I'd never been so cold in my life.

Fuck. What am I doing out here? Other than almost getting myself killed in a freezing rainstorm, in the middle of nowhere.

The sleeping bag wasn't near as warm as I'd hoped, or maybe I was colder than I realized. Either way, I wasn't going to complain. Not given my options.

"Please tell me you still have a dry sleeping bag out there." My savior's voice rang loud even through the nylon and insulation. "Because I'm pretty sure we won't both fit in mine."

"I have a sleeping bag in the top of my pack." I pointed in the general direction even though she couldn't see my hand under the covers. "Not sure about the dry part."

The rain pounded on the tent. My body quaked. Fear and acid roiled my gut.

"Shit. Okay. Be right back."

I curled smaller, as much for warmth as to give her room to get out of the tent. The zip and snick of the door warned me she'd gone and returned.

"You're fucking lucky."

"Not usually."

"Well, you are tonight, because your pack was sitting upright and wide open, but your rainfly kept everything from getting soaked."

The shush of a sleeping bag sliding out of its stuff sack filled me with a ridiculous amount of excitement. I could've happily huddled under five sleeping bags.

Cool air and light wafted in and tremors ran from my head to my toes. My savior's body slipped into my cozy cocoon, blocking the sudden draft. She spread my bag over the top of us, filling the gaps, and I prayed I'd start to feel warmer soon.

"Straighten your legs, would you? I need at least a little room."

Much as I didn't want to give up any possible body heat, I stretched out long. She spooned in behind me, the scratch of her clothing on my bare skin making me hyper-aware of my nudity.

"Aren't you supposed to be naked too?" My teeth chattered. "To warm me up faster?"

"Yeah…No." She took her hand off my hip. "I think you've gotten lucky enough tonight."

"I mean, that's what always happens in books and movies."

"You're still shivering. And you're talking and making perfect sense. So, I really don't think that's necessary. I can give you plenty of body heat through my clothes." She exhales. "Besides, I make it a policy not to get naked with anyone unless we're on a first-name basis."

"Funny. So do I. Yet here I am." I'm pretty sure I tried to shrink inside myself. Vulnerable didn't even begin to cover how I felt in that moment. Stupid and scared and vulnerable came closer.

Her guffaw shot through the tent like a bullet from a gun, but her warm hand landed on my hip again. "I guess there's an easy way to fix that. I'm Jules."

"Evan." My shivers slowed from constant to intermittent. "Thank you for coming to my rescue, Jules."

"I couldn't leave you out there in the rain. You'd have kept me up all damn night." She curled in closer, her head against my mid-back, her knees hitting my hamstrings.

I settled into her welcome heat. We barely fit in her tiny tent like this. No way could we lay side-by-side. She was giving up a comfortable, good night's sleep for me. A total stranger. "I still appreciate it, even if you did it for selfish reasons."

"You're welcome, then. But don't get too comfortable. I'm kicking you out at first light."

"Roger that."

She might've saved my life, but I had zero plans to spend any more time with her than absolutely necessary. So far, this backpacking adventure had given me more blisters and discomfort than personal insights or inspiration. I was done being cold, wet, dirty, hungry, sore, tired, and under-caffeinated.

All I wanted to do was survive the night, speed run the rest of this damn trail, and get the hell out of here. Hot meals and hotter showers beckoned.

CHAPTER 3

EVAN

Hot. Why am I so hot?

I peeled open my eyelids to a green nylon wall dappled gold with sunlight. And a mound of sleeping bags. And a pint-size, fully dressed body splayed over my naked one.

My brain tilted and swirled. I scrubbed my hand over my face. Then it clicked and I cringed.

I'm not sure this backpacking trip was the worst decision I'd ever made, but it wasn't anywhere near the best, or even middle of the pack. I needed to get out of here. Out of this tent. Out of this goddamn forest. Out of Washington.

I should've gone to the beach.

Standing in my climate-controlled apartment in Boston, a week-long backpacking trip on the other side of the country had seemed like a fun and exciting way to change up my life and reconnect with my better self. How hard could it be if I'd done it when I was twelve with no problem? Ha. Funny.

Somehow, I had to extricate myself without waking this woman and get on the trail. Bad enough she had to rescue my pathetic, freezing ass, the last thing I wanted was to relive all that glory with her in the bright light of day like some weird walk of shame.

Or listen to a laundry list of what I'd done wrong. I got enough of that at home.

Only one problem. We were two people sardined in a one-person tent. I couldn't slip out from under her without her noticing.

I put one hand on her shoulder, solid muscle firm under my palm, and gave it a little shake. "Hey, Jules. Wake up."

She stirred and lifted her head, her frizzy brown hair a dark halo surrounding a pair of amused, dark brown and amber eyes. "You're right. You're bigger than I thought."

"Sorry." Heat ran to my face. "I have to pee."

She slid off to the side, her back bowing the wall of her tent. "And I thought your morning wood was because I'm so damn sexy."

"No! I mean, I wasn't thinking of you like that. Or thinking about sex."

"So, you don't think I'm sexy." She fluttered her eyelashes.

Shit. "It's not that. I'm sure you're gorgeous—"

Her eyes widened. "You're sure I'm gorgeous? You can't tell?"

"No. It's…I…I don't know. I was too busy freezing my ass off last night to even look at you."

"Ah, so I'm not pretty enough to catch your eye. Not even now, in broad daylight?"

I squeezed my eyes shut. *How was I supposed to respond? What did she want to hear? Why did women always trap me into these conversational corners—with no good answers and no way to escape?*

Jules snorted. "I'm fucking with you, Evan."

I opened my eyes to her smirk. "Not funny. Do you think you could let me out of here?"

"I'm not keeping you in here."

I glanced at my sleeping bag covered body and back at her. "I'd love a little privacy."

"Fine," she grumbled, moving toward the door. "It's not like I didn't see it all last night."

"Let me at least pretend like I have some dignity."

"Good luck with that." The zipper snicked open, and she crawled out.

Sitting up, I scanned the tent. "Hey, what'd you do with my clothes."

"I shoved them down in the foot of your sleeping bag to dry out."

I reached into the depths of our bags and found my shirt and shorts and boxer-briefs. Not only were my clothes ninety percent dry, they were warm. Well maybe not warm, but definitely not early morning icy. *Brilliant. Why didn't I think of that?*

"Thanks."

At least fully clothed I didn't feel completely at the mercy of mother nature, or kind strangers—even if it wasn't true. Backing out of the tiny tent, I pulled my sleeping bag along with me. Packing up and getting out of there couldn't happen fast enough.

JULES

I took a deep breath of fresh-washed forest. Of Christmas trees and damp pencil-shavings. Rough rock bit into my ass, but I needed a dry-ish place to sit in the sun and crank up my stove. One affording a front-row seat to view the random guy I'd rescued.

That, and I couldn't convert my sleeping pad into a chair with Evan laying on it.

Naked.

Turning on the gas I flicked my lighter. Flames leapt up with a soft *foosh,* burning blue and hot. I placed my pot of hot water carefully on top of the tiny burner, trying not to wonder what Evan looked like in the light of day.

Or who he was. Or why he was out here in the middle of nowhere—apparently without many backcountry skills.

None of which was my business. Except maybe the "what he looked like" part. Not because I wanted to see him naked in all his glory. Just to put a face to the name.

Other than that, I did not need to get involved.

A fine, tight ass backed out of my tent. Evan turned to face me, sapphire eyes beaming from beneath a mop of dark, unkempt hair, longer on top than on the sides. My breath caught.

Fuck. Me. This man is gorgeous.

He flashed his pearly whites and I struggled for focus. And composure.

"Thanks again for saving me from freezing to death last night. I hope you slept okay, despite me crowding you in there."

"No biggie." I shrugged and fiddled with my stove, ignoring the energy crackling between us. "I would've slept worse knowing you were dying in a rainstorm, feet from my tent."

No way was I about to tell him it was the best sleep I'd had in eight years.

Though it probably had more to do with getting in the backpacking groove, and long days on the trail, than anything else. Certainly not because I spent a night squeezed into a too small tent trying to keep some rando guy from freezing.

He'd be on his way in a few minutes. This would become nothing more than an entertaining story to laugh about over drinks with Bryn and Aly when I got home.

Evan scanned the clearing. I pulled a tea bag out of my stuff sack and set it alongside two packets of instant oatmeal.

"I put your gear over there, at the base of that tree." I pointed at the neat bundle that was his backpack and tent wrapped in his rainfly.

"Oh. Wow. Thanks." He crossed the clearing. "You didn't have to do that."

I let my gaze roam his lean body. His ass and legs were nicely muscled, but trim and fit like a runner versus seriously built. Still, he was more than good-looking by most any woman's standards.

Something inside me heated. Just a little. And I hadn't even had any tea yet.

"No. I didn't. But if the wind had picked up you might've lost something important—like your tent. If nothing else, I wanted to make sure your shit stayed dry. I don't have spare gear to loan you, and I'd rather not have you sharing my tent again."

At least not if we're only sleeping.

I crushed that thought.

"Good points. The state of my gear was the last thing on my mind—aside from the unusable state of my tent."

"What's wrong with it, anyway?" The water on my stove burbled. I dumped my oatmeal packs in my bowl and my tea bag into my mug.

"Well, let's see. I'm pretty sure I broke a pole…" He reached for the pile of aluminum tent poles, opening the segments and fitting them together one-by-one. The steady click-clack filled the morning quiet. "Yep. This one is broken off at the end. And when it broke…" He

Wild at Heart

flapped open the pile of nylon and stuck his fingers through a jagged tear along one seam. "It ripped a hole through my rainfly. Looks like I'm sleeping under the stars from here on out. Unless it's raining." A shiver ran down his arms and out his fingers.

"Let me be the judge of that." I poured and held up the pot, cinnamon and mint steam wafting warm across my face. "Hot water?"

"No thanks. I've got cold breakfast."

"Suit yourself." Crossing the clearing, I picked up the broken pole. "You're lucky. It broke below the hub and I've got a pole splint in my repair kit. Easy fix."

"That still leaves a big, gaping tear in my fly. No matter what you do, it's going to leak."

"Eh. Most every gear problem is fixable with the right tools and a little know-how." I met his too-intense gaze and the hairs on my neck did a little dance. Evan was far sexier than he should have been.

Especially since he looked at me like a potential savior he wasn't sure he could put his faith in, not like a woman he wanted to sleep with. Or even found mildly attractive.

"I'm guessing you have both of those."

"In spades. But it's going to take a few minutes to get you fixed up. Why don't you grab your mug and have a cup of tea?"

"Oh, that's all right." He waved a hand around. A worn leather bracelet, studded with stones, wrapped his wrist. Totally at odds with his shiny-new, high-end trail runners and hiking clothes.

"You sure?" Between the cold of last night, and the damp chill of the morning, I expected him to jump on the chance for a hot beverage.

"Positive. Especially since I don't have any tea."

"I've got extra."

His face, his whole body really, tensed. I set down the broken pole and got out another pack of tea. "Grab your mug."

"Are you sure?"

"Positive. Or I wouldn't offer." I gave him my warmest smile.

"Why are you being so nice to me?" He dug around in his pack with one arm.

"Why wouldn't I be?"

"Because you don't know me."

"You're right, I don't. But I'm a nice person." I stirred my oatmeal. "And we're two people in the middle of nowhere, where every piece of gear, every decision, can mean the difference between life and death. You look closer to the dying side of that equation. I told you, I don't want that on my conscience."

CHAPTER 4

EVAN

Jules sat on a boulder in a pool of sunlight, bent over my rainfly with a needle and spool of dental floss. Short and compact, she was not at all my type, but kind of cute with her freckles and her pert nose and her wild curls escaping from her braids. And her smartass sense of humor.

I focused on her fingers, deftly looping floss through nylon. Here she was helping me and I was checking her out. Wholly inappropriate given the circumstances.

"You know, I really thought my tent was sturdier. It's supposed to withstand a monsoon or tornado, according to the sales guy." I tossed a handful of granola and dried fruit into my mouth, washing it down with tea. Minty heat seeped in a blissful spreading pool through my chest.

Warmth flowed into my hands from my bowl/mug—an item I'd barely used since I forgot to pack tea or coffee, and I didn't bring enough fuel to use my stove at breakfast anyway. All to save weight.

Saving weight had seemed critically important at the time. With each sip heating my insides, staving off the chill of the morning air and the bone-deep cold I struggled to shake, I recognized the error of my decision.

Just one of many. Starting with this stupid trip. No, starting with taking that job and moving in with Lainey. Or maybe before that—

"It is strong, but only if you set it up right. You have to insert the male end all the way into the female, or it'll break when you bend the pole."

"That's what—" I clenched my jaw against the rest of the catchphrase out of habit.

Jules's dark brown eyes glinted. Her lips quirked.

No. She couldn't be…No way.

"—she said?" She smirked.

A chuckle burbled up my throat. It morphed into full-out guffaw that rolled out in peals until my stomach cramped and my ribs ached.

Jules stared at me, grinning, while I spluttered and chortled and struggled for control.

I wiped the tears from the corners of my eyes and took a long, shuddering breath. I couldn't remember the last time I'd laughed like that, deep and unreserved. Laughing meant I was still alive. Thanks to Jules. If she hadn't been there last night…I'd never come that close to dying before and I never wanted a repeat.

"You okay there, Evan?" She lifted her brows.

"I'm good." I wiped my eyes again. "It's just, I don't think anyone has said that to me since my brother, when I was about twelve."

Her wry smile, along with the mischievous glint in her eye, took her from cute to gorgeous in a heartbeat. At least, gorgeous in that wholesome, fresh-scrubbed, perky girl-next-door way.

Not like the rail thin, perfectly blond, perfectly mannered types from 'good families' my parents loved to set me up with. Definitely not like Lainey. Then again, you'd never find any of them sewing a tent with dental floss in the middle of nowhere, sans makeup or a fresh manicure.

"Right. Anyway..." She held out her handiwork in one fist and rummaged in a burgundy stuff sack with the other, pulling out a tiny plastic packet. "Here. When you set up your tent tonight put a thin bead of sealer along the repaired seam. Make sure you cover the holes where the floss goes through the fabric."

"Will do. Thanks." I spread out my rainfly, inspecting the tight, even stitches of her impromptu repair.

Impressive.

She picked up my tent pole, studied the broken end, and dug into her magic stuff sack again. "So, if you don't mind me asking—or even if you do—what were you thinking hiking in that rainstorm in the dark last night? Why didn't you stop and set up camp earlier?"

"I needed to make another four miles to stay on schedule." I shrugged. "Probably not the best call, I realize now."

Jules slid a short tube onto my tent pole. Using her teeth, she tore a strip of duct tape off a tiny roll, the rip loud and grating in the quiet of the forest. "Yeah. If the sky goes dark with clouds, and the birds stop singing, it's time to call it a day and set up shelter. Especially if you're above tree line and can't descend fast."

"I'm pretty sure I won't make that mistake ever again. Not that I'll have much of a chance once this trip is over. Seven days out here is enough to last me a lifetime."

"That's a shame." Her gaze met mine, warm and filled with sincerity. "I could stay out here the rest of my life."

"You must be a glutton for punishment. I'm so sick of the damp and the cold and waking up sore and achy from sleeping on a thin foam mat on the ground. And scarfing the same granola twice a day."

"Yeah, I don't blame you. I'd hate backpacking too, if I did it that way." She wrapped the tape around the pole splint.

"What do you mean, that way?"

"You're focused on hard goals. Stuff you can quantify. Super-light pack weight. High mileage. Speed. I'm not." Jules waved a hand at her pack and pile of gear, almost twice the size of mine. "I'm focused on enjoying being out here. So, I'm willing to carry a few more pounds and travel a few miles less each day. I prioritize hot breakfasts, stopping to take in the scenery, and taking a day off due to weather. Or because I just damn want to."

"Huh. But your pack must weigh a ton."

"Sub thirty pounds, with water. When you're only hiking twelve to fifteen miles a day, it's totally doable. And when you're out here for a month or more, a little camp comfort trumps ultra-light pack weight in my book. But to each their own." She shrugged.

A month? She had to be insane. Handy and smart and cute, but certifiably crazy.

"Sounds lonely."

"Why? I like being in the mountains and I enjoy my own company. Five weeks away from clients and phone calls and emails and traffic and everything else is bliss in my book." Her forehead crinkled. "Have you been lonely on your trip?"

Had I been lonely? Scared, worried, stressed, focused on making my mileage, but not lonely. Or at least, no lonelier than I was back home. "Not really, now that I think about it."

"You're probably too focused on your goals to be lonely anyway. They can fill up your brain, and your day, like nothing else. Which is a shame, because you end up missing the best parts." She pressed a second strip of duct tape around the pole "Okay, this section won't fold

Wild at Heart

anymore, but you can strap it to the outside of your pack, and it should get you through the rest of your trip—as long as you're careful."

I took the pole from her and folded the unbroken sections. "Seriously, thank you for all your help. I'm pretty sure you saved my life last night, and now the rest of my trip. I wish there was some way I could repay you, but I don't have any cash—or really much of anything…" I glanced at my tiny backpack and she giggled. "And I need to get moving if I'm going to get off this trail anytime soon."

"No big deal. I'm just glad I could help." She pointed at my tent. "Oh, when you pack up that fly tomorrow, put it at the top of your backpack and leave the repair hanging out so the seam sealer can finish curing without sticking to anything else."

"Got it." I loaded my pack and slung it on my shoulders. "Well, I guess this is good-bye."

She picked up her mug and raised it in a salute, seeming in no hurry to hit the trail. "Have a safe hike out."

"I'll do my best." I turned and trotted down the sun-dappled trail, steam rising from the needle-covered dirt.

I should've been happy to be on my way, gear repaired, and one day closer to civilization. Except…Jules. So skilled and confident. So clearly able to take of herself—not to mention my dumb ass. And the fact that she went out of her way to help me with nothing to gain for herself?

I couldn't figure her out. In my world, very few people did anything unless they stood to benefit. But the only benefit she got was not finding me frozen on the side of the trail. A pretty substantial benefit, but still, it wasn't like she was making money or burnishing her reputation off her good deed.

Usually, my spidey-sense would be going off, alerting me to ulterior motives. Not with Jules.

Something about that was…Refreshing. Appealing. Even more than her big smile and her salty comments. Not that I'd ever see her again. I was making faster time, and in a few days, I'd be freshly showered and on my way back to Boston.

The trail tilted towards the sky. I focused on my pace, on making my feet beat an even thump, thump on the soft trail. Warm, loamy air filled my lungs with each ragged breath.

The towering evergreens became shorter and sparser. The sun beamed. Sweat trickled a line down my neck and between my shoulder blades, making my shirt cling to my damp skin.

I topped a rise, and the jagged, flattish top of Mt St. Helens filled my view. To my right, Mt Adams towered over a skirt of forested foothills in all its awe-inspiring glory.

Intellectually, I knew these old volcanoes were huge. My map showed them rising more than nine and twelve thousand feet from sea level, respectively. But seeing big mountains on a map, and seeing them in person, were two different things. They dominated the skyline and everything around them. Gray mottled with white, they could've been giant pieces of the moon dropped out of the sky eons ago.

I'd never felt tinier and more inconsequential, or more dazzled.

Even with ten miles still to go before I made camp; I couldn't sprint past this view. I dropped my pack and sat on a rock, letting the hot sun dry my shirt. A stream burbled in the distance. A bird twittered.

Life went on, whether I moved or not, because it didn't depend on me. Nature didn't care about my career or my arbitrary deadlines. The pressure that lived in my veins fizzled out a little. I breathed in the fresh, clean air.

Okay. This I could get used to.

With the right gear.

Maybe.

　　　　　　　　Wild at Heart

JULES

Evan had shot off down the trail like a rocket, the muscles in his calves pumping and rolling. Not even topping off his water before leaving. Probably already far behind schedule and trying to make up time.

I never understood the speed hikers. Or the thru-hikers wearing earphones.

Being out here should be about being out here. Not about distracting yourself or getting through it all as fast as possible. If you're going to do that, what's the point?

That's how you got through modern life. Being in the mountains, far away from civilization, should be an escape from that.

I mean it's one thing to go ultra-light and fast on a long day summit, or maybe an overnighter. But a week of that sounded less-than-fun to me. Especially the deadlines—the having to make too many miles to get to a specific spot every day. Nope.

Plenty of deadlines waiting for me at home. This trip was all about being here now. Living in the moment.

An image of Evan smiling at me, the corners of his cobalt eyes crinkling, floated through my head. And a small camp stove lit itself in the bottom of my stomach. Which was weird.

Shorter and lean with dark hair wasn't my type. Judging by the quality of his brand-new gear, he either made a lot of money or came from a lot of money. Or had tons of credit card debt. And he'd definitely never spent much time in the woods. But something about him drew me in.

Maybe that he laughed at my jokes. Or maybe I just liked saving wounded animals. Because he had wounded written all over him in giant, neon letters. I'd certainly dated enough of those to recognize the signs.

Why else would a guy who clearly knew almost nothing about backpacking do a seven-day trip through the middle of nowhere solo? I squeezed my eyes shut, praying to the universe and Mother Nature he'd make it out all right.

Speaking of…High time I broke camp and hit the trail too.

Grabbing my bowl, water filter, and hydration bladder, I wove through the tall sword ferns, their fronds slapping wet and cool against my legs. Bending at the edge of a small stream, I scooped my hands through the frigid water and splashed my face. My skin tingled in the best possible way.

Well maybe not the best possible way, but right up there with sinking into a hot spring or having hot sex. Since I'd taken a one-year vow of celibacy, and I wouldn't get to the hot springs for at least another week, I needed to get my excitement where I could.

Using a little water and sand I scrubbed my bowl, my fingertips going numb. Bladder refilled, I strode back to camp, stowed the last of my gear, and shouldered my pack.

Tightening my hip belt, I ignored the ache of bruises I knew from experience would fade as the trip wore on. With a final scan of my campsite, I headed up the trail, blue skies peeking out from between the treetops.

Black-capped chickadees whistled from their perches in the Douglas Fir and Western Red Cedar trees. I smiled.

I couldn't identify many birds by their song, but their piercing refrain of, "Cheeeese-burg-er. Cheeeeese-burg-er" was unmistakable.

The miles disappeared beneath my feet. The trees opened and the high alpine greeted me with peaks for days. St. Helen's with its blown-off top stood directly ahead and the dome of Mt. Adams towered higher to my right.

I wonder what Evan thought of this view. Or if he even noticed.

Not that it mattered. I'd never see Evan again. At least I hoped not. Because if I did, it meant he was in some kind of trouble. A guy like that needed to get back to the safety of the big city before he got himself hurt.

Dropping my pack on a flat rock, I grabbed a snack bar from my hip belt pocket, biting into sweet nuttiness and thinking back over all the men I'd dated since Justin. They all had one thing in common… They were absolutely nothing like him. Maybe that's why none of them stuck around.

Justin had been funny, and smart, and sensitive, and made everything a good time. He was athletic and a little artsy, with the lean build of a soccer player. And he was always up for anything—any adventure—in bed or out.

Every guy since had been bigger, more beefcake, and much more blond. While they might have been athletic, or smart, or funny, none of them had that dynamic combination that meant life was full of fun surprises and silly escapades.

Most were either hard-core focused on work, or hard-core focused on working out. None of them were bad guys, but they weren't Justin—not that anyone ever could be.

Even my ex-husband. Mark wasn't the right guy either, just a port in a storm. And I'm pretty sure he realized it.

But I'd been young and hurting too bad after Justin to think things through. Sex with Mark had been mind-blowing. Like a drug. For a few hours he could make me forget everything else. For a few months he was a blessed escape from reality. Then our relationship soured.

All that was years ago though and didn't help me solve the mystery of why every guy I'd done more than slept with in the past few years left me for their ex-girlfriends. Twelve of them. In a row.

Seriously. This shit ends now.

With a last look at the snow-splotched peaks, I followed the trail down into deep green forest again.

EVAN

My shoes thumped the trail in a steady cadence. The woods grew dense. The shadows from tall trees kept the sun off my shoulders, while the downhill pitch lengthened my strides. I kept my pace as close to a run as possible. I needed to make up miles and get this ridiculous, stupid, uncomfortable trip over with ASAP.

Stopping for a quick snack I surveyed my surroundings. The trail wound down and out of sight through the forest.

I unfolded my map, the waterproof paper snapping and crinkling, and tried to pinpoint my location. I found my last campsite and followed the trail with my finger. It meandered up and down, sometimes above tree line, sometimes below—at least if the green shading was an accurate indication.

My finger came to a junction. I should've started climbing again at that point. An access trail angled away from the Pacific Crest Trail, descending five-ish miles through treed zones to a dirt Forest Service road.

I checked my watch. Anger and frustration clenched my gut. I was three hours out from camp and had spent half that headed in the wrong direction.

Wild at Heart

My life has become a series of misguided choices and idiotic mistakes.

Shaking my head, I squeezed the last of the gooey, sweet energy gel into my mouth and headed back the way I'd come, doing my best to pick up my already fast pace. Unless I made it at least a few miles past the river crossing before dark, I'd be spending an additional, miserable night out here, where I didn't belong any more than I belonged in a suit, sitting in an office, analyzing financials.

I'd been so positive I would find peace and serenity in the wilderness, the way I had when I was a kid. Or at the very least some sort of purpose to my life. Instead, all I kept finding was discomfort and defeat and my own damn ignorance.

The trail gained elevation fast, steeper than I'd realized on the way down. The burn in my quads grew in intensity and my calves ached until they were just this side of cramping. I slowed my run to a speed walk and kept going, hoping I'd make up time later.

I intersected the PCT, wide and well-traveled and clear as day, and yet I'd somehow made the wrong turn. Picking up speed at last, I vowed to pay better attention going forward.

Brown and grey tree trunks flew by. The sun arced across the sky, changing the angles of the shadows. Rapids rushed and rumbled in the near distance, growing louder with every step.

My trail made a hard left. I stopped.

Far below, a river sparkled through the branches. My needle-covered path followed it in a slow, steady descent. I could hear, and often see, the water but a dense green thicket of brambles and ferns and blackberries and some prehistoric-looking, thorn-covered plant stood between me and shore.

I remembered seeing a bridge on the map. As long as I stayed on this trail and kept going, I'd come to it eventually.

The trail flattened. I sped up, my feet moving smoothly over the soft earth, and smiled. If I could keep up my pace, I had a shot at making it all the way to the site where I'd originally planned on camping—even if it meant finishing my hike by headlamp.

I popped out on a broad, cobbled bank, lit golden in the afternoon light. Wider and calmer here, the river burbled and sang its way around boulders and under downed trees. Upstream a ways steel cables and a splintered and broken board trailed in the current.

Shit. Guess I'm not going that way.

Walking past the nonexistent bridge, I searched for a likely crossing. A beaten, sandy path led into clear, smooth flowing current and out the other side. I surveyed both banks of the river, downstream and up.

A few fallen trees lay tangled in the water downstream, either not quite big enough, or not quite long enough to walk across on. High walls closed in upstream. This was the only obvious way to cross.

I toed off my running shoes, stuffed my socks inside, and tied them to the top of my pack to keep them dry. Two steps in on the slick cobbles and my feet tingled like I was barefoot in the snow. I shuffled forward, slipping and sliding awkwardly on the round rocks.

The water rose to my knees, then my mid-thighs. My legs went numb and heavy. The smooth flowing current shoved at my hip. I slid out my right foot, searching for bottom and—

Cold water swirled over my head.

Swooshed around my ears.

I couldn't breathe. Couldn't think.

My backpack dragged me to the bottom like a lead weight. Daylight swirled bright and gray above my head. Out of reach.

I flailed and thrashed under the water, pack bouncing off the riverbed, the current pulling me downstream towards logs, and bridge parts, and rapids, and who knows what.

Panic flooded my veins with fire and my lungs clenched hard. Pain seared my chest.

I'm going to die. If I don't ditch this pack, I'm going to die.

I fumbled at the buckle on my sternum strap with numb hands, kicking at the river bottom, trying to shove myself to shallower water. My feet slammed into a boulder, stopping me. The pressure of the current threatened to flatten me against it underwater. Curling into a ball I rolled off the rock, losing track of up and down.

My world became the stabbing pain in my lungs and that damn buckle.

I grappled at it with both hands, squeezing from every possible angle with unfeeling fingers, hoping to hit the release clips.

It let go and my shoulder straps spread wide. White lights popping against my eyelids, I grabbed the waist belt buckle with both hands. It clicked open. The current tumbled me downstream.

I shrugged and twisted and somehow got my arms out of the straps and kicked. Hard.

My head broke the surface. I sucked in deep breaths of sweet, clean air and fought my way to shore, collapsing half out of the water. Relief flooded every inch of my body.

With a sudden wretch, my gut heaved, and a burning stream of water flooded out of my mouth and nose. Twice.

Curled like a shrimp in the shallows I gasped and sucked and just fucking breathed—each lungful the most amazing thing I'd ever tasted in my life. I didn't care that my feet and legs were numb, or that I'd surely find a hundred bruises on my body later.

I was alive.

CHAPTER 5

EVAN

I sat up, feet and legs on fire with cold. Somehow, my backpack rolled lazily along the edge of the current, one shoulder strap briefly breaking the surface like a breaching whale. It took a second to realize what that meant. Scrambling to my feet I plunged back into the frigid water.

My fingers scraped rough nylon. I closed my fist and the weight of my waterlogged pack threatened to drag me in again.

No. Fucking. Way.

Pulling from some deep reserve I didn't know I had, I gripped the strap with both hands and planted my heels, letting the weight swing downstream until I held it steady. Muscles screaming, heart pounding, I edged toward shore.

My bare heel clipped a round cobble and slid sideways.

Time slowed.

My sodden pack tugged at my arm.

The world tilted. Icy water covered my head again, stealing my breath.

 Wild at Heart

I clung to my pack and scrambled against the slippery bottom, rocks bashing my feet and shins.

My lungs burned. My shoulders burned. But I needed that god-damn pack.

My foot found a large cobble. I shoved against it, pushing toward the light, and broke the surface, cool air filling my lungs like the world's best beverage.

I glanced downstream and my pounding heart filled my throat. About thirty feet away most of the river disappeared under a huge log.

Fuck.

I let go of the strap. With my hands free I clambered and slipped and somehow dragged my body to shore once more. Crumpling on the ground, cobbles biting into my hip, my thigh, my shoulder, I took a deep, shuddering breath, laying there for I don't know how long.

Long enough for the shadows to stretch across the river. Long enough to realize I was freezing my ass off and I'd better do something before it got dark—especially since I no longer had my pack. Or my tent. Or my sleeping pad or my stove or any food or a change of warm clothes, or pretty much anything I needed to survive out here.

Rolling over with a groan, I crawled to a sunny spot high on the riverbank and collapsed again.

I thought I'd pushed myself to my limit in a few triathlons. God was I wrong. Exhausted, aching, and sore, I still had to make it through a cold night in the mountains. And I didn't have anything more than my soaked shorts and t-shirt. Not even my shoes, let alone a jacket.

My family would never let me live down my stupidity and inept-ness. If they ever found out. I didn't intend for that to happen. I didn't intend for anyone to ever find out I almost got myself killed out here.

More than once.

Lifting my head, I peered downstream and considered my options.

If I found my pack before it got dark, everything in it would be drenched, but at least I'd have my stove and headlamp and sleeping pad. If I didn't find it, I'd be even worse off.

"Fuck. Me." I let my head drop back. It hit rock with a stinging smack.

JULES

The miles disappeared behind me. Each uphill made a little more sweat drip down my spine. Each stream-crossing numbed my feet until they tingled and ached.

I lost myself in the shush of the light breeze in the treetops and the burn of my quads, moving through space and time at a speed humans were built for. Not zooming along too-fast-to-think in a metal box.

The shadows stretched longer. My stomach rumbled.

Next campsite has my name on it.

The roar and tumble of rapids reached my ears, louder than the burble of uncountable smaller streams I'd hopped across or waded through so far. My trail made a hard left and kept going, high on the steep bank of large river. The next campsites wouldn't be far off.

When I was planning my hike, I'd heard the bridge here had been taken out in the last big floods. Walking slow, I kept an eye on the river, searching for a downed tree to cross over on safely tomorrow morning.

The trail dropped closer to the water and flattened. A faint track parted the fat ferns and prickly devil's club, more like a game trail than a human path. But in a place as wet as Washington, it never took long for even well-used trails to get overgrown.

Wild at Heart

I pushed through the greenery, soft fronds flapping against my arms and legs. As I suspected, a giant cedar tree spanned the river. Worn spots on its root ball showed me the way.

Grabbing a rough root in each hand, I planted a boot and heaved myself up. A smooth reddish-brown track ran the length of the broad trunk, disappearing into the gloom on the far side. If I crossed, I'd have to cover a few more miles to get to the next campsites.

My stomach rumbled again. I turned to climb down the way I'd come.

Something bright green flashed on the upstream side of the root ball, bobbing gently in the water. Up a couple centimeters, down a couple centimeters. It niggled at my brain. Changing course, I dropped down the other side of the tree, smaller roots cracking and breaking as I pushed through their dense weave.

I shucked my pack and edged out on another, smaller trunk lying in the water. Just shy of the object, the end of my tree bridge dipped hard and fast. I leapt back to shore, the toes of my boots darkening with moisture.

Scanning the bank, I spotted a medium-sized branch and slammed my foot down on it. With an echoing snap the limb broke off at about a three-foot length.

Coarse bark crumbling in my hand, I shuffled out onto the small tree again. I strained and poked and prodded. The object rolled, revealing a shoulder strap. The niggling in my brain clicked into a knowing. My heart raced.

No fucking way. That can't be Evan's pack.

CHAPTER 6

JULES

The waterlogged backpack weighed a ton. I drug it backwards through the shrubbery, my heart jackhammering so loud it drowned out the river's rumble.

The pungent, green scent of broken stems filled the air. Leaning it against a cedar tree, I ran back for my own pack in case I needed cord, or God forbid, first aid, and bushwhacked upstream fast.

Shoving through dead tree limbs and prickly devil's club, I searched the strainers and shallows and shadows for splashes of color that didn't belong. Red shorts. A blue shirt the color of his eyes.

The centerline between my eyebrows throbbed.

What if it is Evan's? What if he's dead? What if he's stuffed under one of these strainers and drowned?

I pushed the negative thoughts down. Because negative thoughts are no help in a search and rescue situation.

An image of a handsome but too-pale face surrounded by white satin floated through my head. My boot slipped on a wet root. I

     Wild at Heart

grabbed the nearest thing on my way down. Sharp stinging pains shot through my hand, and a dull ache rippled from my right butt cheek, up my spine, to the already tight spot between my eyebrows.

Burying my fingers in damp moss I pushed to standing and picked at the tiny, ridiculously-hard-to-see-or-grab spines embedded in my palm. Which was a waste of precious time. I'd need a ball of sap to get them out anyway.

Get a grip. It's probably not even Evan's. But somebody needs help.

Resettling my pack on my back I trudged upstream, eyes peeled.

The forest thinned. The late afternoon light brightened.

I pushed through a few last, big sword ferns, the fronds slapping my legs like cold damp fingers, and out onto the cobble-strewn banks of the river. The trail followed the shore around a gentle curve. Upstream, sagging cables and a couple boards hung in the current.

And a man stood naked, his back to me, wringing something out. Water dripped onto the rocks at his feet. I froze, relief flooding my veins. I shouldn't have stared, but I couldn't help it. The lines of his body drew me in.

I ran my gaze up his lean, muscular legs to his tight ass—whiter than the rest of him. Watched the ripple of muscles in his back and shoulders each time he twisted the fabric in his hands.

Déjà vu made the world tilt and wobble a little.

Medium height. Medium build.

Dark hair, windstorm messy on top.

No. Fucking. Way.

A ray of sunlight caught his wrist, along with the leather bracelet wrapped around it.

Yes, fucking way.

He shook out a blue shirt. Laid it on a boulder in the sun. I picked my way along the rocky riverbank, footsteps masked by the rushing water, and stopped ten feet from Evan's firm, muscled, and very bare backside.

I might not have gotten a great look at it last night, but I did spend a number of hours spooned around it, serving as his portable heater. In broad daylight his naked ass, and frankly every part of him, looked even better than he'd felt.

Hot tension flared at the base of my gut. My heart kept beating high speed, but in a different way than before. He leaned over to grab another ball of wet fabric.

Evan might not have known shit about backpacking, but his build screamed athlete. Something endurance, maybe running. Or swimming.

Whatever it was, he did a lot of it shirtless and in a sunnier part of the country, because he definitely had a darker tan than most people in the Pacific Northwest.

I could've stared all day, admiring the lines and ripples of his body, but that wouldn't have been polite. He probably wanted his backpack. And much as I believed in enjoying the scenery, I needed to avoid temptation.

And a sexy, naked man in the middle of the wilderness was one helluva temptation.

I cleared my throat. "We have to stop meeting like this."

Evan startled and pivoted, holding his red shorts in front of his for sure shrunken peen like a shield. His gaze met mine and electricity zapped down my spine.

"Oh, ah, hey Jules. How's it going?" His tone said, 'nothing to see here'. The hot flush running up his neck said, 'My life is a never-ending nightmare of calamity and I'm mortified you're seeing me like this.'

My stomach twitched. I worked to keep the laughter from rippling all the way up and out of my throat.

"Better than it looks like it's going for you." He didn't seem to have anything with him other than his shirt, spread out catching the last rays of the sun, and the soaked shorts in his hands. The only things on his body were the dark leather bracelet wrapped around his wrist and the droplets of water glistening on his cut abs. "Unless you're tanning your lily-white ass on purpose, in which case maybe you're doing great."

"Pretty sure my ass hasn't seen sunlight in at least a decade, and I wasn't planning on it happening today." He shifted from one bare foot to another. "How long were you standing there, staring at me?"

"Just long enough to make a positive ID." And be positive Evan was smokin' hot. Much hotter than I'd realized crammed in the tent with him. Or even this morning. "Shouldn't you be, oh, about ten miles up the trail already? What with your schedule and all?"

"Yeah. I should be." He shrugged and shifted feet again, one hand still holding the shorts in front of his dick. "I took a wrong turn…and an unintentional swim." His last words were barely audible over the rumble of the river.

"How bad are the damages?"

"Other than a few bumps and bruises, I'm fine. At least for now. I'm not sure how I'll feel in a few hours though since I lost my pack with all my gear in it." He stared hard at the ground, going a little green around the gills. His next words came out shaky. "Even my shoes were tied to it."

Everything about Evan drooped. His head, his shoulders, his chest. His body crumpled until he sat on a boulder, hands clutching his suddenly way too pale face.

The guy really was a sad news story waiting to happen. I wanted to grill him. Find out what the hell made him commit to a trip he was so clearly unprepared for—and what the hell he was doing crossing here. But I wasn't the type to kick a man when he was down. Besides, it'd be getting dark soon. And cold.

"Could be worse." I shrugged.

"How?" He glared at me.

"Could be raining." The corners of my lips quirked up. "Also, lucky for you, I found your pack less than a half-mile downstream."

His eyes went wide. "Seriously?"

"Seriously." I let the smirk grow and take over my face, and Evan's return smile, while small, made my heart speed up. Just a little.

"There are supposed to be campsites on this side of the river, somewhere up there, I'd bet." I waved at the forested bluff just upstream, glowing gold in the evening sun. "Why don't I get your pack while you do a little recon? I'll leave mine here so I can carry yours. I don't have anything that will fit you, but you should wrap up in my sleeping bag."

"I don't know how to thank you, Jules." His gaze pierced me. "I'm not sure where I'd be if you didn't keep showing up to save me. I owe you again, bigtime."

"You'd be freezing your ass off on the side of the river all night. But you still don't owe me anything." *Like I'm ever going to see you again after tonight.* I yanked my gaze away from his. "Just help someone else out of a jam or two sometime."

I dropped my pack on the rocks and walked away, eyeing the sun's angle. Calculating how much time I had to grab Evan's pack, hike back, cross the river, and find my own site—preferably with a few miles between us.

Helping someone out on the trail was one thing. I didn't need another night of company. Especially the company of a man I'd already enjoyed seeing naked one too many times.

　　　　　Wild at Heart

EVAN

Fuck me. I dropped my head back into my hands and squeezed my forehead with my fingers. *This trip keeps going from bad, to worse, to shittier.*

I didn't know how many times my ego could handle me screwing up, or Jules coming to my rescue. And somehow, I kept ending up naked in front of her. A nauseating flood of vulnerability washed over me, stronger than any other time on this ill-fated trip.

Worse was finding Jules behind me smirking, knowing she'd been staring at me for who-knows-how-long, and blood going to all the wrong places. All I should've felt was ashamed, embarrassed, mortified, and really, really stupid— all the emotions coursing through me now — except my dick twitched the second I laid eyes on her.

Not that Jules wasn't attractive, with her warm brown eyes, and shit-eating grin. It's just, standing naked in the middle of nowhere, with night coming on and no gear, was not the time to think about sex. Especially not after a bad breakup. Or with a woman who kept seeing me at my worst.

A woman who would never find herself in these kinds of situations.

She must think I'm a complete imbecile. Everything in my chest folded inward. *Yeah. Vulnerable doesn't even begin to describe it.*

The shadows reached dark, cold fingers into my sunny spot. I pulled on my damp shorts. My skin twitched and goose-pimpled every place the chilly fabric touched, and a few places it didn't.

I grabbed my wet shirt, the cool fabric clinging to my hands. Shivering, I spread it back out on a rock, pretty sure my meager body heat would never dry it before the temperature dropped.

Rummaging around in Jules's pack, I yanked out her stove, water filter, and food bag. My hands hit a fat, tight, nylon stuff sack at the bottom. *Gold!*

Her sleeping bag settled around my shoulders like a warm hug of mint and vanilla and cedar and moss. Sunlight lit the tops of the trees and my nose and toes tingled.

I didn't know how I would dry the rest of my gear, other than lay it out and hope for the best. Open fires weren't allowed here, even if I knew how to build one without the wax-filled egg cartons we'd used as fire starter in Scouts. But I could find a campsite.

Loading everything back in Jules's pack except her sleeping bag and my wet shirt, I slung it over one shoulder as best I could. I picked my way upstream, the smooth cobbles still warm under my bare soles, to a path leading uphill at the base of the bluff. The loamy, needle-strewn trail cushioned my bruised heels.

One empty campsite perched on the edge of the bluff where the trees opened to a view of glittering river snaking into dark forest. The last rays of the sun gilded the high peaks on either side rosy gold.

I dropped Jules's pack, sat on a convenient fallen log, and wrapped her sleeping bag tighter around my shoulders. Even given my damp chill and general discomfort, I couldn't deny the view.

The sun disappeared and the alpenglow faded. A bright, white light flashed in the murky shadows of the woods downstream. Out of the gloom Jules reappeared. Or at least the glow of her headlamp and a general body outline did.

"Evan?"

"Up here." My voice rang out over the open riverbank below.

Her headlamp bobbed and bounced towards me. Even with my water-logged pack she powered up the hill, dancing over roots and rocks like she belonged out here. Wild and free and in her element.

Despite my dispiriting, damp, and dick-shrinkingly cold circumstances, I smiled. "Over here."

Jules dumped my pack on the log behind me with a squishy thud. "Nice spot."

"Thanks. A woman I met earlier recommended it."

She snickered. "Well, that same woman would probably tell you to pull out your wet gear ASAP so it has at least a small shot at drying."

"Damn." I reached for my pack, my shoes somehow still tied to it, and relief slid through my veins. "That woman sure is smart."

My hand closed on cold, wet nylon. *She must be freezing after carrying this thing.*

"Here." I unwrapped her bag from my shoulders and reached to drape it over hers. "You've got to be cold."

She pushed it back. "Not really. I'm still warm from the hike. Besides, I've got dry layers I can put on and I have a feeling yours are soaked."

"You sure?" I held out her sleeping bag, bare feet aching against the cold ground. Now that I had my own gear back, it seemed wrong to take advantage of her generosity.

"Positive." Jules pulled the cord on her pack and dug out a stuff sack of clothes. "I told you before, I won't sleep well if I think you're outside dying of hypothermia."

The chill air on my naked chest stole what little heat I'd built up in my core. She took off her headlamp, set it on the log between us, turned away and pulled off her T-shirt.

In the dim, peripheral light her back muscles flexed and rolled. Light and shadow. They weren't masculine muscles though. They were about as feminine, and sexy, as muscles could possibly be.

Not that I was attracted to her.

At least not any more than most people are attracted to their rescuers. She slipped a long-sleeve and a fleece sweater over her head. I shivered. *This is stupid.*

Wrapping the bag back around my shoulders, I got out my headlamp, which somehow still worked, and reached into my pack for the first dense, sopping item.

Jules was right, my gear was soaked. Doing my best not to get her sleeping bag wet I rang out everything, laying each piece over the supple branches of nearby bushes.

The river gurgled and chortled below us. The sky to the east went denim blue and the first few stars popped out. Life went on around us.

Jules shifted, took a deep breath, and pushed to standing. "I'd better set up camp."

CHAPTER 7

EVAN

Jules leaned back in her camp chair, a few frizzy curls escaping from under her wool stocking cap. I leaned against a still-warmish rock, my damp sleeping bag draped over my lap in the hopes my body heat would help it dry, and spooned steaming, rehydrated beef Stroganoff into my mouth. Hot and rich and a little bit salty, my meal in a pouch tasted so much better than I'd ever have believed before I started this trip.

It beat out every five-star restaurant meal I'd ever dined on—by a long shot. With the river rushing below us, and the stars blossoming overhead, even the ambience scored higher.

Then there was the company.

In less than twenty-four hours, Jules had quoted Wayne's World and Young Frankenstein. I hadn't known anyone who admitted to watching those old comedies since high school. John outgrew them years ago. My parents considered that kind of entertainment unintelligent, immature, and certainly not useful to my future financial success. Lainey agreed.

"You really are lucky, you know."

I half snorted. "Why? Because the top third of my sleeping bag is semi-dry, so if I curl up in a tiny, shrimp-like ball I should make it through the night."

"Nope. Because whether it's wet or not, you still have all your gear." She shrugged. "You'll survive."

"So, I got that goin' for me. Which is nice." I scraped at the bottom of the bag.

She laughed, scooping another sporkful of her own dinner. "I'm guessing it'd be best if I don't ask you what the hell you were thinking, trying to wade across the river there."

"You'd be guessing right. But in my defense, it looks like a regularly used crossing." I licked creamy, peppery goodness off my spoon.

"It is a regularly used crossing—for horses. The old bridge wasn't built to hold that much weight. Since horses are taller and stronger swimmers than people, riders use the ford. It's a little deep and swift for the rest of us."

"I noticed." Pulling my nylon-covered knees up, I let my head forehead drop onto them.

Jules scraped the last of her meal out of the pouch and set it, and her spork, on the needle-covered earth. "Listen, I hope this doesn't come out wrong, but... What the hell are you doing out here?"

What the hell am I doing out here? Other than apparently trying to get myself killed.

"That, is a damn good question." I raised my head, hugging my knees to my chest for warmth. "I guess the last time I remember being truly happy was camping as a Boy Scout. I wanted a piece of that back."

"But there's a big difference between driving up to a manicured campsite with a carload of food and gear and Scout Masters, and hiking through remote wilderness alone for a week carrying every-thing you need."

"Pretty sure I figured that out all on my own. Thanks, though." I cut the light on my headlamp and stared up at the glittering sky, lay-ered with more stars than I realized existed. "Backpacking seemed easy and fun when I was a kid. And I figured if Bill Bryson could hike eight hundred miles on the Appalachian Trail, out of shape and with all the wrong equipment, I could make it a hundred and fifty. All I needed was the right gear. Which makes me a grade A dumbass."

"Oh, man. I loved A Walk in the Woods. When his buddy starts throwing critical food and gear he's tired of carrying off the side of a mountain?" She chuckled. "Classic."

"Yeah. That has to be one of the funniest scenes in the book. It's less funny now, when a big part of the reason I went super ultra-light was to avoid doing that very thing. Except, in retrospect, I took the ounce-counting a little too far for comfort. Literally."

I eyed Jules, leaning back in the comfy, insulating chair she'd folded her pad into, using the same pad and chair kit I'd refused to buy to save weight. Envy tightened my veins.

"I did bring one frivolous item though."

"What's that?"

I dug in my food bag, wrappers crinkling, and held up a pouch. "Double chocolate cheesecake. I was planning to have it on my last night, but tonight seems like a better call…Assuming you like that sort of thing."

She sat up straighter, her headlamp beaming the trunks of the surrounding trees. "Oh, hell yes. I never turn down dessert."

And I'd never met a woman who did anything more than take one, tiny bite of the dessert I'd ordered. Go figure.

She cranked up her stove and poured fresh water in the pot. The guilt of using more of her fuel bit at me, but at least this time I was giving her something in return. Even if it was only rehydrated cheesecake. "It's not much, but it's the least I can do."

"Hey, when you're this far from civilization, cheesecake's value shouldn't be underestimated."

"True." I snorted and she giggled.

Our laughter died and we sat silent listening to the whisper of the stove. Her glowing headlamp cast her face in shadow, but I could imagine her profile. The pert nose. The smile twitching her lips. Her dark curly hair floating wild around her face.

The plastic lid rattled on the pot. I handed her the opened pouch of dessert.

She cut the stove and poured. "For the record, I don't think you're a total dumbass, just a little naïve. And a whole lot lucky."

"Ha. You keep saying I'm lucky, but I don't feel very lucky. Not with the way my life has been going."

"At least you're not dead."

"Mostly thanks to you." I raised my water bottle in a toast. "Cheers."

I didn't have much more than that to be thankful for out there but being alive was one worthwhile thing. Double chocolate cheesecake was another. And spending a few more hours with Jules seemed like one more.

JULES

I scraped my spoon in the bottom of the bag, passed it back to Evan, and licked the sweet, chocolaty cheesecake off my knuckles. The gesture felt strangely intimate. The kind of intimacy I usually avoided.

Unfortunately, I didn't have time to hike to the next set of campsites. And, well. Chocolate cheesecake.

So, a little too much intimacy it was.

At least he also made me laugh. And he didn't have to share his one and only celebratory dessert with me. Though the fact that once again he'd managed to not kill himself out here was definitely worth celebrating.

Every time shit went shitty in my life, that's what I reminded myself: I'm not dead. I could still breathe and laugh and dance and fuck and cry. My life hadn't been cut short and every day I got to live was worth celebrating—even the shitty ones.

Which led me back to Evan.

I hadn't planned to make camp with him. But by the time I got him squared away, the sun had set and my stomach was grumbling. And maybe, just maybe, I couldn't resist spending a little more time with him—only to try and figure him out, of course.

So far, I'd managed to keep my mouth shut and most of my questions to myself. But seriously… What the hell was he doing out here, aside from trying to die a slow, cold death? His Boy Scouts story was cute and all, but people didn't usually undertake these adventures with so little experience. Not without some outside impetus or something to prove.

I cut my light, turning Evan into a shadow, and let my eyes adjust to the darkness. Even though I couldn't really see him, pain and tension flowed off him in waves, tugging at my heart. At my innate desire to make things better for everyone around me—especially people I cared about.

Not that I cared about Evan. I barely knew anything about him, other than that he was fit, and smart, and got my sense of humor. And he carried around a mountain of issues way heavier than any backpack.

That didn't stop my curiosity from itching like a bad case of poison ivy. The crescent moon edged over the tops of the mountains, casting dim silver bars through the trees.

He blew out a hard breath and shifted, the sleeping bag on his lap rustling.

"Want to talk about it?" I asked.

"Not really."

"Might make you feel better."

"I don't know about that."

"Holding everything in is never a good choice. It's gonna fester and grow inside you until it explodes, destroying everything in its path." That much I knew from experience.

He grunted.

"Fine. Forget I asked." My curiosity itched worse knowing he wasn't going to scratch it.

Probably better he doesn't want to talk. I don't need to get any more involved with this guy and his problems.

The smell of evergreen trees, damp mulch, and sweet earth surrounded us. A rock bit into my ankle. I moved my leg. The air temperature dropped, chilling my exposed skin. "Want a cup of tea?"

His head turned toward me. "Are you sure you have enough?"

"If I didn't, I wouldn't have offered." I always carried extra tea. It was light and small, and sometimes a hot drink in hand made everything else better. I rocked to standing in one smooth motion and clicked my headlamp back on. "Where's your mug?"

"It's in my vestibule. Thanks."

I found it and crouched, lighting the stove, my headlamp casting a bright spotlight on the ground. Evan added water to the pot and handed it to me. His fingers brushed mine. Warm tingles raced along my skin.

 Wild at Heart

His voice came out of the darkness, soft and low. "I told myself I was doing this trip to get back in touch with myself. With who I want to be and what I want to do with my life. Now I think maybe I'm just running away, because when I get back home, nothing will have changed. Not even me."

"What do you mean?"

"I only have a couple more days on the trail and all I've figured out so far is that I don't know the first thing about backcountry camping. And…I never should've come out here."

"Well, that's probably a good thing to learn about yourself, so you don't end up freezing to death in the middle of nowhere on a future trip." The heating water sputtered.

"Unfortunately, those deep realizations do nothing to help me find a job—let alone a new career or a new place to live. I haven't even figured out how to tell my parents I broke up with my fiancé. Though, if I really am lucky, they heard that news from Lainey days ago, and have already moved on from berating me for ruining all their plans to freaking out because they can't reach me."

Oh Jesus. He just broke up with his fiancé. Red flag. Red flag.

If I needed another reason to stay far away from this guy, that was the best possible one. "Sounds like you've got one helluva fun family."

"About as much fun as a razor blade slide with a saltwater pool at the bottom."

"Damn. Razor blade slides are my favorite. And nothing beats the sting of salt in your wounds if you're looking for a good time."

He barked out a single, sharp laugh. "Exactly."

The plastic lid on my titanium pot rattled. I dropped the tea bags in our mugs and poured, chamomile steam warming my cheeks.

"Here you go." I handed him his mug, my light catching his face. Highlighting the creases at the corner of his eyes and the flat, tense line of his mouth.

"Thanks."

"Anytime." I cut my light and wrapped my hands around my mug, heat soaking into my palms. "So, it sounds like you've got a full-fledged middle-age crisis going on."

"Yeah. Except I'm not quite middle-aged. And I'm pretty sure this crisis has been going on for the last twenty years."

"So, what made you suddenly decide backpacking was the solution to all your troubles?"

"I don't know. I guess losing my job—which I hated with every fiber of my being—made me rethink more than a few things. In particular, the horrifying fact that the only time I felt even vaguely happy was swimming or running or biking, preferably alone. So I'd been throwing myself into triathlon training for the past few years, which helped cost me my job, and my relationship."

Well, that explains his hot body.

"What did you do for work?"

"Investment analyst." He sighed.

"What, exactly, is that?"

"I researched companies my firm was interested in adding to their investment portfolio and made recommendations on which ones to buy."

"Sounds interesting. And lucrative."

"It can be. It's also a soul-sucking, ultimately meaningless job where the main goal is to make a very small number of people very rich—ideally yourself included. I didn't really have the drive to make that much money for other people, or myself." His shadow shrugged. "Of course, some people love it."

"Why'd you break off your engagement?"

He blew across the top of his mug and slurped a tiny sip. And another.

Oops. Maybe I overstepped. Shocker.

I stared up at the scraps of star-sprigged sky visible through the branches.

Evan took a deep breath and continued. "Lainey, she's great. Smart, beautiful, driven, successful—and part of my parents' grand plan to connect our two families for financial reasons. It wasn't fair to either of us that I would never be the kind of man she wanted. Not that I even know what kind of man I am or want to be, other than not like that. Thus, my brilliant, get-in-touch-with-myself-by-backpacking plan."

"Excellent choice." I knew all about not being sure of who you are or what you want. And trying to figure it out on the trail. "The get-in-touch-with-yourself-by-backpacking plan almost always works like a charm."

"Right? Unless you end up killing yourself because you don't know what you're doing."

"True. That would throw a bit of a wrench in the plan."

I sipped my cooling tea, surrounded by nothing but shadows and mountains and the faint light of a crescent moon. And Evan. Just two random people in the middle of nowhere trying to figure out what to do with our lives.

"So, if you don't mind me asking…" His rich voice startled me from my thoughts. "What the hell are you doing out here, and for a whole month?"

"Same thing as you. Trying to decide what, and who, I want to be when I grow up." I took another sip of my tea.

"Come on, Jules. I just told you my whole, sordid life saga. You can't leave me with that answer."

CHAPTER 8

JULES

I liked Evan. I didn't want to like him, but I did. I liked sitting next to him in the dark, quiet forest listening to his stories. And I admired his grit.

He didn't complain or freak out when he got into trouble out here. Sure, he shouldn't have been out here alone at all. Not with his total lack of outdoor experience. But he hadn't given up or turned around. Or clung to me like a life raft in the middle of the ocean.

Nope. He kept pushing on, solo, determined to finish his hike. Then there was his water-flecked six pack, on full display today. Those droplets shining in the sun, tempting me to lick them away...

Shit. Don't think about that.

I liked sex. Maybe a little too much. And wasn't usually one to turn down a fun roll in the hay with an attractive, interesting guy— not that Evan was offering. But I'd made a promise to myself I wasn't about to break.

Besides, he wasn't my type. I liked big, burly guys with wild streaks who kept their hearts to themselves. Guys who'd fuck me in weird places or spend all day teasing me and driving me insane but didn't need to get into deep conversations about our hopes and dreams. Or the meaning of life, the universe, and everything.

Evan was too thoughtful, too intellectual, too…nice. He wanted to talk about things. Things I didn't want to talk about.

I never intended to make friends with anyone out here. Definitely not with a pretty man with problems galore and an ex-fiancé waiting at home.

The last thing I wanted to do was strengthen our growing bond by telling him about my personal issues. Which definitely meant not sharing the saga of my love life.

Having twelve men in a row leave me for their ex-girlfriends made me sound toxic at best, anyway. Or like the relationship kiss of death. I planned to keep that info between me and my besties and those twelve assholes, thankyouverymuch.

"It's a long story."

He shifted around to face me, dim slashes of moonlight crossing his face, and set down his mug. "I've got time."

"Right." I parsed what I could safely tell him. "I've been feeling burnt out by work, so I decided to take a sabbatical to recharge."

"What do you do?"

"I'm a freelance graphic designer. And I coach kids' gymnastics on the side."

"Sounds pretty great if you ask me."

"Don't get me wrong, I love coaching gymnastics. And graphic design can be fun and creative. It can also be tedious as hell, and I'm tired of being on a computer all the time. Running my own business is exhausting. And it sounds stupid to complain about it, but the biggest issue is I have more business than I can handle. I'm at the point where I either need to hire another designer or start turning clients away—and I can't really afford to do either."

"Tough choices. Why not coach gymnastics full-time and do graphic design part-time?"

I blew out a breath. "Do you have any idea what a kids' gymnastics coach makes?" I didn't wait for him to answer. "Unless you're Bela Karolyi, it's not much more than a minimum wage gig. I couldn't even come close to surviving in Seattle on that kind of salary."

"That's a shame. Seems like working with kids is always grossly undervalued."

That was an understatement. "Seriously."

Evan shuffled his sleeping bag around. "So…What does your boyfriend think about you being out here by yourself for a month or more?"

Where the hell did that come from? Was he one of those guys who believed every woman's number one priority in life was finding a man?

"What makes you think I have a boyfriend, let alone one I'd need to answer to?"

EVAN

"You just— Well…Ah…Sorry. Sorry. I didn't mean to pry." Except I did. I'm not sure why, but I felt close to Jules. I cared about her. Probably just that weird bond people form with someone who rescues them. I did not need to know about her personal life, though. Tomorrow I'd be on my way early and never see her again.

"It's okay." She didn't sound convincing.

I rubbed my arms, trying to generate a little extra heat. "It's getting cold out here. I think I'm going to bed. See if my tent will keep me any warmer."

"Wait. Let me heat up some more hot water and you can fill your water bottle and tuck it in the foot of your sleeping bag."

"Are you sure you have enough fuel to spare?"

She exhaled hard. "I wouldn't have offered if I didn't."

Her stove whooshed to life. She covered the blue glow of flames with her pot, so I couldn't see her face in the dark, but I could imagine her expression. The same one she'd used earlier—a little exasperated, but not quite eye-roll status. It's just, I still had a hard time believing anyone would offer me so much, without wanting anything in return. But I didn't have anything else to give Jules. Not out here, where she knew what she was doing, had everything she needed, and seemed perfectly happy.

Really, the only thing I could give her was her solitude back. Something I'd do first thing in the morning.

My freshly filled water bottle heated my hand. I crawled into my tiny tent, put on every piece of semi-dry clothing I'd brought, and arrayed my sleeping bag so the wet part could get maximum airflow and the dryish part covered as much of me as possible. Tucking the bottle at my feet, I curled into a ball and closed my eyes, ignoring my periodic shivers.

Zzzzzzzzzzzzt.

That would be Jules, opening her tent door.

Nylon whispered against nylon and her tent zipped closed. Quiet shuffling sounds made their way across the small space separating our shelters.

I'd be so much warmer curled up with Jules again. Not that I would ever ask. That would be way too much of an imposition, and it wasn't like I was borderline hypothermic tonight. Just damp and chilly and uncomfortable because of my own stupid decision.

No matter how much I enjoyed having her splayed across my naked body, it wouldn't happen again. Though I bet it would feel even more amazing if we were both naked.

Did she sleep naked when she was alone?

Images of her bare, muscular body stretched out on top of her sleeping bag threatened to take over my brain, and my dick. I shoved them away.

Jules was a kindhearted stranger who'd thankfully taken pity on me and saved my ass. Twice. Admiration, gratitude, even appreciation were fine emotions to have towards her. Lust was not.

What I needed was sleep. If I made good time and put in extra miles, I had a shot at making it out of here a day early. If I had to start and finish hiking in the dark, I was getting off this damn trail ASAP.

In two nights, I would be tucked in a real bed, in a heated room, after a hot shower. And it was going to be the best night's sleep of my entire life.

CHAPTER 9

EVAN

My eyes opened to darkness. I lay in cozy warmth of my mostly dry sleeping bag, contemplating whether it was still middle of the night, or really early morning. Not that it mattered. I was wide awake, so I might as well pack up and hit the trail.

I could either hike in the dark now, or hike in the dark tonight. The chances of me getting lost would likely be greater after a long day, so the more miles I put in early, the better.

Clicking on my headlamp, I moved as quiet as possible stuffing away my sleeping bag and folding my pad. I unstaked my tent and carried it as far from Jules as I could. She didn't need to be awakened before dawn by the clack of tent poles or the crackle of folding nylon.

Fingertips numbed by damp fabric and chilled aluminum, I shoved my rainfly into the top of my pack, buckled the lid, and shouldered my load. Mostly dry and with four days food gone, it was ridiculously light. I could definitely carry a bit more fuel and food—and more damn tea and coffee.

If I ever did a trip like this again.

Not that I planned to.

No amount of money would've convinced me to go backpacking again.

Ever.

The midnight velvet sky turned faded denim. A bird warbled somewhere off to my right. Another one answered from my left. I picked my way over roots and rocks down to the river, not at all sure how I was going to cross. Wishing I had asked Jules.

I scanned the shore with my headlamp beam, upstream and down. Twenty yards upstream the banks rose up into high bluffs, their dark walls looming over the river, still as unpassable as yesterday.

Downstream it is.

Where the trees and ferns closed in, light and shadow from my headlamp highlighted a thin path toward the river. It led straight to a fat evergreen spanning the rapids. If I'd been paying better attention, I could've saved myself a cold, wet night.

But then I wouldn't have seen Jules again.

My dick twitched at the memory of her finding me naked in broad daylight on the riverbank. I couldn't help wondering what she looked like naked. Not that it mattered. I'd never see her again anyway, naked or clothed.

The flat light of pre-dawn illuminated the makeshift bridge. Barely. Grabbing the cool, slick roots I clambered up and shuffled across, ignoring the dark, swirling water eight feet below.

More downed trees spanned the river not far downstream Their branches reached into the current forming a nasty-looking fence, ready to hook and trap a clumsy backpacker.

My left foot slipped on the smooth trunk.

I teetered.

Wild at Heart

My heart hammered.

Spreading my arms wide, I clenched my abdominal muscles and glutes. The teetering stopped. Steady and slow, I inched the length of the log holding my breath. Moving carefully around broken branches.

The cobbles on the far bank clattered under my feet. Relief ran from my fingertips to my toes. Risk, I'd realized over the past few days, looks a lot different when you're miles from nowhere than it does in the city. I grabbed my water bottle, pouring cool water down my adrenaline-parched throat.

Changing careers or changing my life didn't seem near as frightening as falling in the river, being pulled under by my pack, and almost drowning. Or half as scary as getting lost out here or freezing to death in the middle of nowhere.

Walking back upstream to pick up the main trail again, I considered my history. Each time I'd gotten into trouble out here I'd been rushing. I'd been hyper-focused on mileage goals instead of the world around me.

If I intended to hike out early, and I did, I'd have to cover even more ground over the next two days. I needed to pay attention to my surroundings and the weather, because my life depended on it. I needed to remember I always had options. I didn't *have* to stay focused on the end goal above all else. In fact, I shouldn't.

A good lesson for when I get back home, too.

Jules would never get into the kinds of stupid situations she'd found me in. Nope. Independent and down-to-earth, with confidence in spades—confidence she'd earned through experience, not bought with her parent's money—she had wisdom and her priorities straight. At least straighter than mine.

Not to mention a wicked, slightly juvenile sense of humor. A smile stole across my face.

The chances of meeting another woman like her in the circles I traveled in, were slim to none. I'd never forget her, or what she'd done for me.

Good-bye, Jules. Thanks for saving my naked ass. Again. I glanced in the direction of our campsite across the river and headed into the woods.

The needle-strewn path rolled up and down through towering trees. Miles disappeared beneath my feet. The sun topped the ridge shining hot and fierce in a clear blue sky. I peeled off my long-sleeve shirt and kept a pace fast enough to make my thighs and calves burn, stopping regularly to check my map and grab a sip of water or snack.

Even in the shade of the forest a sheen of sweat slicked my skin. I imagined how good a hot shower would feel. Water beating down on my neck and shoulders instead of the sun and my backpack straps. A week's worth of dirt and grime and stink washing down the drain. Followed by a soft, dry bed to stretch out in.

In front of me, the trail rose in a series of steep switchbacks, disappearing high up the mountain. My calves edged toward cramping. I'd covered twenty miles today already, and still had forty-five more to go to get off this damn trail.

When I conceived this plan, hiking twenty plus miles in one day seemed totally doable. I ran that far and longer in Boston all the time. Staring up at that mountainside, feet and legs aching, my heart sank.

I'd miscalculated. Seven days was barely enough, and I'd never get out early.

Shucking my pack, I plopped down on a log and fished out an energy gel. If I could hike a few more miles today, and get a before-dawn start tomorrow, I could still make it to Highway 12 in two days, as originally planned, and hitch a ride into Packwood for the night.

Ignoring the pain I pushed to my feet, shouldered my pack, and put one foot in front of the other on the sun splotched trail. I climbed one switchback, and another, and another for a solid hour. Maybe longer.

The trees thinned and low shrubs filled the gaps, opening sight-lines into the valley I'd climbed up from. A tiny lake glittered far below, where I'd stopped to refill my bottles around lunchtime.

I metered out a few drops from my dwindling supply, swirling them around my dry mouth. The top of this climb, and a water source, couldn't be that far off. If I could make a few more miles after that, it should be mostly downhill to the highway. Easy.

JULES

The sun hung low in the sky, casting sparkles on the small lake where I crouched, pumping my purifier. My map showed the final climb to the highest, craggiest, most spectacular part of the Goat Rocks Wilderness started a mile or two up the trail.

If I tackled that in the heat of the day, I'd sweat out my weight in water. And after all the effort, I wanted plenty of time to enjoy the views—hopefully without a hundred other hikers around. Getting up there early on a weekday might guarantee me some solitude. Or at least my pick of the most scenic camp spots.

Hydration bladder filled tight like a satisfied tick, I stood, yawned, and stretched my back. Fatigue made my legs heavy.

Despite his best efforts, the crinkle and clatter of Evan breaking camp had woken me early. I'd laid in my sleeping bag trying to fall back asleep, but my brain kept focusing on him.

Wondering how his tent had held up. Wondering if his sleeping bag had dried, and if he'd managed to sleep at all despite the damp cold. Wondering if I should get up and make him a nice cup of hot tea before he left.

I thought about that longer than I'd liked.

I should've been thrilled he hit the trail early, leaving me to enjoy a relaxing breakfast by the river, and a day taken at exactly my own pace and no one else's. Instead, I kept half-looking for him. Half-expecting to find him tangled in a downed tree. Or soaking wet and naked on the side of a river, water dripping down his washboard abs.

Heat and tension quivered at the apex of my legs.

Good thing he's long gone, or I might've made choices I'd regret.

I filled my pot of water to boil for dinner and staked my tent on the loamy ground a few hundred feet from the shore. My stove clicked to life with a hiss and in fifteen minutes I had a hot meal in hand.

Belly full, I watched the last, reddish-gold rays gild the tops of the ridges. Sleep sucked me down as soon as my head hit my makeshift, down jacket pillow.

I crawled out of my tent early, a handful of stars still scattered across the indigo sky. A slight breeze ruffled the dark surface of the nearby lake, carrying tiny splish-splash sounds and the moist, pencil-shaving scent of the forest. I broke camp by headlamp and hit the trail.

The sky turned gray, then peach, then gold, then pale, pale blue. The rising sun warmed my shoulders.

One long, steep, switchback after another climbed through dense forest. My feet fell in front of each other on the kind of autopilot you only get after hiking for days.

My calves tightened. My knee ached in the dull way I'd gotten used to ignoring years ago.

I sipped water, slurped down an energy gel, and kept walking. My brain wandered aimlessly. I sang along to my internal jukebox, considered my dating history for the umpteenth time, and debated the merits of getting a job versus running a business.

The trees thinned, reveal eye-popping views of ridges and spires and forested flanks that went on for forever. Two and a half hours after I left camp, I topped out in the high alpine.

Jagged mountains scraped an azure sky. A few puffy clouds mimicked the white snow of the permanent snowfields tucked into curving, glacier-carved cirques. A marmot's high-pitched whistle rang out.

And not another human in sight.

The angels may or may not have sung.

I sucked at my hydration tube. All I got was a choking sound and a warm dribble. My map showed a series of small ponds about a half-mile ahead and off trail to the right.

Anyone coming up that climb behind me would likely run out of water too and stop at the first one. I set my sights on the second one, hopping from rock to gravel spot to avoid crushing delicate, high-altitude plants and topped a small rise.

Cupped in a tiny basin at the foot of towering peaks, the tarn sparkled in the sunlight. A scattering of late season red fireweed and purple lupine dotted the meadows around it. I pulled out my water filter and pumped, enjoying the views and the solitude and the crisp edge to the rapidly warming, clean mountain air.

A mix of pride, exhilaration, and awe fluttered in my chest. This was what I went out here for. Those moments where I'm completely blown away by mother nature, alone in an awe-inspiring place that I worked my ass off to reach.

Dipping my hands in the icy water, I splashed my face, scrubbing away the dirt and sweat from my hike. My skin tingled. I gazed up at the high ridges and rocks around me.

Not another soul in sight. No voices. No engines. Nothing but me and the mountains and my sweaty clothes and sore muscles. And this clear blue lake calling my name.

I peeled off my shorts, tee and sports bra, dumped them on a nearby rock, and waded into the frigid, clear as glass water. Pushing off the graveled bottom with rapidly numbing feet, I launched a shallow dive. The cold snatched my breath away, tightening my lungs. Surfacing with an exhilarated whoop I treaded water, shoving my dripping hair out of my eyes and laughing with the sheer joy of being alive.

Life didn't get any better than this.

CHAPTER 10

EVAN

I flung one hand over my eyes to block out the light and shifted onto my back. The sun lit the wall of my tent, turning it into a glowing orange mini sauna.

My legs ached. My feet throbbed. My lips, dry and cracked, burned. And my stomach rumbled loud enough to remind me I'd eaten nothing but energy gels for dinner. I swallowed, or rather, pushed a large pebble down the rough scratchiness that pretended to be my throat.

Giving up on sleep, I grabbed my water bottle and sucked at the last few drops.

I'd done one Ironman and it had nothing on last night's grueling hike. Maybe because I hadn't run out of water three-quarters of the way through the race and ended up finishing in the cold and dark.

By the time I hit the obvious top of the climb, I had just enough energy left to stumble off-trail, find the first reasonable spot to pitch my tent, and collapse without cooking dinner—not that I had water left to boil anyway.

Water. That's what I need to deal with first.

I clambered out of my tent into hot, bright mid-morning sunshine.

Shit. It's late. I better get moving, fast. Scrubbing at the crunchy sleep bits in the corners of my eyes, I snagged my toothbrush, water filter, and both empty bottles from my vestibule.

My map showed a bunch of small lakes up here, not too far away from camp. At least, I hoped they weren't too far away. I hadn't been about to start looking for them in the dark. Knowing my luck, I would've walked right off a cliff.

Shoving on my sunglasses I stood and took my first real look around.

My jaw dropped. The scene was…stunning.

Awe-inspiring.

Like something out of National Geographic or The Sound of Music, with snow-flecked mountains rising behind fields dotted with colorful wildflowers. If I listened closely, I swear I could hear Julie Andrews singing. Add in some cow bells clanging and it could be Austria or Switzerland or anywhere in the Alps, except for the three major volcanoes scraping the sky in the other directions.

I'd seen pictures of this area when I planned my trip, and knew it would be spectacular, but nothing prepared me for being out here, in the middle of it. A light breeze blew the cleanest air imaginable across my skin. No gas fumes. No chemicals or perfumes. Nothing but the sweet tang of pine trees and blooming flowers and sunshine.

I threaded through scrubby shrubs and rolling terrain toward the low basin I expected to be filled with water off to my right. Each small rise led to another small dip that wasn't a lake or a pond or even a puddle.

What if I get lost and can't find water? Or find my way back to my tent?

Wild at Heart

Desperation and fear clutched at my gut. Licking my parched lips, I looked back the way I'd come and tried to spot identifying characteristics to help me locate the trail and/or my camp again. Other than the tallest peaks the landscape had an eerie sameness.

A splash and a hoot rang out from somewhere ahead. I scurried toward the sounds, mouth puckering.

Sunlight refracted off bright blue-green water, adding one more unreal element to the scene. One I could almost taste. I searched for the best path down to the small, serene lake.

A dark brown head popped up in the middle and headed for the opposite shore. I scanned for other people…Nothing but a pile of clothes on a rock near the water's edge.

A pale neck and a pair of relatively broad shoulders came out of the water. Followed by a small waist, and the swell of hips and strong thighs. Annnnd, Jules stood naked. Ankle deep. Her back to me. Her body a mesmerizing mix of soft curves and firm muscle.

My dick sprang to life.

And my foot slipped on a loose rock, the clatter of rolling stones echoing in the small basin. She pivoted, hands covering her privates. Which did nothing to hide how incredibly sexy she looked, standing in the sunlight like some rare mountain goddess.

"We have to stop meeting like this," I called out.

"How long were you standing there, staring at me?"

"Just long enough to make a positive ID." And be positive that Jules, even though she wasn't my usual type, was incredibly sexy.

"Ha. Funny."

I tilted my head toward the lake. "Mind if I pump?

She stared at me, wide-eyed, and my chest tightened. Mortified, I held up my filter and empty bottles. "Some water. Pump some water."

"Sure." The corners of her mouth danced. "Go right ahead." She dropped her arms and walked toward her clothes. Instead of getting dressed, she casually gathered everything and waded into the lake.

Maybe I should've done the polite thing and found somewhere else to get water, but I was far too thirsty. And far too entranced by her naked body and the way she moved, graceful and powerful. Comfortable in her own skin out here in a way I wasn't. I couldn't help glancing at her while I filled my bottles.

I also couldn't help the hardening of my dick because every time she bent and dunked her clothes the sunlight caught the planes of her muscles, and the roundness of her breasts, and made a glowing halo of the wild curls floating around her head. And she took my breath away more than the cold water freezing my fingers.

My first bottle filled. I drained it in a few gulps, and I'd swear it was the best water I'd ever tasted, cold and fresh like melted snow. Still, even dirty and sweaty the idea of standing knee deep, let alone jumping into, a glacial lake seemed a little ridiculous. I filled both bottles and used the clean water to brush my teeth.

Jules splashed onto shore and spread her rinsed-out clothing, and her body, across the broad, flat rocks like being out here naked was the most natural thing in the world.

Then again, it really should be. Natural, I mean. At least out here.

I wound the hoses around my filter and tucked it in its storage sack. That was it. I didn't have any good reason to stick around, but I didn't want to leave.

"What are you doing here, anyway?" Jules's voice startled me. "I thought you'd be almost out by now."

My chest collapsed with the weight of embarrassment. "That last climb kicked my ass. I had no idea it would take me three hours to go five miles. By the time I hit the top it was late, and dark, and I was out of water. So, I made camp and passed out."

"Good call. The trail can be hard to follow up here, especially in the dark."

"Yeah. It's not that easy to follow in daylight, either."

"True that." The breeze ruffled the water. She draped a bronze forearm over her eyes to block the sun. "Well, take care. And don't get lost on your way out."

"Thanks." I shifted from foot to foot and stared up at the peaks in front of me, almost close enough to touch. Literally. I wasn't sure what was more beautiful; the mountains and meadows, or the naked woman stretched out in the sun like a cat. So many reasons not to leave. "How was the swim?"

She didn't move. "Fan-fucking-tastic. You should jump in."

"Isn't it cold?"

"Of course it's cold, but in the best possible way." Jules tilted her head and cracked one eye. "If you want to jump in, I promise I won't look. Shrinkage and all that."

"Ha! Funny."

She pushed up to her elbows and stared at me, the pale globes of her breasts shining in the sun. "Seriously, it's amazing. If you've never skinny dipped in a high-mountain lake, you shouldn't pass up this chance. Few things will make you feel more alive—not to mention clean and refreshed."

I moved my bottles and filter in front of my crotch and hesitated, biting my lip. She made a solid argument but getting naked up here in the middle of nowhere seemed weirder than it should—especially for a guy who'd already been naked out here twice. Though it wasn't so much getting naked that was my problem.

It was getting naked in front of a woman I barely knew, when I had a raging hard-on. Talk about inappropriate and uncomfortable. Not sure how I would explain that. And I did still need to break camp and hit the trail ASAP.

"C'mon. Don't be a weenie." She sat up all the way, oblivious to her nudity.

My dick twitched and strained at the seam of my shorts. "I'm not a weenie."

"I'll jump in again with you, if it helps."

"That good, huh?" I was pretty sure swimming naked with Jules was not going to help my current problem, but maybe the cold water would. And the idea of being clean for the first time in five days was pretty damn appealing, not to mention the setting.

"Better." Her smile lit her face.

How many people can say they've swum naked in a high-alpine lake with a gorgeous woman? I crossed half the distance between us.

I can run in ahead of her, or behind her, and be neck deep before she sees my stiffy.

"Okay, then." I angled my body toward the mountains, grabbed the back of my shirt and peeled it off one-handed. The sun blazed on my bare back. "You haven't steered me wrong yet. I guess this is something I need to experience."

JULES

The golden sun brought every muscle in Evan's back into high relief, from his surprisingly broad shoulders to his narrow waist.

Damn. He is way too beautiful for his own good. Or mine.

When he left without so much as a good-bye yesterday morning, I'd been a little devastated. Assuming one can be "a little" devastated. Maybe that was like being a little pregnant. But I couldn't be *that* upset, not when I'd just met the guy and had to keep saving his ignorant ass.

Except, I'd missed him right away. Missed his self-deprecating laugh, and his willingness to keep putting himself out there—and keep accepting my help without it crushing his ego.

The men I'd been dating hid their thoughts and feelings behind broad muscles. Evan's pain and passion and worry and intelligence showed through in his every word and action, along with something indefinable but damn sexy.

Convincing him to go skinny-dipping had to be one of my worst ideas ever. But the universe had brought him to me for a third time. To this tiny, clear blue pool in the middle of the vast wilderness. I wasn't about to look that gift horse in the mouth.

"Last one in is a rotten egg." Standing, I headed for the water without a second glance.

The cold ripped my breath away all over again. I came up facing shore, body tingling, just in time to watch Evan run in. He might've been built smaller than the guys I'd been dating, but he wasn't small everywhere.

No sir-ee. He was plenty big where it counted most. And rock hard.

The tingles centered themselves between my legs. I probably shouldn't have looked, but I couldn't help it.

It's not every day I got to enjoy the sight of a beautiful, naked man in one of the most spectacular places in the world. Far be it from me to ignore the scenery.

He surfaced, spluttering and swiping hair out of his face. "Jesus Christ! It's fucking freezing."

"Just give it a second. You'll get used to it."

He shook his head, flinging glittering water droplets into the sky. "I'm not sure I will. At least not before I freeze to death. Or my fingers and toes fall off."

My laugh rang out over the basin. "If you haven't frozen to death on this trip yet, you probably won't now."

"Thanks for the positivity, I think." He scrubbed at his head, and his arms and legs, and other places I tried my best not to pay attention to him touching.

I swam to shore to give him a little privacy. And to make sure he didn't catch me staring. Because I was having a hard time not staring. Flipping my clothes, I stretched out on my sun-warmed rock again, letting the hot rays dry my still-prickling, goose-bumped skin.

Evan waded out, grabbed his clothing, and dumped it in the lake. I only peeked out of the corner of my eye; I swear. I couldn't help it.

Dunking and twisting his shirt and shorts, he looked a lot more comfortable in his skin. Maybe because the cold water had done its job on his hard-on.

I kinda missed the woody. I liked knowing he had one because of me, even though I shouldn't have.

Aaaaaaand, the warm tingling cranked up between my legs again.

I turned my gaze to the crags looming above me. The scenery I *should* be enjoying. Drenched fabric slapped against rock. Which meant Evan stood feet away in all his naked glory.

Don't look. Don't look. Don't look.

He stretched out on the other half of my flat rock, his hand, hell, his entire bare body, less than a foot away from mine. I gazed at him sideways through slit eyes. The sun turned his already tan skin a deeper shade of gold and highlighted every rise and plane. It wouldn't have taken much effort to reach over and run my hands along his cut muscles.

It took more not to.

I trained my gaze on his face. "So, was it worth it?"

"Totally." He sniffed an armpit. "You were right. I smell much better. And I feel…alive. Energized. Better than I've felt in days. Especially now that my feet are thawing."

"You oughta be used to frozen feet by now." I giggled.

"Not sure I'll ever get used to it, but it's a worthwhile trade-off in this instance."

"Glad you think so."

"Definitely." He sat up and took a long swig from his water bottle. "Thanks for pushing me to get in. I never would have done it otherwise, and now I'm going to remember this moment—swimming in this clear, clean alpine lake with nothing but mountains around me, and you—for the rest of my life." Evan lay back down.

His hand fell right next to mine. Close enough our pinkies touched. He didn't acknowledge the small point of warm contact, and I didn't move. I didn't want to. I wanted to let the heat from his touch run up my arm and down my spine.

It didn't have to go any further, no matter how many warm tingles he generated. It just felt…nice. Companionable.

Okay, maybe a teensy bit sexy. Mainly because of the naked.

But not much.

We lay still and silent. A light breeze whispered over my skin, making the hairs on my arms dance. Marmots whistled. The high keening cry of a red-tailed hawk floated above our heads. I closed my eyes, relaxing into the hard rock. One hundred percent in my happy place.

The lake water lapping against the shore lulled me into a hypnotic, almost sleeping state.

"I'm pretty sure I don't ever want to move from this spot," Evan mumbled.

I sighed. "I know exactly what you mean."

If I could live in a tiny cabin in the mountains, and not have to work on a computer for a living, my life would be complete. Only that dream wasn't so easily realized.

Maybe I could spend a summer as a fire lookout. Or better yet, hot springs caretaker. But eventually I'd have to come back to the "real world" of jobs and clients and credit card bills and my mortgage coming due.

His pinkie skimmed down the outside of mine, the motion slow and small. I held my breath. He slid it back up. And down. Circled it over and skated along the sensitive skin on the inside to the web.

Heat and electricity skittered up my arm. Made it hard for me to think about anything other than Evan touching me.

He twined his pinkie around mine in the world's tiniest hug. "Thanks, Jules."

"For what?"

"For everything. For saving me from freezing. For sharing your tent and your food and your campsites. For talking me into swimming here." His finger squeezed. "My time with you has been, by far, the best part of this entire trip."

The heat centered in my heart. I squeezed back. "You're welcome."

Laying so close to a gorgeous naked man I barely knew, our smallest fingers twisted tight together, I should've been tense and uncomfortable. Except being with Evan felt easy. Natural. Safe.

A puffy white cloud floated in front of the sun, dropping the temperature. Goosebumps rose on my arms again.

     Wild at Heart

"I'd better get going." His voice jolted me.

My heart clenched. Only a little, but more than I wanted. I wasn't out here to get distracted by some random guy. "Right on."

Neither of us moved. A marmot whistled. Another responded. The sun popped out from behind the cloud, warming my chilled skin. Evan shifted but didn't let go. I turned my head to find him on his side, staring at me.

"You're amazing. You know that, right?"

Heat that wasn't from the sun crept up my neck. "What are you talking about?"

"You. You're out here, happily on your own in the middle of nowhere. You came here for solitude and yet you let me barge in on your trip. You've helped me over and over and asked for nothing in return. And you're funny and smart and gorgeous." He shook his head. "Amazing doesn't even begin to cut it, actually."

I flipped to my side facing him. His cobalt eyes peered deep inside me, seeing more than I ever did. I mean, I liked myself and all, but when twelve guys in a row dump you for their exes, it gets hard to see yourself as all that. "Thanks, but don't overdo it."

"I'm not. I'm serious." He reached out, tentative, and traced the tip of one finger along the side of my face, pushing back my still-damp curls.

I held still. I did not nuzzle into his touch.

Because I couldn't do that. I was already hyper-aware of our pinkie fingers wrapped together. And our nakedness. And how close our bodies were to touching.

No need to make it worse.

He brushed a trail of heat along my jaw. My breath hitched.

"If I didn't have a plane to catch in a couple days, I'd love to get to know you better."

"But you do."

"I do." He nodded.

"Well, it's been nice." I gave him a half-smile. "But it hasn't been real nice."

"Could be nicer." His eyes darkened, turning the color of the evening sky as the first stars come out.

His fingers slid into my hair.

Electric tension pulsed between us, tugging like a magnet on steel. I licked my lips.

He leaned in a little, staring hard at my mouth.

I leaned in a little more. Our mouths hovered inches apart.

His warm, minty breath skated across my lips and the mountains disappeared. The sun faded. Even the hard rock biting into my shoulder and hip evaporated. All that existed were our twined fingers, his hand in my hair, and the space between his mouth and mine.

His lips grazed my lips. He inhaled sharp, fingers tightening on my scalp.

Tiny sparks burned down my spine. He nuzzled in. Gentle. Slow. Sweeping and brushing.

Something inside me tightened. Coiling to run. I wasn't ready for this, this…tenderness.

He nipped my lower lip with his teeth and tugged, heat in his eyes.

My breath hitched. He licked into my mouth.

We both moaned. And my weakening resolve headed up the trail without me.

Suddenly, making love on those rocks became a stellar, inevitable idea. I gripped his hip, rubbing circles on the soft, sensitive skin inches above his hard cock with my thumb, and tugged. Almost desperate to close the distance between our bodies.

To feel his bare skin against mine. His hard muscles pressing against me. His hard-on trapped between us.

Instead, he turned the kiss slow and gentle again, and sexy-as-hell. Tasting and teasing until he pulled back with a groan. "I'd better go."

Some tiny, sane part of my brain knew he was right. I clutched at it, clearing my throat. Trying to dislodge the pebbles clogging it. "Yeah. You've got a lot of miles ahead of you."

"I do." He brushed the hair away from my face, too much intensity in his soulful eyes, and dropped another kiss on my lips. "But, for what it's worth, I wish I didn't."

Me too.

"No worries. I get it. I never expected to see you again anyway. So, bonus." I pulled back with a forced half-smile, suddenly too aware of my nakedness and his hard cock and the way my heart kept stuttering when he looked at me like that.

"All right, then." He held my pinkie for five more erratic heartbeats. I know, because I counted them. And because I missed his touch as soon as it disappeared.

I wrapped my arms around my legs and rested my cheek on my knees, shell-shocked. Confused. And more than a little pissed at myself. Not that I was going to let Evan know any of that.

He shook out his shorts and shirt and slid into them. The still-damp fabric raised goosebumps on his skin. Goosebumps I wanted to rub away with my warm hands.

Which was ridiculous. I barely knew the guy, and I wasn't out here shopping for man meat.

Not to mention he wasn't my type. Sweet, soulful, in-touch-with-their-emotions men reminded me too much of Justin. That was dangerous. Any man that reminded me of the love of my life was dangerous. Especially one with an ex-fiancé waiting at home. On the other side of the country.

I'd fall in too deep too soon, make stupid decisions, and end up alone and hurt. Again.

Celibacy. Right. Good call.

Evan needed to move on. Head up the trail. Go back to the big city where he wouldn't have to worry about cold, rainy nights, broken tents, or wet gear ever again.

CHAPTER 11

EVAN

I stuffed the last of my gear into my backpack. My still-damp shirt clung to my shoulders like a cool hand despite the hot sun sitting high in the sky.

How I managed to navigate back to my tent would always remain a mystery. In my head, I still laid on that rock naked with Jules, my hand in her hair, the sweet taste of her lips on my tongue.

Getting up and walking away— No. Ending that kiss and getting up and walking away, took an act of will I didn't know I had in me. It was far harder than pushing through a grueling triathlon in crappy weather when my calves cramped half-way and I puked my guts out at the finish line. Or staying at my crappy job. Or living with Lainey long after I realized we could never be happy together.

Not that I had much choice in the matter.

My flight left SeaTac airport day after tomorrow, I still had a good forty miles between me and civilization, and I was hours late for my pre-dawn start. If I was lucky hiking out, and caught a ride fast, I might get to Packwood with enough time for a hot shower and a good night's sleep before I caught a bus to Seattle. I did not have time to waste.

Settling the familiar weight of my pack on my hips and shoulders, I hit the trail. Jules's Lake (I didn't know the name, so it would be forever Jules's Lake in my mind) sat in a dip off to my right. I glanced that direction a million times walking by.

I could've detoured and tried to find that same little pond again. Taken her in my arms and kissed her and made love to her. If I'd read the signs correctly, she would've happily made love with me right there, on that sun-drenched rock, in the middle of nowhere.

Except, I couldn't use her for rebound sex, and that's all it would've been. Besides, it would be too weird. I hadn't slept with anyone other than Lainey in seven years—not that we'd had sex very often the last few years anyway.

And what if Jules didn't enjoy it any more than Lainey?

My stomach churned. I pushed my pace.

What Lainey liked and didn't like no longer mattered. What mattered was what I liked and wanted—other than Jules, who I couldn't have.

The trail meandered above tree line for miles and the views went on and on. Yellowish-brown cliffs and peaks, swathes of tiny, pink and white flowers, babbling brooks flowing through meadows so green they glowed.

Clean and refreshed, with food and water in my belly, the idea of staying out here longer didn't seem so ridiculous or horrible. I could climb a few more peaks and watch a few more sunsets.

I could swim in more crystal-clear mountain lakes naked.

With Jules.

My dick twitched, hard. Twice. I put a lid on the images bouncing through my brain and focused my attention on staying on the trail.

JULES

Laying on that rock, alone again, I focused on the light breeze riffling over my sun-warmed skin. The way it bent and curled the hairs on my arms. The tang of juniper and snowmelt floating on the air.

And the way Evan's fingers pressed against my scalp, firm and tender at the same time.

And those soft, minty kisses, sweet and sexy and such a fucking tease. And my insides melting in a way they shouldn't have.

And the space between our naked bodies, his hard cock inches from my fingers, and—

I ran my hand up my ribcage, scraping my fingers over the soft skin along the curve of my breast. Circling my nipple. Pinching and pulling, just a little. Teasing it the same way he'd teased my mouth. Bringing those sparks back to life.

Trailing my fingers to my clit, I circled it with light strokes, imagining Evan's fingertips instead of mine. My low back arched off the rough rock.

But I couldn't keep up the teasing. Evan had done enough of that already. I wanted a release.

I rubbed across my clit slow, then faster. The rock bit into my shoulders.

Every muscle in my body tensed and shook. Tiny explosions popped on the backs of my eyelids. Wetness coated my thighs and ran down my ass. I kept going, searching for more satisfaction.

It didn't work.

I guess that's one for the spank bank, then.

Wading waist-deep into the lake I cleaned up, frigid water cooling my hot skin. Too bad it didn't do shit to cool other parts of me.

Slowly, disgust replaced the sexual tension swirling in my gut. Acrid bile hit the back of my throat.

I barely even made it one fucking week without wanting to jump the first available hottie.

The last thing I wanted or needed was a man complicating things. I knew this, and I'd let it happen anyway. I could not, under any circumstances let it happen again. Not for at least a year.

It'd take that long—maybe longer—to figure out how I kept picking guys who didn't want more than a rebound. Or why they kept picking me.

Was I wearing a neon sign? A giant scarlet *R* on my forehead?

I made a mental note to buy a new vibrator when I got home. Vow or no vow, my sex drive wasn't vanishing just because I didn't want to deal with all the other dating bullshit.

The sun floated high above the mountain ridges. Almost noon. Distant laughter echoed off the walls of the cirque. Time to get moving before all the best campsites were taken. I wanted to soak up every bit of the quiet and beauty of the mountains I could before dipping back into the edges of civilization.

CHAPTER 12

EVAN

The trail dropped into the charcoal shadows of the forest. The slope pulled my aching, heavy legs down the mountainside, my feet thwapping loud against the needle-covered dirt.

Engines rumbled in the distance, heralding the highway long before I could see headlights flashing bright white through the tree trunks. I smiled, ignoring the exhaustion permeating every fiber of my body.

The forest opened and cars zoomed past in bursts of light and noise and wind. Dazed, I hesitated, then followed the highway toward the fluorescent glow of White Pass and the promise of a hot meal.

I pushed open the door to the convenience-store-cum-deli-cum-backpacker's-post-office. Bright lights slapped me in the face, along with a weird mix of floor cleaner, fresh coffee, and hot pretzels. I stood in the middle of an aisle packed with cans of tomato sauce and soup, blinking like an owl caught in a headlight. Overwhelmed by all the options. All the colors. All the sounds.

The humming of the light fixtures. The soft pop and *foosh* of cooler doors opening.

The rich, oregano and bread scent of fresh, baking pizza.

I followed my nose over to the deli.

A pot-bellied man on the other side of the counter, with whiskers as white as his skin, wiped his hands on a towel and smiled. "What can I get for you, son?"

"I'll take one of your veggie pizzas."

"That'll be sixteen dollars."

I pulled out my card. "A friend of mine should be coming through in the next couple days to pick up a resupply package, and I owe her dinner. Any chance you can put a twenty-dollar credit on a tab for her?"

He rubbed his beard with his thumb and forefinger, staring up at the yellowed acoustic tile ceiling. "I think we can make that work. Let me go find her package and I can put a note on it to that affect. What's her name?"

I didn't know.

I'd spent hours thinking about a woman whose last name I didn't even know. *Ridiculous.*

"Jules."

"She got a last name?"

"Not that I know." I crossed my fingers hoping her first name would be enough.

"I'll take a look."

"Thank you."

"Sure thing." He shrugged. "We get weirder requests from you thru-hikers all the time."

"That's good." I smiled. "Because I've got one more. Do you by any chance have a pay phone?" I held my breath. Nobody had payphones anymore, something I hadn't considered when I got rid of my cell. All

I'd been thinking about was making sure nobody I knew could reach me and leave irate messages.

"We do. It's out there on the side of the building." He pointed toward the western windows. "Your pizza'll be ready in fifteen."

I walked out into the rapidly cooling summer night air, picked up the handset, crossed my fingers, and dialed my voice mail. One interview request could make all the difference. Surely that wasn't too much to ask. I'd submitted twenty resumes before I left. *C'mon. C'mon. C'mon.*

My voice came through the line, "Hello, you've reached Evan Davenp—" I pressed the star key and passcode.

"You have no new messa—" I hung up the line and stood there, receiver in hand. The idea of calling John, let alone going back to deal with my life and my family and my ex, hit me like a giant boulder smashing down on my head.

Not that I had much choice. I promised him I would check in.

I closed my eyes, the headlights of passing cars flashed orange on the backs of my eyelids. Their engines roaring loud in my ears. I took a deep breath of exhaust-flavored air, clenching my fists and pulling my shoulders up to my ears, and exhaled hard letting everything drop.

It didn't do much to ease the bands of tension wrapped around my head and neck. I took another deep, slow breath and dialed John's number.

"Hel-LO."

"Hey, John."

"Evan. You're alive."

"It appears that way."

"Impressive."

"Thanks for the never-ending votes of confidence."

John's deep chuckle rolled into my ear. "Anytime, little brother. Anytime. How was it? Did you see amazing things? Did you have any major epiphanies out in the wilderness alone?"

Jules wading out of the lake naked, her wet skin sparkling in the sunshine, flashed through my mind. Even though there was nothing sexual about it, it had to be the most amazing thing I'd ever seen. Except maybe Jules, spread out in the sun, naked, on that rock.

The phone line crackled and hissed. "Yeah. It was pretty amazing. I miss being out there already." I realized it was true.

And I miss Jules sarcastic wit, and the way her hair escapes from her braids and curls around her face, and her small hand on my hip, tugging me toward her. Wanting more. Wanting me. "I'll tell you all about it when I'm not standing at a payphone on the side of the highway, waiting on a pizza."

"As long as you had a good time. Because it's not going to be a good time when you get home." His voice came through tight and tense. My shoulders crept back up to my ears.

"How—." I planted my feet and yanked my shoulders down. "How is everything there?"

"'Bout like you'd expect. At least I've been in Chicago for the past few days."

"How many times has Lainey called you?"

"Eleven, no wait…Twelve times counting this morning's blame fest."

"She's still pretty pissed then?"

"It's hard to say. Some days she's pissed at you. Some days she's pissed at herself. Some days she's sorry. This morning, after berating you for twenty minutes, she offered to forgive you and let you come back. Make of it what you will."

 Wild at Heart

I could hear his shrug through the phone. Guilt gnawed at the edges of my gut. I'd bailed and left my brother to deal with my shit. though, in my defense, he did introduce me to Lainey. "So that's a yes on the still pretty pissed?"

"Yeah, but not as pissed as our parents."

Acid burned its way up my esophagus. Standing up to Lainey, breaking up with her, hadn't been easy. Before this trip I'd say it was the hardest thing I'd ever done. Then I'd run away with my tail between my legs because I knew I wasn't that strong. If I stuck around, she'd have somehow convinced me to give us another chance, again.

I'd never in my life stood up to my parents.

I swallowed down the ball of bile. "What did they say?"

"Well, let's see…They started out scared and worried, especially Mother, when they found out you'd left on some 'cockamamie adventure'—Father's words, not mine—and they had no way to reach you. Then the news of your breakup sunk in. That's when his voice went hard and he said something about your trust fund. So overall, it wasn't too bad."

I rubbed my forehead and squeezed my temples, trying to ease the band of tension. "Shit, man. I'm sorry you had to deal with all that."

"That's what family is for. Not saying you don't need to grow a spine, get back here, and deal with your own shit, though." A bottle cap popped and clattered on a countertop. "Speaking of, when *are* you coming back to deal with your shit?"

"Tomorrow night."

"Should I throw you a welcome home party? Invite everyone over?"

"Not funny."

"What should I tell them?"

To fuck off and leave me the hell alone? To let me make my own damn decisions? "That I'll be home soon, and I'll call them when I get in."

"Will do."

"I owe you one, John."

"Bro, you owe me way more than one."

The phone line clicked and emitted a series of long, obnoxious beeps. I heaved a sigh of relief. Confrontation avoided for one more day.

Somehow, I needed to figure out what the hell I was doing with my life before I landed in Boston. If I didn't have a plan, one would surely be made for me.

CHAPTER 13

EVAN

Soap-scented steam followed me out of my second shower in less than nine hours. I rubbed my head with a towel, convinced most people didn't understand this miracle of modern plumbing. After a week without, even lukewarm water did nothing to take away from the sheer bliss of standing under the spray and scrubbing every inch of my body.

Despite the lumpy, bowed mattress, I'd slept better than I had in forever. It would've been even better with Jules there, sprawled across me. I'd been too busy freezing my ass off to enjoy that properly the first time.

First. Like there would ever be a second time. I don't even know her last name.

Shoving those useless thoughts out of my head, I dressed and went in search of breakfast and the first bus out.

Egg and bean burrito warming my hand, I waited at the bus stop on the edge of the highway. A big motorcoach pulled up, engine rumbling. I stowed my pack under the bus, climbed up the tall stairs and picked a seat as far away from all the other riders as possible. The stiff, air-dried fabric of my shorts and t-shirt scratched at my skin, but at least they smelled better from their shower-scrubbing. Or maybe I'd quit noticing the aroma. Either way, I hadn't even thought about bringing a change of clothes for the flight home.

Add that to my list of bad decisions on this trip.

We lurched into motion, swaying on to the highway. If only my parents could see me now, sitting on a common bus, wearing clothes I washed by hand in the bathroom of a random motel in the middle of nowhere—not a maid or granite countertop in sight. If Mother knew I'd been wearing the same shorts and shirt for a week, she'd faint, at a minimum.

Except the idea of needing a different set of clothing everyday seemed a little ludicrous at that point. I snorted and shook my head. I'd come a long way in a week and changed more than I realized, but still not enough.

Miles of evergreen trees scrolled by in a blur of green and brown, beautiful but monotonous, until we pulled into the small town of Centralia, where I caught the next direct bus to Seattle.

I hopped off at the downtown bus stop. The humid air hung thick with salt, exhaust fumes, and fryer grease. With a few hours to spare, I meandered the waterfront with its sweeping views of the rugged, white-tipped Olympic Mountains across the sound. I struggled to ignore the rumble and honk of traffic, and the voices, and the music, all threatening to overwhelm me after a week of quiet.

Grabbing a creamy bowl of clam chowder from one of restaurants straddling the piers, I debated what to do. Nothing came to me.

The closer my watch hands got to my departure time, the further my shoulders inched up toward my ears. And the harder the band of tension around my head tightened.

Going back to Boston and facing my parents and Lainey without a clear plan did not sound like a good time. In fact, it made freezing to death in the middle of nowhere in a downpour sound downright pleasant.

Belly full, I headed toward the train station at Pioneer Square, dodging pedestrians along First Avenue.

The train vibrated and whooshed to a stop at the platform, and I grabbed a seat. *How did my life get to this point?*

I was a well-educated white man from an affluent family. All my problems were first-world problems. I got that.

I wasn't working three mindless, possibly dangerous or hard labor jobs to not even make ends meet. I didn't have a terminal illness, or a terminally ill child, or a mountain of debt. I was a spoiled white guy who hated my well-paying job and my perfectly decorated condo, and the pressure to marry a smart, well-manicured woman from the right family—regardless of whether I loved her or not.

Love wasn't even part of the equation. My parents married because it was a good business merger. They were about to celebrate their fortieth wedding anniversary, and the best I could say about their relationship was they seemed happy to have improved their mutual fortunes and standing in the community.

They didn't particularly like each other. Or respect each other. But they served a need in each other's lives. My head vibrated on the plate glass window as the train rattled past murals and warehouses.

I didn't want to ever live that way. I never cared about money or connections or social status. I was the kid who wanted to wander around outside, exploring and getting muddy, or disappear in a book. I hated putting on a suit and stiff pair of shiny shoes and smiling through Mother's perfectly planned parties.

Unlike John.

He was born with the schmoozing and small talk gene, while I always managed to embarrass my parents, or not live up to their expectations. I also never knew how to get out of striving to achieve their goals. To say no. To let them know I wanted another sort of life entirely.

John was different. He made good grades effortlessly. He was President of his fraternity at Stanford. The life of the party. The good time guy who's smart enough to get the job done. Exactly the kind of guy you like and trust and hire in a heartbeat.

He never struggled to balance who he was or what he wanted in life with our parent's expectations. Then again, he also knew what he wanted in life, he always had, and it dovetailed with their vision perfectly. I didn't have a vision for what my life could or should be, only what I didn't want.

Slinging my pack on my shoulders I strode into the airport terminal. If my week on the trail had taught me anything, it was that I needed a whole let less than I'd ever imagined. And if I didn't need all the stuff, all the trappings of wealth expected in affluent America, I didn't need the high paying job to afford it all, either. Not on top of my trust fund.

But what did I need? What did I want my life to look like?

Something told me if I went back to Boston now, I might never figure it out.

The airport security line folded and stretched down the tiled hallway, voices and boot heels echoed in the packed space. I headed for the shorter, First-Class line.

The woman checking status reached for my ticket. My lungs tightened like I was deep underwater again. My hand refused to lift.

"Sorry. Forgot something." Pivoting, I wove back through the cued-up throngs to the airport entrance, not sure what I was doing other than very definitely not going home.

    Wild at Heart

JULES

The roar of a passing car floated up, audible even though I still had a couple miles to go to hit Highway 12. It's amazing how far man-made sounds carry. Especially the semi-trucks rumbling up and over the pass, making me miss the quiet and solitude and beauty of the trail already.

The last couple days had been particularly spectacular. Even if I did spend every mile looking for Evan. Imagining him naked and in need of a rescue around every random corner.

Or at the very least, naked.

Not that anything would happen. Evan was a fun diversion. He'd given me fucking hilarious stories to tell once I got out of here. And one sexy-as-hell story I planned to tuck down deep inside and keep for myself.

In the meantime, I needed to forget all about the moment where my lame ass almost broke my vow, and the man who inspired it. It was past time I got my solo groove back.

I stepped onto the edge of the highway. The evening sun still gilded the top half of the forested mountains on the north side. Heat still radiated up from the pavement. Dropping my pack in the gravel, I dug out my cell phone and hit speed dial.

It rang once. "Hey, Jules. How goes the hike?"

"Hey, Bryn. It's going great. Just calling to let you know I'm on Highway 12 and headed towards a hot meal now. I'll camp near the trailhead tonight and start the next segment in the morning."

"Sounds good. Thanks for the check in."

"Sure thing. Talk to you in another week or so. Love you, girlfriend."

"Love you, too. Stay safe out there, and don't do anything I wouldn't do."

"No worries." I laughed and hung up the phone. Bryn was by far the more measured of the two of us. If she'd vowed celibacy, she would never have even ended up laying naked on a rock with Evan, let alone kissing him.

Jesus. Have I no self-control at all?

Mortification looped around my stomach in a thin, unnerving line.

I turned toward the bright glow that had to be White Pass proper. A thousand steps and ten minutes later I pushed open the glass doors of the convenience store slash deli slash thru-hiker resupply point, the fluorescent lights searing my eyeballs. Part of me wanted to turn around and head right back to the trail, but the first tangy, toasty whiff of hot pizza made the rest of me reconsider.

A hot meal was enough to coax even the most crusty, anti-social thru hiker off the trail. I wasn't even that crusty.

On the other side of the store, modern plumbing called my name. Besides, I had a resupply box waiting and when I shook my last fuel cannister that morning, it rattled ominously. I wove through shelves packed with snacks to the bathroom.

Face and hands washed, my curly-ass hair finger-combed into somewhat less messy braids, I headed for the counter. An older man with gray hair, gray beard, and kind eyes smiled my way.

"What can I do you for you, young lady?"

"I'll take one of your veggie pizzas. And I should have a package waiting."

"Sure thing. What's the name?"

"Jules Martinez."

"Why don't you have a seat." He nodded toward the row of brown and yellow Formica booths lining the window. "I'll get your pie started then go find your package."

"Thank you."

I did as he said and stared out the plate glass at the bright head-lights rushing by, letting my mind go empty. The whir and hum of the store faded into the background.

"Here you go."

My box thudded on the table; a folded piece of lined yellow paper taped to the top. *Weird.* I peeled off the note, the paper sliding dry against my fingers. Loopy handwriting in blue ink scrawled across the page, not even trying to follow the lines.

—Thanks again for everything, Jules. I wish I could take you out to a nice restaurant and thank you properly, but at least you can enjoy dinner on me. The veggie pizza is amazing! Evan—

"Who's Evan?" A familiar voice came from over my shoulder.

I jumped and twisted in my seat. Two of my favorite faces beamed at me. "Bryn! Aly! What are you doing here?"

They wrapped me in a warm embrace of arms and Aly's lemon and rose perfume, and I realized how much I'd missed them. Missed having Bryn as my sounding board and Aly as my cheerleader.

Bryn's grin practically split her face. "Slow day at the office, so we decided to surprise you and buy you dinner. We even got a hotel in Packwood for the night so you can grab a hot shower."

"You are the best girlfriends ever."

"We know. Though it looks like you don't need us to buy you din-ner." Aly raised one eyebrow and pointed a manicured fingernail at the note still in my hand. "Is he cute?"

I shrugged. "Not really." It was the truth. Evan wasn't cute. He was fucking fine as hell.

Bryn crossed her arms, disbelief replacing most of her grin. "Well, that had to be one of the shortest-lived vows of celibacy in the history of mankind."

"Hey now. I did *not* sleep with him." Unless you counted me wrapping around his bare ass and cuddling him through the night. Not to mention waking up with his steel rod stiffy pinned under my stomach. "Okay, well, I slept with him, but I didn't *sleep* with him."

"So, he *was* cute, then."

"No. Yes. Fuck." I rubbed my eyes. I didn't want to think about Evan anymore, let alone talk about him. "He was hot, in that lean tri-athlete kinda way. He was also freezing to death in the rain, and it was pitch black when I met him. In my defense I didn't discover his hotness until later."

"So, there was a later?"

"Despite my best efforts to ditch him, and his faster pace, he kept making stupid mistakes." The corners of my lips twitched. "Stupid mistakes that resulted in nakedness, which I'll admit was kind of a perk. Even if I didn't take advantage of it."

"So, you're telling us you found a random hot guy in the woods, naked and in need of rescue? How is that even possible?"

"Even a blind hog finds an acorn every once in a while." Aly chuckled.

"Twice." My lips twitched. "I rescued his naked ass twice."

"Cute and naked in the middle of nowhere, twice? And you didn't sleep with him?" Bryn lifted both arms and mock-bowed in my direction. "I am not worthy."

I placed a hand over my heart and schooled my face. "The vow of celibacy is strong in this one."

"I know I told y'all I'd never go backpacking, but this might just change my mind."

We all laughed, but I secretly vowed to hold Aly to that.

"Maybe you'll run into him again, and you could just sort of trip over a root and fall into his arms." she wiggled her eyebrows. "Or onto his penis."

"That'll happen about the same time monkeys fly out of my butt. First off, even if I hadn't sworn off men, he's not my type—" And I planned to keep telling myself that until I quit seeing his sapphire eyes and ripped abs every time I closed my eyes. "And second, he's already on his way back to Boston."

"What do you mean he wasn't your type?" Aly put on her best matchmaker voice. "You like 'em fit as hell. And he backpacks. Sounds like y'all were two peas in a pod."

"Eh, not enough muscle. Plus, I only date blonds."

"Uh huh. But did y'all get along."

I thought back over our talks and jokes and laughs. Even though I never let the topic go deep, being with him was oddly comfortable. More comfortable than I wanted. "Evan was smart and funny and sweet, and wounded as hell with an ex-fiancé he split up with a week ago."

"Shades of your past and your present all rolled into one, huh?" Bryn read right through my words to the subtext. She always had.

"You could say that."

Questions filled Aly's eyes. Bryn knew the whole story. She'd been there when I lost Justin—hell, she was in love with Justin's brother at the time.

Aly only knew the story secondhand. Just the bits and pieces we'd shared over the past few years. She never saw how in love we were, how happy. Or how perfect Justin was for me. Or how destroyed I was after he was gone.

"Well, it's a good thing he's left, then. You wouldn't want to fall hard and have him leave you for his ex. You might never date again, hon."

"My thoughts exactly."

Bryn tapped a finger against her lower lip and tilted her head. "Then again, that would also ruin your perfect record of running away from guys you might actually fall hard for."

I winced. The problem with best friends you've known more than a decade, is they know all your secrets. And they're not afraid to call you on them.

At that moment, I found it a little hard to appreciate.

"Here you go, young lady." My pizza slid onto the table, saving me from saying something snarky I might regret.

It smelled even better right under my nose, all rich tomato, bright oregano, and toasty bread. My mouth watered.

"You two are welcome to share." I waved a hand over the steaming pie. My stomach rumbled in disagreement.

"Thanks." Aly caught the proprietor's attention. "We'll take two more, please."

CHAPTER 14

JULES

Low angle stripes of glimmering morning sun pierced through the tree branches. Belly full of pancakes, heart bursting with girlfriend love, I found my hiking groove again. My mind wandered aimlessly, tuning into the minutiae of the forest—the calls of birds, the buzz of bees, the tang of spruce and Doug firs. Sometimes I sang songs in my head, sometimes out loud.

Turned out telling Bryn and Aly about Evan got him out of my system. And he did provide me with a couple epic-funny stories I could bust out at parties for the rest of my life. And at dinner last night. For those things I thanked him.

I also thanked him for leaving when he did, so I didn't do anything I'd regret. And for leaving each morning on the trail too.

Evan never made me feel like I had to spend time with him or hike his hike. Or even help his stupid ass when he got it into trouble. He thanked me and went on his merry way, leaving me to do my thing.

My kind of guy.

No. He isn't.

A stream burbled across the trail, glittering in the mid-morning sun. I shucked my pack on the bank, sat on the cool ground, and leaned against a big, warm rock. Pulling off my hiking boots, I sank my feet in the cold, clear water, enjoying the tingles.

I dug a bag of dried pears and my map out of the lid of my pack and traced the dotted red line of the PCT with my finger. Breakfast at the cafe this morning meant a later start, but hot blueberry pancakes and good company made it well worth it.

Besides, I only needed to make about eight miles and thirty-five hundred feet of elevation gain to hit the high country. Tomorrow, I'd wake up in the alpine to in-your-face, blow-your-mind views of Mt. Rainier. I planned to relax and take it easy in the morning to enjoy those views.

My feet went deliciously numb. I pulled them out of the stream and sat cross-legged. Closing my eyes, I tilted my face to catch the warmth of the sun. *Bryn did have a point, last night, about me running away.*

If I was being honest, I had to admit that not every guy I'd dated since Justin had left me for their ex. Especially when I first started dating again after my divorce.

I met some sweet, sexy men. Men who seemed really into me. Men who cared about my happiness and did thoughtful things for me.

And it scared the shit out of me. So I ran.

Every. Single. Time.

That's when I started dating men who were in some way unavailable. Sometimes emotionally. Sometimes because they were married to their careers. Or liked themselves more than anyone else.

 Wild at Heart

In the last few years, somehow, I'd developed a nifty knack for attracting men who'd just come out of relationships. Usually unhealthy, co-dependent ones.

While I didn't love any of them, and some I only dated once or twice, when they left me to go back to their fucked-up exes, I thought maybe I wasn't worth loving. Not that I didn't have my own mountain of baggage. But still, I wasn't *that* fucked up. I wasn't needy or jealous or manipulative.

Sure, it was a foolproof way to ensure my heart didn't get broken. But the rejections hurt every time anyway. And I kept picking these guys like they were a punishment I deserved.

Dried pear stuck to the back of my throat. *Maybe I really am that fucked up?* I swallowed hard.

A fat bumblebee buzzed by. The stream babbled by my feet. I closed my eyes and searched for an answer I didn't really want.

Apparently so.

I'd judged Evan for his screwed-up relationships with his fiancée and parents and I wasn't any damn better. Maybe worse. Maybe I was the one with a million red flags popping out of my head, warning every decent guy to stay the hell away and sending the rest running back to their exes.

My eyelids darkened and my cheeks cooled. I opened my eyes to a big, puffy cloud blotting out the sun. Taking it as a sign, I tucked away my snacks and map, laced up my boots, and headed down the trail.

Much as I'd loved seeing Bryn and Aly, I relished the weeks of solitude ahead. Seemed like I'd need every one of those days to work my shit out, anyway.

EVAN

Afternoon light glowed in the treetops. I stared at the trailhead sign and tightened the shoulder straps on my new, larger backpack while cars and semi-trucks roared past behind my back. The weight didn't seem too heavy, certainly less than I expected. I headed into the forest, intent on making a few miles before nightfall.

Not too many, but enough to be away from civilization. I planned to backpack Jules's way. To try and recapture the charm and wonder she'd helped me see out here by way of a little more camp comfort and fewer daily miles. For the first time since I was a kid, I wasn't in a big rush to get somewhere.

Tracing the dotted red line of the PCT on my map with the help of a salesclerk, I'd marked the closest camping to my trailhead, plus potential sites twelve to fifteen miles apart. Where I could, I picked camping near lakes. The views seemed better.

Especially when gorgeous naked women were involved. Or at least one particular, gorgeous, naked woman.

Not that I planned to find Jules out here. That would be one incredible needle in a haystack, and not something I needed anyway. What I needed was more time alone to just be. To try to figure out who I was and what I wanted without anyone else's input. Definitely not Lainey's or my parents'.

Last week I'd been too focused on meeting mileage goals and staying on schedule—not to mention not dying—instead of enjoying being out here and figuring out my life.

With updated goals and strategies, and new gear, I brimmed with confidence. I could do this backpacking thing and not just survive but enjoy it. Savor it.

Handling my family when I got home? That, I was still not confident about at all.

Lucky for me, John wasn't there when I called to tell him I'd changed my flight. He would've tried to convince me to change it back, to come home and face the music before things got worse.

My reasons would never have been enough for him—let alone my parents.

Until I figured out what I wanted and developed a solid argument for it, I couldn't stand up to them face-to-face. I needed something worth fighting for. Otherwise, in their eyes, I'd be running away from responsibility like an immature boy instead of taking all the opportunities they'd afforded me to become the successful man they envisioned and make my mark (IE a ton of money).

If I could find a modicum of happiness on the trail… If I could make small changes in myself and how I lived out here, away from everyone and everything, maybe I could make more and bigger changes when I got back to real life.

My life, my choices. My life, my choices.

The small lake I planned to camp next to came up quicker than expected. Part of me wanted to keep going. Instead, I stopped hiking, set up my new tent, and enjoyed a fudge walnut brownie I'd bought for dessert, while kicking back in my new camp chair.

Shadows enveloped the forest in a rush. I crawled into my sleeping bag and read in the glow of my headlamp, sipping tea. My full-length inflated sleeping pad cradled my hips and shoulder—almost as comfortable as my bed at home, and far more comfortable than that ridiculously thin foam pad I had been using.

I woke to the sky peaching at the corners, shoulders lose, head clear. Warm oatmeal filling my belly, I leaned back in my sleeping pad chair and cradled a hot cup of coffee.

The sky turned rose and gold. The tree limbs whispered in the cool, pine-scented breeze. Birds whistled and tweeted good morning to the day.

At the exact moment I felt like moving, and not a second before, I broke camp and hit the trail. Rolling at first, the further I went, the more it climbed. My calves and thighs burned. My lungs ached.

The sky turned robin's egg blue and the sun peaked over the eastern ridges. Sweat dripped down my spine. All the while Mt Rainier loomed so close, I could almost reach out and touch it.

Walking beneath that behemoth, in the middle of nowhere, my problems shrunk. When one wrong choice could mean death, hating my job or disappointing my parents barely even registered on my worry meter.

The sun beamed on my sweaty head and neck. I switch-backed up the mountainside panting harder with each hairpin turn, sipping water every so often to stay hydrated. Glad I'd gotten an early start.

I didn't think it was possible, but the views kept getting better. At the top, I spun in a slow circle, gawking at the peaks surrounding me. Mother Nature's palace.

This place was at least as spectacular as the Goat Rocks, and I refused to rush through it. Pulling out my map, I pinpointed the next campsites and smiled. I could have my tent set up in time to watch the sunset with dinner.

Sucking a final warm drizzle from the bottom of my hydration bladder with a gurgle, I whispered a silent thanks for that extra liter.

Folding my map, I tucked it in my hip belt pocket, and turned left onto a barely-there side-trail leading into a depression where I thought a lake should be. Flashes of blue sparkled through tree branches. I exhaled relief. The path snaked into a shallow basin and dropped beside a chalky lake the color of morning sky. Across the lake, snow fields like white handprints stretched their fingers into the water.

I filled my spare bottle, guzzling it until my molars froze, then refilled it and my hydration bladder.

Peeling off my shirt, I dunked it in the lake, and swiped it across my forehead and shoulders and stomach. My skin recoiled and goose pimpled. I stared down at my legs, covered in grit stuck to sweat.

Only one remedy for this.

Shucking my shoes and shorts I ran into the lake. Plunging into the frigid water with a resounding splash, I scrubbed at my scalp, shins, and armpits. My feet touched soft, squishy lake bottom. I pushed off and broke the surface with a whoop.

My skin tingled. My soul tingled. My heart filled. I floated on my back in the waist-deep water and grinned up at the clear blue sky.

"You know…" A woman's laughing voice rang out behind me. "We really do have to stop meeting like this."

CHAPTER 15

EVAN

I jumped and spun, searching the shoreline. Jules rocked from toe to heel not far from my backpack, her smile brighter than the sun. My heart took off like I'd been running sprints. "You're right. We do. Because somehow I'm usually the one who's naked."

"True." She stopped rocking and cocked her head. "Though I'm not sure I mind."

"Of course not. Because if I'm naked you automatically have the upper hand."

"Do I?" One side of her mouth lifted. "Then I definitely don't mind. But, since it seems to bother you, I suppose I could do the polite thing and get naked too."

Even standing in freezing water up to my waist, my dick went semi-hard. Jules dropped her pack, peeled off her clothes, and ran into the lake, her laughter echoing around us. And my dick turned into a steel bar.

I tried to determine what was more spectacular, the mountain looming over us, the hazy cerulean water of the lake, or Jules, naked and unselfconscious and so very alive. Her head broke the surface a few feet away and the mountains, the sun, even the ice-cold water lapping at my belly, disappeared.

All I could see was Jules and the way her freedom, her zest for life, radiated from her grin. She did whatever made her happy without worrying about what anyone else thought.

Shaking her head, she flung sparling water into the sun. Cold drops struck my chest, taking my breath away almost as much as the sight of her standing naked, waist deep in the lake, feet away from me.

"What the hell are you doing here, Evan? Shouldn't you be back in Boston by now?"

"A brilliant woman once told me I was doing this whole backpacking thing wrong. I decided I'd better follow her advice and try again."

"Ahhh. I guess you're not as big a dumbass as I thought." Her smartass tone took the sting out of her comment.

"I don't know if I'd go that far. But I'm trying to overcome my dumbassery."

"Considering I found you happily skinny-dipping out here, you seem to be doing a pretty good job." She backed toward shore. "But, while I admire how comfortable you've become, I'm freezing my ass off."

I still wasn't cold. Not at all. Less so when she walked out of the water, her round ass flexing with each step. The muscles in her calves rippling. In fact, I found myself getting very, very hot.

Jules didn't have an ounce of fat on her body. At the same time, she wasn't skinny. With a gymnast's shoulders, and powerful legs built for more than running, she had the kind of build that spoke of hours of using her body to do physical things.

The urge to run my hands over every curve, every line, every ridge almost overwhelmed me. I couldn't move. I couldn't follow her, both because I had a raging hard-on, and because I had no idea what to do, or say. Everything I'd been thinking, everything I'd been planning, no longer mattered.

For the first time in longer than I could remember, I could name something I wanted. Somehow, I had to figure out how to not let her go.

JULES

I practically sprinted out of the lake to put some distance between me and Evan before I fell right into those twinkling sapphire eyes. Because, damn, he'd gotten hotter in the past few days.

It took an act of serious will to not jump into his arms and wrap my body around his like I'd done that night in the tent. Only from the front this time.

The memory of waking up with his hard cock pressed against my belly swarmed into my head. Superimposed itself over my view of him naked in the water, a stunning Adonis. All dark hair, flashing eyes, and sculpted physique.

I'd forgotten how much lean muscles did it for me. I'd told myself I liked big, beefcake dudes. Really, what I liked most was avoiding men that brought shades of Justin back to life.

Evan did that, and then some. Yet somehow, I didn't want to push him away. Even though I knew I needed to.

I plopped down on a rock, the rough, warm stone biting into my bare ass, and wrung out my braids. Evan still stood waist deep in the water, the curve of his pecs covered in a dusting of chest hair and water droplets. Half the dark hair on his head stuck up in every direction, the other half lay plastered to his skull.

He stared into the distance, I assumed at Mt Rainier towering behind me.

"You must've built up one helluva a tolerance to cold last week." I pulled off my hair bands and combed my fingers through my braids.

"Wait. You mean it's cold in here? Funny, I can't feel a thing."

"That's 'cuz you've gone numb from the waist down." I giggled. "Careful. If you stay in there much longer, the shrinkage might become permanent."

"Oh, well, that wouldn't be good." He waded toward me, revealing the deep vee of muscle at his abdomen. It led my gaze downward. My clit tingled.

I focused on dividing my hair into sections instead of the way the dropping water line exposed a few more inches of his naked body with every step. I did not need a better visual. No, I did not.

Finding him here was a pleasant surprise, and a good excuse for a quick dip. That was all. Past time I got dressed and got a few more miles down the trail before sundown. Alone.

I stared at my toes, my fingers twining course sections of my hair like they'd done a thousand times before. The whole point of this trip was to spend time thinking about my career and my love life. I wouldn't make much progress if I spent my time thinking about screwing Evan.

And damnit, I would not, could not, break my vow of celibacy. Especially not after Bryn's comment the other night.

Not that I blamed her for saying it. I wasn't exactly known for being a prude. I liked men. I liked sex. Nothing wrong with either. Except when getting laid kept screwing with my head. Well, not so much the getting laid part, but what happened after.

Much as I always said I didn't want anything serious; it didn't make it any easier when they walked away. The worst part was that I'd started doubting whether I was worth it. Whether anyone would ever want to be with me again in a serious way. Risking my heart and falling in love again seemed pretty impossible after Justin. More so if I wasn't worth loving anymore.

Maybe I'd become too independent. Too used to living life my way and not accommodating anyone else.

Maybe I really did have a giant neon *R* for rebound blinking on my forehead.

Or maybe, just maybe, I'd become a hard-ass bitch. Good for a fuck or two, but not the kind of woman you'd take home to mother.

For years I'd been telling myself that was my choice, and I was good with it. Except keeping my heart under lock and key hadn't made me happy.

Not that letting someone in was any guarantee of happiness either.

Evan's bare feet entered my field of vision. His shadow sat on a rock across from me. The tension from our kiss a couple days ago tightened low in my gut.

Normally, I wouldn't have hesitated to go for round two. But I couldn't let anything happen between us again, no matter how good it might be.

"What are you thinking about?" he asked.

"Not much, really. Just life, the universe, and everything."

"Don't hurt yourself."

"I'll try not to." That was the problem. I'd spent years doing everything possible to keep from getting hurt, only to feel like I'd done the opposite.

"Forty-two. In case you didn't already know the answer."

"Ha. Thanks. If only it was that easy." A tiny bug trundled over the cobbles toward my big toe. "So, how's it going so far? Following my backpacking advice, I mean, not the shrinkage."

"Pretty damn well on both fronts." He chuckled, and his shadow disappeared. I looked up.

Evan lay on the rock naked, staring up at the sky with hands tucked his behind his head. I let my gaze roam up his tanned legs to his pale, defined thighs. Skipped it quickly up to his torso, where the horizontal lines of his abs formed ridges like a mountain range stretching into the distance.

I definitely did not even once glance at his definitely not shrunken dick.

"Let's see…I've realized a chair kit is worth its weight in gold. And putting in fewer miles makes the hiking much more enjoyable, even with a slightly heavier pack." He pushed up onto his elbows. "Not to mention, you would never have run into me if I was still putting in twenty-mile days. That alone makes it a better way to go."

A kaleidoscope of butterflies battled it out for space in my chest while my brain struggled with what to make of that comment. I couldn't remember the last time a guy told me, point blank, he was happy to see me again.

"I'm glad to hear it's working out for you." I wrapped a rubber band around the end of my second braid and ran my hands over my head, searching for stray hanks of hair. "By the way, thanks for dinner. I didn't expect anything, but I did appreciate it."

"You're welcome." He shrugged without meeting my eyes. "Least I could do."

Skin dry and toasty, I stood and slipped on my sun-warmed clothes.

Splayed out naked in the sun, feet away, temptation incarnate tugged at me. All I needed to do was take one step forward and reach out to drag my fingers along his tanned skin. Or lean over and press my lips against his.

His cock twitched.

Energy buzzed through me, pulling at my gut, tingling in my lips, zinging through my nipples. Tightening my clit.

Fuck. We haven't even barely glanced at each other. Get a grip.

I ripped my eyes away from all that tempting nakedness and shouldered my pack. My stomach grumbled, but I ignored it.

Time to put some miles between the two of us before my willpower disappeared and I stripped off my clothes again and closed the tiny distance between us.

"Well, good seeing you again. I hope the rest of your trip rocks."

"Thanks. Same to you."

"All right. Have a good one."

"You too."

I counted to three and walked away.

 Wild at Heart

CHAPTER 16

JULES

Tiny puffs of dust exploded beneath my feet with every step. The trail undulated up and down small ridges and valleys, and Mt Rainier still loomed large. But all I could see was Evan's body stretched out on that rock like some kind of delicious entrée on a platter.

I considered going back more than once. Each time, I squashed the thought and kept putting one foot in front of the other, the warm tingling in my lady parts telling me I needed to keep moving up the trail, fast.

At least he didn't seem to be in any hurry to get going. Hopefully I could create a big enough gap between us that I wouldn't see him again.

My stomach grumbled for about the thirtieth time since I'd left the lake. A tiny, murmuring stream lined with pink and yellow wild-flowers and deep emerald moss called my name. I dropped my pack, rolled my shoulders and swiveled my head a few times, and dug out my bag of trail mix.

The salty sweet combo of peanuts, raisins, and chocolate melted on my tongue. I moaned with satisfaction.

GORP might be old school, but it was damn tasty. I shoved another handful in my mouth and chewed, admiring the swath of lavender, pink, white and yellow flowers thriving in the damp along the stream's banks.

A few puffy clouds dotted the sky. A light, dry breeze quivered the needles of the trees, cooling my skin. And visions of a very naked Evan filled my head no matter what I did.

Singing didn't work. Neither did thinking about my business. Or focusing on my snack.

Nothing to do then but put more miles between us. I stuffed the baggie with the rest of my snack mix into the lid of my pack and tightened the laces on my boots.

"Fancy seeing you here." Evan's warm tenor came from behind me, and my heart skipped a beat. "Nice spot for a break."

He stopped next to me, close enough to touch. Not that I was going to take advantage of that fact.

"It was. I'm done now though, so feel free to take it over."

"Thanks, but I'm good. I had a snack at the lake before I left." He scuffed the ground with the toe of his running shoe. "Since we seem to be on a similar schedule, anyway, would you like some company?"

Yes. No. Gah!

Clearly, I couldn't out-hike him. Not without a much bigger lead. Maybe if I agreed to hike with him, he'd get tired of going my pace and dust me.

Then I wouldn't have to worry about finding a way to make camp without him. Because no way could I spend another night feet away from him without at the very least getting an encore of that unforgettable kiss.

     Wild at Heart

"Sure. I'll take some company for a while." I shrugged on my pack, jumped across the stream, and headed up the trail without bothering to see if he followed.

EVAN

I had not been chasing Jules or trying to catch her. Honest. I could've left the lake when she did, but I'd stayed on purpose.

Don't get me wrong. I'd considered it but decided it would be a bad idea. We were both out here alone for our own reasons. Good reasons too. At least, I assumed hers were good.

Besides, I couldn't even look at her naked without getting a stiffy, which was so not appropriate given the circumstances. When you've been skinny dipping with a woman you're not dating, and you're in the middle of nowhere, chances are good your hard-on would make said woman more than a little uncomfortable. That was the last thing I wanted to do.

But for some reason we kept running into each other, we kept ending up naked, and I kept getting harder each time. I didn't believe in God, but whatever kept pushing us together over and over, I was tired of fighting it.

Not that I could let my guard down. Walking behind Jules, staring at her round ass and the way the muscles in her legs flexed? I could've done that all day. Except that looking at her ass and legs made me want to touch them. Made me want to run my hands lightly along every inch from the soles of her feet to the sensitive spots behind her knees.

I wanted to trace the curve of her hamstring until I cupped her firm butt cheeks in my hands, then follow that same path with my teeth and tongue until she quivered and squirmed and begged me to touch and lick her other places.

Except Jules hadn't given me any indication she wanted anything more from me, or with me. Not since that one, mind-bending kiss—and that had been my idea.

She was the one who took off like a shot after swimming, more than eager to put a good bit of distance between us. I didn't go after her, or try to stop her, because she didn't seem to want me to, and I didn't want to want her.

Rebound sex had never cleared my head, and that's what I was out here for…head clearing. Nothing else.

"Feel free to pass me and hike your own hike if I'm going too slow." Jules's voice startled me out of my thoughts.

"I'm good. Thanks, though." Maybe I should've done exactly that. Except, my gut, my chest, even my eyes, tightened at her words.

"You sure? I don't want to hold you back or anything."

"Positive. I like this speed. Gives me more time to take in the sights." *Mainly your fine ass and legs.* "And I've got nowhere in particular to be tonight."

She let out a single guffaw. "No more big mileage days then?"

"Nope. I told you, a wise woman showed me the error of my ways. I try to learn from my mistakes."

Her laughter peeled across the landscape with gusto. "Good to know."

I wished to hell I knew what was running through her mind, though. Was she pissed I intruded on her hike, or happy for the company? More importantly, was she happy the company was me? I wanted to ask, but I was too afraid the answer might be no.

"So, how's *your* hike been going?"

     Wild at Heart

"Great." She didn't change her pace. "I love this stretch of trail. The next section until we get close to Snoqualmie Pass isn't nearly as nice, but after that it only gets better and better."

I tried to focus on her words instead of her legs. "What do you mean?"

"We're headed for clear-cut city." She shook her head. "I know we harvest trees for stuff we all use—toilet paper, copy paper, notebooks, greeting cards, packaging, cardboard, fences, and walls, all that shit. But it's harder to reconcile all the paper that's thrown away when you're strolling through miles of stumps—though I do my best to use less and only buy recycled."

"Huh." It was hard to envision miles of stumps when lush forests and seemingly untouched mountains surrounded us. "I guess I never really thought about it before."

A light breeze teased my skin, fresh and clean and tinged with the damp green scent of moss and snow.

"Most people don't. It's like eating meat. It's easy when it's something you buy pre-packaged in a store. It's not so easy when you see the way the animals are treated and slaughtered." A shudder ran down her back.

"Do you eat meat, then?"

"Nope. Unless it's game meat someone I know shot and killed. I'll eat that. And I still eat eggs and dairy. And fish, though I'm on the fence about that sometimes."

"How long have you been a vegetarian?"

"Ever since I saw a film about factory farms as a teenager. The way we raise and kill pigs and cows and chickens is vile and disgusting."

"So, did you convince your family to get on board with the idea then?"

"God, no." She shook her head. "My grandparents immigrated to Miami from Puerto Rico and my father says they would spin in their graves if they knew I had forsaken our ancestral foods. My mother is third generation American of French descent, but the Criollo recipes got passed down and my family still loves their pork chorizo and *salchichón*. Though they finally gave up trying to get me to eat it."

At every turn, Jules surprised me. Other than my uncle Martin, I'd never met anyone who held on to such a strong moral conviction, even when everyone around them disagreed. Who made their own lives uncomfortable to help someone or something they didn't even know? The only strong moral conviction my parents ever showed was the belief in making more money at all costs—everyone and everything else be damned.

I wanted, no I *needed* to get to know her better. "Have you ever been to Puerto Rico?"

"Only once when I was little, but I still feel like a part of me is Puerto Rican. And not just my last name and my curly-ass hair. Maybe it's all the stories my grandfather used to tell me. I don't know, it's just in my blood."

"Do you speak Spanish?"

"Not as well as I'd like. Since my grandfather died, nobody in my family speaks it, but I took it for two years in college. What about you? Do you speak any other languages?"

"French. Not that I use it. My parents thought a foreign language would be important for my international finance career." I snorted at the thought of my once future career. "I had a choice of French, because it's the language of diplomacy, or Mandarin—which seemed way to difficult. Clearly it was a waste of time."

"Learning a language is never a waste of time. It's a window into another culture. Besides, it's a great way to get a woman interested."

Her chiming giggle floated through the forest and straight into my balls.

"I'll keep that in mind." I imagined walking up behind her, sliding her curls to the side, and nibbling at soft, salty skin of her neck while whispering, "*Tu es si belle. Vraiment spécial.*" Imagined the way she'd tilt her head and lean into me and moan each time I suckled and nipped.

My dick went painfully hard. I shifted it in my pants and focused on the sky, the clouds, the trail at my feet. Anything other than the sexy woman walking in front of me.

We covered the next couple of miles through stunning, high alpine terrain in silence, with Rainier peering over our shoulders. Another stream burbled through another idyllic flower-dotted meadow.

I wasn't sure I'd ever get used to walking through a fairy tale. Hiking slow enough to enjoy it, I realized I could never take this kind of solitude and untouched wilderness for granted again.

Jules stopped. "I'm running low on water. And I'm hungry. Stop for a break?"

"Sounds good." Dropping my pack, I pulled out a block of cheddar, a stick of sausage, and my pocketknife. "Piece of cheese?" I proffered a slice on the side of my blade.

"Thanks." Jules popped it in her mouth and crouched to pump water. "So, if you don't want to work in finance, is there anything you've ever really wanted to do?

"You mean, like, did I ever dream of being a firefighter, or an astronaut?"

"Something like that."

I searched back in my head, pulling up memories I hadn't thought about in years. "Camp counselor. When I was in Scouts, that was my dream job. Spending time in the woods, away from my cold, demanding home life, was the only time I felt peaceful and happy, and the counselors were my heroes."

"I take it your parents would not have approved."

"That, is an understatement." I chewed a piece of salami, the salty, peppery fat melting on my tongue. "What about you? What was your dream job?"

She didn't hesitate. "Olympic gymnast. It's all I ever wanted to be growing up."

"What happened?"

"I competed for years, and I was good. Looking back, I'm pretty sure I never would've been Olympic good, but I did well enough in state and national competitions to keep the dream alive. Then I landed a vault wrong and shredded my knee—MCL, ACL, PCL. You name it. Full blow out. The surgeon did a great job putting me back together, but my competitive days were over."

Crouched in a squat, the scar glowed white in her golden skin, a long, straight line down the center of her kneecap with smaller dots along each side. Hard to believe she was out here hiking with a full pack after that kind of injury. No doubt about it, Jules was tough.

"I'm sorry."

"It was a long time ago, and really it could've been worse." She shrugged like it didn't matter, but I couldn't miss the tightening at the corners of her eyes. "It gets achy when it rains or I overdo it on steep terrain, but I can still hike and run and backpack, and do a solid round-off back handspring. The only difference is, now, instead of competing, I share my love of the sport with other kids."

We nibbled a few more snacks and packed up. Conversation flowed between us like a stream through a mountain meadow, sparkling and bubbling. Our favorite books and movies, favorite foods, places we've visited.

All too soon the sun hung above the ridges to the west.

Jules stopped in the middle of the trail and twisted her arm to reach into one of the mesh side pockets on her pack. "I think it's about time I make camp. What's your plan?" Her map crinkled as she pulled it out and unfolded it.

"No plan, really." I peered at the map over her shoulder and pointed. "Though earlier I'd been thinking that set of campsites about a mile away looks good."

She stood silent, gnawing her lower lip. I'd swear the temperature dropped ten degrees instantly.

What the hell just happened?

CHAPTER 17

JULES

Oh my fucking God, does he have to stand so close?

Looking over my shoulder with his breath tickling the curls around my ear, with the heat of his body burning into mine even from half a foot away, all I wanted to do was turn around, shove my fingers in his hair, and kiss the shit out of him.

Mostly just to make sure it was even half as good as I remembered, of course. Partly because if it was, I wanted more, even though I shouldn't.

Instead, I stared at my map, frozen in place. Except for the hairs on my neck and the backs of my arms. They stood at attention every time his warm breath caressed my skin, like they were a million tiny compass needles, and he was my magnetic north.

"If you don't want me to camp with you, just say the word and I'll hike on." His words startled me.

"It's not that I don't want you to camp with me, I'm just not sure it's a good idea."

　　　Wild at Heart

Understatement of the year.

"What do you mean?"

"I like you Evan, don't get me wrong." *Too much, that's the problem.* "But I'm not out here to make friends. You're—It's—distracting."

"No problem. I get it." His tone stayed warm and friendly, but his lips pressed into a flat line. "Mind if I take a closer look at your map?"

I handed him the creased, slick waterproof paper and stepped away, trying not to notice the muscles flexing in his arms. He traced the trail with his fingertip. I tried not to imagine him tracing the lines of my body the same way. And failed miserably.

His finger stopped beside a triangle marking the next set of designated campsites, about five miles away. "Oh good. I can make a few more miles, easy."

Half of the sun disappeared behind a knife's edge ridge. "It'll be dark long before you get there."

He stared at the sky. "The weather looks fine, and the trail has been easy to follow. I'm sure I'll be all right."

Worry clogged my throat. Evan had already gotten lost once in broad daylight, not to mention borderline hypothermic and almost drowned because he didn't know what the hell he was doing out here. If he hiked on and… "Nope. Not gonna happen. I'd never forgive myself if anything happened to you."

"Are you sure? I don't mean to push myself on you if you want to be alone."

"Positive. It'll be fine. I've got weeks to be alone." My heart hammered in my chest like a rabid woodpecker. It didn't have anything at all to do with the fact that I'd been enjoying his company. A lot.

Too much.

Or that part of me wanted one more night of talking and laughing with him. Of having a smart, sexy man look at me like he saw straight into the deepest, realest parts of me—and very much liked what he found.

"Maybe there'll be two sites available. Then we won't have to camp together."

"That would just be weird." I snatched the map out his hand. "One more night of company won't kill me. Come on."

Much as I didn't want to admit it, I liked getting to know Evan. And the more I got to know him, the more I liked him.

I liked that he hadn't even tried to kiss me today. Except it meant I couldn't stop thinking about our one kiss, and how sweet and sexy and unassuming and utterly spine-melting it had been. And whether he thought about it.

Not that it would, or should, happen again.

I was saving him from almost certain danger. Saving myself from needing to rescue his ass again. And enjoying the company of a short-term trail friend. That was all.

With at least a few yards of dirt and layers of nylon between us nothing would happen anyway.

The flat rectangle of a brown carsonite post marking the desig-nated camping area materialized out the gray evening light. Tents and voices occupied every site except one.

Evan shucked his pack in front of me. "I guess this is us. Thank you again for sharing." His gaze met mine loaded with sincerity, and something else. My lungs froze. My body leaned toward his.

He squatted and unclipped his top lid. I sucked in a deep breath.

It's my pleasure.

"You're welcome."

We set up tents in companionable silence as the gray evening light faded. I laid out my stove and dehydrated dinner pouch on a wide, flat rock twenty yards away. Folding my sleeping pad into my chair kit, I made myself comfortable and filled my pot with water.

Evan joined me, reclining in his own chair. "I just want you to know, once again you were right."

"About what?"

"A chair kit is worth its weight in gold. I love this thing, my back loves this thing, and it's so small and light I couldn't imagine ever back-packing without one again."

I smirked and clicked on my headlamp, tilting it so it wouldn't shine directly in his eyes. "And I love a man who isn't afraid to tell me when I'm right."

He laughed. "Hopefully I'm not the first man smart enough to tell you that."

"Not the first, but close to it. Because, you know, most guys aren't as bright as you." I chuckled, turning on the gas and flicking my lighter. Blue flame came to life with a whoosh and hiss. "Seriously though, does this mean you might actually go backpacking again?" I perched my pot of water on top of my stove.

"Absolutely. That's another thing you were right about." Evan cranked up his stove. "Enjoying backpacking is all about having your priorities straight. That, and having proper equipment."

Another chuckle bubbled up from my chest. "Pretty sure that's true in life, too."

"I think you're right about that as well." He shook his head. "In fact, I think one of my problems is I've never had my priorities straight."

"How so?"

"I've let my parents and their priorities dictate my choices instead of figuring out my own. And their main priorities are accumulating wealth and burnishing their reputation, and all the privilege that goes with that." He poured water into his pot and set it on the burner. "If those were my priorities, my job, my fiancé, and my life would make sense. The problem is, I couldn't care less about making loads of money. Though maybe I only feel that way because I've always had enough."

I rested my chin on my hand and studied his face. "What's so wrong with making money? I wouldn't mind making more, that's for sure."

"Nothing." He met my gaze, his eyes harder than I'd seen them. "There's absolutely nothing wrong with making money, even a lot of money. But at a certain point, when you're making far more than you could ever need or spend, and your main goal in life is to make even more at any and all costs, there's a problem." He sighed. "My parents aren't philanthropists. They don't have a foundation or donate one cent more than they can deduct from their taxes. They wouldn't donate anything if their accountant didn't tell them it was good for the bottom line. And having all that money has never seemed to make them happy. In fact, it's done the opposite."

"What do you mean?"

"They're always so focused on making money they don't need and making sure everyone knows how much money they have, they never had time or energy for anything else. Certainly not spending time with their children, or hobbies, or travel, or even each other."

"That sucks. I always figured having a ton of money would give you the time and ability to enjoy life more." The lid on my pot rattled. The water inside churned. I turned off the stove and tore the top off my pouch of dried cheesy tuna casserole. "At least, I'm pretty sure it would for me."

"What would you do if you made far more money than you needed?"

"Assuming I already owned a house free and clear and had paid off all my debt?"

He nodded, steam glowing in my light as we poured boiling water into our dinners.

"Then the first thing I'd do is set up regular donations to charities that support children and the environment, like Nature Unlimited, Family Planning, and Inner City Outside. I'm sure I could find some other worthy causes too… Maybe buy a big piece of land for conservation."

"What's Inner City Outside?"

"It's a non-profit that gets underprivileged city kids out hiking and backpacking. My best friend Bryn and I volunteer as trip leaders a few times a year." I smiled. "Seeing those kids gain confidence and self-esteem and an appreciation for being outdoors—it's life-changing for them."

His eyes went wide. "Wow. I bet it's life-changing for you too."

"It is. Few things are more fulfilling."

"So that explains why you're so good at saving my ass out here. I bet I don't have many more skills than those kids."

"Maybe a couple more. Now." Sealing the pouch up tight, I shook my dinner and squished it in my fingers, mixing the hot water and ingredients. Double-checking the seal, I tucked it between my low back and my chair to wait for it to hydrate. Heat from the pouch seeped through my layer and into my tight muscles.

"You're being generous."

"Maybe a little." I grinned and he smiled back.

Evan followed suit with his own dinner and groaned. "Oh my God, you're a genius. This feels amazing!"

"Glad you like it. It's one of my favorite secret backpacker tricks."

"I am honored to be your pupil, sensei." He bowed in my direction.

My laughter bubbled up for the hundredth time that day. I liked that he wasn't too full of himself. That he wasn't afraid to make fun of himself or own his weaknesses. "What about you? What would you do if you had all the money you ever needed, and then some?"

"I used to think I'd take off alone and travel the world. Now I'm not so sure."

"Why not? Nothing wrong with traveling. I'd love to go to Europe and Asia and Africa, and pretty much anywhere else."

"I'm not knocking traveling. But I'm realizing maybe life shouldn't be all about me and what I want. That it might be good to find ways to help other people, too."

"There is that."

We pulled out our pouches and ate. The fatty, salty, carby goodness melting on my tongue took all my attention. Nothing but the scraping of sporks on plastic, and occasional voices from the other campers broke our companionable silence. The sky darkened and stars popped out, first one-by-one, then by the thousands. A sliver of a moon did little to hide them, exactly as I'd hoped.

Dinner finished, we hung our bear-resistant food bags from a high tree limb, and I boiled more water for tea.

"Hey. Was that a shooting star?" Amazement filled Evan's voice.

"Most likely. We're in for quite a show tonight."

"What do you mean?"

"It's the peak of the Perseid meteor shower. Which means seventy to a hundred shooting stars an hour, on average."

"Seriously?"

"Seriously." I nodded, more excited than I should have been to share one of my favorite natural phenomena with Evan. "They'll only get better as the night goes on."

A bright white light streaked the midnight velvet over our heads. "Oh my God. There's another one." He pointed, his arm a darker silhouette against the multiplying pinpricks of stars. "And another one. How did I not know this existed?"

I shrugged, even though he couldn't see it. "Most people who live in big cities don't."

"And I thought the Milky Way was impressive. This is amazing. It's like something out of a movie."

"It really is spectacular." Joy swirled and sparkled in my chest. "I try to make sure I get far enough out of the city to enjoy it every year."

"This happens every year?"

"Yep." I grinned. "Grab a sleeping bag, I'll pour tea, and we can sit back and watch one of Mother Nature's best spectacles."

"Deal."

Water steamed from our mugs, bright mint mixing with the pungent spruce and earthy loam. I cut my headlamp. Evan scooched his chair close to mine and spread his unzipped sleeping bag over our legs. We tilted back in our seats and he counted each star that flew across the sky, bubbling over with childlike excitement.

"One hundred thirty-seven." He turned toward me and tangled his fingers in mine, giving my hand a squeeze. "Thanks for sharing this with me, Jules. I know you were looking forward to time alone, but this is…It's incredible, and I probably would've missed it if it wasn't for you."

His enthusiasm ran through our palms and right into my chest, making it tingle. "Don't forget to make a wish on at least one of them."

"Oh, I've made a wish on every single one."

His knee pressed warm against mine, like he didn't realize it. Even with the stars raining down over our heads, I could barely focus on anything other than the heat passing between us where our skin touched.

"What are you wishing for? A new job? Clarity?"

"If I tell you, it won't come true."

"That's an old wives' tale."

He snorted. "Old wives were smart. That's why their tales have stood the test of time."

"Fine. Be that way." I harrumphed and pulled my hand out of his, crossing my arms. What I didn't do was move my leg and break that last point of physical connection.

His fingers slid down my arm and he took my hand again.

"Maybe I could show you, instead." His voice wavered a little and he cleared his throat. "That probably wouldn't break any wish-upon-a-star rules."

"Okay. Should I turn on my headlamp?"

"Definitely not." He shifted. His hand slid behind my neck and his lips brushed mine.

Just once.

Light as a butterfly.

And delicious sparks shot from his lips like a handful of the stars arcing through the sky. Only these flew straight to my core.

He hesitated. His mouth hovered an inch away. His breath puffed warm gusts across my tingling lips. All my focus shifted to our mouths and how badly I wanted to close that gap between us.

Except, if I kissed him again, I had a feeling this would go much farther than was wise. I also had a feeling sex with Evan would be pretty damn spectacular. Maybe even worth a one-night stand—vow of celibacy be damned.

The big question was, could it be no-strings-attached?

     Wild at Heart

CHAPTER 18

EVAN

Jules didn't move. Didn't react to my kiss at all. My heart dropped into my gut like a waterlogged backpack and sloshed around, heavy and wet.

Maybe I'd been misreading her the whole time. If so, I was a grade A asshole and needed to apologize and give her some space. I shifted, pulling away.

"I'm sorry. That was presumptuous—"

Her hand landed on my shoulder, jolting heat through me. I froze, worry and confusion and desire fighting for dominance.

"I thought you said you wished on every shooting star," she whispered. It took a second to register her words.

"I did." My voice came out rough.

"Did you make the same wish on all of them?"

"I did."

Her hand tightened. "Maybe we should make those come true too."

"Mmmmmm. Probably a good idea. If you're willing."

"Well, you know, it'd be a shame for all those wishes to not come true. Especially when they're so easily granted. I'm willing to take one for the team."

"I appreciate the sacrifice." I dipped my head and nuzzled in, and her tongue tangled with mine, and bright white lights streaked across the sky.

It could've been a dream, the way the stars fell from the heavens and I fell into that kiss with Jules. Perfect didn't even begin to describe that moment, everything so quiet and still, the air crystal clear, her mouth tasting of mint tea and something much, much sweeter.

I slid my tongue along her lips and into her mouth. Swirled it against hers. Tasted, nipped, explored. Her small hand slipped up my neck, lighting my skin on fire. Twining into the back of my hair.

When we'd kissed at the lake, I'd been sure that was the best kiss of my life. I was wrong.

This was…unreal. Surreal. Something out of a romantic movie with bright white stars tracing lines in the inky sky like silvered rain drops, and my heart flying up, out of my chest to beat against hers.

I didn't need anything else other than our lips touching, her breath in my mouth, the way her tongue slicked and flicked against mine. All I wanted was to keep kissing this funny, intelligent, sexy-as-hell woman forever and my life would be complete.

Then she moaned and arched, and pulled me closer, and I wanted more. I wanted everything. I wanted to be with her. Against her. In her.

With one hand, I released the buckles on my chair kit and hers, each click loud in the quiet of the night, and lay her back until I could press our bodies together.

She turned into me, and her hand traced a hot path down my spine. Cupping my ass, she drew me in closer. Wrapping one leg over mine. A fire lit in my soul that ran out to my fingertips, matching the trails of the stars flashing high above.

I gripped behind her knee, my fingers kneading the soft, sensitive flesh, trying to control the desire ripping through me. Nothing, nobody, had ever made me feel like this. This wanted. This connected. This in tune with another person and everything around me.

With a tug, she trapped my hard-on between us and rubbed against it, and my groan came from somewhere deep inside where the fire built. I wasn't sure I could keep it together. I didn't want to push her, but I didn't want to stop.

Her hands came up to cup my face, gentle and sweet, the exact opposite of the way she rubbed against me.

"I want you, Evan," she mumbled against my mouth.

I pulled back a little, trying to look into her eyes but all I could see was a reflection of the stars. "The feeling is mutual."

"So, what do we do about it?" She nipped my lower lip and a line of heat zipped straight to my cock.

I moaned into her mouth and ran my hand up the back of her thigh. "What do you want to do about it?" I traced the line where her ass met her leg and followed it around to the front of her hiking shorts, rubbing light circles and hard lines up the seam.

Jules bucked against my hand. I increased the pressure, teasing out a long groan. "Make my wish come true."

"What's your wish?"

Her hips twitched. "That by some dumb luck you're carrying a condom."

"Good thing I seem to have a lot of dumb luck lately, because yes, I believe I do have one."

She cleared her throat, but her voice still came out gruff and needy. "Maybe you should get it."

"I can do that." I struggled with letting her go, raining kisses down her neck and chest. Caressing the soft swell of her breast. Taking her nipple between my teeth through the smooth nylon fabric of her shirt and bra.

Her fingers gripped my head and pulled it up. "You're killing me, Evan."

"Killing is not exactly what I was going for." I went in for another long kiss, like I was searching for the meaning of life in her mouth. With a light brush of my lips against hers I drug myself away.

The night air chilling my bare legs, combined with the sudden distance, let reality seep in. I was in the middle of nowhere, about to have sex with a woman I barely knew. The first woman other than Lainey I'd even kissed in more than seven years.

I rooted in the depths of my pack, searching for my wallet. *What am I doing? What if this is another bad idea in a long, long line of them?*

Plastic crinkled against my fingertips, my dick twitched, and a switch flipped in my brain.

Lainey and I were through. The most incredible woman I'd ever met wanted me. Responded to me, to my every touch, like no woman had before. I couldn't let this moment slip away, not when I had a chance at something so special with someone so special. I wanted to make her feel as amazing as she deserved.

Fisting a condom, I shoved the other one in my pocket and stumbled my way through the dark to where Jules lay sprawled under my sleeping bag, her unbraided hair a wild, dark mass around her head. Her eyes sparkling in the starlight.

I slid my legs into the quilted warmth, savoring the heat of her calves against mine. "Sorry I took so long."

"That's okay. I'm just glad you're back. I was getting cold and lonely over here watching shooting stars by myself."

I had the feeling Jules was rarely lonely, but I appreciated the sentiment, nonetheless. "I can fix both of those problems."

"That's what I'm counting on." Without warning she climbed on top of me and dropped her hips, grinding against my suddenly rock-hard dick and diving into my mouth like a starving woman. She snatched the condom out of my grip with one hand.

Threading my fingers into her hair I tugged her face away from mine a little. "Hey. Hey. Relax. Slow down. We've got all night."

JULES

I closed my eyes and took a deep breath, cold air cooling my lungs. If this was going to happen, it needed to be fast and passionate and wild and impersonal. Because tomorrow he'd be gone, and I'd be nothing more than a fun rebound story for him. Part of his big backpacking adventure.

"Are you okay?" Evan's low voice sounded sensitive. Caring. Worried.

I cringed.

He was a nice guy.

The kind of guy who wanted to make slow, tender love then cuddle all night. I didn't do all night. Or cuddling. I had hot sex and went on my way. It was better, safer, that way.

All night meant something else. Something I wasn't ready for. Something I realized I hadn't been ready for since Justin.

Evan made me feel special and beautiful and like I deserved more than just a fuck. Out here in the middle of nowhere, with shooting stars falling all around, it was intoxicating. He was intoxicating.

I wanted to be the person he thought he saw, at least for a little while. But that didn't mean it was safe to let this get all emotional. I didn't deserve anything more than I could give. If we were going to do this, I couldn't let him into anything other than my body. Not any more than I already had.

"I'm sorry, Jules." Evan's fingertips drifted along my cheekbone. "Did I do something wrong?"

I shook my head, hoping he'd stop touching me like that. Hoping he wouldn't. "You didn't do anything wrong. It's not you, it's me."

"It's okay. We don't have to do anything else. We can just lay here and watch the stars fall and it'll still be the best night of my life." He stroked my hair gently and I fought the urge to lean into his hand like a cat desperate for attention.

Shifting and tugging, he moved me off him and tucked me against his side. One hand wrapped tight around my shoulders, the other caressed my face, my neck, my arm. It was sweet. He was sweet. Too sweet. And too romantic. And nice. And sexy.

I pressed my cheek into his chest and squeezed my eyes shut fighting against the rush of memories of other moments too much like this one. His spicy, masculine scent swirled around in my head.

It's probably better this way. He's not Justin and he never will be— even if he sticks around longer than tomorrow.

His heart thumped in my ear, slow and steady. "Do you want to talk about it?"

I shrugged. "Not really."

"Might make you feel better."

"I don't know about that."

     Wild at Heart

"Okay." He kissed the top of my head and cuddled me closer.

His arm was strong and warm. Every inch of me screamed this was safe. He was safe. "Thank you."

"For what?"

"For not pushing me. To talk. Or have sex."

"My pleasure."

"No. It's not."

"I told you, laying here with you in my arms, watching this unreal, super-cool meteor shower…This is the highlight of my life. Anything more would be a bonus I don't deserve." He dropped another light kiss in my hair.

Fuck. Everything about Evan, everything he said, everything he did, made me want him more.

"You deserve all this and more." I nuzzled in and pressed my mouth against the pulse in his neck, tasting the salt on his sun-kissed skin. "You're sweet and thoughtful and sensitive and funny, and I'm nothing special."

He tilted my chin up with one finger. "No. That's where you're wrong." The rough pad of his thumb drew a warm line down the center of my lips. "You're bright and independent and hilarious and thoughtful and incredibly special. Anyone who's ever told you different—or didn't recognize it—is a fool."

My heart swelled. Nobody had said anything like that to me in years. "I guess I'm a fool then. But thank you." I shifted and brushed my lips over his. "It's good to know somebody thinks so."

"I don't just think so, I know so." He pulled me in for a deeper kiss, his warm hand cupping the back of my head like he held a delicate treasure. "You're the most amazing person I've ever met."

His words. The way he touched me, kissed me. Like he meant it. He melted me, my resolve, everything.

I couldn't resist any longer. I opened my mouth and flicked my tongue against his lips.

He gasped and tightened his grip, and the kiss shifted from sweet to sexy. I climbed on top of him again and pressed my chest to his, this time melting into his rhythm. Letting him take the lead. Reveling in the slow, sensuous sweeps of his lips. The gentle strokes along my back, my sides. The warm tingles racing across my skin.

Our hips rolled together, his cock pressing hard and sweet against my clit. We both moaned. His tongue slid in and out of my mouth in time to his thrusts.

He slipped his fingers under the hem of my shirt, drawing it up. Tugging it almost over my head. I sat up long enough to pull off it and my sports bra.

Cold air hardened my nipples. His warm hands covered my tits, fingers trapping them, the contrasting temperatures making my quiver.

White trails of shooting stars reflected in his eyes. "God, you're incredible."

His rough voice caressed my ears. His words caressed a part of me I'd forgotten existed.

If ever there was a time to break a vow of celibacy, that was it. For sure.

He pulled me down and rolled until we were both on our sides, tugging the sleeping bag over our shoulders in a rustle of nylon. "I don't want you to get cold," he whispered.

"I won't," I whispered back, sliding my leg up on his hip. His fingers went to the hottest part of me, stroking and pressing and circling through the fabric of my shorts.

Tiny sounds came out of the back of my throat. I grappled at his shoulder blades, trying to pull him closer. Trying to get him to rub harder and take me over the edge.

His fingers pressed against my clit and his thumb curled into my waistband and tugged. "I think these are in the way," he mumbled against my lips.

"Mmmmmmmmmmm." I circled my hips to meet his hand. "Agreed. But you have too many clothes on, too."

"Don't worry about me. Lay back. Hold on to my sleeping bag." He shifted me underneath him. "This is all about you right now."

With a tug, the snap on my shorts snicked open. Each tooth in my zipper ticked loud in the quiet of the night.

Crouching between my legs, under the warm cover of his bag, Evan slid my shorts and underwear down and off my ankles. Trailed his fingers up the insides of my thighs in sizzling lines.

His tongue swept over my clit, hot and slick, and he moaned and I moaned and I quit thinking about everything else.

"Mmmmmm…You taste so good."

He spread my legs wider and stroked me with his fingertips while his mouth did incredible things to my most sensitive parts. Sliding a finger inside me he picked up the pace on my clit, flicking it quick and light as a feather.

My hips bucked and twitched. I twisted my hands in the sleeping bag. Cold air bit my nipples.

Tingles started at the top of my head and my toes and spread to every part of me. He added a second finger and I levitated off the rock, lights shooting behind my eyelids brighter than the stars. I clenched hard around his magic fingers and exploded like a firework.

Slowing his pace, he licked gently, teasing my clit with barely-there touches, still moving his fingers in and out.

I clawed at his shoulders. "Come here."

CHAPTER 19

JULES

Evan crawled up my body, low and slow and sexy as hell, wiping his mouth with the back of his hand. I wrapped my hand around his neck and kissed him, my orgasm tangy and sweet on his lips.

Peeling his shirt off, I arched my back until my skin met his, hot and electric. "I need you inside me. Now. Please."

With one hand I pressed divots into his firm deltoids. With the other, I gripped his hard-on through the fabric of his shorts and squeezed.

"Fuck." Evan groaned and lifted his head, panting above me. "Jules. Are you sure? We don't have to—"

"Positive." I squeezed again. Slipping my other hand down, I shoved at the elastic of his waistband, gripped his smooth, rigid cock and slid my hand up and down until precum slicked his head. I brought my thumb to my mouth. Evan tasted like warm salt and hot sex.

"You're killing me, Jules." He handed me the condom and braced himself on his elbows.

I rolled it on, fisting him and gliding my hand up and down. "The feeling's mutual."

Centering his head at my entrance I lifted my hips. He slid home in one long, drawn-out thrust, resting his forehead on mine. I wrapped my legs around his hips and pulled him in to hit my deepest spots. A few sparks flashed behind my eyelids.

He stilled, his breath puffing across my cheek. I ran my fingers through the coarse silk of his hair.

He dropped his lips to my mouth, my cheeks, my neck, then, just when I couldn't stay still any longer, he slid out and in. Not fast, not slow. I met each of his strokes. "Please, Evan. More. Harder."

"Not yet. I don't want this to be over too soon."

Reaching between us, he rubbed across my clit. I slammed my hips against him, trapping his hand for an instant. His fingers picked up speed, strumming. His tongue slid into my mouth. Each thrust hit a little harder, a little faster.

My pussy clenched and his thrusts went erratic.

I thrashed underneath him vibrating and bucking. Each time he sunk deep a tingling, electric wave of pleasure flooded me, from my scalp to my toenails. And everywhere in between.

His cry rang out loud in the night and he collapsed on my chest. Hand trapped between us. Hips still pumping and circling and making me quiver.

I held him tight, reveling in the firm heat of his body flattened on mine, his cock still twitching inside me. I didn't ever want to let him go. So, I didn't. I held on like my life fucking depended on it.

Until we both went still. Until his breathing steadied, and my heartbeat slowed.

"That." He rained kisses on my lips, my cheeks, the tip of my nose. "Was incredible."

"I couldn't agree more." I flexed my fingers against his shoulders, trying to decide what to do. Because damned if I didn't want more.

Not that it mattered. In a few days he'd go back to Boston—and his ex—and we'd never see each other again.

I was a fool. But it was worth it for one night like this. At least, I hoped it would seem worth it when I looked back later. After he'd gone.

EVAN

Laying there, Jules's skin hot against mine, our bodies still connected, that was heaven. Or as close as I'd ever been or would likely ever get. If I'd figured out one thing on this trip, it was that I wanted more of this, more of her. More of everything Jules had shown me and everything she offered. For the first time in my adult life, I felt good enough—and not because of my name or my money.

My dick softened, forcing me to move. I gripped the base, making sure the condom stayed on, and shifted to my knees.

"Be right back." Palming her cheek I bent down, pressing my lips to hers because I didn't want to get up at all. Not that I had a choice. Some things needed to be handled no matter how badly you'd rather not.

"Me too."

We went to separate sides of the clearing to take care of our respective business. Cleaned up, I crawled under the sleeping bag again.

It didn't seem possible, but even more shooting stars streaked across the sky than before. So close together I had trouble keeping count. Making wishes was easier, since I kept wishing for the same thing, over and over. *I wanted Jules and this life she'd shown me—somehow, someway.*

I counted my fortieth shooting star and she hadn't come back. "Are you okay?"

"Yeah. I'm good." Her voice came from the right, ten or so feet away but quieter than it should've been. "Be right there."

Something in her tone made my gut clench. She wasn't all right. She hadn't been all right before we made love, and she wasn't after.

Shit. Did I just make another bad decision?

Twenty stars streaked the sky. Finally, her dark silhouette blocked my view. I lifted the sleeping bag and scooched to the side. "Count more shooting stars with me?"

She hesitated. My gut twisted into knots.

"Okay," she whispered and lay down beside me.

I tucked my sleeping bag around our shoulders and pulled her in until her head rested in the crook of my arm and our sides pressed together, naked skin warm against naked skin.

"Are you sure you're all right? Did I do something wrong?"

"I'm sure. And you were perfect." She kissed my chest. "Just hold me, okay?"

CHAPTER 20

EVAN

Something cold and wet hit my face. Eyes closed, I swiped at it with my hand.

It happened again. And again. Tiny splats on my forehead, my cheeks, my nose.

I opened my eyes to the flat, dull light of a cloudy pre-dawn. Strike that—a drizzling pre-dawn. I huddled under my sleeping bag and looked around, my sleep-fogged brain struggling to work out what was going on.

Except for our mugs sitting on the ground, it was just me, and my sleeping pad and bag, laying out in the open.

I blinked into sprinkling raindrops.

Shit. It's raining.

Scrambling up I tossed my bag over my shoulder, grasped my pad in one hand, mugs in the other, and beelined for my tent. Jules's orange tent stood silent at the edge of the clearing, a few yards from mine.

I froze, the night before washing over me in a rush of images and emotions. The meteor shower. Jules, shirtless and gorgeous in the starlight. Her body quivering in my hands, against my mouth. The sweet, musky tang of her on my lips.

The sadness and pain in her voice when she curled into me.

And the undeniable fact that she'd gone to sleep in her tent alone at some point during the night.

My stomach churned. The rain picked up force, pattering my head with a soft rat-a-tat.

Setting my stove in my vestibule I clambered into my empty tent, knowing full well I wouldn't be able to fall back asleep—not until I talked to her and found out what I'd done wrong and how to fix it. Because I'd had enough experience with relationships to know I'd probably done something wrong.

Leaving my door half-unzipped I stared at her tent, willing her to wake up. Waiting for the rustle and shift that meant I could try to talk to her.

Raindrops beat louder on the roof. I slipped on my jacket and headed for the tree where we'd hung our food for the night—figuring I might as well get it down in case the rain turned into a downpour. I lowered the stuff sacks and trotted back to my tent as quick as possible. The wet rope chilling a line on my palm as I wound it.

Shivering, I dropped my wet rain jacket and pulled on my fleece. With a too-loud rustle of nylon I tucked my damp bag over my crossed legs, trying to keep the chill from settling into my bones. It did nothing to stop the frustration and worry and fear churning in my gut.

Rain drummed my tent fly, making the walls quiver. Other than that, nothing moved.

If she was sleeping, I didn't want to wake her, but I needed to know what was going on in her head.

Maybe she just got cold and headed to bed in the middle of the night, but I didn't think so. After what we'd shared, why would she suddenly want to be alone? Why didn't she at least wake me and let me know?

I'd tried so hard to make her feel incredible, and I had a sinking feeling I'd done the opposite. At a loss, I cranked up my stove in the vestibule just outside my door. It hissed and spluttered to life. Nylon crackled inside Jules's tent.

The lid on my pot rattled. I poured steaming water into my mug and hesitated, pot poised over her cup.

"Are you awake?" I kept my voice barely louder than a whisper and waited. Nothing. Not a sound. But I'd swear I could feel her laying there, staring at the ceiling. "Do you want a cup of tea?"

Another rustle. "Okay. Thanks."

I exhaled the breath I didn't know I'd been holding and tilted the pot. She didn't sound happy, but at least she was awake and talking to me.

A mug in each hand, rain pummeling the hood of my jacket like a drum line, I stood in front of her tent door and debated my next move until water streamed cold down my bare legs.

I gathered my courage. For once in my life I was going to confront an issue head on. "Tea's ready. Can you let me in?"

"Ummmmm…Sure." I waited for her to unzip her door, shifting from foot to foot, trying not to wimp out before I even started this conversation.

It's just talking. I've survived everything else on this trip, surely I can make it through a damn conversation with a women I slept with. I owe us both that much.

Besides, how could I possibly face my parents if I couldn't even talk to someone I'd only known a few days? The zipper snicked and

   Wild at Heart

the flap fell to the side. Jules scooched back to the far end of her tent, making room for me.

"Here you go." I handed her our mugs and sat just inside, shaking out my jacket, taking off my shoes, and sluicing chilly rain from my legs. I should've pulled on long johns, but it hadn't seemed near as important as listening for signs of Jules waking up, or making her tea, or getting this chance to talk to her.

Zipping everything closed, I settled in. She handed me my tea. I shuddered from the chill, both in the air and in the tent, and cupped the warmth of my mug. The aroma of damp wool and chamomile filled the small space. "It's really starting to come down out there."

"Yeah. Looks like it might be a rest day." Her voice came out flat. My mistake slapped me in the face.

"Shit. I'm so sorry, I didn't even ask if I could come in. I hope you don't mind…"

"No. It's good." She didn't meet my eyes. "Thanks for the tea. It's nice."

"You're welcome." I stared at her face, trying to figure out what the hell she was thinking. The woman in front of me didn't bear much resemblance the vivacious, in control person I'd gotten to know. Not with the way her shoulders hunched, and her head hung over her mug.

We sat three feet away from each other with miles of space between us. Nothing but the hammering of the rain broke the silence. Worry and tension coiled in the pit of my stomach like a snake about to strike. Unfortunately, I knew from experience ignoring the problem wouldn't make it go away.

"Are you okay?"

"Fine." She nodded. "Just cold."

For once in your life, don't play it safe. Talk to her.

"Bullshit." The word slapped out, flat and hard.

Her gaze met mine, filled with as much surprise as I felt, and flicked away. She didn't say anything, just huddled in the corner like a scared mouse.

"Come on, Jules. Talk to me. Last night was the most mind-blowing, incredible, amazing night of my life. I thought it was pretty great for you too. Then I woke up alone and now you won't even look at me." I reached out to push the curls away from her cheek, but she recoiled. I dropped my hand.

She pressed her lips into a thin line and shook her head. "I told you last night, it's not you, it's me."

"How so?"

She sighed from deep inside. "It's a long story, and not one I like to share."

"Maybe it's time you got it out." If she could've curled inside herself and disappeared, I'm pretty sure she would've. "Look, Jules, I really enjoy your company, and it freaks me out you're pushing me away right after we had most spectacular sex of my life. Not that I expect more sex. I just want to make things right between us."

"I'm not sure you can. It all happened a long time ago, and it's never gotten any better."

"Well I'd love to try, if you'll give me a chance."

She sniffled and stared at me; her soft brown eyes bright with tears. "I was in love once, madly in love, and sometimes you remind me so much of him it hurts. Like a knife stabbing me in the soul."

I didn't know what to do with that. "I'm—I'm so sorry. I thought you were enjoying hanging out together, talking, making love."

"That's just it. I was. Too much. And I don't know how to handle it. Especially not the making love part. That's not something I do." She paused. I waited for her to go on. "I mean, I've had sex. But I've never made love to anyone other than Justin, my first real boyfriend. I've never loved anyone like I loved Justin. And I've never been with anyone else who made me feel even half of what I felt with him. Or

 Wild at Heart

I never let anyone get close enough to try because it hurt too much when I lost him."

"What do you mean? How did you lose him? I can't imagine any man falling in love with you and walking away." I wasn't even in love with her, though I didn't think it would take much to fall the last few feet, and already I didn't want to walk away.

She didn't answer. She just looked at me with pain in her eyes and tears streaming down her face. I didn't know what else to do, so I set my mug down and gathered her in my arms.

"It's okay. You don't have to tell me if you don't want to. I'm here either way." She curled into my chest, and I stroked her hair and held her close and willed the pain to go away.

JULES

Fuck. I don't want to talk about Justin. Not with Evan. Not with anybody.

Even after all these years I didn't even want to think about Justin, because when I did, all the agony came rushing back. Every cell in body tightened. My eyes burned and I couldn't breathe.

When I'd crawled into my tent last night, I'd planned to pack up my shit and hit the trail at first light. Only when I woke up, rain drummed my tent. Then Evan was there, stroking my hair and holding me like he'd never let go.

Except sometimes you were forced to let go whether you wanted to or not. That's what made it hurt so damn much.

Swallowing against the giant frog in my throat I searched for the right words, knowing there weren't any right words for what I was about to say.

"Justin died in a car accident," I mumbled into the soft, pine-scented fleece of his jacket. "We were in our senior year of college, wild about each other, and planning to get married and be together forever. Forever never happened. And sometimes you remind me too much of him and what I lost." My eyes burned hot. I squeezed them shut.

"I'm so sorry, Jules. That must've been terrible, and I didn't mean to bring up all this pain for you. I just wanted you to feel beautiful."

"But I'm not beautiful. Because of what I did, after." I gulped and blinked, trying to keep my emotions from overwhelming me before I got it all out. "I tried to cancel Justin out. All my love for him, every-thing we shared, I tried to make it not count."

"What do you mean?"

"I slept around, a lot. Then, six months after Justin died, I got married. Like he'd never existed. Like that could fix anything." A harsh laugh tore up the back of my throat, searing a line of pain from my chest to my mouth. "I mean, how could I do that? After the kind of love we shared—and we shared everything—how could I do that? Not even a year later I was saying vows I'd promised I'd only ever say to Justin, and I said them to someone I didn't even love at all. What kind of fucking heartless monster does that?"

"A human being who's hurt and in shock from suffering a trau-matic loss."

"You don't understand." I lifted my head and looked him in the eye, waiting for the moment disgust filled his face. "I never even cried when he died."

Evan's expression softened, and he brushed my cheek. "You really loved him, didn't you?"

"Yeah." I sniffled. Tears pushed at the backs of my eyes. I blinked against them.

"Well, you can still cry for him. It'll count, even now."

He curved his arm around my shoulder and held me close. He kissed the top of my head and the tears wrenched up, out of my gut. I quit trying to hold them back for the first time in eight years.

"It's okay. It's okay. Let it all out. I'm here," he whispered, over and over while I poured out more tears than the Pacific Northwest sky dumped rain. Choked sobs twisted up from the depths of my soul that hurt. So. Fucking. Much.

All the tears I never cried the night I got the news. Or at his funeral, when I was in too much shock to feel anything. The tears I never cried after my divorce, or any of the nights I laid alone in bed wishing he was still laying there with me.

The whole time Evan held me. Rocking me. Wiping the snot from my nose with the soft sleeve of his fleece.

Somehow, eventually, my eyes ran dry. Evan lay us down and curled behind me, pulling my sleeping bag over our shoulders.

I sniffled. "I'm sorry I cried and snotted all over you."

"Don't be. I didn't mean to make you so upset." He pushed the damp curls off my forehead.

"It's not your fault. Like I said, it's not you, it's me."

"Maybe. But I triggered it." His chin settled on my shoulder, his cheek resting against mine. His beard scratching my skin. "If you need me to go, if you want to be alone, I understand. Just say the word."

The thought of him leaving right then ripped through me like a stab wound. But I'd just dumped a truckload of shit on him and I wouldn't blame him if he wanted to run. No other guy had even stuck around for half as much. "Do you want to go? I know this is a lot to handle. More than you bargained for last night, I'm sure."

"Everything about you is more than I bargained for, Jules. And I want it all. As much you're willing to give me."

CHAPTER 21

JULES

I peeled myself out of Evan's arms and shifted to face him. "What the hell is that supposed to mean?"

"It means I think I've figured out one thing I need in my life." He scooped up my hand and stared into my eyes, expression serious. Too serious. "You."

A wry snort shot out my nose. "Yeah. Sure. Easy to say here. Now. But in a few days, you go back to Boston. That's the other side of the country, remember?"

"I could move here."

"What?" I sat up.

"People move all the time." He shrugged a shoulder. "I'm not happy in Boston. I like Seattle. I like these mountains. And I like you a whole lot. There are worse reasons to relocate." He smiled, warm and gentle. His eyes so hopeful.

My insides collapsed and knotted, and bitter bile flooded the back of my throat. Old habits screamed run. Instead, I searched for every reason why falling for him would be a bad idea. "You don't even have a job. And what if it doesn't work out between us? Or you hate the rain? Or your family freaks out at the idea?" I didn't say the one that kept screaming the loudest in my head—*What if I let you in and you decide to go back to your ex?*

"I can find a job. My family will survive without me. And we won't know what we could be if we don't try." Evan pretzeled his fingers into mine. "Then we're over before we even start. Which would be a shame, because I think we could be amazing together."

Metallic adrenaline coated my mouth. "Look, Evan, I get you mean that now. But we're in our own little bubble out here on the trail. This isn't real life. Chances are you'll change your mind once you get home."

"Bullshit. I've never felt more sure of anything."

I searched his eyes, finding nothing but truth, honesty, and a boyish earnestness that threatened to break my heart before I broke his.

"Then there's something else you should know about me."

"What's that?"

"I've made an art of keeping men at arm's length. The last twelve guys I've dated have all left me for their exes, and it's my own damn fault. I push away any man who starts getting close to me, and I'll probably do it to you, too. And—" I closed my eyes and made myself say the next words, pushing them out fast and hard. "And while I like you a lot, I know you've got your own shit to deal with back home, and I'm not sure I could handle it if you didn't come back any more than I could handle the regret if you did, and I pushed you away, too."

Evan's eyes tightened. My pulse thudded in my ears loud enough to drown out the drumming rain. I held my breath waiting for him to respond. Feeling like I'd just handed him my heart on a platter and stood waiting for him to dump it in the dirt at my feet.

EVAN

I sat up cross-legged and faced her, clearing my throat. "You're right, Jules. I've got a lot of baggage waiting for me at home. Things I've been running away from for a long time that I'm going to have to deal with. But I want to be a part of your life, and I'm going to do everything in my power—including move to Seattle—to make that happen, because I'm pretty sure I'm falling for you. And for the record, I have zero intention of walking away or going back to my ex—even if you push me."

Jules stared at me with pain and fear rolling through her dark brown eyes, not saying a word. I held my breath, hoping I hadn't just ruined everything by putting too much on her.

Honestly, I'm not even sure where all that came from. I hadn't planned on saying any of it. I definitely had not planned on feeling one hundred positive moving across the country and being with Jules was the most logical, most right, most perfect choice in the world—even though she was right about all the things standing in our way.

But maybe she didn't want me the way I wanted her. Maybe this was just a safe and easy fling with a guy who lived a few thousand miles away.

"I'm sorry. I didn't mean to drop that on you, and I don't expect a response." The words tumbled out, not too different from the way I'd been pushed and bounced off the bottom of the river, out of control. "All I meant was that if I had the chance, I'd love to be with you for the rest of this hike, and hopefully longer. I'm not entirely sure how I'll make that happen, but I want to try, if you want me to. But not if you don't. If you don't, I'll leave as soon as you say the word."

    Wild at Heart

She sat still as a statue, but something in her eyes changed. "I don't want you to go. I'm not sure what I want beyond Snoqualmie Pass, or the end of the trail for me in a couple weeks, but I'd love to hike with you for now."

It wasn't exactly the response I hoped for, but at least I still had a chance to convince her I was serious. And time to figure out how I could make our future together more than a promise. "Then I'll stay as long as you'll have me."

Her lips curved into the smile I remembered from all our other days together, and the tension dissolved in the tent and my chest. Her voice went deep and breathy, "And I'd like to have you as often as possible, for as long as you're hiking with me." Her hand slid around my neck, pulling me in until our lips brushed.

This was much closer to the response I'd wanted. "Pretty sure I can work with that." I angled my head and slid my mouth over hers.

She smiled against my lips, then let her tongue slide out to find mine. With one hand, I stroked along her waist, her ribs, taking it nice and slow. It'd been an emotional morning and I didn't want to push her.

I trailed my mouth along her jaw to her neck, nibbling salt-tinged skin. Getting high off her mint and almond scent. Her head tilted, giving me better access and she lay back on her pad, taking me with her. I nipped and sucked at the silky skin behind her ear.

Moaning, she grabbed my hand and moved it to her breast.

Okay. Maybe I wasn't being too pushy.

I trapped her nipple between my fingers and tugged. Her gasp ran an electric line to my dick. Working my mouth down her neck and shoulder, I sucked her nipple through her shirt. She moaned again and arched her back. Her fingers clutching at my skull. I pushed up the hem and traced the vertical line down the middle of her flat stomach with my tongue, licking at her waistband. Making her hips twitch.

"You are such a tease."

"Only because you seem to like it so much." And because I wanted to give her ample opportunity to stop me. I pressed my mouth against her fabric-covered pussy and blew a soft stream of warm air through her long underwear. She squirmed and groaned.

"Please, Evan." Jules pushed gently on my head and rocked her hips.

My gaze met hers. "Please, what?"

She bit her lip, eyes wide and clear. "Please lick my clit and fuck me with your fingers until I come all over your hand."

My dick turned into a concrete post and I almost came right then and there. "As you wish."

She giggled. I slid her long johns down her muscled legs and off her ankles, dragging my fingers along her soft skin. Shirt shoved up, naked from the waist down, she pulled up her knees. The smell of sex made me dizzy. My rock-hard dick pulsed.

I skimmed my fingers through her wetness. Bent and dipped my tongue into her slit. She spread her lips wide with both hands, wanton and sexy as hell. Making it easy for me to flick her clit and slide my finger into her, pumping slow and dragging across the rough patch on the wall of her pussy.

"Oh. God. Yes." She panted and rocked her hips. "Don't stop."

Moisture flowed around my fingers, and I lapped it up, sweet and musky.

"Put your cock in my mouth. I want to suck you off while you eat me."

"I'm not sure I'll last if you do that." I'd never had a woman so into sex, or so willing to take control. I didn't know how to handle it. It was hot. She was hot.

"Don't care." She tugged on my hair, zapping a line of electricity from my scalp to my balls. How could I say no?

I shoved off my shorts and spun to hang my dick over her lips. She arched up and sucked me in, her mouth hot and slick and very, very sure of how to turn me on.

The tip of my hard-on hit the back of her throat and I almost lost it right then. I focused on tasting every inch of her glistening, pink pussy instead of the tightness in my balls and the way her tongue swirled up my shaft. I groaned from somewhere so deep inside it almost hurt.

She clamped a hand around the base of my dick. "Do you have another condom?"

"One." I flicked my tongue across her clit. "Because I'm lucky like that."

"Oh, thank God. I want you closer to me. Inside me. Please." Her voice struck a high, keening note on that last word.

Sitting up, I fumbled with my free hand for the other rubber I'd stowed in my pocket the night before. Jules lay on her back, knees wide apart, rubbing herself with two fingers. "I want you to fuck me from behind and play with my clit."

That image…Oh my God. I gripped the base of my dick hard, trying to hold back. After years of grudging missionary once or twice a month, Jules kept blowing my mind, among other things. "As you wish."

I might not know if she wanted this to continue after, but I knew for damn sure she wanted me right then. That was more than enough. We could figure the rest out later.

CHAPTER 22

EVAN

Jules and I lay in the dim green glow of her tent, limbs twined, listening to the barely noticeable whisper of mist rain falling on taut nylon. Our hearts beat slow and steady, in time together. Like we were two halves of a whole.

The last person I clicked with like this was my tent mate at Scout camp, Steve. We both loved camping, we were obsessed with *Home Alone*, and we both desperately wanted dogs. We also both came from families that didn't have much time for us. We got each other, accepted each other, without explanation or negotiation.

That was me and Jules, only with mind-blowing sex added in. I couldn't help wanting more.

I stroked her back and shoulder and kissed her, slow and sweet, pouring all my thoughts and feelings into that connection. Her mouth responded, soft and gentle, but her muscles tensed.

"You okay?" I pulled back, wondering for the umpteenth time if I was moving too fast. If every time I let my emotions out, it brought up too many old memories for her to handle. But I didn't know how else to convince her I was serious about her. Us.

"More than." She snuggled in closer and laid her head on my chest, but her hand clenched the edge of her sleeping bag to pull it up and never let go of the tight grip.

Given my baggage—and hers—I understood why she wouldn't trust me or this situation. But I refused to believe I had no chance with her. Somehow, I would earn her trust.

The only way seemed to be to go big or go home. Or in my case, go home and go big. Even though the thought of standing up to my parents still made something in my stomach curdle.

Until Jules, I'd always played it safe, doing just enough to get by but never committing all the way. Largely because I never wanted to be doing what I was doing.

That's the reason I'd been so unhappy with Lainey, and the reason I'd lost my job. I didn't love either of them.

Sure, I was a perfectly fine investment analyst, but I wasn't a star. I didn't take big risks or jump at opportunities. I came in, did a good job, and went home. I didn't eat, sleep and breathe investing, or buy rounds of drinks when I hit a big win—because I never had a big win. I won sometimes, but not big.

I wasn't going to make the same mistake with Jules. For the first time in my life I'd found someone worth going all in on. And maybe, just maybe, if I opened my heart to her, made myself vulnerable— hopefully more vulnerable than she felt—maybe she'd be willing to risk hers with me.

First, I had to go back home and take care of business. I was twenty-nine years old and could do what I wanted with my life, including move to Seattle.

What if Jules is right? What if it's easy to say all this out here in this bubble, but not so easy when I'm faced with finding a new career, and Lainey and my family demanding I do the opposite?

Except I couldn't go back to Boston and be even remotely happy. I needed a plan with solid arguments my parents couldn't refute—something more than *I'm in love and happy.*

Thankfully, a few ideas were forming. Because love and happiness did not rank high on their scale of priorities. Not when their son wanted to throw away the life they'd invested in and built for him.

JULES

Evan's heart thumped slow and steady in my ear. His hand slid up and down my shoulder in a smooth caress. Slowly, my muscles relaxed.

I'd been so afraid of ever admitting to anyone what a horrible person I'd been after Justin's death, sure they'd reject me. He hadn't even blinked let alone recoiled.

Nope. He'd done the exact opposite. We'd talked and laughed and done pretty much everything we could do. It'd been easy and fun, and a part of me wished it could go on forever.

The other part knew it never would. Otherwise, I would've been more freaked out that he wanted to move to Seattle to be with me. But the chances of that actually happening? About as likely as a snowball surviving in hell.

Evan didn't think so, though. He didn't believe me about life and relationships being different out here.

I'd hiked for days with people I met on the trail, people I instantly clicked with, until we seemed like best friends. And we all swore we'd stay in touch once we returned to civilization, for sure.

Never happened. Not once.

So, enjoying the rest of this section with Evan seemed like a no-brainer. I mean, since I'd already broken my vow of celibacy I might as well enjoy it. Because no matter what he said, or how much he meant it, once he got home, he'd stay there. That's just how trail romances worked.

And men I dated.

I lifted my head from his chest, listening to nothing. "I think the rain stopped. Want to pack up and hike?"

"Sure. Sounds good. I'll get hot water going for breakfast." He unzipped the door to a misty-gray world. Silver droplets clung to the spruce needles and moisture hung in the air like a thick curtain.

It didn't take long to pack up sleeping gear and shake out our tents to a reasonable level of dampness. I sipped my tea, eyeing him over the lip of my mug. Evan kicked back in his camp chair, ankles crossed, enjoying his steaming oatmeal. Like he didn't have a care in the world.

Compared to the shivering, unprepared guy I'd first met, he'd turned into a backpacking pro—competent with his equipment and comfortable out here in the wilderness. With his rumpled hair and rumpled shirt and rumpled smile, he looked ridiculously appealing.

There's something extra-sexy about a man that isn't afraid to take advice and try new things. A man who learns from his mistakes instead of doing the same stupid shit over and over.

Unlike most people.

Me included.

We cleaned our dishes and loaded our gear. I shrugged on my pack and he kissed me. Starting sweet and taking it hotter and deeper until I was on the verge of dropping my backpack, and my clothes, in the needle-covered dirt.

He broke the kiss and slapped my butt cheek. "After you."

I lifted my eyebrows. "You just want me to go first so you can stare at my ass."

"Of course I do." He chuckled.

"Good to know." Turning on my heel I headed down the trail before I peeled down his shorts and gave him head again. Cool, damp fog wrapped around my legs, contrasting with the spreading warmth across my butt and the heat of his gaze.

Damn, that sex under the stars might even be the best I'd ever had. Not to downplay what I had with Justin. But there's a difference between the giddy newness of sex in your early twenties, and the deeper want and knowing and skill that comes from years of practice.

And Evan didn't just fuck me. He'd looked at me like I was worth more than any other thing on the planet. Touched me like I was made of something special and rare. Focused on my pleasure with a single-minded intensity that would've been terrifying if he wasn't so good at making me quiver and shake and tingle and explode.

On top of that, he was so open with his thoughts and feelings. It blew my mind. That he could be so willing to put himself out there, shot raw terror through my veins.

It was all I could do not to run. But like an adrenaline addict I wanted more despite the dangers. Though the only real danger was that I'd miss him for a while once he was gone. A little bit pain for all this pleasure seemed worth it.

The clouds broke, and the air turned hot and humid. We skinny-dipped surrounded by dark green spruces and Doug firs, kissing and fondling each other until our feet and legs went numb. Then we hiked some more.

     Wild at Heart

I propped my foot on a boulder and bent to tighten my boot laces. Evan slid his fingers between my legs and I forgot how to tie a bow. When we stopped for a snack, he kissed me senseless by the banks of a babbling brook. That night we did everything you could do without a condom. And the next night. And the one after that.

CHAPTER 23

JULES

Every time Evan smiled at me, every time he looked at me with all that intensity in his too-blue eyes, I melted a little bit more.

I couldn't help it. Especially as the days passed in a haze of laughter and the sex-filled glow that comes from fooling around at every opportunity. Each one another in a string of days to end all days, except I didn't want them to end. At least not soon.

I counted fifty steps, took a deep breath, and spit out the question I'd been ignoring. "So, when do you fly out?"

I didn't turn, or stop, or even glance at him over my shoulders. Just kept counting steps.

"Day after tomorrow."

"Damn." *Too soon.* I readied my head and my heart to take a big leap, like prepping for a hard vault.

"What?"

"Remember those hot springs I told you about?"

"Of course. They sound incredible—probably on par with the meteor shower."

"Oh, they are." My heart shoved itself into my throat, I put one foot in front of the other, eyes focused on the brown ribbon of trail. "And if you had another day or two you could totally hike into them with me for a night, then hike out and thumb a ride back to Seattle the next day."

For fifty-four steps, the only sounds were our footfalls and the caw of one loud raven.

He inhaled. "Maybe I can move my flight again. I can't make any promises until I check my voice mail, but I'd love to stay."

My heart dropped out of my throat and flitted around on fairy wings inside my chest. I stopped and turned so fast he came this close to running into me. "Seriously?"

"Seriously. I would love nothing more than to spend another couple of days out here with you." His rough palm cupped my cheek in warmth. "Being naked with you in a natural hot spring would be a huge bonus."

The pad of his thumb drew a sizzling line down the center of my lips. One that ran straight to my clit.

"Along with a fresh box of condoms."

One side of Evan's lips lifted, begging to be kissed.

Bryn was going to give me a raft-load shit about breaking my vow of celibacy. But she was the one who always said it was past time for me to take a chance and let someone in.

"Thank God there's a store between here and there." His smile broadened, flashing in his eyes. "Using the last condom seemed like a brilliant idea the other morning. For the past few days, I haven't been so sure."

The tip of his tongue drew a scorching line down the same path his thumb had taken. I quivered in my hiking boots, lifting on to my toes to get closer to his mouth.

The weight of my pack combined with my singular focus of Evan's lips.

I teetered.

He caught me, sliding one hand into the tight gap between my pack and the small of my back and yanking me against him. Plunging his tongue into my mouth in long, slow thrusts. Lifting my leg and bending his knees to press his hard cock against me.

My insides went molten and I moaned, pretty sure I was losing my mind. Not enough to have sex without a condom, but damn close.

"Ahem." A throat cleared behind me.

EVAN

We jumped and broke apart. Jules stumbled, and I grabbed her hand to keep her from falling.

"Excuse me. Didn't mean to startle you."

"That's okay."

"Mind if I pass?"

"Sorry. Sorry." Jules released my hand and stepped to the side of the trail to let the youngish, bearded guy go by.

Inspiration struck. I stood mid-trail, still blocking the hiker's way. "Hey, man. How's it going?"

"Good." A sly smile crept across his face, and he glanced between us. "But not as good as you."

     Wild at Heart

"Well, actually, that kind of depends." I placed my hand on the guy's shoulder and steered him off the trail a few feet, talking quietly so Jules couldn't hear. "I'm hoping you can help me out."

I explained my predicament, and he dug out his wallet with a big, shit-eating grin.

"Thanks, man. You're a life-saver." I clapped the hiker on the upper arm.

"Enjoy." With a final glance at each of us, the hiker headed down the dirt ribbon and disappeared into the woods, whistling.

"Is he whistling—"

"Sexual Healing by Marvin Gaye? Yup." I thanked the universe I wasn't a blusher, or generally prone to embarrassment, because this idea was genius. I only hoped Jules thought so too.

"Did you just—"

"Borrow a condom from that random hiker? Yes, yes I did." The corners of my lips quirked, and I put my hands on her tiny waist, right above the constricting band of her waistbelt, tugging her close. "I hope that's okay." My voice came out low and rough. "I didn't want to wait another day to be inside you."

"Okay. Seriously? It's fucking brilliant."

CHAPTER 24

JULES

The trail meandered through a peaceful old growth forest of wide, gray trunks and crystal-clear ponds. The sun climbed toward the tops of the trees, making the leaves of the huckleberry bushes glow. Evan stopped and pulled me in for a kiss, cupping my cheek. Holding me close.

He released me and walked on. Lightheaded from euphoria and lust, it was all I could do to keep hiking instead of kissing Evan some more. Because I should. While I could.

A loud chime rang out. It took a second to register the sound as my cell phone. And what it meant. And what it *really* meant.

That Evan would be leaving soon.

Of course, I'd become firmly addicted to having him around. To making him laugh. To making him come. Not to mention the way he made me feel smart and sexy and funny and like we were equals. Two halves of a whole.

     Wild at Heart

Every chance he got he let me know he liked me, and desired me, and wanted to be with me—baggage and all.

How can I resist that? Him?

Already I could barely remember LBE—life before Evan. But even if he stayed the extra day, I'd still be hiking the next two sections of trail alone. While that'd seemed exciting and freeing at the start of my trip, now almost two hundred miles stretched in front of me, lonely and long. Some of my euphoria drained out like helium from a balloon, leaving me barely floating inside.

At least he promised to come back.

Right?

We crested the ridge overlooking Olallie Meadows and I gave in and took out my phone. "I need to give Bryn an ETA real quick."

"Sure thing." Evan dropped his pack and sat on a boulder, staring at the forested flanks of Mt. Catherine.

I texted. He shifted and fidgeted.

"Okay. All set." I bent to stuff my cell into my lid pocket.

"Mind if I use that to check my messages?"

"Here you go."

He stepped away and dialed. Each time he pressed a button to save or delete a message, his shoulders climbed higher toward his ears. The veins and tendons in his forearms popped out in greater relief.

He white-knuckled my phone. A deep furrow ran between his eyebrows. My gut churned.

"Everything okay?" I worked to keep my voice neutral.

His lips pressed into a thin line. I couldn't tell if he was trying to get his emotions under control or decide what to tell me.

EVAN

John's voice ran on repeat in my head.

—Bro, you better come home and clean up your mess. Mother is freaked that you 'ran away and left that poor girl,' and Father keeps threatening to revoke your trust 'because you don't deserve a dime of support from them, if this is how you're going to behave when you've had every advantage given to you.' I can't hold them off any longer. —

Giving him my voice mail number had clearly been a huge mistake. I didn't want to leave Jules but hearing that meant I didn't have a choice. It wasn't fair for John to handle the wrath of our parents.

I refocused on the moment. On the warm sunlight, and the birds warbling, and Jules, chewing the corner of her lower lip. "I'm not going to be able to move my flight again. I'm sorry."

"Sure. Of course. It's okay." She twisted the loose ends of her shoulder straps in her fingers. "Do what you have to do. I'm sure Bryn can give you a ride into town, that'll give you time to get cleaned up and get a good night's sleep before your flight. Maybe even see some of the—"

"Hey. I wish I didn't have to go." I wrapped my fingers around hers, stilling them, and stepped in close. I swept my mouth across hers. "But I promise I'll be back soon."

"I know. I get it. Go deal with your family and figure your shit out." She stepped back, waving a hand, putting too much space between us. "Maybe you can be back by the time I finish the trail."

"How about I do better than that and finish your hike with you?"

Her eyes lit with possibility. "What do you mean?"

"How long is your next section?" I stepped forward, closing the gap.

          Wild at Heart

Her lips parted with a minute gasp. "About seventy miles. Should take me six days. Seven if I have a layover day."

"I bet I can meet you at Steven's Pass and we can do your last section together." I nuzzled her lips, tasting, inhaling her breath. "If you want."

"Seriously?" She kept her voice even, but her fingers clutched my arm.

"Seriously. If I can't get my family on board in a couple days, more time isn't going to help. And I don't have much to pack." I dragged my mouth over hers, inhaling, tasting her breath. "Besides, I'm not sure I can be away from you longer than that."

I slipped my tongue into her mouth. She gasped and rocked onto her toes.

"I'd love it if you finished the hike with me," Jules mumbled against my lips.

I smiled against hers, heart soaring. "As you wish."

It took everything in me to pull away. But I had a flight to make, and we still had a few miles to go.

The roar of cars zooming by on the highway filtered through the forest far too soon. I wanted to keep going, maybe forever.

Instead I was heading home, and somehow, I needed to concoct a reasonable business proposition and plan of action before I got there. At least I'd had some ideas on the trail, thanks to Jules.

My feet hit pavement like walking into a wall. I snagged Jules's hand and stopped her next to me, weaving my fingers into hers and tugging her in close. Nose to nose. Tangling my other fingers in her coarse, curly hair I breathed her in, a heady combination of mint and cedar and woman.

"You are the most amazing person I've ever met, and I'm not letting you get away." I lifted my head enough to look her in the eye. "One way or another, I'll be back in time to meet you at Stevens Pass."

She shifted her weight from foot to foot and chewed her lip. "Promise?"

"Promise." I took her chin in my fingers. "Jules, I'm not going back to my ex. I'm coming back to you."

I closed the inches between us and kissed her like she was the last woman on earth, and I was going into a battle from which I might never return. Pouring my heart and soul into her mouth. Tasting her like she was the richest, most decadent dessert. Devouring her like I could never, ever, get enough.

A car horn blared, and we leapt apart, laughing. I pulled her back into me and finished what I'd started, taking our kiss from hot and heavy to slow and sweet. Nibbling and sucking at her lips because I was having serious difficulty stopping.

"We better go," she mumbled against my mouth, breathless.

CHAPTER 25

EVAN

The tallish, athletic brunette squeezed Jules until she almost couldn't breathe.

When she turned my way, I held out my hand. "Hi, I'm Evan. You must be Bryn."

With a glance at Jules, she took my hand in a firm grip. "Nice to meet you. Are you the Evan I can thank for part of my dinner at White Pass last week?"

"That would be me. And you're welcome. Except now I'm afraid of what Jules already told you about me."

"Only good things." A sly grin made her eyes glitter. "Of course, first impressions are everything."

I peeked at Jules, standing to my side with her lips pressed together and her chest convulsing like an alien could pop out at any moment. Bryn's eyes went wide. Jules nodded almost imperceptibly and twitched an eyebrow. Bryn smiled.

My palms itched. They had to be talking about me, but I had no idea what they were saying. "I'm starving. Why don't we go in and order food?"

"Sounds good." With a last, pointed look at Jules, Bryn led the way to the food truck. We dropped our packs against a battered trailer with Armadillo Eats hand-painted on the side.

Jules slipped her hand in mine and squeezed. "The curry here is amazing. That's what I'm getting."

"Perfect. Will you order me a bowl? I'm going to go to the restroom and clean up." I dropped a quick kiss on her lips.

She smiled and my heart leapt. "Sure thing. It's inside the gas station."

Those two needed a few minutes to themselves or they were going to burst. Not that I liked being talked about when I wasn't there, but it was better if Jules told Bryn about us. Otherwise, I'd be trapped in a car with my girlfriend's best friend for an hour, with no idea what, or how much, I should share.

JULES

The steep, metal stairs leading into the old RV-turned-food truck creaked under my weight. Stepping inside, two things struck me instantly.

The weirdly inviting aroma of rich and creamy mac and cheese mixed with coconut milk and curry, and the beige.

Beige counters, beige paneling, beige floor that might've once been white. But it was clean, and the food was always damn good. In the winter the RV would be packed with hungry skiers. This time of year, we had it to ourselves.

We shuffled through a handful of mismatched chairs and two tiny tables and ordered three curries from a middle-aged guy wielding ladles behind a crock-pot covered counter.

I stared out the window. Across the wide gravel parking lot, Evan sauntered into the gas station, all tanned muscles and dark, mussed hair. Looking every bit the scruffy, sexy outdoorsy guy. The kind you want bending you over a log on the shore of a sparkling lake and—

"Holy hottie." Bryn's words jolted right through me. She tucked her credit card in her bag, and we took our bowls and sat. "I thought Evan went back to the East Coast. Explain."

"He started to but decided to hike another section instead. We ran into each other again on the trail." The image of Evan, naked, up to his waist in clear blue, high mountain water floated through my head. The corners of my lips twitched.

"Please tell me you found him naked again. Aly will die."

"Maybe." I shrugged one shoulder, trying for nonchalance and failing spectacularly when my smile spread. "Okay, yes."

"Judging from the way you two were kissing when I pulled up, it seems to be going well." Her eyes glittered with joy, humor, and curiosity.

"The universe brought me the same hot guy, naked in the wilderness, three times. I couldn't turn my back on that kind of a gift."

Bryn's laughter rocketed through the small trailer. "I take it you didn't turn down any of the other, ahem, gifts he came with, either?"

"Would you?"

"Hell no." Her lips quirked on one side. "So much for your vow of celibacy. I knew you wouldn't last a year, but I figured you'd make it longer than a week. Not that I can blame you. I mean, damn."

"Yeah. And I did wait a few days because of it. Maybe Evan wouldn't have stuck around if I'd jumped right into bed with him."

"The way he looks at you, I don't think that made a bit of difference." Her voice went quiet. Serious. "Speaking of, I haven't seen a man look at you like that since…"

"Since Justin. Yeah. I know." A delicious shiver ran along my skin, but with a sharp edge to it. I was foolish to take a risk with Evan. But nobody ever said falling for somebody was a smart thing to do.

"Have you freaked out yet?" She searched my face.

"Some. But he always seems to know the right thing to say or do. When I quit stressing over it, being with him is amazing. So good it's hard to believe it could be a mistake."

"You look happy."

"I am. But it's easy to be happy out here." I wave at the mountains outside the window.

"True." Bryn tilted her head. "So, what now? Is he going to keep hiking with you?"

I shook my head and blinked against the sudden tightness behind my eyes. "He needs to go home and take care of a few things. But he's promised to meet me again in a week for Section K."

"That sounds pretty serious."

"Feels that way too." I swallowed a lump of jagged, metallic fear mixed with the sweet marshmallow fluff of excitement. "Especially since he says he's moving to Seattle."

"Holy shit. Is he moving just to be with you?"

"Sort of." I peered out the dusty, scratched RV window at the gas station. "He says he likes it out here, and he's ready for a change. So why not Seattle? But I'm not sure what scares me more—that he'll actually come back, or that he won't."

"If he seems worth it, I think you should take the chance. Roll with it and see what happens."

"I'm trying. When we started hiking together, it felt safe because it would be short-term. Except now I don't think I want it to end and he's leaving." I glanced at Bryn.

"So, you just have to do your thing until he shows back up, and, assuming he does, figure out how to not run away."

"Exactly. Easy. Right? And if he doesn't, it's not like we've been together for years and he's the love of my life. I'll survive." The gas station door swung wide. Evan squinted at the sun, pulled his sunglasses down, and ambled across the lot like he didn't have a care in the world.

"Yes, you will. Piece of cake." Bryn grinned. "You deserve a fabulous relationship with an amazing guy who looks at you like you hung the moon and the stars. It's been too long."

"I could say the same to you." I gave her a pointed look.

"You could, but I don't have a man mooning over me and you do." Bryn wrapped her arms around me and squeezed. "You've got this, girlfriend. It'll be hard and scary, but you've got this. And him."

Fear clawed and clutched at my insides with icy fingers despite my bravado. "What if I don't have him? What if he doesn't come back?"

She released me and hitched her head toward Evan, stepping into the beige Formica and harsh fluorescent lights of the janky food truck serving the best curry for miles around.

"He will."

I hoped she was right.

CHAPTER 26

EVAN

I heaved my pack into the hatchback of Bryn's car and closed it with a thunk of finality. Leaning my ass on the warm metal, I wrapped Jules in my arms and held her close. Drinking in her mint and cedar scent.

"I don't want to leave. Not now. I'm pretty sure not ever." I searched her eyes, trying to read her thoughts, worry and fear and excitement doing the butterfly stroke through the curry in my stomach. "I know it's only a week, but it's going to be a long week without you."

She took a deep breath and blinked twice. "I don't want you to go either, but I get it."

"I'll see you in seven days, max. I promise." I swept my lips across hers, tender and sweet and full of even more promises. She kissed me back, but the stiffness in her shoulders told me words and kisses weren't enough. "Here. So you don't forget about me."

Spinning my leather bracelet, I undid the knot and tied it on her wrist. "My Uncle Martin gave me this the year before he died. It means a lot. I'll be back for it, and you."

        Wild at Heart

She fingered the blue and brown stones, spinning the loose, worn strap around her wrist. "Are you sure?"

"About what? Loaning you my bracelet, or coming back here?"

"Both."

"Very."

"Okay, then." She stood on her tiptoes, wrapped her hands around my neck, and kissed me hard and fast. She broke the kiss, slung her backpack on her shoulders, and took three steps back. "See you soon. Travel safe."

I'm not sure what was harder, saying good-bye to Jules, or getting in the car and driving away. Her face fell in the sideview mirror and something inside my chest caved.

Bryn glanced at me. "You really like her, don't you?"

"I do." *More than I ever thought possible.*

The pavement rumbled beneath the car. Trees flew by in a green blur. I leaned my head on the window, the glass vibrating against my forehead, and saw Jules's face instead of the mountains.

"So, what, exactly, are your intentions with my best friend?"

I jolted upright, mouth falling open. "I'm sorry, what?"

"You heard me. What are your intentions with Jules?"

"I plan to move to Seattle and be with her."

Bryn didn't respond.

"I mean, I don't expect to move in with her, or push her in any way. I'm moving to Seattle because I need to move somewhere, I like Seattle, and it's the only way I can have a shot at convincing her I'm serious."

"If you're so intent on showing her you're serious, why are you leaving now?"

Bryn was fishing, but I didn't want to get into my personal life with someone I didn't know. "Family emergency."

"Jules told me you're coming back in a week. I hope that means your family emergency isn't too bad."

"It could be worse." Jules's voice rang in my head, "*Could be raining.*" I held back my smile. It was true. Things could be quite a bit worse. Nobody was dead or hospitalized. All I risked was the wrath of my parents. "And since I'm currently unemployed, and I don't have much stuff, it shouldn't be a problem to be back here in a week."

"So, you're going to move across the country, just like that, for a woman you met less than two weeks ago?"

"I know it sounds impulsive, but yes."

She looked at me again, a little longer this time. "I'm probably overstepping boundaries, but Jules is my best friend, and I don't want to see her get hurt. When you're isolated on the trail, it's easy to get caught up in a fantasy where everything seems to make sense. Sometimes it doesn't make the same sense after reentry."

"So I've heard." Except something deep inside—a calm, knowing, a sense of completeness— told me we were meant to last. "These past two weeks I learned more about myself and what I want than in the past ten years combined. Stripping my life down to the gear in my pack and the miles under my feet—and Jules." I waved my hand like I was trying to physically pull the right words out of thin air. "It gave me clarity."

She harrumphed, knuckles tightening on the steering wheel.

"People move across the country all the time. It can't be that hard. Pack up my stuff and ship everything, find an apartment, start a business. Easy." If only I felt as positive as I sounded.

The click-whir of tires on pavement filled the car again. We passed one exit, then another.

"What kind of business?" Bryn's voice broke my thoughts.

Wild at Heart

"A non-profit summer camp for underprivileged youths. Something like that Inner City Outside program you two volunteer for, but a stay-away camp."

"I thought you didn't know the first thing about camping?"

I brought my hand to my chest in mock indignation. "How dare you malign my camping skills? I am an excellent camper."

"That's not what Jules told me last week."

"I've improved. I swear. Please say you won't hold it against me." I shook my head. "I didn't even get a chance to make my own bad first impression."

"Oh, don't worry about that. You made a fine first impression, from what I heard." She worked hard to keep the smile twitching her lips from taking over her face. "Seriously though, why do you want to open a camp?"

"It's not about my level of technical camping skills. Anyone can learn those. Even me." I grinned at her. "And I can hire experienced counselors."

"True…"

"I want to help kids get out in nature and leave the screens and the hustle behind. I want them to have the chance to test themselves a little, in a safe environment, and do more than they expected. Show them the stars, all the millions of them you never see in the city." My voice grew stronger. Excitement zinged through my veins. I'd never said all this before in so many words, but every word felt right. "I want those kids to experience a completely different way of life full of challenges and wonders they'd never expect—and gain the confidence that comes from getting out of their comfort zones and surviving. You know?"

"I do know." She changed lanes and turned on the stereo, keeping the music low. "And I think it's a noble and worthy cause."

"Thanks. Though even the idea of launching something like this is overwhelming." I focused on the mental checklist I'd started on the trail. "I've got to find a location, raise money, hire a branding and marketing firm, create curriculum, hire staff, and I don't even know what else. Honestly, I'm way out of my element here."

The highway widened and flattened. Houses sprouted from between the trees on both sides.

"You know, I have a friend who runs a nonprofit camp for kids with disabilities. I bet he could answer a few questions or point you in the right direction."

"Really? That would be fantastic. I don't fly out until tomorrow night. Red eye. You think there's any chance you could put us in touch before I leave?"

"Sure. I'll give it a shot. If he's around I can have you both over for dinner."

"Are you sure you don't mind?"

"Not a bit."

My heart zoomed around in my chest on hummingbird wings. My stomach vibrated with anticipation and possibility.

I twisted toward Bryn, staring at her profile, trying to figure out her angle. Like Jules, she didn't seem to have an ulterior motive. Nothing specific to gain. She didn't know anything about me other than Jules liked me. She was just a nice person doing something nice because she could.

"Thank you, then. I really appreciate it, and the ride." Hopefully, I'd be able to get enough information to formulate a reasonable, if bare bones, business plan. One that would give me a real shot at convincing my parents I wasn't shirking responsibility.

 Wild at Heart

JULES

Sunshine slipped through the branches of the trees, dappling the trail. The muted roar and acrid exhaust of cars on the highway wouldn't disappear for a few more hours. Not until I'd gone far enough to put a high ridge between me and I-90.

And Evan.

I pushed that thought down.

Relax. He'll be back in a week. He promised.

Rubbing the smooth stones in his leather bracelet, I put one foot in front of the other, counting my steps.

Justin made promises too.

Fuck.

Dropping my pack on a rock, I unclipped the lid and dug out my food bag. I grabbed the bar of dark chocolate, because chocolate makes anything better. Thankful that past me had decided to stash a good bar in this particular restock box.

The day I packed it seemed like a lifetime ago. That bitter, hurt woman making a vow of celibacy didn't jive with the one falling head over heels on the trail.

Being with Evan changed me in a fundamental way. Even out here by myself, I wasn't alone anymore. We were together in our heads and hearts, even if we were on separate sides of the country. And I wasn't freaking out about it.

Maybe thirteen was my new lucky number. I cracked off a square and popped it on my tongue, savoring the velvet texture and rich flavor.

Except another week of solitary trail time didn't hold quite as much appeal anymore. I mean, it would be great no matter what. But having Evan as a trail partner was so much better than hiking alone. He even beat out Bryn—mainly because I couldn't have mind-bending sex with her.

He might even beat out Justin.

I waited for guilt to wash over me in a nauseating wave. Nothing happened. I rolled the idea around in my head and my stomach didn't tie itself into a pretzel. My palms didn't sweat. My scalp didn't tighten.

Tucking away my bulging food bag, I picked up the book I'd sent myself. The crisp, clean copy of *Learning to Love Yourself* seemed wrong. I didn't need that. I needed to learn how to love someone else. Namely Evan.

Shoving the paperback deep into my pack, I hefted it, extra-heavy with fresh food and full water bladder and settled it on my shoulders. My waist belt and sternum strap buckles clicked loud. With a last glance to make sure I had everything, I tugged all the straps and hit the trail.

It was time for me to quit playing it safe. If he was going to move across the country for me, then I needed to meet him halfway—maybe not geographically, but emotionally.

No more guarding my heart. I needed to be patient. And trusting. And give him, and me, a real shot at something amazing.

CHAPTER 27

EVAN

Cars honked and slowed, red taillights blinking. My shoulders hit my ears, though I couldn't tell if that was due to the Boston traffic, or the fact that I was on my way to family dinner.

In Seattle, on my flight, and all day at John's condo, I'd worked nonstop getting everything organized and printed. I hoped it was enough. Having my parent's financial support, not to mention their connections, would be a tremendous boost for my nonprofit.

While I didn't need money to be happy—I knew that for sure now—it would help me get my new business off the ground. What mattered more, though, was my parents believing in me.

One step at a time. I've got a lifetime to make them proud, first I need to get them on board.

At least Jules and Bryn seemed to have faith in me, because even John was skeptical when I explained my ideas on the phone yesterday. Or maybe Bryn was just a nice person who wanted her friend to be happy, and my success was key to that. Not that it mattered either way. I'd take support anywhere I could get it.

All too soon I pulled around my parent's u-shaped, flagstone driveway.

Stepping out, I flapped my arms and peeled my shirt away from my damp armpits, glad I'd left a duffel of spare clothes in my car at the airport. I didn't want to have to see Lainey before I was ready. Forcing my leaden legs up the three stairs to the intimidating, enormous dark oak doors, I slipped on the requisite blazer and steeled myself for battle.

The cold metal knocker vibrated in my hand with each dull thwack. On the third knock I released it and waited, praying the maid would open the door. The maid was always a good sign. It meant my parents were happily enjoying pre-dinner cocktails.

The door swung wide with a swoosh, like a black hole opening and exerting a magnetic force, dragging everything in sight into its desolate, bleak space. The painted and shellacked face of my mother filled the gap. Her smile only moved her lips.

I braced against the pull, not wanting to enter the bottomless pit of despair that surely awaited me, and knowing resistance was futile. Nobody can withstand the force of the Davenport black hole.

"Evan, dear. I'm so glad you're home safe. I've been worried sick about you." My mother grabbed my elbow and dragged me into the two-story foyer, tastefully done in white marble and crystal chandeliers, patting my arm and prattling on. "What were you thinking, leaving us all like that, without a word? We've all been terrified something awful happened to you."

"I left a note saying where I was going, you know." I never understood how the house could stay so clean, and yet be odorless except for my mother's omnipresent, floral cloud of Chanel No 5.

We crossed to the hall, her heels clicking loud and hollow on the stone floor. "Your father has been beside himself. And Elaine, that poor sweet girl, so worried you wouldn't make it back in one piece. What would she do if you lost an arm or a leg out there?"

"Ummm, be glad that I'm alive?" The hall was a good sign. Maybe Father was out back having drinks. That would be ideal. He'd be at his most relaxed, and willing to talk business.

"How could you be so thoughtless, so selfish, putting us through all this so you could go gallivanting in the mountains?"

That did it.

The spine I never knew I had before snapped ramrod straight. I yanked my arm out of her clutches. "If you want to make a big deal out of this, I suppose that's your prerogative, but let's get the facts straight. I have no job and no commitments, so I decided to take a trip. I left a note, so you knew where I'd gone, and I checked in with John and let him know I was extending my trip another week. Which means I was neither thoughtless nor selfish, and any stress it caused you, you brought upon yourself."

Her eyes widened, and her perfectly manicured hand flew to her perfectly lip-sticked mouth. "How dare you be so rude? After everything your father and I have done for you—"

"Emily?" My father's voice boomed down the hall from the formal dining room and straight into my bones. *Speak of the Devil.* "Was that Evan at the door? Dinner is about to be served."

"Yes, dear. We're coming."

Dinner? This early? The hairs on the back of my neck stood at attention.

My mother clutched my elbow again. "Come along, dear. We'll talk about this with your father later. You know how he hates anyone being late for dinner."

We stepped into the open doorway of the dining room. My father glowered at the head of the table, in the ornate carved cherry-wood chair situated under the portrait of his namesake, John Theodore Davenport I. My great, great grandfather. Painted by the famous M. Shrine.

On one side of the table sat Lainey, all smiles. On the other, John IV, my oh-so-supportive brother, glanced at me and gave a tiny, almost imperceptible shake of his head.

This time, the hairs on the back of my neck vibrated with a fatalistic sense of deja vu. The unmentioned early dinner hour. Inviting Lainey and John. It was a set up.

This whole production was purpose-designed to torture me. To make me sit through hours of small-talk and passive-aggressive jabs, with no opportunity to defend myself, so that by the time I was alone with my father I would be practically guaranteed to lose my cool. *Not this time, dammit.*

Lainey scooched out her chair and crossed the room, throwing her arms around my neck and pulling me in tight. "Oh, Evan. I'm so glad you're home. I was worried. I've missed you."

I stiffened. Lainey should've been giving me the cold shoulder not welcoming me with open arms. Unless she thought my return meant I'd had second thoughts, and we could get our impending nuptials back on track. She curled her hands around my forearm, towing me toward her chair. "Let's have a seat. Dinner is about to be served."

"So I heard." I scooted her chair in, flashing John "The Look".

"Hey, little brother. Long time…" He got up and circled the table, big enough for ten—twenty with all the leaves on—and met me halfway in a bro-hug, slamming my back with his fist, and neatly separating me from Lainey.

    Wild at Heart

If I was going to be trapped here, at least I could pick the spot. And it was not going to be right next to my ex-fiancé, pretending everything between us was fine.

"Good to see you. How was your trip?" John made his way back to his chair. I followed and sat next to him. "I can't wait to hear all about it."

Father cleared his throat. "Have you kids heard the latest news on the Hollowell-Foley merger?"

Personal topics were forbidden at the table. Personal issues were simply always forbidden. Clearly my trip was both personal, and an issue, and he certainly didn't want anyone putting a positive spin on it before he reamed me for it.

"That the FCC has decided it can proceed? Of course," John chimed in. "Half my clients own stock in one or both of them, and the other half own stock in their competitors."

"I don't think the merger is going to hold up in court." Lainey waved her manicured hand in the air like shooing a fly. "And you know it's going to end up there."

Lainey, John, and my father launched into a detailed discussion of the pros and cons of the merger. Mother ran off to herd the kitchen staff.

I knew how this went. For the rest of dinner, everyone would pretend I wasn't there. Later, it'd be like I never left, and never broke up with Lainey. As long as I went on with this charade, I'd receive a stern warning from my father to never worry my mother like that again, life would go back to normal, and my entire little escapade would be swept under the rug.

If I insisted on continuing with my "selfish, immature behavior", there would be consequences. It remained to be seen what, exactly, those consequences might entail. I wouldn't find out until we retired for cocktails, or possibly later, since Father liked to keep people waiting as long as possible.

Make them frustrated and emotional so they weren't thinking logically by the time the meeting occurred. I squeezed my eyes shut for a second and exhaled, searching for calm.

Mother click-clacked into the room, followed by two, formally attired servants. Tiny China plates with amuse-bouche appeared on the silver-plated chargers in front of each of us. Beneath the table, John pointed at me, made a circle with his thumb & forefinger, and poked his other pointer finger in & out of it. The corners of his mouth flicked up.

I pressed my lips into a line and tightened my eyes at him.

Not funny. I already know I'm fucked, bastard. No need to rub it in.

CHAPTER 28

JULES

The flat charcoal-gray of pre-dawn had turned into the flat smoke-gray of a classic Pacific Northwest fall day. Squatting on my heels on the needle-covered ground, I shoved my remaining cheese, GORP, and dried mangoes into my food bag. Every swish and crinkle too loud in the cloud-muted forest.

Solitude settled heavy on my shoulders along with the damp fog. Something I'd never experienced.

I loved being alone in the mountains. Always had.

But somehow, the past three days of hiking through some of the most spectacular wilderness in Washington had dragged on endlessly. At the hot springs I couldn't settle in and relax. All I could think about was Evan.

I barely noticed the clear blue lakes reflecting puffy clouds and craggy peaks, except to imagine a very naked Evan swimming in them. Or standing on shore all ripped abs and shaggy hair, with droplets sparkling on his bare skin. Wearing nothing but the bracelet that he'd wrapped around my wrist when he left.

Settling back with a steaming cup of tea and looking at the stars? No way could I think about anything other than Evan.

And me.

And what would happen when I saw him again.

If I saw him again.

Fuck.

Throbbing swirls of emotion and excitement—along with a spicy dash of sheer terror I tried to ignore—crashed through me. Hit so hard I swear a part of me could've drown.

But I could push through it. Had to push through it. Pretend it didn't exist in favor of the rush of falling for him.

And I wanted that. More than I'd wanted anything — anyone — in too many years. My life, especially my love life, had been on autopilot for forever. Time to change that.

All I had to do was keep hiking, and in a few more days Evan would be waiting for me at Stevens Pass. Standing there with his cobalt eyes and tousled hair and hot mouth.

I bit my lip until it stung and focused on Tetrising the rest of my stuff sacks into their allotted spaces. Balancing my pack on my upper thigh I slung it around onto my back.

My feet fell one in front of the other on their own. A chilly mist hung in the air, wrapping around trees and peaks, and prickling my skin. Growing denser and wetter with every passing mile. Ignoring thoughts of Evan, I turned my focus to my business dilemma. Because I couldn't handle another year of sixty-hour weeks of screen time plus managing contractors.

I considered my goals. If I kept just my three biggest clients, I could make enough money to get by. That would free up my time to

     Wild at Heart

find a new career to ease into. Maybe something outdoors. Though finding an outdoor job that paid enough to survive in Seattle might be a bigger fantasy than imaging Evan and I could work out.

At least, no matter how I turned it around my head, my plan seemed workable. Graphic design work didn't exactly make my heart sing, but I could deal with doing it part-time until I found something more fulfilling.

The mist coalesced into a fine drizzle. In no time, itty bitty droplets clung to my hair. I pulled on my rain jacket, the thin, crinkling fabric clinging to my bare, clammy arms, and picked up my pace.

Droplets tapped a sharp rhythm on my hood. Chalky brown puddles formed in the trail. Mud fused to my boot soles making them slick and heavy. Slowing my roll.

Raindrops stung my face and bounced off my jacket. Hard. I gave in and dug out my rain pants, unzipping the sides and pogoing around to pull them on over one boot, then the other, without sitting down on anything wet or busting ass in the mud.

Not that they would keep me dry. With the warmish temperature and high humidity, wearing rain gear was like hiking in my own, personal sauna. I unzipped the thigh vents and kept going, head down, climbing a series of switchbacks up the side of a mountain.

My legs swooshed with each step. I watched my feet, keeping the rain out of my eyes and making sure I didn't slip.

Out of the corner of my eye, something flashed in the underbrush. Just a glimpse of neon, brighter than the hunter green ferns and berry bushes covering most of the hillside. It didn't seem right. Or natural.

I hit a turn in the trail and bushwhacked forward, scanning for whatever I'd seen. Wet leaves and branches slapped my nylon-covered legs. The pungent scent of freshly broken branches brightened the air.

A lime green blob, far too bright in the gloom, flickered in and out of view about twenty yards below me. I slipped and stumbled downhill, breathing hard. In the middle of a tall patch of sword ferns lay a muddy, torn, ultralight backpack.

My breath hitched. My throat turned into the Sahara. My heart thundered in my ears, drowning out the rain beating on my hood.

I knew that pack.

It's not possible. Is it?

What if he was hiking in to surprise me?

Dropping to my knees I scrabbled at the buckles and draw cord. The pack opened and I upended it, anonymous stuff sacks thudding and clattering onto the muddy ground around me. Food, clothing, toiletries.

Fuck, fuck, fuck.

EVAN

My father turned toward the liquor cabinet. Ice cubes clinked. Whiskey sloshed. The clock sounded eleven resonant bongs. I'd been home five hours and we were alone at last. I set my file folder on the chair in front of his imposing mahogany desk and stood, pretending to review the spines of the books filling the shelves.

If I sat, he'd stand, one hip on the corner of his desk, and loom over me. I'd turn into a twelve-year-old boy again, cringing against the elegantly worn leather. My father never yelled or hit. He didn't need to. He remained calm and commanded respect. Then he told me exactly what he expected me to do, and what would happen if I didn't.

Wild at Heart

All the while implied consequences hung above my head like a well-honed hatchet. Because I had all the right opportunities and doors opened, and I needed to appreciate what was afforded and take advantage of it, not be an ingrate, or a stain on the family.

Horrible things were going to befall us all if I didn't behave like a proper Davenport—especially now that Father was planning to run for Governor—and I'd be the sole reason. At which point I'd cave.

I'd been down this road more times than I could count. After Uncle Martin, my champion, passed away when I was fifteen, it became harder and harder to fight for what I wanted. By the time I started college I didn't know what to fight for anymore, so I quit fighting.

At last, I had something worth fighting for again, and I intended to win.

"Have a seat." My father handed me a low-ball glass. "It's good to see you've come to your senses and returned home. I know your mother and Elaine missed you."

I pulled myself up to my full height and looked him in the eyes. My heart pounded in my ears. "But you didn't?"

"Why must you always attempt to put words in my mouth?"

"Because you don't." I clutched the cool crystal and took a sip trying to add moisture to my parched mouth. The whiskey burned a sweet line down my throat. *He can serve me alcohol like an adult. It's past time he treated me like one, too.* "And for the record, I have not come to my senses and returned, like some long-lost prodigal son. I'm not staying."

"Have a seat and let's discuss this."

"I'll stand, thanks."

"Suit yourself." Father pivoted and strode behind his desk, picking up a sheaf of papers. "You have a meeting tomorrow with Len Blackstone about a position with his firm. Nine a.m. sharp."

I blinked and blinked again. Blackstone Investments was one of the most prestigious firms in Boston.

"Please tell Len I appreciate the opportunity, but it's not a good fit for me right now."

The muscles in my father's neck corded. Nobody told John Theodore Davenport the IV no—especially not me. Definitely not when he was pulling a big favor for me with one of the wealthiest, most successful men in Boston.

"You can tell him yourself when you meet him in the morning. I'm sure he'll be shocked to discover my youngest son is an ingrate." He swirled the brown liquor in his glass, ice cubes clinking. "Frankly, I'm not surprised you'd make such a poor choice."

I'd been dubbed an ungrateful screw up more times than I could count. Still, a sharp pain pinched at the corner of my heart.

This time though, the pain reminded me why I needed to fight. Because relationships shouldn't be about controlling others.

I wanted to be around people who genuinely liked me and wanted me to achieve my own goals. People like Jules, and Bryn.

Taking another sip of whiskey, I let the warmth—and the image of Jules laughing, naked in an alpine lake with the sun in her curls— shore up my resolve. "No. You can tell him. I did not ask you to set up a meeting, nor did I agree to one. And it's not because I'm ungrateful. I truly appreciate everything you've done to set me up for success, but it's success as you define it. You've never once asked me about my goals or plans."

"It is not for children to decide what success looks like. It is a parent's job to make those decisions and set children on a path of achievement." His gaze met mine, lips pressed tight. "Your mother and I have worked incredibly hard to give you every possible opportunity, and you're choosing to squander that. I cannot abide by your attitude, and I expect you to meet with Len in the morning."

He returned his attention to the papers on his desk, dismissing me.

Every ounce of my body wanted to cringe and shuffle out, apologizing ad nauseum. My mind, my soul, and most of all my heart, had zero interest in following along with his rules or even playing his game. I gulped another slug of whiskey, for courage.

"I am not—" I cleared my throat. "I am not a child. I am a twenty-nine-year-old man." My father didn't move. "I've followed your guidance my entire life and you know what? I'm not happy or successful—even by your standards—as you so generously like to point out. In fact, I've been depressed and anxious and stressed and everything except happy for years. Doesn't that matter at all to you? Don't you want your children to be happy?"

My voice went up more than I would've liked on that final question. Giving away my emotions wouldn't help my cause but controlling them wasn't easy.

His jawline hardened, the muscles tensing and rolling. My heart rattled in my chest like a car on an old wooden roller coaster. I could count the number of times I'd seen my father this angry on my thumbs.

"How dare you? Everything I have ever done is to ensure your happiness. And you dismiss it all because you don't like your job?" He stalked around his desk and toward me across the expensive oriental carpet. I held my ground. "Happiness is an illusion you can't afford to chase, because it makes you soft. Complacent." The knuckles of his fist thudded into the leather planner topping his desk. I flinched. "Life is about working hard and providing for your family and making something out of yourself. The rest is a bunch of woo-woo mumbo jumbo designed to siphon money out of poor fool's pockets by promising them what they'll never have."

I kept my voice smooth. Steady. Calm. "Respectfully, I disagree. I believe I can be both successful, and happy. But not as an investment analyst, and not married to Lainey. I want to do something with my life that makes a difference, and I've put together a plan—" I reached for my folder.

"You already have a good plan for your life and your career. If you cannot follow the path your mother and I have laid out for you, then I cannot support you. And your grandfather would not care to support you."

"What?"

"You heard me. If you're going to embarrass me by getting fired, standing up one of my long-time friends and colleagues when he's willing to offer you a job, and walking out on your fiancé to go traipsing around in the woods, you can do it on your own dime. I'll be contacting our lawyers regarding your trust fund tomorrow night."

"So, you're cutting me off without even giving me a chance."

"I'm not doing anything to you. You put in little effort at work and lost your job, leaving a black mark on the Davenport reputation. You shirked your responsibilities to go off on some ridiculous camping trip; and you left Elaine so concerned she's had difficulty focusing, and she has a quite a big criminal case in court right now."

Guilt settled over me in a suffocating, heavy fog. He was right, all of this was my fault.

His eyes narrowed for an instant, and he went in for the knock-out. "Make no mistake young man, this is all your doing. Nothing in life comes free. If you want the benefits of being a Davenport, you have to do what's best for this family. You claim to no longer be a child, so act like an adult. The choices are yours. So are the consequences."

Wild at Heart

"What about Uncle Martin? Grandfather didn't throw him out of the family because he went to work in Africa. All I want to do is help people, too."

Maroon splotches mottled his neck, like he was about to physically explode into millions of oozing red bits. "This isn't about your uncle," he ground out. "It's about you and this family and your lack of respect."

"No." I planted my feet. "It's about my life and my career and my choices. It has nothing to do with this family."

"As long as you're a Davenport, it has everything to do with this family. Either show up for the interview tomorrow morning, or you're on your own. End of discussion." He turned his back again, reaching for a leather-bound volume off a high shelf.

In that moment something became crystal clear. Something I'd thought a million times but deep down never wanted to believe true… My father didn't love me or anyone else. He wasn't capable of it. All he loved was making money, amassing power, and upholding the sanctity of the Davenport name so he could get his long-overdue Governorship.

Mind reeling, I picked up my folder and walked out of his perfectly appointed office. Every part of me ached, raw and painful like I'd run three triathlons back-to-back. The vomiting was bound to start any second.

Stopping down the hall, I listened for voices, footsteps, general signs of life. Other than a muted clatter from the direction of the kitchen, the house seemed quiet. I breathed a sigh of relief and tiptoed toward the front door.

Heels clicked on marble. I picked up my pace.

Going into this, I'd known it would be tough. I'd known my parents would be less than thrilled, but after almost six hours of suffering, it was all I could do to even muster coherent thoughts. Let alone the desire to come up with any more words to state my case.

With just feet to go before I reached the doorknob, Lainey appeared in the foyer, still crisp and put together in her conservative suit and careful updo. My chest caved.

"Evan, please. We need to talk."

"No, we don't." My fingers dug into the dark blue folder in my left hand, creasing the cardboard. I gritted my teeth and shoved my shoulders back, striving to hold on to any semblance of conviction possible. "We talked before I left. You read my note. Nothing's changed. There's nothing else to say."

"I have things I want to say." She crossed her arms.

Of course you do. I shut my eyes and rubbed my eyelids, hard. *Closing arguments, every time.*

Lainey was brilliant and she knew how to play emotions, manipulate people into seeing things her way. It's why she'd already made Junior Partner at her firm, and a big reason why she'd make a terrific Davenport. In no way was I prepared to withstand her interrogations or reasoning.

"Please, Counselor. It's late. I'm exhausted. Can we talk tomorrow?"

"Of course." Her voice softened. "Why don't we go home now, and we can talk over breakfast? Before I go to work."

It'd be so easy to go home to our place, beg forgiveness, and slide into my side of the bed. I'd done it so many nights, how hard could it be to give in and do it for that many more?

Easier than fighting this fight. Easier than walking away from my family and their support and my inheritance, that's for sure. The easy way called to me with its familiar, soothing voice.

 Wild at Heart

I shoved the words out fast, before I lost the rest of my confidence. "I don't really think this is a before breakfast discussion. Can we talk tomorrow night?"

A door shut with a low whump. Heels clicked somewhere in the house.

"I'm working late prepping for a case." She pulled out her phone, staring at the screen and tapping. "I won't be free until the end of the week."

"I'm leaving day after tomorrow." My words hung in the air.

She looked up; the corners of her mouth tight. "I'd really like to talk before you leave. I won't be able to sleep until we do. And after all these years, I think you owe me that much."

A thick blanket of guilt threatened to suffocate me.

"Fine." I rested my hand on the door handle. "I'll meet you at the apartment."

CHAPTER 29

JULES

Rain splatted on my hood. My shoulders. I stared at the pile of gear on the ground. The air smelled like drenched wood and decay.

My gaze caught on a small brown tent bag, a little bigger than a water bottle, and all my breath came out with a heavy whoosh.

Oh, thank God. Evan's tent is orange.

Rocking back, I put my hands on my knees and sucked in deep breaths, trying to control the tremors wracking my chest.

It took who knows how many minutes of water dripping off my nose to get my shit together. Longer than it should have. I searched the pack for an ID that wasn't there, and loaded all the gear into it again, not sure what shook me more…

The idea that Evan might be out here lost and hurt—or dead. Or the creeping realization of how much the idea of losing him freaked me out.

Either way, I didn't have time for it. Evan was not out here injured, but somebody else might be.

Standing, I sucked in a deep, damp breath and yelled, "Hellllllooooooooo?" The clouds and rain muffled my voice. And I'm sure the voice of anyone else out there. But I stood still, listening.

Rain tapped and pattered and splatted on the wet leaves and needles. In the growing puddles. On my jacket.

"Hellllllooooooooo?" I tried again.

In fifteen years backpacking I'd dealt with one sprained ankle and one slightly melted sleeping bag. Until this trip. When, for some unknown reason, the universe decided to even up the score.

Peering uphill through the silver mist and raindrops, I searched for clues in the lush greenery. With a sigh, I grabbed handfuls of wet branches and stems and leaves to keep from slipping and worked my way uphill in a grid pattern, stopping and calling out every few minutes.

Each traverse revealed another handful of broken branches and divots in the needle-covered mud in a direct line uphill of the pack. Nothing else.

Moisture dripped. Inside my rain gear and out.

I reached the base of a high cliff and gazed up the craggy, dark brown face. At least I assumed it was high since dense grey clouds hid the top.

A backpack could survive a fall from up there. A person? Not so much. A hard line of tension wrapped my spine.

What the fuck do I do now?

I couldn't risk leaving someone here injured without their gear. But everything told me nobody was here. That the pack must've fallen from up on that cliff a while ago.

Muddy and drenched, knee complaining, I stumbled and slid down to where I'd left the backpack. I called out into the mist one more time. Nothing but raindrops tapping leaves and wet earth in a steady hiss replied.

With no better plan coming to mind, I strapped the abandoned pack on my own, stretched my rain cover over both, and shouldered the awkward-ass bundle.

Either I'll meet the owner coming down the trail looking for it, or I'll find them up top.

The cliff couldn't have been more than a half mile above me as the crow flies, but the trail sure as hell didn't follow a crow. It followed the contours of the mountain crossing from one facing to another. Every so often, it switchbacked up. Not climbing near fast enough.

All the rain made it hard to be sure—because God knows it doesn't take long for everything to be drenched out here—but something told me the pack had been sitting there for at least a couple hours. Probably long enough for the person who lost it to hike down and find it.

Unless they were injured. Or unconscious. Or maybe they'd fallen too, and somehow, I didn't spot them in the rain and fog and foliage. The tension around my spine stretched to cover my ribs.

About every hundred squelching steps my brain came up with another scenario for what could've happened to the backpack's owner. What I might find at the top of the cliff. And what might happen if I didn't reunite them with their gear.

At last, the trail leveled off and meandered through bent, scrubby trees. I searched for signs in the mist. A footprint in the muck. Broken fern fronds. A faded trail. Anything.

A body.

An image of Justin laying in his open casket flashed into my head. Icy dread replaced the tension. I packed that old, all-too-familiar vision away as quick as it came and kept walking.

Don't freak out. Don't freak out. Don't freak out.

I had to stay clearheaded and unemotional until I found out what happened to the backpacker or could call for help. Whichever came first.

Once I knew they were safe I could lose my shit.

The trail widened and curved left. No treetops poked up through the mist to my right. Just endless gray and an airy emptiness I'd swear was a drop off. Not that I could see much more than ten feet in front of my face.

Shucking my pack, I inched out on the rain-slicked rocks I thought were the edge. It felt like the right spot, but the fog hid any landmarks. I could've been five feet up or fifty.

"Hellllllloooooooooooooo," I yelled out into the void. I turned and yelled again. Louder. And again. The icy fear and worry clamped around my heart.

Not sure what to do next, I dug out my map and a snack bar from a side pocket. Tiny raindrops tapped against the waterproof paper. If I didn't figure something out soon, I wouldn't make it to the next camp-sites before dark—let alone the one where I'd planned on staying.

Squinting in the dim light, I traced the trail. Counting switch-backs. Noting where I'd found the pack. Trying to decide if I was on top of the right cliff based on that and my average hiking speed.

Hard to say for sure, but I thought it was.

If I took the backpack with me from there, I might leave some-one stranded in the mountains with no gear. If it was the wrong cliff, I might leave someone stranded without gear anyway.

Then again, even if the pack hadn't fallen from there, whoever owned it would have to pass by to retrieve it.

I worked at straps and buckles with damp, wrinkled fingers. The random pack toppled into the mud with a splat. I righted it and fished inside the lid pocket. My fingertip scraped the familiar roughness of a coil of paracord I'd noticed earlier.

Perfect.

Grabbing the pack, I walked back the way I'd come, hunting for a reasonably high tree branch and a fist-sized rock. It took fifteen minutes to find a suitable spot, and two tries to toss the cord over the branch, but I got the pack hoisted out of reach of nosy black bears where a passing hiker would see it.

Hopefully the one who lost it.

Next, I needed a high point with enough cell signal so I could call 911. The faster I found one the better. For my missing backpacker, and for me to make it to Stevens Pass in three days.

EVAN

The rust-colored brick of our building filled my car window far too soon. I sat outside, a fist of anxiety clenching my gut, and clutched my new cell phone. The one with a Seattle area code.

Even though I knew she couldn't answer, I dialed the first number I'd saved in my phone. The one she'd scratched on a napkin at that curry shack when I'd given her the number for my voice mail that was no more.

"Hey Jules. It's one a.m. here in Boston, and I'm sitting in my car, in the middle of a noisy city, sweating. It was unseasonably hot and humid here today, followed by frigid at family dinner. I really wish I was still on the trail with you. Where it would be hot, but in a different way. And I guess you could say humid, too. But not in a sweaty gross way, in a sexy way." I pinched my temples with my forefinger and

Wild at Heart

thumb, took a deep breath, and started again. "Well, anyway, I really just called to tell you I was thinking about you. Also, now you have my new cell number in your phone. If you want to reach me, call this instead of my voicemail box. Okay. Well. I'd better go. See you soon. Miss you. Travel safe." I hit the end call button shaking my head.

"Travel safe." What the fuck was that?

I couldn't sit outside the building like a weird stalker any longer. Shoving open my car door, I inhaled the cool, briny air. With every step toward the door, the overwhelming desire to turn tail and run tugged harder.

Avoiding this whole conversation would be so much easier. We'd had it so many times before I already knew the outcome—and it wasn't an outcome I was willing to accept anymore.

That's why I'd left a note. But after seven years together Lainey did deserve more. Even if more meant me getting barraged with all the reasons I shouldn't leave. I winced and stepped off the elevator, turning left.

The red wooden door of our place stared me in the face. I knew every crack and chip by heart. The curved scratch where the edge of our bed frame drug against the door when we moved in (I thought Lainey was going to sue the movers over that one). The gouge where my key slipped after a drunken wedding reception years ago, when we were too busy making out for me to pay attention. Back when things were still good between us.

Low jazz oozed out around the edges. Jazz was part of her rebellious streak, the side of her that fought against her parent's love of all things stodgy and proper—like chamber music.

We grew up in the same social circles but didn't spend any real time together other until college. When I started getting to know her, I thought it meant she was cool, interesting, and in search of something different than the paths our parents set for us.

Shaking my head, I planted my feet, squared my shoulders, and rapped on the door. In less than three seconds the sparkling glow of our foyer chandelier washed over me, along with Lainey's gaze and an uncomfortable sense of deja vu. That unnerving sensation was fast becoming the norm on this trip.

"Hi."

"Hey, Evan. Thank you so much for coming over." She used her work voice; chipper and friendly, yet professional. Like a lawyer greeting a client, or maybe the opposition lawyer she's about to eviscerate. "Come in. Can I get you a drink?"

Padding across the hardwoods in bare feet, hair falling around her face in lush gold waves instead of pulled up tight for work, she looked so much like the coed I first met.

Except for the outfit. Her prim gray suit with a skirt that fell to just below her knees insisted everyone take her seriously. A far cry from the jeans and sweatpants she wore on campus.

I leaned against the wall and folded my arms over my chest. It was late, I was exhausted, and my emotions were slingshotting all over the place. I wanted to give her, and I'm pretty sure myself, the impression I wasn't staying long.

"I've got…" She opened the fridge door and peered inside. "Skinny margaritas, a Corona light, and water. Or I can make you a martini."

And this is what you find in a high-powered lawyer's fridge when you leave her alone for two weeks. The corners of my lips fought to rise.

"What?" She crossed her arms. "I had the girls over the other night."

"I didn't say a thing." I shook my head. "I'm good, though. Thanks."

     Wild at Heart

Her brows came down in a hard vee, but she turned and filled two glasses from the filtered water tap on the sink, set them on mirrored gold tray, and headed for the living area. Placing the tray on the leather ottoman that was supposed to serve as a coffee table, she perched on the edge of the couch, straightened her skirt, and patted the firm cushion next to her. "Come sit. We can be at least friendly and civilized, can't we?"

No. No we can't. Because you're going to get the upper hand and I'm going to let you convince me to stay.

My shoulder stayed glued to the wall. "I've done enough sitting tonight."

"Evan, I gave you seven years of my life. Don't you think you can spare me thirty minutes of your time?"

Guilt shot a hole through my gut. And I was so incredibly tired of feeling guilty. "Fine, thirty minutes."

I peeled my shoulder off the wall and crossed to the couch, sitting as far from her as possible. My butt barely sank into the smooth leather.

We'd fought about that couch—one of the few fights I'd ever won, more-or-less. She wanted something light-colored and modern in a soft fabric. I wanted comfortable, distressed brown leather I wouldn't worry about staining all the time. Where I could eat popcorn while watching movies with my feet up or drink red wine without fear.

We'd compromised on this gray leather modern style, and for the first time I admitted to myself how much I disliked it. Yes, it was leather and not white, but it was uncomfortable as shit.

Another perfect reflection of our relationship.

Exhaustion permeated every fiber of my being, settling deep in my bones. Exhaustion from the red-eye, and the adrenaline, and the hour, and dealing with my father. "Lainey, it's late. What did you want to say?"

"How could you break off our engagement with a note?"

"I'd told you I was unhappy, and I was leaving, before. More than once. You chose not to hear me, so I put it in writing."

She sat silent, spinning the engagement ring on her finger. "You're right. I'm sorry. And I can't change that, but I'm listening now."

Shock rippled through me. My mouth went dry. Never, ever, had I heard Lainey apologize, for anything. I took a sip of water.

"Please, Evan. Let's talk." Her blue eyes were wide and clear and genuine.

What if things could change? What if my leaving had been a wake-up call? "About what."

"Well—" She cleared her throat. "I was hoping you might reconsider."

"Reconsider what, exactly?"

"You and me. Us. The wedding." She waved her hand around, the pink, square-cut diamond glittering in the light. "I haven't told anybody why you left, so we can just pick up where we left off."

"Why would I want to do that? I wasn't happy before and I don't see that changing. In fact, not happy doesn't even begin to describe how I've felt." I clutched my water glass, knuckles white and aching.

"I know you've been unhappy since you lost your job, but everyone needs a purpose. Once you take the position with Blackstone, you'll feel better."

"I turned down the interview at Blackstone."

"What?" She blinked two, no three times in rapid succession. "Why would you turn down a plum position like that?"

"Because I don't want to be a financial analyst anymore. No." I shook my head. "That's not right. I never wanted to be a financial analyst and I'm not doing it anymore."

Lainey patted my knee like I was a small child. "Well, I'm sure your father, or mine, can you help you find another position in the industry. What are you thinking of switching to?"

"Running a non-profit camp for children."

"It's nice you're feeling philanthropic." She patted my knee again. "I'm sure you could find time to serve on the board of a non-profit."

I moved my knee away. "I don't want to serve on a board. I want to start my own camp. Outside Seattle."

Her laugh tinkled like glass wind chimes. "What do you know about the outdoors? Or camps? Or running a non-profit?"

"Enough to know it's what I want to do." My voice hardened. "And what I plan to do."

Her mouth formed a tiny O. "But you don't know anyone in Seattle. And you'll never make any money running a non-profit."

So much for changing. "And your point is…?"

"My point is that we've spent seven years together. We live together. We're engaged. I'm about to make partner and finally have time for a wedding. This was our plan from the beginning, and now that you're home, we can get right back on track." The passion of a lawyer in the middle of closing statements buoyed her voice. "Doesn't what we've invested in this relationship mean anything to you?"

It does. It means I had my head firmly planted up my ass for seven years.

"Not in the way it does to you. Besides, spending more time on a lost cause just because of sunk costs is always a bad business decision."

"How can you say we're a lost cause?" Her voice cracked. "Don't *I* mean anything to you?"

"Lainey, do you love me?" I angled toward her.

"Of course I do." She sat up straighter and lifted her chin. "I wouldn't marry you if I didn't."

"Let me rephrase that…Are you in love with me?"

She laughed; the sound pinched instead of ringing. "What does that even mean? What matters is that we're good together. I care about you. You care about me. And it makes sense for our families and our careers."

I'll take that as a no.

"We might have been good together in college, but when was the last time you wanted to spend time with me? Just me? Not at a function or a dinner somehow related to work."

She stammered and cleared her throat.

"I want to be able to laugh and talk and watch dumb movies with someone. Or go for a hike or a run together. I want to look forward to romantic dinners, or just coming home and hanging out together. That's not us." I waved my hand between our bodies. "Other than the last seven years, all we share are similar backgrounds and upbringings."

"Isn't that enough? It's where both of our parents started, and they're still married." Her hand fell on my arm, fingers gripping a little too tight, denting my skin. "We're building a life together. A good life, with all the things we both wanted. And I *have* missed you."

Missed me picking up takeout.

I took my arm back. "I'm sorry, Lainey, but we're on two different paths, with two different sets of priorities. If I'm going to spend the rest of my life with someone, I want them to love me for who I am, not despite it. And definitely not for my last name and family connections. You deserve the same."

She gripped my hands in hers. "Evan, I get that you needed some space to process being fired and consider your career direction, but

 Wild at Heart

you're too old to be acting so impetuously and too young for a mid-life crisis. It's time to come back to real life and make good on your promises—to your parents and to me. I'll forgive you, and we can forget this ever happened."

I shuddered, amazed how much her words echoed my father's, and pulled out of her grip.

"Forgive me for what exactly?"

"Well, for leaving me out of the blue like that. And for—" She looked at the blank, dark TV screen on the far wall. "Whatever it was you did while you were out there."

"What, are you talking about?"

She picked at her skirt, smoothed the fabric. "With her." Her gaze met mine. "Because I know you were with someone. That you cheated on me."

"Again, what are you talking about?" My heart slammed into my throat. I wracked my brain to figure out how she knew. Only one answer came to mind, but I'd deal with that later. "I broke up with you. So, I couldn't cheat on you even if I wanted to."

"Semantics." Her face betrayed nothing. Not a scrap of emotion.

Despite our crappy relationship, I didn't want to hurt her. I never wanted to hurt her. But a part of me wanted her to at least get angry so I'd know our relationship had meant something more to her. That I had meant something more to her.

Lainey continued in the same calm tone. "We'll call it an early mid-life crisis. And now that you've gotten it out of your system, we can move forward."

Bile flooded the back of my mouth. "You're still not listening…I want to marry a woman who wants to be with me because she loves me, not because it's good for her career, or our families. And I sure as hell don't want to marry a woman who doesn't care if I've slept with someone else—even if we were broken up at the time. And you should want the same."

"What about my career?"

"What about it? You're a damn good attorney. You're going to make partner with or without me." I faced her, wrapping her hands in mine. "Lainey, you're intelligent, hardworking, gorgeous, and know how to do the high society song and dance. You deserve a man who appreciates you for all that and more. Someone with the same goals. Someone who makes you happy. That's not me, and it never will be. I'm sorry."

She stared at me in silence, glistening eyes pinched at the corners.

"Come on, Lainey. I'm not right for you. You're not right for me. We haven't been right for each other in a long, long time, and I think deep down you know it's true." I mustered all my conviction. "This is your chance to find someone who can make you truly happy. Take it."

After an eternity of heartbeats, she exhaled. "How long until you leave?"

"Two days. If it's okay, I'll come by tomorrow while you're at work and pack my things." Most of what we owned Lainey had picked out. It wouldn't take more than a few hours to pack my clothes and box and ship the few things I wanted. John promised to be in town to meet the auto transport people next week, and that would be everything.

"So, your mind is made up?"

"It is. I'm sorry. I didn't mean for things to turn out like this."

She sniffled, and a single tear drew a clear line through her perfect makeup. "Neither did I. But I think I like you more with a little back-bone. So maybe this *is* the right move for you." She twisted the ring off her finger and held it out to me.

The five-carat stone caught the light from the floor lamp, throwing rainbows. I fisted it, cutting off its shine, and shoved it in the front pocket of my jeans with a small nod. "It's the right move for you, too, Lainey."

"I hope she makes you happy, because once your father finds out it'll be the final nail in your coffin."

"Pretty sure that coffin is already in the ground." I let one side of my mouth twitch up.

"True." Her smile was tiny, but real enough to glint in her eyes.

"He'll probably be more pissed he can't swing the axe over my head anymore, but I won't miss it."

CHAPTER 30

JULES

The weather hadn't budged overnight. Dense clouds swirled in somber shades of gray and white. Suspended raindrops hung thick and heavy. And the mountainside in front of me rose straight up.

Shoving my dripping curls out of my face, I focused on placing my feet on rocks instead of the slippery, delicate tundra plants, and gaining as much as elevation as possible. Fast.

That, and keeping my sense of direction firmly honed on the trail below.

It'd been almost twenty-four hours since I first spotted that backpack. Even the best survivalist wouldn't fair too well with no tent in this weather. Worse if they were injured. The sooner I got cell service, and Search and Rescue on the way, the better their chances.

Assuming they're still alive.

All night long, my brain had a glorious time tossing out suggestions for what might've happened to my missing backpacker. Then generously mixing in images of Evan, injured and shivering and alone.

          Wild at Heart

Plus adding a dash of Justin, so white and still in his coffin. Just for spice.

Like having my very own montage of death and loss and horrible accidents running on repeat.

Good times.

Peering through the thickening clouds, I searched for a decent wind break with a little cover from the rain. This high up nothing much presented itself. Not that I could see more than twenty feet out, anyway.

I stepped up onto a rocky shelf, a dull ache pulsing in my knee. I'd already climbed two peaks trying to get a signal with no luck. Nothing like bushwhacking up and down a few mountainsides in the damp, chilly weather to make that bad boy grumpy.

A few smallish boulders loomed out of the mist to my right. I slipped off my pack and tucked myself in best I could, my shoulder and back pressed into the rock.

Pulling back my rain cover I dug through my pack lid. My wet fingers slid over the smooth surface of my phone. Clutching it, I worked it out from under the ditty bag, hit the power button, pocketed it, and huddled.

Waiting.

Hoping.

Drizzle-mist whispered against my hood. I closed my eyes and focused on my breath. On the tiny hairs at the base of my nose moving. In. Out. In. Out.

The sharp ding of my voice mail chime sliced through the near silence, jerking me back to the task. It took three tries for my wet fingers to unlock the damn thing. The onscreen notification showed an unknown Seattle number.

Probably a junk call.

I checked my service, fingers and toes crossed.

Two bars. Better be enough.

"911. What is your emergency?"

"I'd like to report a missing backpacker."

The connection wasn't solid, but with only a few repeats I managed to relay the details to the dispatcher. The line went dead. SAR was on the way.

I took a slow breath, sucking the moisture-rich air deep into my lungs. Dropping my head, I exhaled. Like that, the responsibility for the missing backpacker's survival had been taken off my shoulders. If only my macabre montage, and the tightness of pain and loss, would go with it.

Hopefully Evan could fix that. Remind me he was alive. And wonderful. And committed to being with me. Because all my old worries and fears kept gnawing at me. Pinching and poking at my heart and soul. Reminding me exactly how bad it hurt every time I got rejected. Or lost someone I loved.

Not that I loved Evan.

Not yet anyway.

Leaning my head back, I let the mist hit my face. Focused on the cool static of a million tiny raindrops washing over my skin and my deep breaths.

Something smooth slid through my fingers, slick and slow.

What the fu—?

My phone!

I clutched and scrabbled. Grabbed the rain-slicked corner. Fumbled. Missed. It flipped through the air, smacked a boulder with a nauseating crack, and disappeared between two rocks. Shoving my hands in the narrow gap did nothing to mute the splat when it hit bottom.

My gut lodged in my throat.

"Fuck." I closed my eyes and took a deep breath. Opened them and assessed the situation.

The boulders were too big to move. Pushing up my jacket sleeve I squirmed one hand into the narrow crevice. The rough rock scraped a stinging rash into the skin on my wrist. My forearm. My elbow.

I grunted and stretched my fingers. They dipped into cold water. Not deep, less than inch, but definitely enough to soak my phone. I shoved my arm in a little further, ignoring the rock pinching my bicep, and scrabbled blindly. My fingertip tapped something smooth and hard.

Exhaling, I smashed my shoulder and chest into the rock and strained, hooking the edge of my phone case with my fingernail. Eyes closed, holding my breath, I worked at the lip, dragging it toward me millimeter by millimeter.

I scissored the case between two fingers and, holding on tight as possible, lifted it off the ground. My knuckles ground against the rough rock and wedged. I twisted my wrist.

Annnd the phone slid from my fingers and splatted into the puddle again. "Fuckity fuck fuck."

I wiped the rain from my eyes and rocked back on my heels. Somehow, I needed to grab my phone without using my hand. Digging out a mini-stuff sack from my pack, I emptied my lip stuff, small tube of sunscreen, compass, spare hair band, and a few other necessities into the lid pocket.

I shoved the stuff sack into the crack, followed by my hand. Slowly, I worked the stuff sack open and nudged my phone in with two fingers.

Cold water ran down my face. My neck. My spine. My arm ached where the rock pinched it tight. My knuckles burned from scrapes.

Wrapping the draw cord around one finger I pulled my arm out. The sack wedged against the crack.

With my free hand, I stuffed the muddy cord between my teeth. Grit grated the enamel. I prodded the phone with one finger. It turned. Slipped through. And the stuff sack dangled from my smiling mouth.

Pulling out the phone my smile faded. A crack spiderwebbed across the pitch-black screen protector. I pushed the button on the side. Nothing. Not even a flash of lights.

"Shit. Fuck. Damn." I stood and stretched, relieving the cramps from contorting my arms and legs and back.

If I was lucky, it would come back to life once it dried out.

I rummaged in my pack for my tiny pack towel and a bag of freeze-dried orange chicken. It was almost impossible to wipe anything dry out there, but I did what I could. Tearing open the bag with my teeth I dropped the phone in the rice, sealed it, and stashed it in my backpack.

Shoving the damp towel in my pocket, I started the long, slow process of picking my way back down the slippery mountainside. In the dim light and clouds, it was hard to tell time, and I'd forgotten to check on my phone, but my spidey-sense told me I still had a few solid hours of daylight.

Given how long I'd spent searching for a signal, I'd still never make it to my planned campsite. And I hadn't made up any lost time from the day before. But if I could cover decent miles this afternoon, and put in extra tomorrow, I could still make it out on time.

Fuck, I needed to make it out on time. Because the sooner I saw Evan, the easier it would be to cram the bad old memories and over-blown fears back into a tiny little box deep inside.

Because in two days, I'd be starting a new, happier phase of my life with an incredible guy.

EVAN

For the third time, I unclipped the lid of my backpack, opened the drawcord and took out the top few stuff sacks. Swapping the food bag with the clothes bag, I tried to get the weight distributed the way Jules had shown me, wanting everything well-organized so I'd get to the trailhead as soon as possible and ready to go.

"Bro, you have got to stop that." John stood over me, shaking his head. "You're driving me nuts."

"Sorry. I guess this whole leaving the family and everything I've ever known behind to start a new life on the West Coast is a little more stressful than I expected." I didn't bother to meet his eyes—or stop what I was doing. I let the sarcastic tone speak for itself.

He took a sip of coffee and pointed at my open suitcase. "Those your running shoes?"

"Yeah." I tucked smaller stuff sacks into my pack.

"We've got a few hours until we need to leave for the airport. Let's go burn off some of that stress energy."

I paused, considering the idea. "Okay. Give me a minute to load everything again."

He checked the time on his phone. "You've got fifteen for me to finish my coffee and you to get ready."

Ten minutes later we walked out the front doors of John's building and into the unseasonably warm August air. Turning, we headed for the Back Bay at a slow jog.

Running along the waterfront, the smells of rotting seaweed, hot dogs, and car exhaust burned my nose and throat on every breath.

Even with the sun still low in the sky, sweat beaded the back of my neck.

We hit the shade of the tree-lined Esplanade and John picked up the pace. I trailed behind him, dodging people strolling along the river, my knees and ankles slow and stiff. My brain, on the other hand, flicked between memories of being on the trail with Jules, and how the hell Lainey knew about Jules. Only one rational explanation presented itself.

The crowds thinned and I found my rhythm, joints loose, feet pounding a steady cadence. Breathing easier I caught up to John.

He glanced at me, a small smile on his lips. "Better?"

"Better. Thanks." My stride matched his, though my tone wasn't as light. Seagulls cried overhead, but the silence between us hung as heavy as the humid air.

"Spit it out, Evan."

Shoes thwapping against pavement, I dodged a mother pushing a stroller, and a walker with three Great Danes straining at their leashes, searching for the best way to broach the subject.

"C'mon man. What's eating at you?"

"You mean other than the fact I dumped my fiancée, and she didn't really care, and father excommunicated me?"

"Yeah. Other than that."

"How could you tell Lainey about Jules?"

"I didn't."

I pulled up short. John stopped and faced me.

"Well I don't know how else she would've found out." I set my fists on my hips, my chest rising and falling with ragged, deep breaths.

"I swear I didn't tell her. Not outright, anyway."

"Uh huh."

"Okay." He threw his arms up in the air. "She grilled me and wheedled and did everything she could to pump me for information.

Information I did not give her. But I can't be responsible for her reading between the lines."

"So, she used her powers of deduction, then?" My voice came out snarky.

"Yes, she did. You're the one that got engaged to a lawyer, so I don't know why that's a surprise."

"Still, you had no right to say anything."

"Fuck you. You're the one who skipped out and left me to deal with your shitstorm. Now you're not happy with results and that's not my fault." He crossed his arms over his broad chest and raised one eyebrow. "If you wanted to control the narrative you should've come home instead of hanging out in the woods getting laid."

"Fuck you."

"I'm just speaking the truth. It's also not my fault you don't like it."

We stared at each other, neither one giving ground. My fists ached to punch him in his smirking face. Mainly because he was one hundred percent right. *I should've known better than to leave that tidbit of info in that voice mail.*

It wasn't hard to imagine Lainey extracting enough information from John to put together the other pieces of the story. She was a genius prosecutor. And thinking back it became clear she wasn't positive when she broached the subject with me. I was the dumbass who confirmed it.

The mom and stroller we'd passed earlier rattled by. Then the dog walker.

"You're right. I'm sorry. I'm an asshole." I let my arms drop. "I know you fielded a million calls from Lainey when I should've been here to deal with my own shit."

"Yes, yes you are." John's neck and shoulders relaxed, and he grinned with one side of his mouth. "No worries, though. I figured out you're an asshole years ago."

"So, we're good?"

"We're good." His hands dropped to his sides. "Enough talking. Let's run."

Relief washed through me. I pushed off my toes. "In case I haven't said it enough, thank you again for dealing with all that."

"That's what brothers are for."

We slid back into our natural pace, side by side, feet thwapping as one. The slap of my running shoes, the steady cadence of my breath, and the fresh air usually calmed my thoughts and centered me. Instead, something else gnawed at me.

A tiny, questioning voice in the back of my head made my shoulders creep towards my ears. One that, once I thought about it, had probably been there since I was a teenager.

"Why was Uncle Martin almost thrown out of the family for going to Africa?"

"Wow. Is it tough question day, or what?" John picked up his pace, running in silence a couple feet ahead of me.

"Wait." I caught up. "What do you know?"

He stared straight ahead, lips thinning.

"Spill it, John."

"You really think Grandfather almost kicked Uncle Martin out of the family for going to Africa?" He glanced at me.

"That's what Father always said."

John slowed his pace. "But why would he get kicked out for volunteering as a doctor overseas? Think about it…Everyone always touted his bravery and service to others like he deserved a gold star medal. Like his time doctoring people in horrific, post-destruction conditions was proof positive of our entire family's selflessness and Catholic devotion."

"I don't know, but it doesn't add up." My legs churned along automatically. "I always assumed he wasn't happy Martin defied his wishes and walked away from a lucrative medical career."

John shook his head. "Grandfather didn't kick Uncle Martin out because he joined Medicine for the World. His leaving was part of the deal."

"Deal? What deal?"

"You know Uncle Martin got engaged to Lizzie Lassiter a few months before he left, right?"

I riffled through childhood memories. "Ummm, sure. I think I knew that."

"From what I understand, about a month after the engagement, Grandfather caught Uncle Martin in bed with Lizzie's older brother."

"Wait a minute." I took two more strides and my legs quit functioning while my brain went into hyper-drive, struggling to process this mind-blow. "You mean Uncle Martin was gay?"

"Bingo."

I wandered towards a shaded bench overlooking the river while the pieces clicked into place. "So that's why he never married. But why did Grandfather let him come back? That old man was about as prejudice as they come—even for his time."

"All those accolades Uncle Martin got for pioneering new procedures. Those were worth parading out." John sat next to me. "That, and they could pretend not having a wife was just one of the many sacrifices of his dangerous but much-lauded volunteer work."

"And the Davenport reputation was not only saved, but burnished."

"Pretty much."

Boats puttered by on the St. Charles. Sunlight reflected bright white off the buildings across the river. Turning this new information over in my head, I struggled to piece together the puzzle. No matter how I looked at it all, something still didn't make sense.

"Doesn't it seem like Father overreacted with me, then? I mean, it's not like he walked in on me fucking a dude."

John rubbed his palms on his thighs. A pair of seagulls squawked and fought over a piece of hot dog.

"I think he was bluffing. Father expected you to cave right away, not challenge him and walk away. Nice going on that by the way." He held up a fist.

I bumped it with my own. "Thanks, though I'm not sure it worked in my favor."

"Well, then you're pretty much screwed. Unless you want to toe the line."

"Yeah. No. I'll figure my life out on my own, thanks."

I angled towards John, the warm bench hard under my ass. "There's one more thing I don't get. You're the oldest, you're the most success-ful, and you're the one carrying on the full family name. Why do they even care what I do? They should be pressuring you to get married and take on the Davenport mantle, not me."

He rested his elbows on his thighs and stared out at the water with blank eyes. Sweat darkened his yellow shirt in deep vees, front and back. Children chased pigeons, laughing. Seagulls screeched. John shoved his fingers through his hair making it stand in uneven rows.

He exhaled hard, with a small groan. "The difference is, he didn't catch you giving Todd Belman a blowjob in your bedroom when you were fourteen."

Time stopped. The seagulls hung in the air, frozen. My heart quit beating.

"No shit?"

"No shit." John's voice was flat.

Time clicked back on and like a dam breached, a rush of sounds and thoughts overloaded my brain. My heart pounded like a bass drum in my ears.

I stared at John, trying to find something about him that looked different. That would give me any hint this part of him existed. He looked like my brother. The same person I'd known my entire life. "So, you're gay?"

He stared at a sailboat floating by. "I don't know. I've had relationships with women too, though not in a while." A small smile teased the corners of his lips. "Mostly I'm attracted to people I have a good time with. I'm not picky as long as they make my dick hard."

Classic John. He enjoyed the things and opportunities he was given to the fullest. Dove into them and rolled around like a dog scratching his back in the grass. And he'd always had this pragmatic, direct logic, and singular confidence in himself, I'd never been able to emulate.

Still, how could I not have known? Why did he hide it from me? A bolt of pain shot through my chest. The one person I'd always relied on, that I'd always been closest to, had been lying to me for twenty years.

"I wish you'd told me. I would've kept your secret." I shrugged and stretched out my legs, striving for nonchalance. "I never cared who you fuck anyway, as long as you're happy."

"I know, bro." He met my eyes for the first time since we'd sat on the bench. "It's not that I didn't trust you, but it's my cross to bear, not yours. And if I was going to hide it, I needed to hide it from everybody."

Logically, I understood. Emotionally, I had a feeling the sharp sting would take a while to go away. "I'm surprised Father never tried to marry you off, for cover, if nothing else."

"I told him if he did, I'd come out of the closet. Very publicly. But as long as he didn't, I'd work hard and be a model son in every other way. And of course, keep my indiscretions, discreet."

"So, you show up at every social event with a different woman on your arm, everyone thinks you're some kind of lothario, and you keep your real sex life far away from Boston."

"Pretty much." He tipped his head my way. "I've kept up my end of the bargain, and he's never mentioned it again."

"Seems like you've done a better job living life your way than I've done."

His shoulders sagged. "If you don't mind hiding who you are from the whole world—including people you love."

"Fuck. Yeah. Good point. I mean, I can only begin to understand how hard it's been. You had to sever the two parts of your life to make it work." Pieces clicked in my head. "That's why you bought the condo in Chicago, isn't it? Not business."

"Yeah." He gazed across the river. "Bro, you realize you're the only person who knows. I'm not even sure Mother knows."

"If Mother knew, she probably convinced herself it never happened years ago. But thanks for finally telling me." I nudged his firm shoulder with mine. "It's ridiculous though. In this day and age, it shouldn't even matter. Hardly anyone cares if you're gay anymore."

"Except Father and most of his cronies."

"You think it would hurt his big run for Governor?"

"Who the hell knows? It doesn't matter anyway. I'll live up to my part of the bargain until the day he dies. Though I'm glad the cat is finally out of the bag with you. And you finally stood your ground for what you want." John nudged my shoulder with his. "I don't think any of us saw that coming."

"Yeah. Though for some stupid reason I thought he might treat me like an adult and at least hear me out, for once." I stood, paced a few feet out and back, stopped and met John's eyes. "I swear to God, I am never setting myself up to be let down by him again."

"Good luck with that."

The theme from Psycho rang out from John's arm band. We stared at each other, wide-eyed. He shrugged and touched one Bluetooth headphone.

"Hello, Mother. What can I do for you today?"

The hysterics in her voice came through loud and clear even though the words didn't.

"It's okay. Calm down. Everything is going to be okay. We'll be there as fast as we can." He hung up and leapt from the bench. "Shit. We've got to go."

"What's up?"

"Come on. I'll explain on the way." John took off, sprinting back towards his condo.

CHAPTER 31

JULES

The sky shifted from steel blue to dark denim. I took out my head-lamp. The bright, circle of artificial light stung my eyeballs, but at least I could see the trail. And it wasn't raining.

My knee barked every time I took a big step up, or a jarring step down. The throbbing ache in my calves and quads became impossible to ignore. I'd covered thirty-five miles in two days and still had at least six more to go.

So much for making it to Stevens Pass today.

My heart fell. If I kept going, Evan would've already found a camp-site or hotel room, and I would have nowhere to camp.

What I wanted more than anything was Evan. I wanted to wrap my arms around him and press my lips to his. I wanted him to hold me and kiss me and fill me and convince me he was real and alive. That our relationship was real and alive.

I needed him to remind me opening up, being with him, was worth the risk. Because I'd been having trouble reminding myself—especially after crossing paths with the SAR team headed in on horseback to find the missing backpacker.

Explaining how and where and when I found the backpack made the chances of the backpacker's survival shrink from reasonable, to slim, to none in my head. I'd given the team lead my number and asked him to let me know how it turned out, but it didn't stop my worrying.

If the missing person didn't make it, I hoped they wouldn't leave behind a significant other or kids. Unlike Justin. Who'd left me, and his brother and father, wrecked and broken.

A sharp pain sliced through my chest. *What if Evan didn't come back? What would happen to me then?*

Would I fall apart again, trust forever shattered? Would I splinter into a million pieces I'd never be able to put back together? The sharp pain settled into a low ache. Quieting the evil, negative voice whispering in my head got more impossible with each passing mile.

He'd promised to come back. And I believed he meant it—at the time. Still, I knew how easy it could be to settle into the comfortable inertia of a life you didn't love but could live with. How hard it was to pick up and move across the country, leaving everything you know behind.

I clicked my headlamp off and closed my eyes, letting them adjust to the silver moonglow, then scanned ahead. A light flickered in the near distance. The last designated campsites before the pass weren't much further.

I'd find somewhere to squeeze in my tent come hell or high water, get up at the butt-crack of dawn, and be making out with Evan before lunchtime. And all would be right in my world.

Holding on to that thought, I made camp, scarfed dinner, and settled in for the night.

Excitement woke me before dawn. I shook out my damp tent and packed up, the dark sky fading to charcoal, then smoke. The quicker I got to Stevens Pass, the sooner I'd be with Evan.

Clouds had moved in overnight, wrapping the tree trunks in damp gray quilts. Moisture dripped from their needles. Carpets of mosses glowed vibrant kelly and emerald green, contrasting with the other, muted colors.

A soft buzz vibrated through air and into my bones. It grew louder and stronger, settling into my molars.

I rounded a curve in the trail. Massive, high-voltage power line towers loomed out of the clouds. Cutting the valley in two with their procession of spindly metal legs.

How can people live under these things?

The ski runs of Stevens Pass were obscured by the fog and mist, but I knew they were there. Which meant Evan wasn't far.

Excitement shimmied up and down my body, mixing with the low, humming vibrations. I followed the trail under the transmission lines. My shell pants swished with every step.

On the other side, it switch-backed up through a canopy of spruce and fir dense enough to block some of the rain. Sweat slid down my spine. Beads of cold water dripped off the ends of my braids.

At the top of the ridge, the whir and plash of car wheels on wet pavement reached my ears. Evan was so close I could feel it. I picked up my pace.

A few parked cars appeared in the wet gloom. My feet skittered on gravel. We'd agreed to meet in front of the clock tower by the lift ticket windows on the hour. I trotted across the deserted base area.

The clock hands read five 'til eleven. Evan wasn't there.

Yet.

Maybe he left a message.

　　　　　Wild at Heart

Crossing my fingers and toes, I pulled out my phone and mashed the power button. Nothing. I held the button longer, grateful for the cover of the patio roof.

"C'mon. C'mon. C'mon."

Black screen.

I shoved it back in my pack, waited ten more minutes, and headed inside in search of flush toilets, hot water, and soap. The warm air from the hand dryer worked wonders on my soaked curls. Through three, blissful cycles.

It wasn't like my hair could get frizzier anyway.

The wet, chilly weather had settled in my bones for so many days on this last section I'd forgotten the joy of artificial warmth. Of heated bathrooms and hot water splashing my skin.

Stepping into the main lodge I checked the time. Eleven thirty.

The salty, greasy, aroma of frying potatoes made my stomach grumble. I beelined for the café.

Veggie burger and fries in hand, I settled in next to a window where I could see the clock tower and laid my phone on a heating vent.

My nerves wound tighter with every passing minute.

At five 'til, I bussed my plates and stationed myself under the ticket window overhang, bouncing on the balls of my feet. If it wasn't for the rain, I'd have done back handsprings across the grass in front of the chair lifts to burn off my anxious anticipation.

The hands on the tower clock crawled. With each tick past the hour my heart dropped further into my gut. All I'd been focused on was seeing Evan's cobalt eyes and warm smile. On his arms wrapping around me, strong and safe. On his mouth slanting over mine. It didn't seem like too much to ask.

The clock hit quarter after. My eyes stung. My shoulders drooped.

"Fuck. Fuckity, fuck, fuck." I spun on my heel three times. Flapped my arms. Crossed them, exhaled a hard breath, and stalked over to guest services.

The teenager at the counter smiled. "How can I help you?"

"Do you by any chance have a phone I can use? My cell broke on the trail…"

"Sure thing. As long as it's local." I nodded.

She passed me a handset. "Here you go."

Shaking fingers made it hard to dial my voice mail.

—Beeeeeep. You have three new messages. —

I held my breath. Evan's alto voice came through the line.

"Hey Jules. It's one a.m. here in Boston, and I'm sitting in my car, in the middle of a noisy city, sweating. It was unseasonably hot and humid here today, followed by super cold at family dinner. I really wish I was still on the trail with you. Where it would be hot, but in a different way. And I guess you could say humid, too. But not in a sweaty gross way, in a sexy way." He paused, and his awkward, silly words washed over me like waves of joy. "Well, anyway, I really just called to tell you I was thinking about you. Also, now you have my new cell number in your phone. If you want to reach me, call this instead of my voicemail box. Okay. Well. I'd better go. See you soon. Miss you. Travel safe."

The smile fell from my face. *Shit. He didn't leave his number. Maybe in the next message.*

To erase, press seven. To save, press nine. —

I mashed nine and tucked the receive against my shoulder.

"Hey Jules." The warmth in his tone radiated through me. "I know you're on the trail right now, so I don't expect you to answer, but I wanted to tell you how excited I am to get there and be with you. Anyway, I don't know if you'll get this before we see each other. Which will be soon. In which case you can ignore this message because I'll tell you in person. Happy hiking."

Fuck. He didn't leave his number.

Hope and excitement worked to suppress the voice reminding me I had no way to reach him. Not that it mattered. He'd be here soon.

I saved that message too, looking forward to the third one. The one that would tell me he was back in Washington and on his way to meet me.

"Hey Jules. Ummmmmm…Listen." His muted voice cracked over the line. "I'm really sorry, but I'm not going to make it in time to meet you at Stevens Pass. My father had a heart attack. I'm staying at the hospital until he wakes up." He took a deep breath. "Or something. I don't know. Anyway, you've got my number. Call me when you get to Stevens. I'll update you when I know more. Talk soon, I hope. Bye."

The weight of his words sunk every bit of hope I'd been holding on to. I hung up, handed the phone back, and drifted outside.

Fuck. Fuck. Fuck. Fuck. FUCK.

I didn't have his number. I didn't know when he would get there. I definitely did not know what I should do next.

Somehow, my original plan of hiking the trail solo had been replaced by too many daydreams of hiking the next section with Evan. Showing him some of my favorite spots and watching his eyes light up each time.

The campsite with the bitchin' view straight up a glacial cirque. The looming, snow-topped mass of Glacier Peak reflected in a deep blue tarn. The endless fields of off-white Bear Grass, fluffy like troll pencil toppers after you spin 'em.

Not to mention all the talking and laughing and smooching and fucking we could do in those exquisite places.

Going alone sounded less than fun. And I might never get to hike it with him. Because if his father didn't recover, who knows what responsibilities he'd need to shoulder. In Boston.

Not that I'd blame him. Promises are made all the time that can't be kept. Shit happens. People die.

My sore legs trembled. I collapsed on my pack and stared up at the socked-in hillside. Hot tears streaked my cheeks. The nasty little voice in my head rang loud.

He's left you, just like all the others. And he's Never. Coming. Back.

CHAPTER 32

EVAN

My ass ached on the hard, plastic waiting room chair. I stood, shoved my fists into my low back, and stretched. It'd been three days and still no change. Seventy-six hours of sitting in this damn hospital, waiting for a doctor to tell me something I didn't already know about Father's condition.

One part of me wanted to get the hell out of this hospital, Boston, all of it. Screw him. He didn't want me to be part of this family anymore, so why bother? Another part of me believed I needed to stay, at least until he woke. Or didn't.

I wasn't sure exactly what my role would be if he died, but Mother and John needed all the help they could get either way.

And what if almost dying changes him for the better?

The doors opened with a whispered whir, and like every time that happened, my heart leaped into my throat. John strolled in with two coffees and a pair of gray bags under his eyes. My heart settled back into my chest.

"Hey, little brother. How are you holding up?" He held out a steaming paper cup.

The rich scent of dark roast slid up my nose, pushing out the caustic burn of disinfectants and illness. I took a sip. "Better now. Thanks. How's Mother?"

"Sleeping off the latest round of sedatives." He eyebrows pulled together in a vee. "I really hope Father pulls through. For her sake, if nothing else."

"I just don't get why she's so upset. It's not like they've ever been in love. They've never even shared a bedroom, that I can remember." I plunked back into my chair and rested my elbows on my knees. "She doesn't even have to worry about finances."

John sat beside me. "I don't know. Maybe it's some kind of identity crises. I mean, they have been together more than forty years. They're like business partners for life. If he dies her whole world changes, and she'll have to figure out who she is without him."

"And there's no doubt who's been in charge. She's basically been Mrs. John Davenport all those years." Bile and coffee burned my throat. "Can you imagine spending forty years with someone you don't love? Someone who makes all the rules, too."

"All too clearly, bro. All too clearly." His disturbed gaze met mine. "At least you've dodged that bullet."

"Seems like you have as well."

His lips quirked upward for a second. "Some days it feels like I made a deal with the devil. But I'm trying, that's for sure."

I sat back, my chair legs screeching against the linoleum. "So, what do you think has kept them together all these years?"

"You mean, other than the fact that Davenport's don't divorce, and they're cut from the same cloth?"

"Yeah, other than that."

He sipped his coffee. The squeak of nurses' shoes grew louder, then faded down a nearby hallway. "I think they keep each other's secrets."

"What secrets?" I stared at John, trying to read his mind. "Something other than Uncle Martin being gay?"

"Yeah, but this is between you and me, because I don't know anything for sure. It's just a theory I've put together from bits and pieces over the years..." He looked at me expectantly, his words hanging between us.

Did I want to know? Deep inside, I was always aware my parents had secrets (who doesn't?), but that was abstract.

"Of course. Sure. It's all just your own personal theory I won't share with anyone else, ever. So, spill it."

"I'm pretty sure Mother has had at least one affair."

"Wait. What?" My brain ached trying to imagine my prim and proper mother sneaking around with a lover. "How do you know?"

"My bedroom overlooked the front drive."

"So?" I sipped my coffee.

"She used to leave a lot late at night when we were kids—at least a couple times a week. And far too dressed up to be going on a quick trip to the store. She didn't seem to be trying to hide it, either." He huffed out a breath. "I didn't put it together until I moved out, but now it seems obvious. She was having an affair and Father didn't care."

Hot liquid shot out of nose and mouth, searing down the wrong pipe and into my lungs. I coughed and spluttered and John pounded my back while thoughts and emotions collided inside me with bangs and crashes that should've been audible.

Wiping tears from my eyes I took a shaky breath, "Why do you think he didn't care?"

"Maybe he was having an affair of his own." He shrugged. "Your guess is as good as mine."

I shook my head, fingers denting the sides of my to-go cup. None of this made any sense. At least not in my current state. Gripping my temples with the thumb and forefinger of my other hand, I pressed hard.

John's big hand landed on my shoulder. "I'm sorry, bro. I didn't mean to dump a load of shit on you while you're sitting in this damn hospital. Why don't you head over to my place and grab a shower and a nap? I'll hold down the fort and we can talk about all this later. Once you've had some sleep."

"You sure?"

He threw an arm over my shoulder, sniffed, and scrunched his nose. "Positive. I'll call you if anything changes."

JULES

The dull rumble of passing cars filtering through my window made my teeth grind. The glare of my laptop screen seared my eyes. Everything seemed too loud, too bright, after weeks in the woods.

A droplet of water traced a chilly line under my UW sweatshirt and down my spine. I shivered and focused on the best way to phrase the news of my return.

I did not need Bryn and Aly swooping in to interrogate me. Not yet.

I wanted peace and quiet to deal with my disappointment. Though why I thought catching the bus back into Seattle would give me peace and quiet, I did not know.

—Off the trail. Phone is broken but everything else is fine. Talk later. —

Bryn's profile picture stared at me accusingly. Like she knew good and damn well everything else was not fine. I hit send, closed my computer, and plopped down on floor in a straddle.

The wool rug scratched at the backs of my thighs. I stretched long over each leg, focusing on the tightness in my hamstrings. My calves. Breathing in deep and exhaling slow. Trying to relax down another inch. Hell, trying to relax at all.

The normally cheerful, lemon-colored walls of my apartment squeezed in, dark and confining.

Dismal thoughts spiraled in my brain like mud-specked soap scum swirling down the shower drain.

Lucky number thirteen my ass. Evan isn't coming back.

They never do.

I was a fucking fool for believing a short trail romance could ever be anything more.

Shoving my negative voice in the dusty closet in the back of my head, I got up and opened a window to let in some fresh air.

The rumbles and honks of evening traffic, and the pungent, low-tide aroma of rotting seaweed and exhaust fumes, filled the room. My head throbbed. I slammed the window shut and went back to the couch. My still-packed backpack glared at me from the corner by the door.

I didn't even want to think about finishing my hike, because that made me think about finishing it without Evan. Better to stay in town and get on with my life, than dwell on that shit on the trail alone.

What I needed was food. Lots and lots of food that didn't come in a pouch.

I pulled up the website for the Thai place two blocks down and ordered Tofu Pad Thai. And Swimming Rama. And Pad See Yew. Because they all made my mouth water.

And Mango Sticky Rice. Because dessert fixes everything.

The same way that chocolate cheesecake Evan shared with me on the trail fixed everything. Or fucked it all up, because that was the night I admitted I wanted him.

I am such a fucking idiot. Why did I try to play savior when I know good and damn well I can't really save anyone? Not even myself.

Grimacing, I sank back down on the rug and into a spinal twist. Then a low bridge, a full backbend, and a handstand. Anything to force me to focus.

Knuckles rapped on my door. I jerked and teetered. My feet hit the rug with soft thuds, stomach gurgling. I pulled the door handle. "Wow, that was fa—"

"What are you doing home?"

"What happened, hon?"

Bryn and Aly hustled into my living room.

I swallowed a million different responses. "Nothing's happened, except I broke my damn phone."

Aly stared at me; lips pursed. Like she was eyeing a horse she was considering buying. Trying to see if it's lame. "You sure you're okay, hon? You wouldn't come home early from a backpacking trip unless your dog died." She pointed a perfectly manicured, hot pink fingernail in my direction. "And you don't have a dog."

"I'm fine, I promise." I held up my hands in protest. "I came back to town to get my phone fixed."

Bryn's brow wrinkled. "So, when are you going back out?"

"Depends how long it takes to get a new phone." I stared anywhere but at her face. "A couple days, maybe."

     Wild at Heart

"So, we've got at least twenty-four hours to stuff you full of margaritas and high-calorie goodies, assuming we can tear you away from your man." Her gaze swept over me and the living room. "Speaking of, where's Evan?"

I stared at the wall. "Boston."

"Oh." Her voice went soft. "When's he due back?"

"I'm—I'm not sure. His dad had a heart attack. Evan's waiting to see if he pulls through. At least that's what he said in his voice mails. I haven't actually talked to him." The last word came out wavy and weak.

Two pair of arms wrapped around me and squeezed. Aly's lemon and rose scent washed over me.

"Shit. I'm so sorry, Jules. I'm sure he'll get here as soon as he can."

"Seriously. Because that man is dumber than a bag of hammers if he doesn't come back to you."

"No. I'm the one that's stupid." My heart cracked. The tear duct damn burst.

By the time I told them everything, my eyes were red and swollen and my coffee table looked like a Thai takeout explosion.

"I'm sure Evan is still planning to come back. Once you talk to him, you'll feel better." Bryn took another bite of sticky rice. "Can't you pull the number off your phone and use my cell?"

"I wish. My damn provider only shows the number onscreen. It doesn't say the number on voice mail."

"Well, you'll have a new phone tomorrow. Hopefully he'll call back soon."

My heart dropped like a boulder into a lake, with a big splash and a loud whomp. I shook my head. "He thinks I'm on the trail for another ten days or so…"

"You know, you've got the time. You should go back out as soon as you have a new phone." Bryn looked me in the eye. "I can take a few days off and hike with you partway."

"Thanks. But I'm ready to start revamping my business and looking for jobs. That's the one thing I'm clear on."

"Well, you know I'm not going backpacking until the Devil's butt turns blue and freezes off. But I'm always available if you find yourself needin' a stiff drink or a shoulder to cry on."

"You two are the best. But seriously, I'm fine."

"You sure?" Their voices meshed in stereo.

"Positive." I smiled a little. I had people in my life I loved, who loved me back. "I'm sure Evan is coming back. It's just going to be a while. In the meantime, I've got a pile of dirty laundry to do and I plan to use the extra time to enjoy a slow reentry."

"How 'bout happy hour tomorrow night then? They hired a cute new server while you were gone. We can drink margaritas and check out his fine ass." Aly grinned.

"Done."

The two best girlfriends ever stood and wrapped their arms around me in a final squeeze of warmth and heartbeats and lemons and roses.

"Meet you at six?"

"See you then."

"Enjoy sleeping in your own bed." Bryn smiled.

"I will." *Though I'd enjoy it more with Evan.*

The thunk-click of the door closing echoed through my small condo. An odd, off-kilter sense of displacement slammed into me.

Being inside a building never felt right after weeks in the woods, but it was time to get my career and business on track.

I cleaned up the leftovers, threw my stinky backpacking clothes in the wash, and hung my sleeping bag out to air. With nothing else left to do, I opened email. The name of one of my largest clients jumped out.

—

Dear Jules,

Thank you so much for all your hard work on our branding these last three years. Unfortunately, it is my job to let you know we've decided to bring our graphic design needs in house.

I'm writing to provide you thirty days' notice of termination of our agreement, as stipulated in your contract. It's been a pleasure working with you, and if you ever need a reference, please don't hesitate to get in touch.

All the best,

Stephanie Chase

VP Marketing

Dolen Heinz

P.S. If you know of any mid-level designers looking for a full-time position, please do send them my way.

—

Fuck. Fuck. Fuck. Fuck. Fuck.

CHAPTER 33

EVAN

My shoulder vibrated.

I shifted under the covers.

It vibrated again.

Oh, fuck. My phone.

Sitting, I groped around in the sheets for it. "Hello?"

"Hey, Evan. Time to get up."

I rubbed my eyes and stared into darkness, trying to get my bearings. "What time is it?"

"Four a.m. Father is awake and lucid. The doctors predict he'll pull through with flying colors. Mother is with him now and we should be able to see him soon."

"Ok. Wow. That's great news." The flavor in my mouth turned from soured pasta to cat vomit.

Rolling out of bed, I slid on clean khaki shorts and a plaid button down, brushed my teeth and hair, and raced for the hospital. In front of the main doors, I sucked in a deep breath and searched for my spine.

This was it. My last chance to make amends. At the very least, if he had another heart attack, I didn't want our relationship to end on the same shitty note. That's what I told myself as visions of a heartfelt apology and a too-weak handshake turning into a warm hug flitted through my head.

The doors slid open with a hushed whirr, the sting of antiseptic cleaners and the artificial glare of fluorescent lights far too familiar. My heartrate jumped from a slow walk to a fast jog.

My dock shoes squeaked on the shiny, white linoleum floor. The nurse on duty greeted me with a broad smile. "You must have received the good news. Congratulations."

"Thank you. Can I see him?"

"Absolutely, but your brother's in there now. He's still very weak, so we're only allowing one visitor at a time, and only for a few minutes. You can wait outside his door."

My heartrate sped up to a sprint. "Okay. Thank you so much." I pushed through the double doors to ICU.

Standing in the hallway, the hushed sounds of the hospital echoed way too loud. I shifted from one foot to the other. I counted my breaths.

I considered calling Jules for moral support, even though I knew I wouldn't reach her. Even though I'd have to go to the waiting room to use my phone. Maybe because I'd have to go to the waiting room to use my phone.

The broad door to Father's hospital room opened with a quiet swish and closed with a soft click.

"Hey, bro."

"Hey." I jerked my head towards the room. "How is he?"

"Irascible as always."

"Where's Mother?"

"Gone home to get some sleep." John made air quotes around the words get some sleep. "Pretty much the same thing she's been doing since the heart attack."

"Do you think he wants to see me?"

"Hard to say. That wasn't a hornet's nest I wanted to poke." John shrugged and waved a hand at the door. "He's all yours. Good luck."

"Thanks. I think." I grasped the handle and pulled. The low murmur of news pundits filtered through the growing gap along with the steady, comforting beep of his heart monitor. The room smelled like the old meatloaf and too-sweet applesauce sitting forgotten on a rolling side table.

I tapped with my knuckle, hoping maybe he wouldn't respond. That maybe he was sleeping, and I could come back later.

"Come in." His deep voice didn't boom like usual.

Shaking out my shoulders, arms, and hands, I stepped inside the private room. With the curtains closed, the only light came from the wall-mounted TV set and a small reading lamp hanging over the corner of the bed.

My father, the man I'd always been terrified of, looked small. At least, smaller than I remembered, surrounded by machines and wires and an IV drip. He. The lines in his face seemed etched deeper, and I'd swear his hair had faded from distinguished salt and pepper to mostly white.

"It's good to see you, Father." I reached out and he grasped my hand, his grip surprisingly firm. "How are you feeling?"

"Perfectly fine. Or I would be if these doctors would let me go home."

"I'm sure they're just being cautious. You were unconscious for almost four days, after all."

     Wild at Heart

"Exactly why I don't have time for all this nonsense when I have a campaign to run." He gestured at the tubes and wires. "I assume your appearance here means you've decided to accept my offer."

I winced. That was it. Straight to business. Nothing emotional spoken between a father who almost died and his son.

Anger fired in my veins, scorching and white. Anger I'd tucked away somewhere deep inside since my childhood. Anger with him for setting impossible standards, anger with my mother for never saying a word, and anger with myself for always giving in. "My appearance here means I came to see if almost dying changed your mind. To see if you're at least willing to consider my business plan."

His eyes tightened at the corners. The steady background beep sped up a little. "How many times do I have to remind you that I am doing what's best for this family, and I expect you to do the same."

"And you're the only one who knows what's best for this family, and for me?"

"You can either do what I say, or do what you want, but don't expect me to support your fanciful plans."

"Somehow, I thought having a heart-attack meant you actually have a heart after all. I guess I was wrong." Biting back every ounce of rage and moral outrage, and all the childhood hurts and slights, I turned on my heel and stalked out.

John leaned against the wall of the corridor, giving me a once-over. "That was fast."

"You know our father. Always gets right to the point." I ground the words out between clamped, aching jaws. "You'd think almost dying would change a person's perspective."

"Sorry, Evan." He clapped a firm hand on my shoulder. "It's hard to have a change of heart when your heart is made of stone."

"Yeah. I really should know that by now, and not keep hoping for something that's never going to happen."

"Ah. Well, you, on the other hand, are all too human." He shrugged. "So, what's your plan?"

"Head back to your place and book a ticket on the first flight to Seattle."

I wasn't sure exactly when Jules would be off the trail, a few more days at least, but I couldn't wait to see her. I couldn't wait to hold her and touch her and kiss her and taste her and tell how lucky I was to be with her. I couldn't wait to remind her how good we were together and prove we'd be even better off the trail than on.

CHAPTER 34

JULES

The air on the patio smelled like fryer grease and corn chips. I swirled a salty-sour swig of my margarita and let the liquid burn down my throat, trying to relax. Trying to ignore the rushing roar of cars going by a few yards from the patio. And the constant fucking chatter and clatter of Happy Hour at our favorite Mexican restaurant.

And the stressed-out thoughts circling inside my head. Because every time I made a plan, it managed to blow up in my face.

"Can I pour you another?"

I jumped. My server pointed at the mostly full pitcher sweating in the middle of the table. Less than an inch of yellowish-green liquid pooled in the bottom of my glass, a goblet the size of my face.

Another sounded a-fucking-mazing, but I didn't need to be two drinks in this early. No matter how much getting drooling, weaving, stinking drunk sounded like a great idea right then.

It couldn't go any worse than any of my other recent decisions.

Actually, I guess it could.

"No thanks. I'll wait for my friends."

He trotted off and I wished he could leave me in blissful silence. Except the city was too damn loud. Much louder than I remembered. Thin bands tightened across my forehead.

I sucked down the last of my drink and set it on its coaster with a dull clunk. Bryn and Aly appeared in the patio entrance and waved.

"Hey, Jules." Their voices chimed in unison as they slid their arms around me in a warm embrace. They hopped onto the two empty stools surrounding our tile-topped table.

"How was your first day back in the real world?"

I glanced at Bryn. "Fine. Replaced my phone and went for a hike at Lincoln Park. Busier on the trails than I was hoping, but it was nice to hang out down by the water." I hefted the pitcher, ice clanking, and filled their glasses first.

Aly eyed the remnant liquid in my otherwise empty goblet. "Are we late?"

"Nope. I got an early start." I topped off my glass.

Their gazes burned holes in my cheeks.

"What's the matter, Jules?"

"Did you talk to Evan?" Aly's voice was hushed. She wrapped her manicured hand over mine.

I shook my head. "He hasn't called, and I wasn't able to retrieve his phone number."

Concern knotted Bryn's forehead. "So, what's going on?"

I lifted my heavy glass and slurped down a big gulp, relishing the salt on my lips. Steeling myself so I wouldn't totally break down in the middle of Amigos.

"Oh, nothing much, except—I'm fucked. Every fucking plan I make, every fucking decision I think is right, keeps going sideways."

"Now, hon…" Aly gave my hand a gentle squeeze. "You don't know what's up with Evan yet. I have a feelin' that's gonna work out fine."

"I hope so. But my whole new business plan already got shot out the window." My voice boomed out and my hands flew up in frustration.

The knot in the center of Bryn's forehead tightened. "What do you mean?"

I grabbed the hard, cool stem of my glass. Forced my voice to stay even. "Dolen Heinz fired me." I shifted my butt on the hard, wooden stool and looked at Bryn, then Aly. "They were forty percent of my income. I'm pretty much screwed unless I land a few more clients ASAP. Which makes my idea of letting all my smaller clients go, and doing less design work, fucking laughable right now."

The weight of my words slammed down on my shoulders like an overloaded backpack. Doing more marketing and more networking to land more clients for a business I no longer wanted sounded awful.

"Maybe it's a sign you're supposed to take a big leap to something other than graphic design." Bryn rubbed my arm. "You've been burnt out for a while, anyway."

The weight got heavier. My shoulders drooped further. I spoke to the mosaic tabletop. "I did some job searching online last night. Nothing jumped out that looked interesting. Or that I'd be qualified for. Not without going back to school."

"Aw, honey. Jobs are like men and houses—if one doesn't work out, there's always another. You'll find something. It just might take longer than a month of Sundays."

I took another salty-sweet, burning slug of my drink. And sent a silent thank you to the tequila gods for creating something so wonderful.

Fresh chips and salsa appeared on the table. "Can I get you ladies anything to eat?"

We order our usuals. The waiter walked away.

Aly's gaze followed him. "I bet he'd be a tasty snack."

I glanced at his ass, which was indeed fine. And realized I'd been there more than thirty minutes and hadn't even noticed. *I AM a hot fucking mess.*

Bryn stared at me over the rim of her glass.

I met her gaze. "What?"

"You should go finish your hike."

"What the hell are you talking about? I need to find more work, like, yesterday."

"No. You don't."

I opened my mouth. She held up her palm.

"Seriously, Jules. If you hadn't broken your phone, you'd still be on the trail. Which means you wouldn't even know about Dolen Heinz for more than another week. So, go finish your hike and get your head on straight. You can deal with all this when you get back." She smiled. "I promise it'll still be waiting, and hopefully Evan will be too."

"I don't know, Bryn." I shook my head. "Between this whole Evan thing, and worrying about the lost backpacker, I wasn't exactly in the best headspace out there. Adding in more issues isn't exactly going to help."

"She's right though, Jules. Ain't much you can do right this second, and I've never known you to give up vacation days." Aly took a sip of her marg.

"I don't want to leave until I talk to Evan."

She raised one eyebrow. "Seriously? You're going to put your life on hold for a man you just met? That fits you 'bout as well as socks fit a rooster."

Annnnnnd…someday I'm going to tell her grandmother exactly how much I appreciate her passing on all these ridiculous sayings. "I guess I was just really looking forward to finishing the hike with him."

"And when you started, you were really looking forward to finishing it alone." Bryn gave me a pointed look. "Besides, Evan might not even call again until he thinks you're off the trail. So, you might as well be on the trail, enjoying fresh air and glorious sunsets over endless jagged mountain peaks. It beats moping around your condo."

She was right. They both were. I hadn't put my life on hold for a living, breathing man ever.

Just a dead one.

The ring of my phone blared through the patio noise. My throat clogged and I scrabbled for it in my bag.

The screen showed a 206 number. I swallowed down the Chickadee nesting in my esophagus and slid off my bar stool, heading toward the street. "Hello?"

"Hi, is this Jules Martinez?" An unfamiliar voice came through the line.

"Yes, it is."

"I'm with Snohomish County Search and Rescue. I just wanted to let you know we found that missing backpacker you reported and she's going to be fine."

Weight I didn't know I'd still been carrying slid off my shoulders. "Oh my God. That's great news."

"It is. Not everyone gets so lucky. She had a broken collarbone and a concussion, but your phone call and smart thinking likely saved her life. She found her backpack when she came to and managed to set up shelter, so she was in pretty good shape when we got to her. And she said to tell you thank you."

"I'm sure anyone would've done the same. But I'm glad I could help. Thank you for letting me know." Relief made all my limbs lighter.

"It's always a pleasure to make the good kind of calls."

I trotted back to the table, grinning from ear to ear.

Aly stared at me. "Well don't you look happier than a tornado in a trailer park."

"Evan?" Hope brightened Bryn's voice.

"Nope. SAR. Which is almost as good. They found the missing backpacker and she's going to be okay."

"That's terrific."

"It is." *And maybe a sign.* "Any chance one of you can drop me at the downtown station in the morning? The Stevens Pass bus leaves a little before nine."

EVAN

The other line rang twice. "Teller Jones Realty. How can I help you?"

I worked to find enough spit to speak. "Bryn Jones, please."

"One moment."

The line clicked, and the unplugged version of Nirvana's "Come as You Are" played in my ear, reminding me I now lived in Seattle. Not that I needed the reminder.

Laying in my hotel bed last night, excitement warring with worry, I realized for the first time exactly how ridiculous my life sounded—moving cross country to a city I didn't know, to be with a woman I'd barely spent time with and start a non-profit in a subject area I knew almost nothing about. And I'd walked away from the family fortune to do it.

Maybe I was reckless, or foolish, or stupid—or all of the above—but a calm spot deep inside told me it would all work out. Of course, there was a fair chance that calm spot was nothing more than the eye of an enormous, destructive hurricane.

"This is Bryn."

My brain stuttered and reengaged. I cleared my throat and slapped on a smile I hoped would float through the line. "Hi Bryn, it's Evan Davenport. Jules's friend. From the trail. How are you?"

"Hi, Evan. I'm good, thanks. I'm so sorry to hear about your father. Is he doing better?"

Depends on how you look at it.

I sucked in a deep breath, using it to push down the acrid bitterness creeping up from my chest. "He was last time I saw him. Thanks. I'm in Seattle now, though, and I was wondering when Jules is due to get off the trail."

"Not for another week or so. Her phone broke, so she came back to town for a couple days to get it fixed before starting the last section."

I didn't want to wait a week to see Jules walking out of the forest, hair a mass of wild curls, her smile huge when she laid eyes on me. I didn't want to wait to feel her arms and legs wrapping around me like she never planned to let go.

Maybe I could catch her, or meet her partway by hiking down from the north end?

Finding her along one hundred and seventeen miles of wilderness trail wouldn't be easy. Memories flashed of the night we met, and me, freezing my ass off in the rain-soaked darkness, and the day I made the wrong turn and lost my trail.

"I'd be happy to pick her up at the end…" I swallowed hard, closed my eyes, and crossed my fingers. "If you think she'd like that."

Bryn's laughter chimed through the line and into my veins, sparking a high like the best drug ever. "I think you should absolutely pick her up. She'll be way happier to see you than me or Aly. Be forewarned, there is no cell service in the par, and only a couple campgrounds on highway 20. If you don't see her by eight p.m., she'll camp at the last group of sites about five miles up the trail and finish the hike out in the morning. You may have to overnight in Winthrop, or crash in your car if all the campsites and hotels are booked."

"No problem." Nothing, absolutely nothing, would be a problem if it meant I got to see, and hold, and kiss Jules even a few hours sooner.

"You should stop by my office sometime this week and pick up the change of clothes Jules left. Hold on a sec and I'll connect you with Aly. The two of you can coordinate a handoff. Be sure to give her your number so we can all stay in touch."

"Sounds good. Thanks, Bryn."

"Sure thing. And if there's anything else I can do to help you get settled out here, just let me know."

CHAPTER 35

JULES

Sunlight beamed through the green walls of my tent turned it into a sauna. Groggy, sweaty, and a little disoriented, I rubbed crumbs of sleep from my eyes.

I'd managed to snag the last available campsite a few miles from Hwy 20 right as the sun set, made dinner, and crawled into my sleeping bag with a plan to be up early. Except, instead of passing right out I spent half the night having incredible, panty-wetting, anything-but-restful dreams about Evan. The other half I spent worrying about what I would say when I saw him again. Or if I would see him again. And debating which would be worse.

I rubbed the smooth, blue and brown stones of his leather bracelet. The one that said he'd have to come back for. I had no idea if we'd be even half as good together off the trail. But if he actually left his family and fiancé and moved to Seattle, I'd have to try. With a click of my lighter, my stove hissed to life.

If he showed up, I'd have to admit my world view had been skewed. And that I needed to at least give us a chance. I could take it slow, but I needed to take it.

Slow wasn't my usual style. All or nothing, or rather nothing but sex, was my style. For good reason. I could date and fuck and have fun with guys and not get my heart broken if I kept my walls up. Except I'd already let Evan in too far to stick with that. Steam dampened my face as I poured boiling water into my mug and bowl.

If he didn't show up, I'd be off the hook. I'd also be adding a thirteenth tick-mark in the column of "left me for his ex" and nursing a crushed heart. But life would go on.

It might not be pretty for a while, but I'd survive. Because I'd survived worse.

Voices carried through the sunlit forest. I rinsed out my oatmeal bowl and tucked it away. I still had tea to finish. And my tent to pack up.

It would be easy to stall another night. Nobody would start worrying about me for at least two more days.

A bright, cheery, "Cheeeeese-bur-ger, cheeeeese-bur-ger" whistled through the trees. A slight breeze riffled my hair. I closed my eyes and savored the fresh scents of spruce and pine and mountain top.

If I could stay out here I would.

In the woods, my life was reduced to a minimum of options. I didn't have to deal with finding clients or figuring out a new career direction. Or Evan.

Or there not being an Evan.

Too bad living in the wilderness isn't really feasible.

I sucked down the bitter dregs of my green tea, and had camp broken sooner than I wanted. With one last look around I hit the trail

Hiking the final few miles of my trip, all I could think about was who would be waiting at the end of the trail.

Bryn or Aly, or Evan? Bryn or Aly, or Evan?

The sun arced higher into the sky, heating my aching shoulders. Beads of sweat formed along my hairline. The trail curved left, and the occasional whir of a car driving by filtered through the narrow strip of forest separating me from the highway.

Which meant less than a mile lay between me and the trailhead.

Too soon, the flat, straight edge of a picnic table caught my eye through the trees. Man-made items always stuck out after weeks in the woods, where shapes are organic and straight lines rarely run straight for long.

My heart fluttered. My palms slicked.

The clearing behind it had to be the parking lot.

I scrubbed my hands on the rough nylon of my shorts and tramped through the picnic area, trying to hold on to every shred of peace and tranquility I'd found on the trail.

Sunlight glared off windshields, harsh even through my sunglasses. I didn't recognize any of the cars in the parking lot. The rugged peaks of the North Cascades that hadn't been visible in the dense forest towered over me. I turned a circle, enjoying the view one last time.

Fuck. I'm going to miss being out here.

Walking toward the kiosk in search of shade, I passed a dark green van. On the other side sat a small white SUV. A slender man with shortish dark hair leaned against it. Hands in his pockets. Staring at his flip-flops.

I sucked in a breath.

He looked up. Sapphire eyes met mine and I froze. Except my heart, which went into overdrive.

He came back.

The ramifications threatened to overwhelm me. Crush me straight to the ground. Or maybe I was about to float into the stratosphere.

I couldn't tell if the bubbling in my gut was from fear or excitement. Or both.

Take it slow. Take it slow.

Clean-shaven, in long gray shorts and plaid snap front shirt, sunglasses shoved up on his head making his hair stick up in five directions despite being trimmed neat on the sides, Evan cleaned up well. Really well.

And that shy smile. Holy hottie.

I could try all day to say he wasn't my type, but I'd be lying. He'd turn my head anytime, anywhere.

Especially when he stared at me like that. Like he wanted to devour me. Something vibrated inside me, low and deep. I licked my lips.

In two steps he closed the distance between us, stopping not even a foot away. So close I could see his pupils dilate and contract. Count the charcoal lines in his cobalt irises.

His teeth bit into his lower lip. He lifted a hand like he wanted to brush the curls off my face, but let it drop, scooping up my fingers along the way.

His thumb brushed light strokes over mine. Every inch of me quivered.

"Hey," he said, staring at my mouth hard enough to make my lips tingle.

"Hey." I remembered the way we wrapped around each other in the tiny space of my tent. I remembered the laughing and the talking and the skinny dipping, and all the things I'd missed after he left.

Things I'd been doing my best not to think about for the past ten days.

Except with him right here, in front of me, close enough to kiss and touch, I wanted to do all that and more. So, fucking, bad. More than I wanted to protect my heart.

He cleared his throat. "I hope it's okay that I'm here."

"It is. Of course, it is. More than okay. Thank you for coming to pick me up. I hope you haven't been waiting too long. Camping around here can be pretty hard to come by and I'm sure you have better things to do than sit out here in the middle of nowhere waiting on me." I gulped a breath to stop my verbal diarrhea.

"Nope. I just got here yesterday morning. And I can't imagine a more beautiful place to wait. Or a more beautiful person to wait for." He leaned in a little closer. Or maybe I leaned toward him. All I know is the gap between us shrunk. Heat and electricity hung in the air, pulled tight like a web of cords connecting us. "How was your hike?"

Fuck me. I didn't want to talk about my hike or make pleasant conversation. I wanted his lips sliding over mine. His tongue thrusting into my mouth.

His thumb to stroke something other than my thumb.

Slow, Jules.

I forced my brain to come up with an answer. "Good. Fantastically beautiful. Long. A little rainy. A little lonely."

"I'm sorry I couldn't get back sooner. I missed being out there with you." He raised his other hand, trailing his fingers along my cheek in tingling lines. His warm palm cupped my jaw. I nuzzled it, savoring the roughness of his callouses.

"I missed you being there with me." My voice came out husky and hoarse.

Evan's mouth hovered over mine. His minty breath blew warm gusts across my skin.

He licked his lips. "I really want to kiss you right now."

My breath hitched. My lips tingled. The vibrations at my core turned up a notch. All thoughts of going slow vanished

I took a wavering breath. "So kiss me."

EVAN

Jules slid one small hand behind my neck and tugged my head down, closing the gap. The ball of tension in my stomach melted. I brushed her mouth with mine, breathing her in, and traced the tip of my tongue across the pad of her lower lip.

She gasped, and her tongue met mine, warm and slick, and I lost myself inside her mouth. Rising up on her toes she kissed me hard and deep and like she'd missed me as much as I'd missed her. I'd been dreaming of this moment for weeks, and in the first few seconds, the reality beat every one of my dreams by a hundred miles.

I trailed my lips along the salty skin of her jaw to her neck. Her fingers tightened in my hair, and a barely audible, high-pitched whine escaped from somewhere in the back of her throat.

My head bumped into her backpack. I pulled away. "Fuck. I'm sorry, Jules. I bet you'd like to drop your pack and get cleaned up."

"Yeah. As long as you promise to pick up where you left off after." Her fingertips grazed her lower lip. "And to never apologize for kissing me like that again."

"Done." I dragged my mouth across hers one more time, because I could, savoring the tingling pinpricks of electricity.

My heart soared around in my chest, doing a dance with my stomach. I'm pretty sure everything in my chest cavity flip-flopped at least twice. Jules was there and happy to see me, and our connection was there, and the way she melted when she kissed me told me everything I needed to know.

Wild at Heart

I pecked the tip of her nose, wishing I could see her eyes behind her sunglasses. "I picked up a change of clothes for you from Aly. Let me grab them."

"Awesome. Thanks." She unclipped her sternum strap and slid her pack off her shoulders and down to the ground with a thump while I grabbed the bag out of the backseat of my rental, trying to act nonchalant and failing miserably, I'm sure. Especially since the giant grin on my face appeared to be a permanent addition.

Because with Jules by my side everything would work out fine, and what didn't work out fine we'd get through together. Screw my father. We were going to be happy and successful together—on our own terms.

My ass heated more than could possibly be caused by the sun. Turning, I caught Jules staring with a broad smile. She wolf-whistled and my grin spread larger (if that was even possible).

I tipped an imaginary cowboy hat. "Why, thank you ma'am."

"No. Thank you." Beaming like a kid in a candy store, she plucked the bag from my fingers. "For the view, and the fresh clothes."

My face officially split in two. "My pleasure."

A car roared by, and another. We grinned at each other like we'd won the lottery—which I guess we had. My already overwhelming desire to kiss her and touch her and tug her into the woods and slide inside her grew stronger. It pulled me toward her.

She shifted, clearing her throat and pointing a thumb over her shoulder at the forest. "Um, I'm just going to go change. Be right back."

I couldn't take my eyes off her legs, her ass, and the way her strong, defined muscles bunched and rolled in that mesmerizing way, until she disappeared between tree trunks and shrubs.

I also couldn't stop smiling. Or looking forward to my new life here in this beautiful place and my future with this amazing woman.

CHAPTER 36

JULES

Peeling off my clothes, I dropped them piece-by-piece in a pile on the forest floor. Each cool swipe of baby wipes left a light-colored line in the brown dust on my skin, along with the faint odor of baby powder. Nothing quite like getting clean at the end of a long hike.

Except maybe having a smart, thoughtful, sexy-as-hell man pick me up.

A part of me still couldn't believe he actually came back. That Evan was standing in the parking lot, not twenty yards away, waiting for me. The rest of me quivered with an intoxicating mix of excitement and fear and desire.

My lips tingled from the kiss a few minutes earlier. From the way electricity shot through every nerve in my body when nothing more than his lips brushed mine.

I wanted more of that. A whole lot more.

We'd fucked like rabbits before he left, but the connection between us seemed bigger now. Stronger. Pulsing in a way I wasn't sure I could keep a handle on.

Taking it slow would make it easier to hold on to at least a teensy bit of control. Then again, it'd take more than a little control to go slow. But I wanted to make this work.

With one last swipe around my ankle, I balled my third wet wipe and dug in the bag. Instead of the rough cotton of the shorts and t-shirt I'd packed, my fingers met a thinner, silkier fabric. I pulled out my green sundress. The flirty one that came to just above my knee, with crisscross straps that showed off my shoulders.

The one I wore for date nights and dancing.

I turned the bag inside out. Empty.

Aly. You didn't.

I shook the dress out. Still nothing.

Since I wasn't about to put my sweat-stained, crunchy hiking clothes back on, I pulled the dress over my head and smoothed the soft cotton over my bare ass and down my thighs.

The breeze blew cool fingers up my skirt. I felt Evan's warm ones instead. My clit tingled.

So not helping me take it slow.

Aly was going to get an earful next time I saw her. I shoved my dirties in the empty bag and wove through the trees back to the car.

Evan sat in the rear hatch with my pack tucked behind him. Sunlight poured through the windows picking out the highlights in his dark hair. Making the edges of his sculpted profile glow gold like the perfect boyfriend in a rom-com, right before he admits his love and kisses the girl.

And for the first time in a long time, I wanted to be that girl so, damn, bad. The one the man looks at adoringly while he pledges his undying devotion. And not even a shred of guilt tried to quiet the trembles of excitement in my chest.

I swiped my damp palms on the front of my dress. Gulped down the nervous birds fluttering in my throat. *Take it easy, Jules. Don't screw this up.*

"Hey." I dropped my bag in the hatch

"Hey." He turned toward me. "Feel bett—?" The word died on his lips. His gaze roved from my knee to my waist. Lingered on my chest until it went hot.

A large pigeon took up residence at the top of my esophagus. My breathing went shallow and fast.

"Much." I sat, trying for nonchalance. Not easy with his knee inches from mine. Or with every inch of my skin prickling and itching for his touch.

And God, that sounded so weird. His touch. Not just anyone's touch. That's why I didn't want to go too fast. I knew once I leapt into that water I wouldn't want to come up for air. Much as I wanted it, him, the idea still freaked me the fuck out because I knew I could drown in the emotions.

But I could handle it. Would handle it. With baby steps.

Because deep down I knew being with Evan would be worth the risk. I mean, hell, he'd come back. And that connection between us hadn't dimmed one bit. This had to be right.

He pointed at a soft-sided cooler. "I wasn't sure what you might be craving so I brought cold beer, Gatorade, and sparkling water. And chips and salsa and hummus and some weird yellow cherries I found at a roadside stand. What's your pleasure?"

His voice dropped an octave on that last word and his gaze heated, and oh, Jesus, every moment of fooling around on the trail rolled through me in one long, steady rush.

The way he'd held me and looked at me, pulsing inside me while I melted down in his arms. How we tasted and teased each other for days when we ran out of condoms. His hard cock in my hands, my mouth. His fingers and tongue taking me over the edge again and again.

"Sparkling water sounds great for starters." *Then you.*

He rustled around in the cooler and handed me an icy can. The heated brush of his fingers contrasted with the cold aluminum. A delicious shiver backflipped up my arm and down my neck, raising goosebumps.

I took a long sip that did nothing to cool down my body. Not with his tanned hand resting on the tailgate three inches from my bare leg.

My thigh got busy recreating the sensation of his fingertips trailing over my sensitive skin. Tracing the line of muscle up the inside of my leg until I squirmed and begged him to go higher. *Touch me more.*

I shifted and crossed my legs, ignoring the ball of nervous tension and desire rolling around in my gut. Ignoring the prickling and wetness at the apex of my thighs. Determined to at least wait a few hours and find our footing together before I jumped him.

Because having sex too soon usually resulted in a guy leaving me. I would not fuck this up by falling into my old patterns. *At the very least, I can wait until we get back to my place.*

Taking another sip of soda, I stared in the direction of the mountains towering over us. But I watched Evan from the corner of my eyes.

He stared at me. Or at my legs, anyway. His gaze heated and traveled up my body to my chest. He captured the corner of his lower lip with his teeth.

The shimmer of electricity running down my spine and straight to my clit reminded me I wasn't wearing any underwear—like I needed any reminder.

Instantly, I wanted Evan inside me. As soon as possible.

EVAN

I'd never seen Jules in a dress before. And, wow.

She stared up at the snow-tipped peaks and ridges, and I let my gaze roam over her body, admiring the way the sundress exposed just enough cleavage, and highlighted her muscular shoulders. And the way it hitched up higher on one thigh than the other when she crossed her legs. Legs I was more than ready to run my hands along.

My balls tightened and my dick twitched, but I didn't want to scare her by coming on too strong, too fast. I settled for tugging on a couple of her curls and tucking them behind her ear. Then sliding my fingertips down the soft, sensitive line of her neck to her collarbone.

Goosebumps broke out across her topaz skin.

She tilted her head and met my gaze. "You are a cruel, cruel man."

"I'm cruel?" I traced the hard line of her collarbone with one finger.

She nodded, licking her lips.

"You're the one sitting there in that way too tempting little dress, with all that soft, freckled skin calling my name, when all I've dreamed about for the past three weeks is touching you." I followed the edge of her shoulder strap down with a barely-there touch. Her breath hitched. "Being with you."

She captured my hand, stopping me, and I thought for sure I'd gone too far, too fast. Then she brought my fingers to her lips and I melted. Except for my dick, which stood at full attention.

The heat of her mouth wrapped around my first two fingers, and if I thought I was hard before, I was wrong. So, so wrong. Stealing my fingers back, I slid my other hand into her curls and drew her closer.

Our mouths met in a greedy kiss and an explosion went off inside my chest. A mix of relief and desire flooded out to my finger and toes. She still wanted me as much as I wanted her.

Sliding my hands to her waist, I tugged. Jules straddled me, twining her arms around my neck and grinding against my rock-hard dick while she kissed me like I'd saved her life.

I ran my fingers along the hem of her skirt. Skated them up the inside of her thigh. Stroked the bottom curve of her ass. She quivered and ground into my hard-on, making it ache and throb.

Circling my thumbs around to the front of her hips I traced patterns in the hollow where thigh meets hip. Sliding down, I met the springy coils of her pubic hair.

She's not wearing underwear?

Fuck. Me. She's not wearing underwear.

"Do you have any idea what you do to me?" I whispered against her mouth, stroking down either side of her pussy. She rocked into my hands.

I rubbed across her clit, once. Twice. She whimpered into my mouth, hips twitching.

A semi-truck roared past, buffeting us with hot, pavement-scented wind. I jumped, remembering where we were, and tugged her skirt down. Shifting her off my lap, regret and need roughened my voice. "We probably should get you home before we go any further."

She stood and smoothed the front of her skirt, biting her lip. "I don't think this can wait."

"But what if a carload of kids drives by?" Just the thought made my stiffie go soft.

"Fair point." Jules tugged my hand. "Come on."

Giggling, we ran into the woods until the sun's bright reflection off car windshields disappeared behind us.

"Sit." She pushed my ass onto the rough bark of a downed tree trunk and climbed back into my lap. "Now, where were we?"

With a sexy grin she wrapped her arms and legs around like I'd imagined all those times in Boston, clinging to me like she never wanted to let go, and kissed me deep and hard.

Nothing had ever felt so good.

"Here?" I mumbled, cupping her ass. Slipping my fingers down to her pussy. Spreading her wetness all around and sliding one, then two, inside her heat. Reaching between us with my other hand I flicked her clit.

"MMMMMMmmmmmmm." She slid her lips to my cheek, my jaw, my neck, leaving a trail of fire behind.

"Please tell me you have a condom, Evan." Her whisper came out hoarse. Her breath tingled in my ear.

"I have a condom, Evan." Her giggle sent my heart fluttering. Something about making her laugh did it for me as much as anything. Standing, I set her on her feet, holding her close with one hand. She worked the buttons on my shirt, her tongue tracing a hot line down every inch of newly bared skin. Her teeth caught my nipple, sending shock waves to my balls.

I growled and picked her up, standing. Capturing her mouth with mine I spun us, sitting her ass on the fallen trunk and grinding into her. Rocking my hard-on against her sensitive clit.

Somehow, with one hand and no functioning brain, I fished out my wallet.

"Here." She snatched it from me, found the foil packet, and tore it open behind my back. The crinkle of a wrapper never sounded so good. "Unzip your shorts."

Smiling against her mouth, I let her legs drop. "As you wish."

"Fuck, I love the way you say that."

     Wild at Heart

This wasn't exactly how I imagined our first encounter would go. I'd been picturing hours spent giving her orgasm after orgasm in an actual bed, with an actual shower nearby to clean up and fuck in again after. But I wasn't about to say no.

The idea that she wanted me bad enough to drag me into the woods for a quickie before we got to her place was hot. We'd have plenty of time for long, slow, lovemaking later.

The snick-snick of my zipper descending vibrated against my hard-on. Jules's hand wrapped around my dick, warm and firm, and tugged it out of my pants.

I ran my fingers up her thighs, her hips, her ribs, taking the hem of her dress with me. She lifted her arms over her head, and I tugged the thin material off, and she stood naked in the sunlight like she didn't have a care in the world.

My ability to breathe disappeared, because I was staring at the most beautiful woman I'd ever seen, naked in one of the most beautiful places on earth. And she was mine.

Jules bent and sucked my dick into the wet heat of her mouth, staring up at me with those big brown eyes. The sun gleamed on her bare back, tiny dust motes floating in its rays like snowflakes. I dropped her dress on the ground and traced the silky skin on the sides of her breasts. Ran my hands down to her ass. Slid my fingers to her clit, making circles in the dampness.

Groaning, she pulled back and rolled the condom on. "Do you have any idea what you do to me?"

"Some." I smiled and turned her around, pressing between her shoulder blades until she braced her hands on the trunk. "Spread your legs."

She did as I asked, the swollen, pink folds of her pussy glistening in the sun. The sweet musk of sex swarmed my brain, overriding any thoughts. I bent and took a taste.

One long, slow swipe of my tongue along her crease. A circle around her entrance.

I caressed the curve of her ass, the pale skin smooth under my fingers, and slid my finger up and down her slit, collecting moisture. I let it slip in and out of her, so slick and wet.

"Damn, Evan." Jules glared over her shoulder. "Are you going to fuck me, or are you just going to tease me?"

My dick throbbed. "I'm not sure yet. It's a tough call."

I swirled my swollen head against her wet lips, dipped the tip into her, pulled back. She tossed her head back and moaned, low and deep, more like a growl.

Wrapping one hand tight around the base of my dick I stroked. Not to keep it hard, but because I couldn't help it. I slid one finger deep inside her, pumping it in and out in time to my strokes.

"Evan?"

"What? Can't you see I'm busy?"

She glanced at me again, eyebrows raised. One corner of her lips twitched. "Too busy to fuck me?"

"I'm getting to that. Just be patient."

"Patience is for suckers. I want you inside me now." She rolled her hips against my hand. "Pretty please?"

"Well, since you put it like that…" Stepping forward I pressed my head against her entrance. Jules grabbed my ass with one hand and tugged.

I slid into the hilt and froze, sinking into her tight, wet heat. Letting the shivers and spasms settle low in my gut. Taking a few deep breaths to gain at least a modicum of control, I eased out, and back in. Nice and slow.

Her nails bit into my skin. "Harder."

She didn't have to say please this time. Gripping her hips, I slammed into her, grunting, shock waves of pleasure radiating out through my body. Both hands braced against the trunk she rocked back, meeting every thrust.

My balls tightened, and I grit my teeth, holding back my release. Wanting to give her one first.

Reaching around, I slicked my fingers in her wetness and found the firm nub of her clit, rubbing it back and forth with light, fluttery strokes and pumping into her hard as I could.

"Oh. God." She moaned and bucked and shook. "Fuck. Evaaannnnnn."

Wrapping my other arm around her waist I slammed into her again and again, moving my hips faster and harder. Moving my fingers faster and harder. She clamped down on my dick and cried out, a low, guttural, scream. My orgasm unleashed bands of pleasure and tension tightening and loosening around my dick, my balls, my chest, my head.

I collapsed over her muscular back, holding her tight. Dropping kisses on her neck, her shoulders. Her scent filled my nose, a heated mix of pine, mint, baby powder and hot sex I couldn't get enough of.

"That, was amazing." I grabbed the base of my dick and pulled out, standing us up and holding her close. Nuzzling her hair.

"Mmm." Jules twisted around and kissed my chest. My dick twitched in my hand.

Laughter rang out in the near distance. Her gaze met mine and we both giggled. We couldn't be far from the parking lot, or even the trail. A frisson of excitement ran down my spine as I tied the condom in a knot. She stepped away, picking up her dress and shaking it out.

The sex we'd had before was fun and playful, or sweet, or emotional. This was different—raw, and needy, and hot as hell. I never realized sex came in so many flavors, and with Jules, I liked them all.

Pulling her dress on and smoothing the skirt down over her luscious bottom, she sighed. "I suppose we should hit the road. I am beyond ready for a hot shower."

"As long I can join you." I smiled at the image of her naked and wet, with runnels of soap coursing down her back, and her ass, and my slick hands gliding over her skin. My dick twitched again.

"Will you scrub my back?"

"I, am an excellent back scrubber."

"Deal." She smiled back, the gleam in her eyes making me giddy. I floated along behind her to the parking lot, like a balloon on a string, my gaze glued to her ass and the swaying hem of her dress. Knowing she wasn't wearing underwear, and we'd be in car together for the next couple hours, made me rock hard. Again. Already.

Though that did nothing compared to knowing she wanted me, and we'd have all the time in the world to laugh and tease and fuck and make love in Seattle.

CHAPTER 37

JULES

Maybe I should've been upset I gave in so easy. But that was impossible. Not when I was sitting in the passenger seat of Evan's rental car with full-on post-orgasm glow, his fingers tracing lines and circles on my knee. Up my thigh.

The way he smiled like he'd won the lottery every time he glanced over would've been enough to make it worthwhile. But damn, I couldn't wipe the grin off my own face either. The same one that had been stuck there since our first kiss in the parking lot.

Especially when he practically exploded with excitement about his summer camp idea.

His enthusiasm was infectious. I peppered him with question and had to admit he'd thought it out pretty well. If I was sold, surely other people would be too.

One tanned hand gripped the steering wheel. "Ok, so are these cherries any good? I've never seen a yellow cherry before."

"Oh my God, Rainier cherries are the best. Yellow on the inside too, and super sweet. They don't taste anything like a Bing cherry." I pulled two small, round fruits out of the bag resting next to my leg and held one out to him. "Try one. But watch out for the pit."

He popped it in his mouth, pulled out the stem, and chewed. His face went slack and his chewing slowed. His eyelids drooped a little. A drop of cherry juice trickled from the corner of his lips. He licked it away and smiled. "That's amazing. How have I never heard of Rainier cherries before?"

"They're a smaller, local crop that got hybridized here. I don't think they get shipped very far outside of Washington. I'm surprised you even found any this late in the season."

"Lucky me." He squeezed my leg.

"Lucky us." I squeezed his hand, grinning so hard my face ached.

We rolled down our windows and spit our pits, the cool, asphalt-scented wind whipping my curls in my eyes. I fed him another cherry. "So, how's your dad doing? Is he out of the hospital yet?"

"No idea. Haven't talked to him." Evan shrugged and spat his pit with a soft thwpth. His nonchalance couldn't cover the cool tension radiating off him. Or the way his palm stilled against my thigh.

"What do you mean?"

"Well, he came out of his coma before I left." He moved his hand from my thigh to the steering wheel. "That's all I can tell you, consider-ing he basically disowned me."

"Wait. What?" I twisted in my seat to look at him. "Did you talk to him before you left?"

"I guess you could say that, though I'm not sure how much he heard." He shook his head. "You'd think almost dying would make a father want to be closer to his kids, to support them and love them unconditionally. Not mine."

"Shit. What happened?" I reached over and squeezed his leg, not really knowing what else to do or say. He flicked his gaze to me, eyes tight at the corners instead of wide and sparkling with excitement.

"We had an argument the first night I was home. I wanted to show him my plans for the camp. He wanted me to stay on the path he'd mapped out without even giving me a chance. Instead, he gave me an ultimatum…Either toe the family line or lose my inheritance. I walked out."

"Oh, no." I struggled to process his words. I mean, how could a father do that?

"Oh yes." His knuckles whitened on the wheel. "When he woke up from the coma, I hoped he'd have a change of heart—because doesn't the villain always? But apparently it doesn't work that way in real life. So, I left. At this point, Father can go to hell for all I care."

"I'm so sorry, Evan." My fingers caressed his knee on their own, sliding across the springy hairs in circles, while I worked to parse this news. "What about your mother?"

He rolled his eyes. "She'll do whatever Father tells her, so I don't expect to hear from her anytime soon."

"So—" I croaked. A bald eagle with at least a six-foot wingspan had taken up residence in my throat. I swallowed it down and tried again. "So, basically, you gave up your family, your fiancé, your career, and your inheritance to move out here and be with me?"

I held my breath, waiting for the answer. Emerald evergreen trees whizzed by my window.

"Not exactly." He glanced at me. "My brother and I are still on good terms, and he's the only person I really care about."

My hand stilled of its own accord. I pulled it into my lap. "That's good, I guess, but it still seems like a lot to give up."

"Not when you consider everything I'm getting in exchange. Money isn't worth much if it doesn't make you happy. I'd rather have a career that's fulfilling and do something good for the world." He lips tilted up. He captured my hand and brought it to his lips, brushing a soft, sweet kiss on the back. "And be with you."

Those last words held the most weight. Tons of it. All of which came crashing down on my chest until I couldn't breathe. Because right then he didn't have the career or business. He just had me.

The interior of the car shrunk, and my heart expanded to watermelon size and throbbed inside my ribcage. My throat.

He kept talking, something about finding an apartment and his business idea. I tried to focus on his words, but my mind whirled.

This was supposed to be my chance to prove to myself I could love someone again, and I deserved love. But I couldn't be his everything. The pressure was way too much, especially since I couldn't be trusted not to fuck this up.

If I did, on top of getting his heart broken, he'd have ruined his life for nothing.

Fuck.

EVAN

Cool wind whipped into the car through our open windows, balancing out the warm sun beaming on the windshield. My mouth held the sweet taste of those amazing Rainier cherries.

"Okay, enough about me." I gave Jules's small hand a squeeze. "Tell me all about the rest of your hike. How was it?"

"It drizzled pretty much the entire Stevens Pass section, starting about a day after you left for Boston."

"That's a bummer." I shivered at the memory of huddling under my rainfly in a downpour the night we met, wearing shorts.

"Not really. Even though you can't always see the peaks, there's a tranquil beauty to the swirling fog and pattering raindrops that fits the whole rainforest motif. The weather was sunny most of this last section, though."

"It still blows my mind you hiked over four hundred miles. I really wish I could've been out there with you for the last part."

"Yeah. You would've loved it. This last week alone I saw maybe five hikers, and one bear across a drainage. And I ate enough huckleberries to last me until next year." Her voice had an odd flatness. Or maybe I was reading her tone wrong.

"So, with all that solitary trail time, did you decide what you want to do career-wise?" I popped another cherry in my mouth, savoring the sugar and caramel flavored juiciness.

"Sort of."

Jules's voice had definitely gone flat instead of following its usual, excited up and down pattern. I glanced over at her, sitting in the passenger seat, slowly chewing a cherry and staring out her open window.

"I'm sorry. I didn't mean to pry." What I really wanted to do was ask, "Is something wrong?", but I was scared to know if something was wrong—especially between us.

"No. It's okay." She spit her pit with a forceful thwap. "It's just, I thought I had it all figured out—I would fire all my small clients and live off the large ones while I made a transition to something else. Only while I was home, I found out my largest client let me go. So now I'm back at square one. Or maybe square negative one, since my bottom line is taking a pretty big hit."

"That sucks." I squeezed her hand again. It stayed limp in my palm. "I'm sorry I brought it up. I'm already ruining your post-trail glow and you haven't even made it home yet."

"Yeah. I could happily not think about my business for at least another couple of hours."

I wanted to talk more about my business plans but sharing my excitement didn't seem right. I wracked my brain for another topic and came up empty. We'd talked for hours on the trail, and we hadn't seen each other in more than three weeks, yet somehow, we'd run out of things to say.

"Mind if I take a nap? I didn't get much sleep last night."

"No. No. Go ahead."

She shifted, leaning her head back and closing her eyes. I released her hand. In a few minutes her breathing evened out. Trees and mountains whipped by. We sped past the shimmering, blue-green waters of Ross Lake.

Every chance I got I glanced over, studying her pert-nosed profile, and the freckles sprinkled across her nose and cheeks. Memorizing the way her hair curled around her cheeks. Resisting rubbing her neck or stroking her thigh might've been harder than walking out of Father's hospital room.

We hit I-5 and all my attention went to navigating traffic and following my phone's directions to her condo. I parallel parked in front of a tallish brick building. "Hey, Jules. You're home." I gave her shoulder a small shake. "Time to wake up."

"What?" She rubbed her eyes, confusion clouding her features, and looked from me to her front door. "Oh. Okay. Thanks."

I popped the hatch, slung her pack over one shoulder, and headed for the entrance. The air smelled like hot coffee and the musky salt of low tide.

"You don't need to carry that." She grabbed her dirty clothes bag from the back seat and trotted after me.

"I know. But I want to."

Her hand landed on my shoulder. "Seriously. I've carried that pack for miles with way more weight in it. I'm good."

"I'm not trying to carry it because I think you can't." I smiled. "I just don't believe chivalry is dead yet."

Her mumbled words were obliterated by a car horn, but I'm pretty sure she said, "Maybe it's time to shoot it, then."

Jules cleared her throat, shuffling from one foot to the other. "Ummmmm…Listen, I'm exhausted. If it's okay with you, I think I'm just going to go up and crash."

"I can snuggle you until you fall asleep, if you want." I brushed the curls away from her cheek, the way I'd wanted to in the car. "And take care of dinner."

"Thanks, but I really need some alone time. To adjust." She looked at the wall over my shoulder, her backpack sitting on the pavement at our feet—everything except my face.

"You sure you don't want your back scrubbed."

"Thanks, but I'm good." She still didn't look at me. "Maybe a rain check?"

A band tightened around my chest. "Sure. How about breakfast tomorrow, then?"

She huffed out a breath. "I'm not sure what time I'll wake up."

"Lunch, then? Or a hike? Or dinner? I'm wide open, so whatever works for you, works for me." I tried to keep the needy whine out of my voice, but I wasn't one hundred percent successful.

"I'm meeting Bryn and Aly for dinner tomorrow night—it's tradition. And my knee needs a break from hiking. Why don't you text me in the morning and we'll see?"

My heart hammered in slow motion, each beat reverberating like a gong, shaking me from head to toe. "Are you sure you're not trying to take a break from me?"

"No, no. It's not that at all." She grabbed her pack by the carry strap behind the top lid and pivoted toward the wood and glass door of her building.

"Then what is it?" I dropped my palm on her bare shoulder, stopping her. "Talk to me, Jules."

She turned back, lips in a hard line, eyes holding a mixture of sadness and fear. "I'm sorry, Evan, but I need some time to think."

"Think about what?" I tangled my fingers in hers. "All I'm asking you to do is hang out."

"I'm not sure I can." She pulled her hand back and stared at the pavement. "I mean, I like you. A lot. And I really wanted to make it work. But we barely know each other, and you gave up everything — literally everything — to move here and be with me. That's a lot of pressure…"

"I like you a lot too, Jules, but there's no pressure. While you were certainly one good reason to move to Seattle, you weren't the only one." I slid a finger under her chin and tilted her face up until her gaze met mine. "I also like Seattle's combinations of mountains, city, and ocean. It seems like the perfect place to start my non-profit, so I'd probably be here whether we'd ever met or not. But I'm really glad we did, and I'm hoping you'll give us a chance."

"I want to, Evan. I told myself I would. I just don't know how. I'm sorry." She closed her eyes and took a deep, shuddering breath. When she opened them, they glittered with unshed tears. "I'll just end up breaking your heart. And you don't deserve that."

"I'll take my chances."

"What if I'm not ready to take mine?" She swallowed, throat rolling hard. "I thought I was, I really did. I wanted to be. But a big part of me didn't expect you to show up. Now that you're here, and you gave up do damn much to be here, it's a lot. I need some time to come to terms with all of this."

My lungs wouldn't expand enough to take a decent breath.

She wanted to be ready. Past tense.

"How much time are you thinking?"

I'm not sure." A single tear slid down through her freckles as she undid my leather bracelet and pressed it into my hand. "Here. I'm sorry."

"It's okay. I know you're scared. You have every right to be. You've been dealt some shitty hands in the past." I brushed the tear away with my thumb and blinked against the sting behind my own eyelids. "But something tells me we could be amazing together. And I live here now, so I'm not going anywhere."

She blinked a few times fast. I couldn't tell if what I said made her feel better or worse, but at least she didn't try to leave. I clutched my bracelet, the beads digging into my palm.

"I don't know when, or if, I'll ever be ready, Evan. It's not fair to you."

"I get to decide what's fair to me." I looked into her eyes, trying to let her know how much I cared about and supported her. "But I'm not sure you're being fair to yourself either. You can't keep running away every time someone gets close."

"Maybe I'm not ready to let someone get close yet."

"Maybe you're not. If that means you're going to struggle with this for a while, that's okay. If it means we end up being friends instead, that's okay too. Just don't cut me out of your life completely." The last few words reverberated in my head, too tight and high-pitched.

Thoughts and emotions ran across her face like a stream down a mountainside, mixed together in a white froth so I couldn't distinguish any single one.

"I won't call if you don't want me to, but I like you. As a person, a friend. I'd like to be able to text you." I took the deepest breath my tight chest would allow and continued. "You don't even have to respond, if you don't want."

Cars rumbled by. Horns honked in the distance. My heart slammed around inside my shrunken chest cavity at high speed, like a gumball machine super ball bouncing erratically in a too small space.

"Okay."

"Okay."

CHAPTER 38

EVAN

I slid my keycard into the lock. The light flashed green, and I shoved open the door to my brown and gold hotel room with my hip. Wrinkling my nose at the musty, bleach-tinged air, I dropped my soft cooler and overnight bag by the door and flopped across the king-size bed.

My head throbbed. My heart ached.

Walking away from Jules hadn't been easy. Everything inside me screamed I needed to stay. That if we spent time together everything would go back to the way it was—natural and fun and easy. Except it didn't matter that I knew we were perfect together. She had to let me in.

I slid my phone from my pocket and speed dialed. John picked up on the second ring.

"Hey, bro. What's up? How are things in Seattle?"

"Generally speaking? Good. With Jules, I have absolutely zero clue. One minute she's hot—and I mean scorching—and the next she's glacial."

"So, I'm guessing you slept with her before you told her about losing your trust fund."

Groaning, I threw a pillow over my face, wishing I could hide my head under it like an ostrich and wait for this situation to go away. "I didn't plan to, but I couldn't turn her down."

"Well, then can you blame her? You did leave everything and move across the country to be with her. That's pretty heavy when you've only been dating for a couple weeks."

"I know, but it seemed like one hundred percent the right thing to do when I left. It didn't occur to me it might be a problem for Jules. Now she's completely freaked out and doesn't want me around." Rolling to my side, I cuddled the pillow, the soft cotton cool on my cheek.

"Did you talk to her? Ask her what she wanted?"

"I tried, but I don't think she knows." I pinched my temples with my thumb and forefinger. "She's got issues she's working through, and I just made them worse, not better. I get that. I'm willing to give her time, I just wish I knew what's going through her head."

"You, and a few billion other people on the planet trying to navigate relationships." He laughed, more rueful than happy. "That's been the one good thing about my situation. I haven't had to worry about serious relationships in years."

"I admit I'm a little jealous. My life would be easier, and I could use something going easier right now." I got up and closed the curtains.

"But it wouldn't be near as exciting."

"True."

"Speaking of things going easier..." He hesitated. "What would you say to a fundraiser for your camp? I've been putting out feelers, and I think we could generate plenty of support from the usual open-checkbook crowd. When you're ready."

A spark of excitement crackled somewhere deep inside. I tamped it down. "Why would they support an excommunicated Davenport?"

"Well, Father isn't exactly shouting about that from the rooftops. Wouldn't be good for our reputation." John snickered. "You know, if you make this happen, you could become the new, celebrated altruistic hero of the family."

"I don't know how I feel about shouldering Uncle Martin's mantle, but a fundraiser would be terrific." I ran dates in my head. "Let's plan it for early November, before the holiday season gets in full swing. That should give me enough time to get ready. Especially since I have nothing else to do."

Except pine for Jules. I gripped my scalp, pressing hard enough my fingertips ached.

"Relax, Evan. Everything is going to work out. I've got a good feeling."

"Good like that time you made a mint on the Rexler IPO?"

John's deep, ringing laugh rolled through the phone. "Better, bro. Better."

If only I could believe that. "So, what should I do about Jules? She agreed to let me text her, but she didn't want to, so should I text her? If so, how often? Or should I wait for her to text me?" John was always good at navigating people. Another of his traits I didn't inherit. "I don't want to be a stalker, but I think time apart is the problem. When we're together, everything works. When we're apart she overthinks it and gets scared."

"Text her when you have something to share. Be her friend— whatever that would normally look like if you moved to a new town where you only had one friend."

"So, every hour on the hour then?"

"Bro—"

"Kidding."

JULES

Vanilla-scented steam surrounded me. Almost-scalding water pounded my neck and shoulders. Neither did a thing to relax my over-tight muscles. But I'd spent most of the day moping around my condo in sweatpants and I needed to do something. Anything.

Other than spend another minute trying to decide which was harder, being with Evan, or pushing him away. Or why all the parts of me couldn't get on board with the same plan. Cutting the water, I grabbed a towel, scrubbing my skin with the rough fabric until it turned pink and tingled.

Heartache and regret swamped my mouth with a flavor a lot like burned coffee. When we'd been on the trail, everything seemed clear. We were perfect together. Meant to be. When he left for Boston, I thought the hard part would be waiting for him to come back.

Now nothing seemed clear, and everything seemed too damn difficult.

My body wanted him, bad. My heart was on the fence. My head was a definite hell no.

I yanked on jeans and a long-sleeve cotton shirt, snagged my phone off the counter, and hit speed dial.

"Good afternoon, Teller Jones Realty. How can I help you?"

"Hey, Aly."

"Jules! Welcome back. What's up?"

"Are you and Bryn busy tonight for happy hour?" I held my breath, hoping.

"No. Why? Aren't you busy gettin' busy with your hottie?"

Closing my eyes, I searched for an answer that wouldn't start a phone interrogation. "I needed some alone time to unpack and get my head together. Take care of a few things."

"Well, hopefully you took care of plenty of things with him already." She giggled, and images swarmed through my head of Evan, shirt open, chest golden in the sun. His fingers, his cock, pounding into me. The tenderness in his eyes, his touch, his voice, when he held me close and told me how much he wanted me.

Fuck.

Too many things. And it's all your fault.

Aly's emotional radar turned on with an almost audible click. "You all right, hon?"

"Honestly, I'm not sure."

"Well, nothing like margaritas and girlfriends to help figure it out." Her voice came through bright and cheery. As always. "Bryn's free as soon as she finishes up with her last clients. I'll drop her a text and we'll meet you at Amigos in thirty."

It took me ten minutes to get to the restaurant, grab our favorite table, and order drinks. And less than ten to suck one down. I hefted the thick glass pitcher, ice cubes clinking, and refilled my glass.

"Hey, hon."

"Hey, Jules. Good to have you back."

Aly and Jules wrapped me in a double hug, their arms warm and strong and safe. Aly's familiar lemon and rose perfume cut through the hot corn chip and melted cheese aroma.

Relief coursed through me, and my shoulders dropped more than they had since Evan's big revelation in the car. Letting me go, they pulled out barstools, the legs screeching on the concrete floor.

"Pour a couple more of those, would you?"

I filled their empty goblets. Taking a seat, Aly picked up her glass. "To fantastic vacations and hot men." She watched me over her rim, questions in her eyes.

Bryn echoed Aly and we all clinked. The salt on my rim burned my lips and tongue.

"Okay. Spill it. What's going on?" Bryn stared at me.

Much as I wanted their support, I didn't know how to explain it. And I wasn't sure I wanted to try. It was all still too raw and confusing. "Spill what?"

Aly plunked her glass down. "Don't play innocent. You just got back from more than a month in the woods—which you claim to love better than a beach vacation, not that I'll ever understand why—and the sexy naked man you met, who's crazy about you, moved here to be with you. So why are you sitting in the henhouse with us instead of boning his brains out?"

"It's not that simple."

"Maybe it could be that simple if you let it." Aly waved her peach-painted fingers around.

"No, it can't. It's more than I can handle. The way he looks at me, the way he touches me, the things he says to me…I want to kiss him as much as I want to run away screaming because it feels like something inside me is going to break open." I pointed at Aly. "And this is all your fault, you know."

"And you, are making about as much sense as a chocolate teapot."

"You switched my change of clothes." I glared at her, her oblivious smile pissing me off more. "How was leaving me with a sundress and no fucking underwear supposed to help me take it slow with Evan?"

Bryn eyes widened to margarita goblet size. "Aly! You didn't?"

"I was just trying to help." She ducked her head and spun the stem on her glass. "I mean, you put that bag together pre-Evan. Seemed wrong to greet your new hottie wearing baggie ol' shorts and an over-sized t-shirt. So, I popped by your apartment and grabbed your favorite dress."

"Fine. Okay. I get that part. But no underwear?"

"Oh, come on Jules. Y'all were fuckin' like bunnies half the trip, and I haven't seen a man that head over heels for you, ever. Why on God's green earth would I think you'd want to do anything other than jump his bones immediately?"

"Because you know my history." I slammed my glass on the table too hard. "You know I'm scared of diving in too fast and getting hurt."

"I also know it's high time you gave someone a chance again."

"But we all agreed I should take it slow—if he even showed up again."

Aly raised one eyebrow. "I agreed to no such thing. We did agree that *when* he came back, you'd give him a chance."

"I tried. Except, I found out he not only left his friends and family, he had a fight with his dad and gave up his trust fund to move here. To be with me." I slid my fingers up and down the damp sides of my goblet. "That is way too much pressure. More than I can handle. So, it isn't going to work out. And now I'll never be able to wear that damn sundress again, thanks to you."

"Wait." Bryn's hand landed on my forearm. "Tell me you didn't dump him already."

"Not entirely, but that's my plan. He wants to stay friends, and I agreed to let him text me." My eyeballs stung. I took a big, sour swig of my drink, letting the tequila burn its way through the lump in my throat.

"So, you're saying God, or the universe, or whatever you want to call it..." Aly waved her peach nails around again. "...put a smart, sexy, naked man in your path in the middle of nowhere not once, not twice, but three times, and he blew your mind—"

"Sort of."

"—and he's crazy about you, and you're crazy about him, and he moved to Seattle to be with you, and you're just going to walk away on the first day because he gave up a trust fund for you?"

When she put it that way, it sounded stupid and shortsighted. I looked to Bryn for support.

"She has a point, you know." Bryn gave my arm a squeeze. "It sounds pretty romantic, and it's not often you get that many chances. Especially with a man you're really into, who clearly adores you. Even after he's seen the fucked-up parts of you."

"Hey now." I balled a cocktail napkin and threw it at her. "I don't have any fucked-up parts. I am perfect, and you know it."

"If you were so perfect, we wouldn't be sitting here, and you know it. Lucky for you, your imperfections are a big part of why I love you." Bryn grinned and threw the napkin ball back, pegging me in the shoulder. "And I think they're part of what Evan loves about you too. Maybe you shouldn't be so quick to throw that away."

I topped off my glass and considered her words. When I broke down bawling in the tent, Evan didn't shy away. He held me and soothed me and made love to me like I was the most wonderful, precious thing on earth.

And today, he'd been nothing but sweet and supportive, even I when I confused the hell out of him. Even when I could see the pain tightening the lines on his face.

Ironically, the problem was that sweetness. That caring. It's what scared me most. Evan wanted to hand me his heart on a platter and I was all thumbs.

I shook my head. "I'm bound to fuck this up because I always do. He doesn't deserve the heartbreak. Better to cut both our losses now, before it hurts more."

"Shouldn't Evan be the one who decides whether or not to risk his heart?" Bryn's words echoed Evan's a little too closely.

"Maybe…?"

"Besides, you know it's bad luck to kick a gift horse in the nuts, Jules." Aly's bright voice cut through the bar noise. "Especially one delivering love right to your door. Do that too many times and the gift horse might never come back." She finished with a flourish and swig of her drink.

"Can't really blame him either." Bryn snickered into her glass. "The gift horse, I mean."

I snickered a little too, then sobered.

Aly had a point. A couple of them, in fact.

Points I would've wholeheartedly agreed with except every time I was alone and let the emotions roll through me—Evan's, mine—I lost my equilibrium. My head spun and I got disoriented, like losing sight of the landing on a hard vault.

Then the walls closed in. My heart raced. My palms went clammy. And painful cracks ran through my heart.

Aly's expression went serious. "I think you should give it a chance, hon."

"If I could ever get the panic attacks to stop, I would. So, if you've got any bright ideas on that front, I'm all ears. Until then, Evan and I are dead in the water. And I'm hungry." I flagged our server, and we ordered our usuals.

Bryn tapped her lower lip with one short fingernail and stared wide-eyed at the wall across the room. A wall that held nothing more interesting than a plant in a painted pot and a pair of sconces.

I knew that look. She was parsing options. I couldn't decide if that made me nervous or relieved.

Fresh chips and salsa landed on our table. Bryn blinked.

Hoisting the heavy glass pitcher, she topped off our drinks. "You know, you two don't really know each other off the trail. So maybe he's right. Maybe you should try being friends for a bit. Take the pressure off and find out if you're really compatible before you stress out about the future of your relationship. Or lack thereof."

"Honestly, I'm not sure I can even be around him without wanting to either jump his bones or run away and curl up in a corner." I clutched the bowl of my glass, pressing my fingertips into it until they went flat and white. "Sometimes both in less than an hour."

"So, don't spend time with him in person. Take baby steps." Bryn twirled her glass. "Commit to texting with him for a month. That's long enough to figure out what you want to do, but not so long it feels like forever. You might find you have nothing to say to each other, and viola, problem solved."

"I don't know…" I closed my eyes and imagined texting with Evan. The jokes and movie quotes and deep thoughts. My heart sped up, but I couldn't stop the corners of my mouth twitching. "I'll think about it."

"What's there to think about, hon? Seems like a good way to keep your anxiety at bay and still give y'all's relationship more than an ice cube's chance of surviving hell."

I looked from Bryn's thoughtful expression to Aly's smiling, supportive one, searching for a good argument. My fingertips ached against the hard glass.

"Fine. I'll try. But just texting. And just for a month—no longer."

"You got this." Bryn patted my hand.

"Ain't nothing to it but to do it." Aly raised her glass with a lascivious smirk. "So here's to doing it!"

"Here's to doing it," we echoed.

Bryn voice held way more enthusiasm than mine, but I clinked glasses with both of them. Inside, I vowed to not let it go any further than a distant, electronic friendship that I could let peter out in a few weeks.

That was the safest course of action. For both of us.

CHAPTER 39

JULES

Stretching out in my bed, I cracked one eye open. Bright sun seared my tequila-laced brain. I winced and slammed it shut. Cobwebs and cat crap covered my teeth and tongue.

Shots for dessert had seemed like an ideal way to forget about Evan for a while. I'd come home drunk enough to pass out without brushing my teeth, but unfortunately, not drunk enough to avoid dreaming about him.

Dreaming that he'd been here, making love to me. That he'd slept in my bed, and I had the best night's sleep of my life splayed naked across his chest, his arms wrapped tight around me.

Grumbling, I peeled myself out of my twisted sheets and shuffled into the kitchen, shading my eyes with my hand. Normally I loved all the natural light in my condo.

I should've bought blackout shades.

My coffee grinder tried to split my head in two, but it was worth it for that first sip of hot, dark, acrid brew. And the second and third sips, too.

On the trail I drank a lot of tea, but this hangover called for the strongest, blackest coffee. And a handful of ibuprofens chased down by a very large glass of water. Followed by a large, greasy breakfast of eggs, toast, and hash browns at the café down the street.

My phone light blinked. I flipped it over, glanced at the notifications, and dropped it on the counter with a clatter. My heart took off at full speed, like it was sprinting toward the vault horse.

It's just a text. It's not like he's at my door, looking all sexy and fuckable with that mussed hair and those soulful, dark-wash denim blue eyes.

My heart picked up the pace again, but in a different way.

Slow, Jules. Slow.

Ignoring temptation, I picked up my mug and took a sip. And another. Sucking in deep, smooth breaths of coffee-scented air, I worked to calm my still-racing heart.

Thanking the universe my clients didn't know I was back yet, I focused on my plan…Grab breakfast, pick up groceries, maybe fit in a run.

The ding of my phone snatched all my attention.

Fingers tingling, I leaned my hip on the counter and counted to twenty. If I was doing this, I was doing it on my own terms. With boundaries.

That meant not answering his texts immediately, like I had nothing better to do than wait for him to message me.

I sipped my coffee until nothing remained but a dark brown stain in the bottom of my mug. I drummed my fingertips on the counter. I debated a shower.

In a moment of weakness, I grabbed my phone and opened my texts.

—Lease signed on new apartment. As of today, I am officially a Seattleite! —

—Where's the best place to buy furniture cheap around here? —

A combo of, "Ohmygod, he's really serious about staying!", and "Oh. My. God. He's really serious about staying.", ran in circles in my head.

The coffee in my stomach rolled, launched a double back flip, and totally missed the landing. Closing my eyes, I ignored the caustic churning and searched for the right response. The one a friend would give another friend. Because the least I could do was be supportive since he didn't know anyone else, and he'd moved to Seattle for me.

Grimacing, I thumbed my keypad.

—Congrats! Where? —

—Fremont. 39th & Aurora. —

Not even two miles away. Close enough to run or bike over.

Close enough for a quickie.

NO!

—Nice. Great neighborhood. Try Design on a Dime for good consignment furniture cheap. —

The little dots kept spinning, but no text came through. I flipped the phone face down and ran water into my mug.

DING

I jerked. Shutting the faucet, I wiped my hands dry on my t-shirt and checked the screen.

—I'm headed out for a run+drink to celebrate this afternoon. Let me know if you're interested...—

My thumbs hovered over the keys while I imagined Evan in nothing more than running shorts and shoes, droplets of sweat glistening on his ripped abs. Tight tingles raced along my skin.

Boundaries, Jules. Boundaries. Stick to the plan.

—Sorry. Super busy day. Enjoy your new place and congrats again! —

Plugging in the charging cord, I abandoned my phone, and all contact with Evan, and headed for a hot shower. Evan and I, we were just trail lust anyway. If I kept him at arms' length for a few weeks the attraction would fade, and I could ghost him.

Then he'd head back to his wealthy family, his trust fund, and his beautiful ex-fiancé.

CHAPTER 40

EVAN

The rush and whir of traffic filtered through my apartment window at a steady, low hum. Sitting at the kitchen counter, I stared at the six black and white design concepts on my screen and scratched my head.

None of them came close to portraying Aspire Academy the way I envisioned. Because, with a stronger focus on leadership and communication skills, and environmental stewardship, Aspire offers more than the usual climbing, backpacking, orienteering curriculum. It would offer kids the chance to test themselves in new situations, lead groups, and make a difference. At the same time, a sliding fee scale letting at least half the kids attend for free would help ensure a more diverse group of campers.

Thinking about it got me more excited than I'd ever been about anything—other than Jules. These designs did the opposite. Not that I knew how to create my vision yet.

Even though I'd spent the past two weeks trying to figure out.

So far, I knew I wanted to help these kids develop their communication, teamwork and interpersonal skills, and self-esteem and curiosity and ingenuity. And I knew I wanted kids from all walks of life together.

I just didn't know how to portray all of that in a logo. Or explain it in a way that a designer would understand so they could put it in a logo, apparently.

Jules would get it right away.

Too bad I couldn't hire her to work on the project with me. I might not have the highest emotional IQ in the world, but even I knew that would be breaking her rules.

That's why I'd contracted two of the best outdoor industry specific branding firms in Seattle to come up with initial concepts. Except half of the logos looked like they were for either day care or new age centers, and the other half looked either too fancy and expensive, or too modern and hip.

I wanted something earthier, more old school but still youthful. Something that said trust *and* adventure, with a focus on leadership and success.

Gray morning fog swirled outside my apartment window. The dregs of my coffee pooled in the bottom of my plain, white mug.

I'd promised Jules space, and I kept my promises. Even though giving her space over the past two weeks was about as much fun as almost drowning during a river crossing. Because her definition of space meant I sent her amusing and personal tidbits daily, and she responded every couple of days with the most polite, vague, and evasive texts ever.

Each time she seemed just this side of ghosting me, and I didn't know what to do or say. I wanted to be the new, stronger version of me that went after what I wanted. Except the new Jules didn't want the new me. She wanted space.

Asking for her professional opinion seemed like it might be fair game, though. I wouldn't be asking her to actually work with me, just look at what I had and give me some advice and direction.

My heart thumped and banged around my chest. Before I could chicken out, I texted her the logos.

—First round designs. What do you think? —

The instant I hit send, my heart rate tripled, and worry rippled down my spine like I was halfway through a tri with a bad calf cramp forming, instead of sitting at my kitchen counter. I wanted to sit there and fidget for however many hours until Jules responded.

Instead, I headed to the bedroom, grabbed my swimsuit, goggles, and towel, and gathered my road biking kit. A hard workout would do me good. And the saltwater swimming pool in West Seattle I'd heard about seemed a perfect distance away to combine with a training ride.

My phone chimed. One leg in my bike shorts, I speed-hobbled across my apartment and snatched it off the counter.

—Third from the left isn't horrible. —

A hard guffaw shot out of my throat.

—How very diplomatic of you. Now tell me what you really think? —

The dots in the corner of my screen spun.

—Based on what I know about Aspire, none of these comes close to hitting the mark. Who did you hire? —

—Not telling, but I agree. Any thoughts on how to steer them in a better direction? I'm lost. —

     Wild at Heart

JULES

One glance at Evan's logos and I knew they were way off base. Sitting on my couch I clutched my phone, watching the dots spiral. Visions of a school shield whose outline formed a mountaintop raced through my head.

I could nail it in a heartbeat.

Not that I would.

Evan was lost. Again. And every ounce of me wanted to rescue him.

Again.

Partly because I couldn't forget the slow, delicious build of sexual tension between us every time I'd rescued him on the trail. Or how damn good it felt when I finally gave in to it.

Partly because I missed his company. His laugh. His movie quotes. The way he held me when I broke down crying.

A little bit because I loved that he asked for help.

Not that it made any difference. Working with him would only make things harder.

Fuck.

I took a deep breath, all the way down to the depths of my gut and exhaled loud. It didn't help. I'd thought a couple weeks apart would be enough for the attraction to fade. Only the more I texted with him the more I missed him.

I missed his sense of humor, and the way his brain worked. And I liked that he didn't push. He gave me the space I asked for but didn't disappear.

The more I liked him, the more I missed him, and the harder it became to keep up my walls.

My phone screen didn't hold any answers. No matter how badly I wished it would turn into an enchanted mirror and tell me what to do.

Aly and Bryn would say I should help him. As a friend. And because Aspire was a good cause.

Except being around him would be too risky. Make it too easy to get closer. I couldn't do closer. Not yet. Maybe not ever.

Thumbs poised, I considered what to say. Typed words and deleted them. For twenty damn minutes.

I threw the phone face down on the couch beside me with a growl.

If I was going to help him communicate his vision, I needed more info about Aspire. I'd learned years ago if I sent prospective clients a questionnaire, I wouldn't get near enough info to do my job well.

That's why I met with clients in person, or via video chat, to go through the questions together. No way was I ready to hear Evan's voice or his laugh. Let alone see his face, with those twinkling lapis eyes, and that oh-so-kissable mouth with the power to make my toes curl.

Still, ideas for his logo kept banging around in my head, demanding attention. And I did want to help.

Since he wasn't actually a client, I didn't need that much info. Just enough to make sure I pointed him in the right direction. I snatched my phone off the cushion.

—What's your email? —

He texted back in seconds. I grabbed my laptop and forwarded a copy of my usual client intake questions along with instructions.

Once I had his answers, it'd take a matter of minutes to send him my thoughts. Then he could go back to whichever design firm he preferred and get a better result. Win, win.

CHAPTER 41

JULES

Searching for the right combo of hip, fun and outdoorsy, yet serious and trustworthy, I clicked on my screen and changed the logo font again. I stared at the Trajan font, assessing, and bolded it. Using my mouse, I tugged the top corner of the mirrored triangles forming the shield, creating a little more white space for a cleaner look.

Perfection.

All three of my designs fit the bill, but this one made my heart race in the best possible way.

Evan had sent the intake questionnaire back to me later that day. Amazingly, his answers were damn detailed and complete. Each time I read through his mission statement, goals, target market—even his planned sales and marketing channels—I was more impressed. And more excited.

That's what going to business school does for you.

That, and being smart as shit.

If he accomplished even a fraction of his goals, Aspire had the potential to make a huge difference for kids lucky enough to attend.

I couldn't believe his initial designs were so far off base. If his designers didn't understand what he wanted based on this info, a little feedback wasn't going to do the trick. "Scrap these and start over." wasn't going to be super helpful either.

Instead, I'd worked on fresh logos a few hours last night and this morning. Smiling, I attached my three designs to an email.

—

Evan,

I thought it might be easier to show your design firm one or two sample logos to get them on the right track. So, I whipped these up super quick.

They're rough, but I'm guessing they're closer to what you're looking for. I hope this helps.

Good luck!

J

—

Short. Friendly yet professional. I reread my email one last time and clicked send.

Part of me wanted to sit right there at my kitchen counter until he responded even if it took all day. I wanted to know his thoughts and feelings—about the logos, of course.

I mean, I always felt that way with my clients. So it wasn't that odd. Even if I was more impatient than usual.

Shaking the thoughts loose from my head, I headed for my bedroom and running clothes. Sitting around waiting for Evan's response

Wild at Heart

was stupid. What he thought didn't matter anyway, since I wouldn't be finishing any of those designs.

Besides, Bryn would be waiting for me in an hour, and I needed serious exercise—or maybe an Evan exorcism—to get him out of my damn head.

I shoved my ID and some cash into the tiny zip pocket of my running shorts and eyed my phone warily. If Bryn needed to reach me, leaving it would cause a problem. But I sure as hell didn't want the temptation of watching for Evan's reply.

In a flash of brilliance, I turned off email notifications. Sliding my phone into its holster, I popped in my earbuds, scooped up my water bottle, and headed out the door.

A pumping beat filled my head and I took off down the sidewalk at a brisk walk, inhaling the rich aroma of crisp battered fish tinged with vinegar. Starting from my place added a few extra miles to my run. I figured I needed every one of them to clear my head.

I picked up my pace, dodging strolling tourists and local families, and closed in on the Locks. My ankles loosened. My knee quit creaking. The warm sun made a nice counterpoint to the cool, salted breeze flitting against my skin.

Slowing, I trotted through the shady, park to the crowded, aluminum walkway leading to the other side of Salmon Bay. The dull buzz of voices and the oily fumes of boat engines filled the air. A big, blue and white tour boat occupied half of the large lock, along with a multi-colored flotilla of sea kayaks and a pair of sailboats, all waiting to get into Lake Union.

Turning sideways, I slid past a family taking photos against the rail. Half my brain focused on navigating the throngs, the other half kept thinking about Aspire. And my designs.

And Evan. And how much I wanted him. And how much I didn't want to want him.

I passed the salmon ladder and headed up the hill away from the water and the crowds. Way too soon, the wide-open pavement of the south lot came into view.

Bryn stood in the grass like a flamingo, one foot pulled up behind her ass in a quad stretch.

"Hey, girlfriend."

"Hey." I popped out my earbuds and dropped into a straddle, focusing on the tension in my hamstrings. "How was your hot date last night?"

"Not so hot. Too much ego, not near enough brains. He spent the whole night talking about his cars, insisted on paying for dinner, then insisted I owed him for it. In blow jobs." Bryn rolled her eyes.

"Seriously?"

"Seriously. I threw a twenty on the table, told him I didn't owe him shit, and stormed out." She switched legs. "That's the last time I'm letting a dating app set me up."

"Beats letting Aly do it."

"Maybe. That girl is a meddlesome matchmaker." Bryn stood, a sly smile spreading across her face. "Speaking of, how are things with Evan? Did you send him feedback on his logos?"

"Sort of." I stretched over my left leg and stared at the blades of grass around my toes. "I ended up sending him a few rough drafts of new designs."

"So, you decided to take him on as a client?" Her voice went up an octave. "That's awesome."

"I did not, so don't go getting all excited." Standing, I faced her and pulled my knee to my chest. "His designs were so off base it was quicker and easier than providing feedback on what he had."

"Sure it was." Her lips twitched at the corners.

"You're worse than Aly, you know?"

"Why? Because I want to see you happy, and I think you'll be happier with Evan than without?"

Hands on my hips, I searched for a snappy comeback. "Yes."

"Right. Okay then. Noted." She beamed. "No more trying to make my bestie happy."

"Fuck off," I grumbled, pivoting on my heel. "Let's run."

Bryn fell in beside me, the soft whump of her shoes hitting the needle-covered dirt path matched mine. "Why aren't you taking him on as a client, again?"

"You know exactly why. I'm a fucking mess, Bryn." I picked up the pace. "The last twelve guys I dated left me for their exes, and you know what the common factor was in all of those relationships?"

"The men were all assholes?"

"No. It's me." I stopped. She stopped beside me. "Something is wrong with *me*. I've picked nothing but losers ever since Justin. Maybe I'm too fucked up to attract a great guy because I'm not ready to let someone in."

"First off, I think Evan is a great guy, and he's head over heels for you. Secondly, he's still here in Seattle, not back in Boston with his ex—in case you didn't notice." She pointed a finger at me. "Thirdly, you can't really afford to turn down a client right now, can you?"

"No, but Evan doesn't have any money. He gave it all up when he moved here. And while I'm happy to help a friend out a little, I can't afford to do any more pro bono work right now." I headed down the trail again, talking over my shoulder. "Besides, he probably won't like my designs that much anyway. They're just general ideas to give him some direction."

Bryn caught up. "Well, he must have some money if he's working with either Marker & Case, or Gilbert. Those firms don't come cheap."

"True…" My feet slowed. "Wait, how do you know who he hired?"

"He called me for recommendations. But if I know you, your designs are right on the money and he's going to love them."

DING

I ignored my phone and Bryn's comment. Crossing the road, I followed the broad trail bordered by dark green sword ferns and pale green alders and maples.

DING

"Do you want to check that?"

"Not really."

DING

"How 'bout putting it on silent, then?"

DING

"Fine." I ran a few more steps and slowed, reaching between my shoulder blades for my phone and unlocking the screen, Bryn hovered at my elbow.

—You're a genius. These are amazing!! —

—Thank you. Thank you. Thank you. —

—I didn't expect you to actually design my logo, but I really appreciate it. Please let me know what I owe you. —

—And I don't mean to push, but you nailed it when no one else even came close. Would you at least consider taking me on as a client? —

My heart sang like a black-capped chickadee, only instead of "cheese-bur-ger" it whistled "Heeee-loves-it."

"Told you so." Bryn did a shuffle in the dirt, hands in the air. "Booyah."

I wanted to do a little dance, too. Because helping Evan help others made me happy.

        Wild at Heart

Making Evan happy made me happy, too. Not that I would admit it to Bryn.

"Doesn't make a difference. He can't afford me."

"Seriously? Pffffft." She glared at me. "Again, he hired either Marker & Case, or Gilbert. He's got the money."

I braced my hands on my hips. "Maybe I don't want to do his branding."

"Bullshit. I saw the look in your eye. You're excited about his business. Besides, can you afford to turn down a big job right now?"

"Not really." I stared at the broad red trunk of the cedar tree behind Bryn.

"So, throw out a large enough number that it'll be worth your while. Either he'll balk, or you'll make bank."

"I'm not sure there's enough money in the world to make me spend time with Evan."

"Why?" She crossed her arms. "Because it'd be such a hardship working with an intelligent, yummy man to help him make his philanthropic dreams a reality?"

I glared at her.

She glared back.

"Aly would tell you that you can't keep kicking gift horses in the nuts. And this time you'd be kicking two at once."

"You suck." I dropped my arms and my gaze. A cloud obscured the sun and the temperature dipped at least five degrees. The breeze rustled through branches, ruffling the hairs on my arms.

"Only because you know I'm right. But you love me anyway." She loped off down the trail and I followed. A ferry boat horn blared in the distance. Bryn glanced over her shoulder. "Everything has a price. So, how much would it take?"

"I don't know."

"A hundred thousand. Would that be enough?"

That would be almost what I brought home in a year. "I can't charge him that much."

"Why not? You're worth it. And if he says no, you're off the hook."

I shook my head. "Still…"

"Okay, fifty thousand, then. Just don't undervalue yourself. Charge what the big firms charge." Sunlight poured through the canopy again, dappling the trail, making sweat roll down my spine and between my boobs.

Or maybe that was the topic.

"I don't know." Doing Evan's branding would bring us way too close. But I'd taken a hard look at my business bank account this morning and it wasn't pretty. "I need to find out more about the scope of work before I get into money."

"But you're going to find out what he wants and give him a bid?"

"I'm going to find out what he wants and give him a bid."

And I'm going to make it so high he'll never go for it.

EVAN

"Bro, you're not going to believe it."

"Believe what." John's thick voice croaked through the line like he'd just woken up.

I'd waited until eight in the morning east coast time. He should've been shaved and showered by now, at least. Anyway, I couldn't wait any longer to share the news with him or I'd burst.

"I hired Jules to do my branding."

"You what? How? That's awesome." Excitement cleared the cobwebs from his voice.

"Yeah." I smiled into my phone. "She's twenty-five thou more than the other firms, but I think it's worth it. If I want people to donate the big bucks, Aspire has to look like a successful, going concern."

"Definitely. Congrats. I can't wait to see it all come together. And the timing couldn't be better." Pages crinkled in the background. "I reserved a ballroom at the Seaport for November twentieth, with A/V, catering, and cash bar. I need your logo ASAP to get your invitations ready, and you need at least a basic website up before I start mailing them—which I'd like to do in two weeks. No more than three."

"I am on it." I put a reminder in my phone calendar. "Thanks for all your help."

"That's what brothers are for. Though you're still going to owe me one." He paused. "So, how's it going with you and Jules? Personally, I mean."

"I'm not sure yet. I miss her, man. I thought she was pulling away until she agreed to do this job. Honestly, I'm not sure why she did."

"But now you're going to have to meet in person at least once or twice to get all this done, right?"

"I don't know. I hope so. She's pushing to work together remotely." I sipped my coffee. "Maybe she's lost interest, now that we're back in the real world."

"In you? No way. You just need to get her to meet you for coffee or something. I'm betting she's avoiding you because she likes you too much." I could picture John, feet planted wide, eyebrows coming together in a deep vee.

"Yeah, maybe. Getting her to commit to working with me was hard enough, though. I don't want to scare her away."

"Well, take it slow, but take it. You're bad about letting everyone else get what they want at your expense."

"Tell me something I don't know."

CHAPTER 42

EVAN

I clicked my mouse, minimizing and maximizing windows on my laptop screen, and swiped at my red, burning eyes. For the past four weeks, sleep had been subsumed by website planning, hiring and working with a copywriter, searching for the right property, calling in every possible favor to get butts in seats at the fund raiser, and about a million other details I'd never thought of before.

Also, excitement. Seeing the pieces come together fed my soul and got me out of bed each day. Not to mention working with Jules. Even if all we did was text and email, at least we communicated regularly.

Pulling up each file, I hit print. It'd be so much easier to choose the right designs for the website banner and handouts, and make sure it all looked cohesive, if I could see all the graphics in front of me at one time.

Though at this stage nothing was easy. I'd quickly discovered trying to put together a top-notch non-profit camp from scratch in three months took more hours than existed.

A grinding clatter emanated from my office. I called it that, even though I hadn't even taken time to buy a desk yet. Just a chair and table I'd picked up at the consignment store and a printer, along with a couple of barstools for the kitchen counter. The couch and TV I'd purchased new and had delivered last week.

Taking money out of savings to buy even basic furniture hurt, but it had to happen at some point. If I was frugal enough, I could cover my expenses for a good nine months before I'd have to sell that engagement ring or find a job. Hopefully the fundraiser would get my business up and running long before I ran out of cash.

I stumbled to the coffee press and refilled my mug for the third time. Big decisions required a clear head, and I had a lot of those to make. Ones that meant hemorrhaging money until after the fundraiser. If they were the right decisions, it would all come out in the wash. If not, well, things would get tighter.

While I'd done okay for myself investing, I didn't have anywhere near the money I'd expected to receive from my trust fund when I turned thirty in January. Money I'd wanted to use to get Aspire off the ground, back when I thought I'd have all the time in the world to create and launch the camp.

The office fell silent. I went to grab the pages, anticipation waking me up more than the caffeine.

A stack of sheets lay in the printer tray, the lines and colors fragmented and spotty. A low ink warning flashed on the screen. I switched out the cartridges and tried again.

Not a single damn page printed clear.

Fuck. Me. I do not have time for this.

Grabbing my phone, I texted Jules.

—Do you by any chance have print versions of my graphics? John needs the finals, my printer died, and my eyes are bugging from looking at my screen. —

JULES

Guilt roiled my stomach. I stared at Evan's text, then up at my wall. The wall currently covered in every one of his potential graphics, all neatly mounted on foam core and ready to hand over to him.

Except I couldn't work up the guts to drop them off in person.

I'd considered mailing him printed samples, but that seemed silly since we only lived two miles apart. So, I'd planned to call a courier yesterday, but even that felt wrong.

He was my highest paying single client project ever, and my friend. The least I could do was treat him the same way I treated smaller clients. Which meant doing all a designer could do to help him get Aspire launched right.

DING

Hissing out a breath, I tapped one finger against the side of my phone.

—If you could print them, I can drop by and pick them up. —

I imagined Evan standing outside my condo with a shy smile and those cobalt eyes piercing right through to my soul. Hot tingles swirled at my core.

Fuck. Two days shy of a month without talking on the phone or face to face, and my attraction hadn't faded one bit.

DING

—I know you're busy, but it would be a huge help. —

Bitter bile burned up my throat. Not giving him the printouts would only screw with his deadlines. I could be a mature, professional business owner and not jump his bones for two minutes.

—Sure. I'm available until 2. Unit 12C. —

—Thanks! You're a life saver!! I'll see you in twenty. —

Annnnnnd, the hyperventilating kicked in. Along with a mad scramble to change out of my ratty old sweats and t-shirt. I riffled through my closet, searching for something casually professional and not at all sexy.

My fingertips skimmed my green sundress and tingles did back handsprings up and down my spine. I shoved my bulkiest long cardigan across the bar to cover it. Pushed down memories of the last time we were together.

Closing my eyes, I took a deep breath. And another.

Client meeting. Client meeting. Client meeting. Client meeting.

All I had to do was let him in, hand him the stack of prints, and it'd be over. Quick and easy.

I threw on my favorite pair of dark wash jeans and a tank top. Over that I layered a striped, button-down shirt and tucked it in.

Even though it was my own home, I reached for a pair of sandals. Meeting with him barefoot felt way too intimate. If I could've covered every inch of my exposed skin, I would've. Except no amount of clothing could protect my heart.

I glanced at the clock on my phone. Two minutes to go. My hands shook. My pulse raced.

Shoving my coffee table out of the way I flipped into a handstand. Forced myself to concentrate on something other than the fact Evan was going to be standing right here, in my living room, in the next few minutes.

Shifting my weight, I turned a circle.

The hollow thump of knuckles on wood made my heart rate shoot up again, ticking and jumping like an old wooden roller coaster that's just topped the big hill. I teetered, barely getting my feet on the floor.

My mouth went dry. Probably because all that moisture went straight to my palms instead. Well, there, and the junction of my thighs.

"Be right there." I took a sip of water from my glass on the counter and walked to the door, wiping my hands on my jeans.

He's just a client. He's just a client. He's just a client.

A really hot client who totally turns my crank.

SHUT UP!

With a hard swallow I yanked open the door. Extra fast. Like pulling off a band-aid.

And then Evan was there, in the flesh. All hard muscles and soft eyes, and luscious, kissable mouth. Citrus and spice swirled into my head. Clouding my thoughts.

"Hey."

"Hey."

CHAPTER 43

JULES

My hand froze on the doorknob. My feet stayed glued to the floor.

A shy smile just like the one I'd imagined crinkled the corners of his eyes. I couldn't stop staring at his face any more than I could slow my racing heart.

"Thanks again for meeting with me. Can I come in?" Evan gestured toward my living room, hand trembling slightly.

"Oh. Yeah. Sure. Sorry." I stepped back. Not enough to break the band of electricity pulsing between us, but enough to let him in. "I'll grab your prints."

He took two strides and froze, staring at the wall covered in potential Aspire branding. I stepped next to him. So close, if I reached out just a little, I could trace my fingertip along his forearm. Up the ridge of his biceps. And—

Be. Fucking. Professional.

I blinked twice, swallowed hard, and found my voice. "What do you think?"

          Wild at Heart

Without taking his eyes off the wall, he dropped a paper bag on my counter and walked in for a closer look.

"Jules, your work. I don't even know what to say." He beamed at me over his shoulder. "I'm seeing my dream come to life, thanks to you."

I floated forward, feet hovering at least three feet off the ground. "Which colorway is your favorite?"

"You mean I have to pick?" His cobalt eyes crinkled with laughter. "Inconceivable."

My lips twitched. "For brand consistency, it probably *is* best to only use three colors, instead of twelve."

"Damn. You're making it hard."

Hard. Like his abs. And his cock sliding into me. And…

"That's what *he* said."

"Nice one." He glanced at me again and smirked.

Crossing one arm to support his other elbow, he rested his chin on his hand and stared at the designs. Annnnd the way his cut biceps bulged under the edge of his short-sleeve button-down should've been illegal.

My fingers twitched, desperate to close the distance and caress his skin. Follow the lines of his muscles up to his chest. Along the creases of his abs. Down the hard vee that led to his waistband and beyond.

Evan pointed. "I like this, but it feels like I've seen it."

I yanked my brain out of the gutter and focused on his words. "Agreed. The brown, green and yellow is definitely more traditional outdoor camp, but with a slight twist. It's not my personal favorite, but I always provide a range of choices."

"So, which one do you like best?" He turned his thoughtful, perceptive gaze on me.

"You have to pick first. Otherwise, I might color your opinion with mine." I let the corners of my lips flick up. "Pun intended."

He groaned. "C'mon, Jules. I need a little guidance here. My head's been swimming in decisions, and I hired you because you're the expert."

"I'm not telling until you do." I grinned. "Seriously though, without thinking, which one do you gravitate towards? Which one feeeeeeels right?"

His eyes bounced from left to right then settled. "The brown, blue, and orange."

A warm flush stole over me, spreading from my chest to my toes to my fingertips. "Same."

"Yeah. It's perfect." Evan grabbed the foam core with the logo, holding it by the edges. "Hip and fresh, but also a with hint of nostalgia. And it looks trustworthy and authoritative. I think it's going to appeal to parents and donors, and kids."

I nodded. "Exactly. It's a bit of a nod to the old Forest Service and Smokey the Bear badges for nostalgia. The brown is earthy, outdoorsy, and that shade of blue screams trust me."

"I love it. But I'm not sure if I like how it works with this Website banner. Is it okay if I mix and match a little…?" He glanced at me.

"Absolutely. Have at it. It's your candy store."

He held the logo up next to one of the other Web banners. The one with the green forest image in the background. "What do you think of this with this?"

Squinting, I stared at it with critical eyes. "That could work really nicely. I can mock it up and print it pretty quick and bring it by later this afternoon if that works."

"That, would be amazing." His gaze met mine and a delicious tremor juddered through me that I did my best to ignore. He stepped closer and his voice deepened. "Seriously, Jules. I can't thank you enough for doing this. For helping make my dream come true."

The air between us pulsed and vibrated.

I waved a hand to break the spell. "My pleasure."

And I meant it. I loved seeing Evan so happy. Especially compared to the slightly lost, definitely over his head guy I'd met on the trail. Or the sad one I'd walked away from on the sidewalk in front of my building a month ago.

That I'd had a hand in creating that joy made it even better.

"Oh, hey, I thought you might be hungry, so I brought sandwiches." He walked to the counter. Opening his paper bag with a loud crinkle he held up a paper-wrapped square and smiled. "Mediterranean Madness. Hummus, roasted bell pepper, eggplant, and feta."

How could I resist?

EVAN

I biked east along the Burke-Gilman path towards my apartment, warm sun on my back. The sparkling, sailboat and kayak filled waters of the ship canal lay on one side, warehouses and old brick industrial buildings sprouted on the other.

Joy and excitement rushed through my veins with every pedal stroke. Because not only had Jules created the perfect visual branding elements for Aspire, samples of which I had carefully tucked in my pannier, something between us, or inside her, had shifted.

I was sure of it. Or least fairly confident.

Maybe she was just being polite and friendly because I was her client, but I'd swear it was more than that. A crack had opened in the door she'd closed between us.

I'd expected her to kick me out in fifteen minutes. Instead, we'd spent two hours looking at design options, talking, and enjoying lunch together.

Her excitement and insights into building, branding, and marketing my business were invaluable. Even more invaluable was her throaty laugh. The way she threw her head back and chortled with gusto and glee at my jokes made me giddy. Making her even a teeny bit happy delighted me.

I wanted to kiss her and offer her a job in equal measure, except if I jumped in with both feet again, she'd run. If I took it slow, like I'd been doing, with no pressure, maybe she'd feel safe enough to open the door a little wider. Meet me for coffee or a run.

The way we worked together, the way it felt to be together, was easily as good off the trail as on. She'd have to recognize that fact eventually.

It would take time to regain her trust, but it'd be worth it. She was worth it. Waiting a few more months was a small sacrifice when I planned to spend the rest of my life making her happy.

CHAPTER 44

JULES

Flirting with Evan was fun. Being with Evan was fun. When he came over, I knew better than to lead him on if I wasn't interested, but I couldn't help being drawn in.

The instant I saw him I was interested. Too interested. And I got more interested the longer we hung out together, laughing and talking and bouncing ideas for his business back and forth.

That was the problem. Which sounded like the most stupid and illogical argument ever—even to me. That shit would never hold up in court.

Yes, your honor, I didn't want to go out with him because we liked each other too much. Got along too well.

How was the sex?

The sex was spectacular, your honor.

And I couldn't stop Aly's words from running on repeat through my head. About the universe. And gift horses.

I didn't want to be the ungrateful bitch who kept kicking hers in the balls, because Aly was right.

Even if he was a total masochist, no way would that horse keep coming back. He'd find someone who appreciated his gifts. Maybe gave him a blowjob in thanks instead.

I snorted into my mug, then sobered.

All my choices seemed as stupid as my reasoning. Then again, I didn't trust my own judgement anymore—especially not when it came to men. Hadn't for a long time.

I dialed Bryn.

"Hey, girlfriend."

"Hey. Got a minute?"

"For you, I've got five. What's up?"

"So..." I hesitated. It was one thing to think all those thoughts about Evan. And Evan and me. It was a whole other thing to say them out loud.

"Evan?"

"Totally." I sighed dramatically. Because this situation deserved a damn dramatic sigh.

"Did you finally break down and actually talk to the poor guy?" Her wry tone spoke volumes.

"Yeah. We talked on the phone." I strove for nonchalance. "He came over, too, to pick up samples."

"Wait. Weren't you going to send those by courier last week?"

I paused, long enough for the silence to grow uncomfortable. "Ummmm, I guess I didn't get around to it. And he needed to make his final color selections ASAP."

"Holy shit." Her voice jumped an octave. "What happened?"

"Nothing. It was a client meeting. We looked at his graphics and picked his brand colors. And he brought over a couple sandwiches, so we had lunch."

"Wow. So, it went well, then?"

"Too well. I'm supposed to drop a couple more off at his place in an hour." I clutched my phone like a lifeline. "I don't know what the fuck I'm doing, Bryn."

"Ummmm, trying way too hard to not admit you're head over heels for the guy, and he's head over heels for you?" She had the tone of a patient parent explaining something to their kid for the umpteenth time.

"I guess I'm not sure if that's a good thing or a bad thing."

"Aha! You admit it." She gloated. "You're still into him."

I pinched the bridge of my nose. "I though not seeing him for a month would fix it. Make me not want him anymore. Well, that plan backfired."

"Big surprise there." Bryn snickered. "Absence makes the heart grow fonder, and all that."

"Thanks for sharing that now."

"You wouldn't have listened before."

"I guess not." I heaved another dramatic sigh. "What should I do, Bryn?"

"Don't ask me what you *should* do. What do you *want* to do?"

The line went quiet, except for the hushed swoosh of her breath. My printer clacked and whirred in the background.

"I don't know." My voice came out a childish whine. "I guess I want to be with Evan, but I don't want to get hurt again."

"What if you could be with Evan and not get hurt? Would you go for it then?"

"Duh. Of course." I shifted the phone to my other ear and grabbed a can of spray adhesive from the closet. "But that's not reality. You know as well as I do even people with the best intentions can disappear from your life in an instant."

"Sure. They can also stick around." Papers shuffled on her end. "You'd have been with Justin even if you knew you would lose him too soon, right?"

"Yeah." My eyes stung. I blinked hard. Hell, I would've gone through losing him again if I could've had another year with him. "In a heartbeat."

"Okay, so hypothetically, if this was your last chance to be with Evan, and you would only get four years together—but they'd be amazing—would you take it?"

EVAN

I rubbed a towel on my hair, draped it over the shower rod, and pulled on my favorite, faded pair of Madras shorts and a t-shirt. Despite the fall air, I'd sweated out my shirt on the ride up the Fremont hill in full sun.

Relaxing into my perfectly distressed, tufted brown leather couch with my feet up, I perched my laptop on my thighs and opened email. One from Bryn caught my eye…

—

Guest Lodge and Cabins for Sale

Former kid's camp on twelve acres with year-round stream, surrounded by National Forest, just an hour and half outside Seattle. Turn this versatile property into a conference center or retreat or maintain it as a camp.

Includes twelve furnished cabins that sleep six each, a main lodge with commercial kitchen and dining room, and an owner's/manager's cabin.

—

A link took me to the full listing details, including photos. Excitement vibrated in my veins. I checked the price. Only two point six million—unbelievable. On the east coast it'd cost triple that.

—

Hey Bryn,

This looks perfect. When can I see it?

-Evan

—

I clicked through the pictures again and again, studying the rough-hewn cabins and big trees. The sunlight sparkling on water and the deer wandering placidly through the forest. Getting more and more amped.

—

Hi Evan,

How about tomorrow morning, leaving my office at 10? We'd plan to be back around 4 p.m.

Best,

Bryn

—

Bryn Jones

Teller Jones Realty

—

—

Works for me. See you then. Thanks, Bryn!

-Evan

—

A harsh buzz blared through my apartment. I leapt up, took a deep breath, and sprinted the three steps to the front door.

Jules stood in the hall in the same green dress she'd worn when I picked her up at the end of the trail. The one she'd been wearing the last time we had sex.

My heart stopped, probably because half the blood in my body went straight to my dick.

The dress she'd been wearing when she dumped me.

The blood in my dick reentered my heart and I struggled to make sense of a cascade of confusion, desire, happiness, wariness, and I'm not sure what else.

I thought I didn't know where the boundaries were when I'd left Jules's apartment, I was wrong. Those boundaries seemed crystal clear; be friendly, yet professional. Make her laugh, but don't touch her.

Seeing her in that dress, hair a mass of curls piled on her head, I had zero idea what to do. How to react.

All I could do was keep my eyes on her face, or anywhere other than her body and that damn dress exposing way too much of her soft skin. The silence stretched and morphed while I gazed into her dark brown eyes, trying to gauge her mood. Counting the amber streaks in her irises.

"Hey."

"Hey." I glanced down. Her chest heaved like she'd sprinted up the two flights to my apartment wearing lead boots.

She fidgeted with the strap on her messenger bag. "Mind if I come in?"

"Oh. Sorry. Of course." I stepped out of the way and Jules walked into my apartment, the hem of her skirt twitching below her ass. I adjusted my dick in my thankfully baggie shorts.

She spun a slow circle. "Nice place. A little bare, but nice."

"Yeah, I've been busy with Aspire." I stuffed my hands in my pockets, "Besides, most furniture is highly overrated. No need to fill a space just because you can."

"True. And you do have the most important pieces—a sofa, a bed, and a TV. Rest, relaxation, and recreation are covered. What more do you need?"

You.

My mouth went dry. My dick throbbed.

Preferably in my bed or on my couch for some rest, relaxation, and recreation. Now.

I clenched my fists inside the fabric, struggling against the urge to grab her and slant my mouth over hers and kiss her until we had to come up for air. To taste every inch of her, slowly and thoroughly, and do all the things I'd wanted to do but didn't have a chance the last time.

She reached into her shoulder bag and pulled out a short stack of foam core boards, her face serious. "Here are the rest of those mock-ups. Do you want to look at them alongside the others?"

Stay professional and friendly. The dress is pure coincidence. Or maybe she has a hot date later. She did say she wouldn't be free after two.

My heart sank a little. "That'd be great." I smiled, but not too big. "Can I get you something to drink? I've got water and fizzy water. Or beer."

"Water. Thanks." She focused on organizing all the options on my counter. I let my gaze roam from her broad, muscular shoulders to her small waist, and along the curve of her hips.

No matter how much I wanted her, I would not give in to my urges. She finally let me in a little, I couldn't be a give-an-inch-take-a-mile guy. I had too much to lose.

CHAPTER 45

JULES

What the fuck was I doing, standing in front of Evan's granite countertop laying out foam core boards in perfect lines, in what used to be my favorite green dress?

When he opened his front door, I'd been hoping his eyes would light up. That he'd make the connection between my outfit, and, well, us. Instead, he'd averted his gaze right away and acted like he didn't find me the least bit attractive.

Yet every inch of me remained hyper-aware of him standing right, fucking, there, looking over my shoulder. If I took one small, diagonal step back I'd be able to press my body against his hard, hot one. My foot shuffled backward.

Shit. No. I pulled my foot in. *What the fuck am I thinking?*

He'd been nothing but professional and polite and I'd come over planning to jump his bones. Or at least kiss and make up. Which was stupid for two reasons…

One, I didn't fuck clients, let alone date them. Though I'd dated Evan before he became my client. But that was neither here nor there.

Two, I had no idea if he was even interested in being with me anymore after I pushed him away. Maybe I was being arrogant, believing my gift horse was still waiting around.

Either way, everything I'd been thinking since he left my apartment was entirely inappropriate. Which led me right back to: *What the fuck am I doing?*

I couldn't quick-change my outfit, but I could quick-change my plan. Go over the new designs and get the hell out of there before I made a fool of myself and lost a client—and paycheck—I needed.

Shuffling to the side I put more distance between us, hoping the tingles pulling at every inch of my skin, every cell of my body, would subside. I took a critical look at the Web banner options with the full-color logo he'd chosen, considering how each played with his brochure, and all the other marketing pieces.

And paying no attention to Evan standing a foot away. Or the hairs on my arms standing on end. Or the way the skin on that side of my body twitched with his every move, his every breath.

No attention at all.

"Okay. First impression. Which banner do you like best?" I gestured at the three versions I'd mocked up with his new logo.

"I still like the green forest background, but this version, with the montage of kids succeeding, is even better." He moved the other two options off to the side. "Yeah. Definitely this one."

"Same." I grinned and he smiled back, and my heart did stupid, fluttery things.

I focused on the graphics in front of me and pointed. "Okay. How about we put that one on the home page, and on the brochure and invite, then use these other images throughout the site and in the slide show and brochure."

"Looks perfect."

"Also, if you connect us, I can work directly with your copywriter to finalize content and put everything together."

"That, would be wonderful." He stepped in closer. Energy thrummed between us. Or at least through me. "I knew you were exactly the person I needed to help make this happen. I'm not sure I could trust anyone else to understand, and support, me and my dreams."

Tingles cartwheeled down my spine to places they didn't belong.

"Glad I could help." I turned away and tucked the two unneeded designs in my bag. Before I made the mistake of closing the shrinking gap and pressed my lips to his.

"Oh, wait." An enormous grin shot across his face and excitement shimmered off him like heat waves off pavement. "Before you go, can I get your opinion on a couple of other Aspire related things?"

"Um…"

"It'll only take a minute. It's not graphic design or marketing, but I'm happy to pay your hourly rate for your time."

I did not need spend more time in close proximity to his cute smile and buff biceps. No matter how much he paid me. But he'd already plopped down on his couch and popped open his laptop. I stood behind him, inhaling citrus and spice, and trying not to run my fingers through his mussed hair.

"Check out what Bryn sent over today." He angled the screen toward me.

"Holy shit. That looks amazing." I scuttled around the couch and sat beside him for a better view, the leather cool and smooth against the bare backs of my thighs. I crossed my legs, hoping to squash the tingles heating up in places they didn't belong.

"It even has winter access, so I could do special holiday camps, maybe for foster kids." He clicked through the images, pointing out all the best details. Stopping on the owner's cottage. "Could you imagine living there?"

The rustic, tin-roofed wood cabin had a covered front porch with two rockers overlooking the stream. Behemoth, old-growth Cedar trees and Doug Firs surrounded it, with the jagged tops of a few snowy peaks poking above the forest.

Inside, old ski paraphernalia, a couple overstuffed couches, their backs draped with crocheted throws, and an enormous wood stove made it look extra cozy. It was the mountain cabin of my dreams.

"Totally." The word came out hushed. Reverent. "It's perfect."

I swallowed down the bitter tinge of jealousy with a big gulp of hoping it works out for him. He'd taken a huge risk with his life. He deserved a place like this.

"Isn't it?" His breath ghosted across my cheek, warm and minty.

I glanced up.

His mouth. My mouth. Only inches of space between us.

My lips caught fire. I licked them, trying to cool them, and the flames moved to his eyes.

"Jules…?"

I swallowed the dry lump in my throat. "Yeah."

"Do you feel that, or is it just me?"

"You mean that tingling tension and heat pulsing between us?"

He nodded. "Thank God, because I was afraid I was the only one, and I really want to kiss you right now, but I'm not sure that's a good idea. And I cannot read you at all and I really, really don't want to scare you away." He paused. "And judging by the look on your face I'm completely freaking you out."

     Wild at Heart

He dumped his laptop on the couch between us and grabbed his head with his hands. His fingers raked his unruly mop of hair into messier contortions. "I'm sorry, Jules. I promised you I wouldn't push, that I'd give you space, and I just fucked that up completely."

EVAN

Judging by the way Jules pupils expanded, and the way her lip trembled, I'd definitely scared her. I dug my fingers into my skull, hoping to use the pain as an anchor for my swirling thoughts. Something, anything to bring a clear idea of what to do, what to say, now that I'd screwed up everything.

She touched my arm.

I practically jumped out of my skin.

"Evan, you're not freaking me out."

Her words didn't penetrate through my sinking thoughts.

She squeezed my forearm, her hand singeing my skin. "Evan, I'm not freaked out."

Turning my head, I peaked at her with one eye. "You're not?"

She shook her head. "I'm not."

"You're sure?"

"Positive." She smiled and moved my laptop to the ottoman. "In fact, I thought you kissing me was the best idea you've had all day. And you've had some good ones."

Shifting around on the couch, Jules straddled me. I froze. Or at least, every part of me except my dick froze.

"Because I've been dying—" She brushed her lips across mine, skimming so light I might not have known it was happening if my eyes were closed. Then again, my eyes were wide open, and I'd still swear it was a dream.

"To kiss—" Her teeth nipped my lower lip, sending sparks shooting straight to my balls. "You."

She slanted her lips over mine and sank down against my hard-on. This response seemed crystal clear. I wrapped my arms around her like I'd wanted to do for weeks and pulled her closer, grinding into her.

She moaned and I dipped into her mouth. Her tongue tangled with mine and her hips twitched against me. Sliding my hands down I gripped her ass, the fabric of her dress crinkling in my palms, and thrust up.

I caressed her thigh, trailing my fingers up the soft skin, catching her skirt and pulling it along. Planning to tease along the edges of her panties. Only nothing stopped the skim of my fingertips, and I lost all capacity for rational thought.

My world shrunk to the silk of her skin and the curves of her ass, and the way she curled and thrust and rubbed against me, her tongue slick against mine.

A moan escaped the back of my throat and she devoured it. And me. And I became nothing more than the sum of every part where we touched.

"I've missed you. This." She panted against my lips, grinding into me again. "I want you, Evan. Now."

Somehow, her voice, her words penetrated the tiny part of me that held my backbone. The part that remembered what happened the last time she'd said those words. The part that needed to know where we stood before this went any further, because I didn't know if I could handle her pushing me away again.

"I want you, too." I shifted, pushing her upright. "But not like this."

Her eyes went wide and bright. "What do you mean? Don't you like couch sex?" Her smile did not erase the worry line between her eyebrows.

I rubbed my thumb over the vertical crease, trying to smooth it. The last thing I wanted to do was upset her. "I love couch sex, and I'm sure I'd love couch sex with you, but I'm not some toy you can pick up and discard on a whim."

"I wouldn't do that—I...I don't think of you as a toy." She scooched to my side and tucked her legs under her, tugging her hem down to cover them. "I'm so sorry, Evan. I didn't mean to hurt you, or make you feel disposable. I got scared. Before."

"I know you did, and I get it, but I've spent too much of life letting other people make my choices for me. I can't do that anymore." I scooped up her hand and held it, rubbing her thumb with mine. "Jules, I want to be with you forever. I can be patient and wait until you're ready, but I can't go through that again."

"You won't."

"How can you be sure?"

She got on her knees and stared into my eyes. I didn't let go of her hand, our one point of physical connection.

"Because you were right—we're great together. On the trail and off. And I've realized I don't want to throw away what we've got, regardless of how much or little time we get together on this earth, just because I'm scared I might lose you." She sniffled. "That's just stupid."

The tight band that'd been compressing my chest for the past month released. I took a deep breath of air laced with mint, cedar, and vanilla. "Totally stupid."

"Also, because you came back. It scared me that you gave up everything to move here, but I can see now I put way too much burden on myself for that. It's your life, and you're finally living it the way you want whether I'm in it or not. I respect that."

"Thanks. I just—"

She placed a finger on my lips. "I'm not done yet."

I nodded, doing my best not to kiss that finger. Nibble along its edges to her palm, her wrist. Except she had more she needed to say, and I needed to hear it. To really listen.

"I want you, want to be with you, because you're thoughtful and caring and funny and smart and driven and sexy as hell. And because you make me want to strive for more—to grow and change in the best possible ways." She dropped her hand to her lap, looking down, then up at my face again. "And maybe the biggest reason I want to be with you is because you came back, and you stayed. You gave me space when I pushed you away but didn't run."

The last person to make me feel even a fraction this good about myself was Uncle Martin. And he had nothing on Jules.

"You're worth waiting for." I tucked a stray curl behind the delicate shell of her ear. "Besides, you warned me you'd probably try to push me away if things got serious, so I knew what I was getting into. I'm just glad you came back."

"Me too."

She tilted her cheek toward my hand and smiled, her gaze never leaving mine. I splayed my fingers and slid them into her curls, cupping her freckled cheekbone, letting the warmth sink into my palm. Realizing how much I'd missed her, and how much I was looking forward to getting to know every inch of her better. Inside and out.

Leaning in, I pressed my lips to hers, soft and sweet and gentle, all my emotions flowing through that one, small point of connection.

Pulling back a little, she smiled. "Does this mean can we get back to the makeup sex now?"

I smiled back. "Yes. Yes, it does."

     Wild at Heart

EPILOGUE

JULES

The wheels of the plane bounced off the tarmac, and nervous tension seated itself on my shoulders. I fidgeted with the end of my seat belt.

Evan took my hand. "Don't worry. You're going to be great."

"Shouldn't you be more nervous? You're the one coming back to Boston and facing all your father's cronies knowing they could make or break your dream."

"First of all, it's now our dream. And second, I don't give a damn what they think, or if they give us any money at all. If we don't do well with this fundraiser, we'll hold another one somewhere else. Or we'll find other investors." He shrugged and smiled. Forehead unlined. Eyebrows relaxed. "Somebody is always willing to give money to a good cause."

"That's not what I'm worried about." We'd worked our asses off for the past couple months. I'd bet my condo that people were going to be thrilled to support Aspire Academy and its mission. I stared at our joined hands. "This isn't my world."

He shifted in his seat, angling toward me. "It's not mine either, but I know how to navigate it and I'll be with you the whole time. Anybody who doesn't love you, and all the amazing work you've done, at least half as much as I do can go to hell."

We filed off the plane and strolled through the airport hand-in-hand, dragging our wheelies. The doors swished open, and crisp fall air nipped at my skin, such a change from the damp November drizzle of Seattle. A bigger, blonder version of Evan stood next to a candy-apple red Audi.

"Hey, bro." John swept Evan up in a man hug and they pounded each other's backs. "Good to see you."

"You too. I've missed you, bro." Evan broke free, slipped an arm around my waist and tucked me into his side. "John, this is Jules. Jules, John."

I reached out my hand. "Great to finally meet you in person."

"You, too." His grip was firm. "I love what you've done for Aspire, and for Evan."

"Thanks, but Evan's done way more for Aspire. And for me, too."

Evan's warm gaze met mine and we shared a smile. "I'd say we're pretty even in that department."

John snorted. "Okay lovebirds, we'd better get moving. Traffic won't get any better and you two need a room." He popped the trunk and reached for my suitcase. I held it out to him with my left hand.

John's face went blank, then lit up like fireworks had just gone off. "Seriously?"

"Seriously." Evan's grin threatened to break his jaw. I swallowed and nodded, still not used to the sapphire sparkling on my finger and everything it symbolized. I loved it, mind you. I just wasn't used to it yet, or the idea that I didn't feel guilty about it. Or guilty for loving Evan. Somehow, being with him had helped make the guilt melt away.

     Wild at Heart

"Congratulations! When's the big day?"

I cleared my throat. "We haven't set a date yet, but maybe next fall if we're not too busy."

"Well, welcome to the family." John scooped me up in his big arms and spun me around. "Thanks for finally making an honest man out of him."

My feet hit pavement and I found my balance. I couldn't help beaming up at his happy face, so like Evan's and so very different. "My pleasure."

"Have you told Mother or Father yet?"

"Hell no. Why would they care?" Evan's expression went blank. "I haven't talked to either of them since the last time I was here."

"I'm honored, then." His lips twisted in a wry smile, and he tossed our carry-ons into the trunk.

Evan clambered into the back seat. "So, what's our plan?"

"The event doesn't start until six, but we can get in to do setup at three. John eased out of the busy airport pick up area. "Tomorrow you two can sleep in, go for a run, hang out, fuck like bunnies, whatever. I'll be up and out early and back by lunch. We should leave around one to pick up the centerpieces, programs, and donation forms on our way to the venue."

Evan clamped a hand on John's shoulder. "Thanks again for putting all this together. I, we, couldn't have done it without you."

"Yes, thank you." I echoed.

"Glad I could help. It's good to see my little brother finally excited about something in his life. More than one something, in fact."

EVAN

Chatter and well-dressed bodies packed the ballroom. White-aproned servers circulated appetizers through clusters of people drinking and laughing beneath the soft light of the chandeliers.

Standing against the wall, I shifted from foot to foot, going over my mental checklist for the millionth time. Every seat had been pre-sold, and I didn't want to screw up in front of a full house of the wealthiest elders and scions of Boston. Jules and I had agonized over every slide in our presentation, our handouts and the donation forms and process. We'd set up the AV and tested it. And tested it again.

Despite what I'd told Jules about not being worried, nerves coiled in my stomach like a snake about to strike. Even the warm goat cheese wafting from the appetizer trays didn't smell appealing. I checked the time and nodded to John. The lights dimmed twice. Attendees took their seats, digging into their salad course.

Rubbing my fingers over the stones in Uncle Martin's bracelet for good luck, I strode to the podium.

We can pull this off. We can pull this off. We can pull this off.

Smoothing my notes, I cleared my throat. "Good evening and thank you so much for taking time out of your busy schedules to join us here tonight. For those of you who don't know me, I'm Evan Davenport, President and CEO of Aspire Academy, where we're creating the leaders of tomorrow in a whole new way. Tonight, I'd like to show the power of making the outdoors accessible to children from all walks of life, and how we can harness that to build confidence and set them on a path to becoming confident, thoughtful, and successful architects of their own futures—and ours."

I spoke about my experiences, and how my time in the outdoors helped make me the person I am today; complete with slides of me as a happy camper. I explained how it helped me understand decision making and consequences, and how it gave me the strength, self-confidence, and conviction to follow my dreams.

Quotes and statistics on Nature Deficit Disorder, and the healing power of spending time in the woods—especially for kids without easy access to the outdoors—flashed on the screen. Finally, it was time for the heartstring and wallet tugging section of the program.

"Now that you know a little more about the inspiration for Aspire Academy, I'd like to introduce you to our COO, Jules Martinez. She's going to share a few stories from her years of working with kids in the outdoors, what our program will look like, and what it will take to make this dream a reality for kids from all walks of life."

Muted clapping echoed in the room. Not quite the reception I'd hoped, but we weren't done yet.

I tugged the wood step stool into position with my foot. Jules stepped up, gave my hand a quick squeeze, and took over the mike. A natural speaker whose passion shone like a full moon glowing on a mountain peak, she had the crowd eating out of her hand in seconds.

The house lights came up to thunderous applause. All around the room people pulled out tissues and wallets.

I stood off to the side with John, staring at the growing number of donors waiting to swipe credit cards.

"See, I told you this would work." He slapped me on the shoulder. "Anything to do with puppies, kittens, or kids is always a winner. The best part is, I bet half of these people are writing checks to get in Father's good graces."

"Oh, the delicious irony."

A throat cleared. "Hello, son."

My gaze met a pair of familiar blue eyes. My stomach, finally uncoiling, snapped back into strike mode.

"Hello, Father." I gripped his hand hard. "Mother." I tipped my head in her direction. "Thank you for coming."

"Your mother insisted. And as usual, she was right." He squeezed her shoulder briefly, shocking me almost as much as his not entirely frozen tone. I'd never seen any physical affection between them. Ever. "I'm proud of you and what you're doing here. That COO of yours is quite the evangelist."

All the words I'd been planning to say to him for months evaporated. "Thank you. I couldn't do this without her."

On cue, Jules bounded over and stood at my side, glowing with adrenaline and joy, hand extended. "Hi there, I'm Jules Martinez. Thank you so much for coming tonight."

"John Davenport." He took her small hand in his large one. It's a pleasure to meet you, Ms. Martinez. This is my wife, Emily." He angled slightly. "We're very impressed with what the two of you have accomplished in such a short time and we'd like to talk with you more about this venture." He glanced at Mother, who nodded almost imperceptibly. "Perhaps over dinner tomorrow night—assuming you'll still be in town."

Jules eyes widened, but she maintained her composure.

I struggled to do the same, not sure what to make of the warm welcome. "We appreciate the offer, but there's one thing you should know first."

"What is that? Please tell me you haven't let some loan-shark investor stick you for massive interest payments or part-ownership."

"Of course not. You taught me better than that." I paused and prepared myself. "In addition to being a brilliant COO and my business partner, Jules is my fiancé."

If he didn't have such a well-honed poker face, I'm pretty sure Father's jaw would have hit the red and gold carpet of the ballroom.

Instead, he looked from my face to hers and continued without missing a beat. "Congratulations. It seems we have much to celebrate. Seven o'clock?"

"Seven o'clock," I responded without thinking, shock rendering my brain unusable.

"That's very kind. I'm looking forward to it." Jules reached out to shake my father's hand once more.

He turned and strode off across the ballroom, intent on doing more business, or keeping up connections and appearances, at the very least. Father was never one to just be social for the sake of enjoying another person's company.

Mother stood where he left her. She reached out and took Jules's hand in hers and smiled warmly. "It's a pleasure to meet you my dear. I look forward to getting to know you better."

Her gaze met mine over Jules's head, and it might've been the light reflecting from the chandeliers, but I could've sworn her eyes glistened. "See you tomorrow night, Evan." She waved at one of her fellow socialites and crossed the room to her side, leaving me gobsmacked, astonished, astounded.

In my head, I took back every disparaging thing I'd ever said about my mother. The woman was secretly a genius and a saint. And right then I loved her more than anything, except Jules.

Jules stared across the ballroom. "Was that—? Did they just?" Her voiced came out two octaves higher than normal.

"My parents, appearing to accept me back into the fold? And you as well. Yes, I think it was."

"Congrats, Evan." John squeezed my shoulder. "I told you I had a good feeling about this. You should listen to me more often."

"When have I ever not listened to you?"

John's smile turned evil, and he opened his mouth to respond.

"Never mind. Don't answer that."

He threw his head back and laughed his deep, rolling belly laugh. "Okay, little brother. Far be it for me to rain on your parade. I'm going to check on a few things."

Jules slid her arm around my waist. "So, it looks like everything is working out even better than we expected."

"It does."

"We should celebrate when we get home. Want to go backpacking? We can share my one-person tent. Like old times?" She waggled her eyebrows.

"Funny you should mention backpacking and naked…How would you feel about hiking into the hot springs for a couple days next week?"

Confusion clouded her features. "I'd love to. But you'll never get reservations for that soon. The office is only open on Wednesdays and Fridays to return messages."

"What if I told you I'd made these reservations months ago?"

"I'd say that's just another one of the many reasons I'm marrying you."

The End

Thank you for reading
Wild at Heart

Your time is precious, and I appreciate you spending a few hours of it with me and the characters inside my head. I'd be thrilled if you could take another minute to leave a review. Reviews are my best marketing tool, and help other people find this story.

Want to be the first to know about new releases, special contests, and freebies? Join the Gold Club at www.stacygold.com/goldclub

You can also stay in the loop by following @AuthorStacyGold on:

Facebook

Twitter

Instagram

Goodreads

Bookbub

Book Club Discussion Questions for *Wild at Heart*

1. Do you find Jules to be a strong female character? Why? How does the author show you she's strong?

2. How does the setting of the Pacific Crest Trail impact the characters and help drive the plot forward?

3. How would the book have played out differently in a different time period or setting?

4. Evan isn't your typical romance novel Alpha Male. What makes him different? Do you find him attractive? Why or why not?

5. What was your favorite part of the book? What was your least favorite?

6. Which scene has stuck with you the most?

7. What do you think Stacy Gold's goals were in writing this story?

8. What did you think of the writing? Did you reread any passages?

9. How did the book make you feel? What emotions did it evoke?

10. Did your opinion of this book change as you read it? How?

11. Ms. Gold addresses a number of themes in this book. Which ones did you notice? Which ones resonated with you and why?

12. How do you feel about the relationship between Jules and Evan? Do you think it's healthy or unhealthy? Why?

13. Both of these characters need to make difficult decisions along the way. What are a few of them and how do you think they handled them?

14. Would you recommend the book to a friend? How would you summarize the story if you were to recommend it?

15. If you could talk to Ms. Gold, what burning question would you want to ask?

Wild About You
Coming in 2023

Without trust, there can be no love.

Bryn Jones has finally built Teller Jones Realty into a business that can thrive without her daily presence. So, she throws herself into her passion—leading kids' backpacking trips for Inner City Outings (ICO) and planning the annual fundraising gala. The last thing she expects is the one-time love of her life to suddenly reappear as a fellow board member.

Climbing guide Jamie Stanton never planned on returning to Seattle, because returning means revisiting his past and the Rainier-size mountain of guilt he carries. But his boss wants to open a Washington outpost, and his Seattleite dad just had a stroke, so he's back. He has no idea volunteering at ICO will bring him face-to-face with the most painful parts of his life—the woman he loved, the reason he left, and the damage done.

Can they move beyond their traumatic shared history and learn to trust and love each other again?

Want more from Stacy Gold right now?

Check out the Emerald Mountain
ski romance novella series and boxed set…
www.stacygold.com/books

Never You
Novella #3 in the Emerald Mountain Series

An enemies-to-lovers story

Emerald Mountain Ski Hut Caretaker Morgan Monroe doesn't do casual relationships. Not anymore. Certainly not with the obnoxious, flirty, too-hot-for-his-own-good chef she's wanted to strangle all season. He's the kind of man she wouldn't date in a million years, even if he were the dating type.

Chef Dan Griffin doesn't believe in relationships. But a one-night stand to celebrate the end of ski season? Hell yes! Especially with the gorgeous caretaker. She's sexy but melt-in-your-mouth sweet, the kind of woman who could convince a man to get serious…if he were the relationship type. She kept her distance all winter, but he's hoping he can convince her to get closer for one night of passion.

When things heat up on a cold winter's night, will they play it safe or follow their hearts?

OKRWA IDA Contest Finalist
2nd Place, Best Erotic Short 2019 & 2020

NYRWA Kathryn Hayes "When Sparks Fly" Contest
3rd Place, Best Erotic Romance

In Deep
Novella #2 in the Emerald Mountain Series

A second chance at love story

Sophie Tremore is trying to build a career in the male-dominated world of Ski Patrol. Hard to do when her new boss is her smokin' hot ex-lover. She hasn't forgotten how he made her body tingle and her heart pound, although he's making it a lot easier by treating her like she's incompetent—when he's not ignoring her existence altogether.

Emerald Mountain Ski Patrol Director Max Demford has been doing his best to avoid working with his feisty former flame, given his judgment is clouded by those eight mind-blowing weeks two years ago. Ski patrol is dangerous enough, and no way could he handle another person he cares about getting hurt on the mountain.

Forced to work together, their simmering attraction becomes difficult to ignore. When Sophie gets caught in a slide, an adrenaline-filled day could turn into a spectacular night they will never forget—one that could risk both their careers.

N.N. Light Book Awards Winner
Best Erotic Romance

H.O.L.T Medallion Finalist
Best First Book

OKRWA IDA Contest 5th Place Finalist
Best Erotic Short

Just Friends
Novella #1 in the Emerald Mountain Series

A friends-to-lovers story

Taya Monroe is trying to pick up the pieces of her failed writing career and broken life after walking out on her cheating fiancé. The last thing she needs is a serious relationship. The last thing she wants is a fling. Then she runs into an old friend and ski partner—the one man she always wanted who never wanted her.

Ski Patroller Jordan Wiley is a single dad with zero time or energy for dating. When he reconnects with Taya, his attraction to her is even stronger than before she left him behind for a career in the city. But with a young son to think about, he's determined to ignore his feelings. Again.

After a magical day on the slopes, a snow storm traps them in an avalanche of chemistry neither can deny. Will their friendship survive the weight of their passion, or will they surface as more than friends?

N.N. Light Book Awards Finalist
Best Erotic Romance

OKRWA IDA Contest
3rd Place Finalist

**Novellas in the Emerald Mountain Series are stand-alone, not chronological, and can be read in any order!*

RESOURCES FOR WOMEN INTERESTED IN HIKING OR BACKPACKING

Your local outdoor shop Many outdoor stores have classes, events, and of course gear available. It's good to shop local!

REI www.rei.com Offers gear, events, and classes in the US
MEC www. mec.ca Gear and how-to articles for those in Canada

Facebook and Instagram Groups – If you're looking for other ladies to hike with, social media is your friend. Just search "women hiking" + your area. There are tons out there these days and chances one is near you.

> **Women Who Hike** www.Womenwhohike.com can connect you to Facebook groups in your area
>
> **Women Who Explore** www.womenwhoexplore.com
>
> **Hike Like A Woman** www.hikelikeawoman.com
>
> **Outdoor Women's Alliance** www.outdoorwomensalliance.com
>
> **Black Girls Trekkin** www.blackgirlstrekkin.com
>
> **Fat Girls Hiking** www.fatgirlshiking.com/
>
> **Girlventures** www.girlventures.org/

Know of another group that gets women and girls out hiking and/or backpacking? Email me at stacy@stacygold.com and I'll add them to my list.

About Author Stacy Gold

Award-winning author Stacy Gold is a compulsive tea drinker, outdoor sports junkie, and lover of good (and bad) puns. She gave up her day job as Communications Director of a nonprofit mountain biking organization to write sassy, steamy, contemporary romance novels. Her stories are packed with independent, kick-butt women finding love and adventure in the great outdoors. When  Stacy's not busy reading or writing, you can find her dancing, laughing, or playing hard in the mountains of Colorado with her wonderful hubby and happy dogs.

Learn more at http://stacygold.com or follow Stacy's adventures on Facebook, Twitter, and Insta @AuthorStacyGold